To Heal and to Build

"Sometimes I have been called a seeker of 'consensus'—
more often in criticism than in praise.
And I have never denied it.
Because to heal and to build
in support of something worthy is,
I believe, a noble task.
In the region of the country where I have spent my life,
where brother was once divided against brother,
this lesson has been burned deep into my memory."
                                    Chicago, April 1, 1968

To Heal and to Build

The Programs of President
Lyndon B. Johnson

Edited by

James MacGregor Burns

Prologue by *Howard K. Smith*

With commentary by *Chester Bowles, McGeorge Bundy,
James MacGregor Burns, Ralph Ellison, Walter W. Heller,
David E. Lilienthal, Eugene V. Rostow, Stewart L. Udall*

Epilogue by *Eric Hoffer*

McGraw-Hill Book Company
New York   Toronto   London   Sydney

Foreword

This volume was handed to the publisher early in March, 1968, just before the extraordinary weeks of political turmoil, beginning with the New Hampshire primary and culminating in President Johnson's statement of withdrawal and his peace offer to North Vietnam. This climactic speech, and a second talk the next day, April 1, 1968, on his more personal feelings about the Presidency, I have added as of the date below. Otherwise not a word has been changed in the speech selections or in the prefatory essays.

It has been easy to let the selections stand, because the volume was intended not as a campaign book but as a summation of the programs of the Johnson Administration—a summation directly relevant to the campaign of 1968 and to an estimation of the place of the Johnson Administration in history. It is still so intended.

"I think the whole world offers no finer spectacle," John Bright said over a century ago, than the selection and the authority "of the freely chosen magistrate of a great and free people." But whether a people can remain both great and free depends in large part on their capacity to distinguish the crucial and lasting problems. Historians know that the burning issues of one era may be the forgotten ones of the next. The supreme challenges to the Johnson Administration may prove to have been Vietnam and civil disorder—or they may prove to have been hunger or space or nuclear proliferation or population or the needs of medical research or of the environment.

I have tried to cope with this uncertainty by including in this volume speeches covering all the issues that, it seems to me, could occupy the citizen today or the historian of the future. They do not by any means embrace the whole range of the Administration's concern and action. Major sectors of public policy—for example, more traditional aspects of welfare, or some of the regulatory functions—have been underemphasized. But the selections are designed to reflect the extraordinary intensity of the Administration's efforts in a score of key policy areas.

The emphasis also is on continuity. The programs of the Johnson Administration have their direct source in the hopes aroused and directions set during the electrifying months of John F. Kennedy's Administration. Those programs stem less immediately but still quite markedly from the Roosevelt and Truman administrations—indeed, from all the twentieth-century Presidents who have faced up to poverty and injustice at home and to threats to American security abroad. The work of not one but of at least four Democratic Presidents—and of one or two Republican Presidents—is on trial in the fall of 1968.

The essayists were selected with an eye to this fact. Several of them first began their public service during the Roosevelt Administration, as did Lyndon Johnson himself. Several began under Kennedy. Several were part of no administration. Collectively, it is hoped, they supply a combination of the participant's insight and the outsider's detachment that may be of use in putting the President's speeches in context.

This is an independent venture. The White House cooperated in supplying speech and other material, without either requesting or receiving the right to pass on the content. The essayists are accountable only for their own contributions. The editor assumes full responsibility for the selection of the essayists themselves, the choice of speeches, and the collateral material in the book.

James MacGregor Burns

Williamstown, Massachusetts
April 14, 1968

Contents

Part Two: The Great Society Today

Part Three: The Frontiers of Excellence

Part Four:　The Reformation of Politics

Prologue:

A Strong Thread of Moral Purpose

By Howard K. Smith

Passing a durable judgment on a live active President is chancy business. However, reporters can rarely resist an invitation to try. I believe that a longer perspective will place Lyndon B. Johnson very high on our scale of Presidents. A large and articulate number of my writing colleagues believe the opposite. So let each who wishes put his assessment down on paper and wait for time and the exhaustion of temporary emotions to tell which is more nearly right.

The literature from which to dissent has grown voluminous in a short time, ranging from the wholly unfunny farce, *MacBird,* across a sizable list of magazine pieces to Robert Sherrill's sour biography, *The Accidental President.* What is particularly significant to me is that the writers are capable observers, with no previous record of malice, and will often in private admit that their arguments are not quite legitimate. In view of the savage treatment by contemporary writers of public figures like Abraham Lincoln and Franklin D. Roosevelt, one is forced to conclude that the abuse of forceful Presidents satisfies some strong public appetite. That calls for a special effort at analysis.

1

I am convinced that for all the study and curiosity we lavish on the American Presidency, most Americans have not really critically penetrated its essential function, that of *leadership*. The British, either by instinct or intent, have been more clearheaded. Long ago they recognized that societies tend to put contradictory demands on their leaders. People want and need a kind of godlike national symbol to keep unsullied and with which to identify. But they also need an altogether fallible human leader to raise hell with. With exquisite comprehension, the British have kept the two roles separate. They have a Monarch, whose sole function is to be a symbol and whom it is bad taste to criticize. And they have an active Prime Minister as clearly imperfect as you or I, and about whom it is all right to say anything that comes to mind.

In America we have never clearly understood the love-hate demands we put on our Chief Executive. We confuse the two in one person and then suffer the normal stresses of human beings trying to do several contradictory things at once. When a President is shown in the movies—an example from the late TV movies: FDR presenting a medal to James Cagney playing the role of George M. Cohan—we feel it proper that only the back of the President's head is shown, the way old biblical movies used to show Christ. Yet at the time that movie was made, displaying our Monarch with mysterious awe, the daily papers were publishing full-face photographs of our Prime Minister and saying insulting things about him. This is not to suggest that there is anything wrong with calling a politician names. But it is unnerving to find that he and God are the same person. To justify the blasphemy critics are apt to go to excess to prove that a public figure who is really just fallible is in fact villainous. They feel less guilty if they can overstate their case.

There are other less basic reasons why contemporary assessments of a President are often wrong. First, current judgments are easily fouled by the fact that what is conspicuous and immediate and simple in a man, subject to our unrelenting stare, often outclamors what may be durable and long-range and complex.

Second, the judgment of reporters, who provide the public with most of what it knows about a President, is distorted by an old journalistic tradition. That tradition is negative. It is geared to seeking out what went wrong. The Pulitzer prize for reporting is given mostly for exposé. This is probably good: a healthy skepticism is as essential to reporting as it is to science. However, since most of our Republic's history has been remarkably successful, the tradition of concentrating on what failed makes for bad history.

And third, current assessments of our Presidents are often untrustworthy because of the ingrained American distrust of power, possibly bred in us from our Nation's first formative war against an English tyrant. "Americans feel rather warm towards a safely dead President," a student of our institutions once said to me, "but they do not like or trust live active Presidents. They think they do, but in fact they really don't."

If the case against Lyndon Johnson has been overstated, the reason lies partly with him. A magazine has observed that the single adjective that suits him best is "more"—whatever it is, he is and does more of it. His style or manner is more conspicuous than that of other men of politics, and it diverts attention from deeper qualities in the man. He has been more accessible to our negative-oriented press than past Presidents have been; there must be few, if any, columnists or White House correspondents who have not been called in for long private talks with the President. And in his case, finally, the American distrust of power is more operative because he, more than almost any predecessor, knows how to use power and does use it with evident effect.

Any writer assessing Lyndon Johnson faces the fact that the first half of his permissible time in office has already made him something of a political monument deserving of awe. When he is safely retired or dead, we shall all doubtless agree about that. He succeeded in the White House a magnificent and beloved young President (many of whose virtues were, however, only discovered after his death)—a hard act to follow in the continuing drama of the Presidency. Yet, within weeks, Mr. Johnson filled the whole stage with his person and achievements.

At that time, Congress had settled down in a state of total noncooperation with the Presidency. John Kennedy's last Congress was, said *Time* magazine, "the longest, most tedious, least effective first session in U.S. history." Walter Lippmann said of the session that "it was a conspiracy to suspend representative government." George Ball said the situation amounted to a full-blown constitutional crisis. This was the time when all those urban and social problems that have lately begun exploding were attaining maturity. That was the situation when Mr. Johnson took office and deftly and swiftly pulled the congressional log jam apart and got things moving again.

In the shortest time ever granted a Vice-President risen to President—eleven months—Johnson faced elections and won the biggest confirmation in our history. Too much is made of the fact that his opponent was Senator Goldwater, who proved easy to beat. It is hard to believe that any other opponent would have fared much better. The switch of high Republicans to Johnson began long before the Republican party had chosen a candidate: Edwin Neilan, the Republican head of the U.S. Chamber of Commerce, told reporters as early as December 1963 that he was thinking of voting for Johnson. Henry Ford announced his switch in May 1964—two months before the Republican Convention and at a time when, just after the Oregon primaries, it looked as though Governor Rockefeller might be the nominee of the GOP.

In any case, on the basis of that election, Mr. Johnson proceeded to launch and pass a legislative program without equal in all our past. Federal aid to education and Medicare, which had repeatedly run into stone walls on Capitol Hill, were now passed. The Voting Rights Act that is still changing our whole national outlook was passed. A cabinet department to deal with our rapidly growing city problems was created. As has been universally true of social reforms, few big problems were wholly solved overnight. But tremendously important beginnings were made in many urgently needy fields. Arthur Krock, often a skeptical observer, wrote, "Of the activists who have served as President of the United States, none has set and maintained such a driving pace as Lyndon B. Johnson."

In foreign affairs, assessment is more difficult because, among other reasons, it may take years before all the results of an act of statecraft are in and it becomes clear whether the act was wise or not. An example was President Johnson's hasty trip to Honolulu in February of 1965 for his first meeting with Premier Ky of South Vietnam. At the time most commentators called the trip an act of folly with no higher purpose than to steal headlines from Senator Fulbright's hearings on Vietnam. It was only the unfolding of events that made it clear that the meeting served two very important purposes. First, it gave Ky the confidence to put down the rash of wholly irresponsible street riots by Buddhist political demagogues. And, second, it forced Ky to begin the constitutional process of nation-building. The process is highly imperfect, as is inevitable in an underdeveloped nation racked by both subversion and aggression. There will be frustrating steps backward before there will be more steps forward. Leaders of the process are destined to change, and conditions to evolve, in unpredictable ways. But the process had to begin, and the Honolulu meeting applied the historic pressure to get it started.

Comment about the way Mr. Johnson has handled crises, such as his very first one in Panama and the more difficult one in the Dominican Republic, follows an interesting rhythm. In such thoughtful books as those by Philip Geyelin, Evans and Novak, and Weintal and Bartlett, flaws in the handling are meticulously detailed. (Finding flaws in crisis tactics is, of course, a bit like shooting fish in a barrel.) But the final verdict of the writers is often that things turned out pretty well after all. What they fail to say is that things turned out well in the end because that is how they were designed to turn out.

In the continuing Vietnam crisis, assessment has to be reserved until there is success or failure, or something reasonably final in between. The only long-range judgment one can honestly make is that no one has yet suggested a serious alternative to what is being done, other than that Mr. Johnson "try harder" either to win the war or to seek peace. Senator Fulbright's frequent comments are not really alternatives but rather expressions of anguish —which everyone, including the President, fully shares. General Gavin's famous enclave plan may some day be fashioned into an alternative by a clearer mind, but a rereading of the original testimony of that great soldier shows it to be a confusing and impractical idea.

There is, in my opinion, one consistent and serious fault in Mr. Johnson's handling of foreign affairs. That is in his articulation of purpose. He does not state his purposes well, or has often simply withdrawn and not stated them at all. At critical periods he tends to abdicate the forum to his critics. Thus false conceptions are fastened onto the public mind which remain long after the crises themselves have been successfully resolved. I am not sure why this is so, but my guess is that Johnson, the genius of action, suffers a basic distrust of the ability of Johnson, the public speaker and explainer— a worry that his manner before cameras, or before a press conference, will not measure up to the substance of his case.

However, I also believe that in time the quiet, long-range developments behind the dramatic and controversial crises will be given greater weight. Insistently and painstakingly, regional cooperation among nations too weak to act alone is being pushed in both Latin America and Asia. The war in Vietnam in particular has been essentially an effort to buy time to allow this process to begin in a region hitherto intimidated into passivity by China and its friends. In years to come, when Johnson has disappeared, this may be regarded as quite an achievement.

The record of Mr. Johnson over the first half of his possible time in the White House is clearly a remarkable one. Yet, the figure who achieved it is uninhibitedly human, with warts and flaws and weaknesses that all humans are subject to.

His chief enemy is his style, which often absorbs attention that ought to be directed to his more substantial features, so let us say something about it. The Johnson manner comes, like all human qualities, partly from what is inborn and partly from what his special environment has shaped in him.

What is inborn in him is an effervescence rarely seen in serious politicians. A man who plays no golf, reads few books, and enjoys no other avocation, relaxes from the world's hardest job by talking about it. In doing so he may pace the room and flail his arms. He may mimic visitors who have irritated him. He pauses to address you nose-to-nose. One of his closest aides, Jack Valenti, once made an effusively praiseful speech about Johnson's qualities in which he said, "I sleep better at night because Lyndon Johnson is my President." The speech was widely ridiculed. But there was one assertion in it that is simply factual. Mr. Johnson, said Valenti, has "extra glands." Of that there can be no doubt.

Mr. Johnson's family tree consists mostly of what is called Scotch-Irish ancestry with a branch or so of German. But I am convinced that somewhere in the foliage there was an Italian, for the President's vivacity is pure Mediterranean, ill disguised with a Texas accent. When he talks in a small circle, *Time* magazine once said, he makes William Jennings Bryan "look like a cigar-store Indian." In after-hours conversation he imitates Stephen Leacock's hero who jumped on his horse and rode off in all directions. In his infinite briefing sessions with people from all realms of life, he does not address his audience so much as he envelops and surrounds it.

When he first met the graceful Southern girl destined to become his wife, her two reactions were typical. "I knew he was something special," she has said, "but I did not quite know what." And in response to his enveloping maneuver, she said, "I did not know whether I wanted to get that intense that early in life." Like many politicians later on, she found that she was not really allowed a choice.

To that inborn enthusiasm one must add the influence of the region of his upbringing. It is a state that seems to excite more animosity than any other, possibly because it got too rich too recently and too quickly—and often shows it. Political fashions in the state are changing, but in Johnson's formative period, rural ways became overlaid with a new urban vernacular. Theodore Roosevelt once said that a political speech is not a painting but a poster; and in the Southwest the poster paints tend to be a little more garish than elsewhere.

Perhaps the simplest way to illustrate the formative effects of Texas politics is to describe some of Mr. Johnson's opponents when he first ran for the U.S. Senate. One of them ran on a platform that promised a gift of five dollars to every man, woman, and child in the state. Another promised he would propose making armaments out of old discarded tin cans. The style of yet another is indicated by his nickname: Lee ("Pass the Biscuits, Pappy") O'Daniel! O'Daniel won. Johnson lost. But he learned how to campaign in Texas so well that he never lost again.

When I came to Washington from a solid twenty-year stint of covering Europe, the Middle East, and Africa, the most evident thing in the Capitol next to President Eisenhower was Lyndon Johnson. His perpetual motion on the floor of the Senate and in its cloakrooms was one of the shows of the city. It was easy to make fun and I did. But after a while it occurred to me that in an era of sleepy government some important legislation was being passed, and in almost every case the causal factor was Johnson.

My first meeting with him was for lunch in the baroque suite of the Senate Majority Leader—called the "Throne Room" by reporters. Everything essential about Johnson was on display. We had a meal of open hamburgers cut in the shape of the state of Texas. The leader talked for two-and-a-half hours solid, miraculously consuming food without stumbling over a syllable. His discourse was punctuated by his receiving little chits of paper from busy secretaries and by his calling out brief answers to the little memos over his shoulder. From time to time a Senator would come in for a brief whispered conversation. Yet the whole performance was one unbroken lecture on the functioning of the U.S. Senate. It was easy to be dazzled by the performance into thinking this was all show and no substance and to forget that all the time he was maneuvering the Civil Rights Bill of 1960 to passage by a conservative and reluctant Senate and thus laying the foundation stones for the rights revolution of our time. I was so fascinated that I never got past Laredo on that culinary map of Texas on my plate.

The faults of Lyndon Johnson are all there pretty much as reporters describe them. He tends to be irritable. He is resentful of news leaks and impatient of criticism. He plays his cards close to the chest and is not above showmanly efforts at petty deception to make a surprise appointment or decision more surprising when he finally springs it in public.

But I have two basic quarrels with the list of faults. First, other Presidents have been guilty of them too. John Kennedy became so impatient with the *New York Herald Tribune* for criticizing him that he canceled the White House subscriptions to that paper. Johnson is given to pungent, descriptive, and sometimes unprintable language; but he has not yet cussed out loud from coast to coast as President Eisenhower so justifiably did when his TV prompting device went awry in the middle of a speech.

The so-called credibility gap doubtless exists. But I am inclined to think that two factors make total candor in a President in our time almost impossible. For one thing, foreign policy, which our Constitution requires the President alone to make, has become vastly more complex than it ever was before. The postwar bipolar world in which only America and Russia really mattered has dissolved into a multipolar world in which every primitive ex-colony is sovereign and is beset by unprecedented problems. No President will ever be able to bare all without giving offense or revealing tactical plans that simply in the national interest should not be revealed.

For another thing, our Constitution, for all its virtues, makes it very hard to pass, and very easy to block, legislation, due to its system of vetoes, which we call "checks and balances." An active President who wants results simply has to master the art of maneuver.

Other activist Presidents of this century have had exactly the same difficulty as Johnson. Professor Arthur Link's biography of Wilson says Wilson was often charged with "grazing the truth," and it quotes a reporter of the time as saying, "It was impossible to rely on anything he said." Professor

James MacGregor Burns, the biographer of FDR, was once asked which of the two—Roosevelt or LBJ—was the more devious. Burns responded: "FDR, without a doubt."

My other quarrel with the list of faults of the present Chief Executive is the weight of value given to them. To me they seem rather trivial when put alongside his positive qualities as a President.

It is often said of Johnson that he is an "accidental" President; it should be added that *all* Presidents are accidental. It would be more distinctive to call him the logical and natural President for his time, for so the leading figures of the time have said. Once when President Eisenhower was conversing with Senator Johnson in the oval office, the President pointed to his desk and said to the Senator, "You may be sitting there one day." John Kennedy, when running for President in 1960, told a reporter that he felt himself to be better qualified for the job than any potential candidate "except Lyndon." After being defeated by Johnson in 1964, Senator Goldwater said to me, "That guy knows that job better than anybody."

The presidential process logically begins with finding out what needs to be done. In this respect, no past President has so exhaustively scoured the nation for ideas as Johnson has. Under no previous administration has there been such a continuous parade into the White House of decision-makers from whom counsel is sought—governors, labor leaders, businessmen, reporters, members of Congress, and even the office assistants of members of Congress.

White House aides have toured campuses to solicit ideas. Task forces of experts have been set up to produce reports on broad fields of action. Just last year the mass of resultant paper was a six-foot shelf of loose-leaf notebooks—a mass winnowed down to produce a program of legislation. This thoroughness of the national canvass for ideas is something wholly new in the American Presidency.

The single task a President must undertake himself is that of making decisions—decisions as to which legislation must be pursued and what action taken in crisis. No President has protected his right and duty to make decisions as jealously as Mr. Johnson has. He has developed a habit of keeping all options open until the last allowable minute and—when a sudden foreign crisis like that in the Dominican Republic does not limit time—until the last piece of relevant information is available. His caution is famous. He has said that the three most important words in the English language are "just a minute." He once told an impatient critic, "When you sit in this chair you think three times before saying 'Go.'"

His almost fierce determination to make his own decisions at his own pace has caused him a good deal of friction with the press. In 1964, he decided where to go and make campaign speeches virtually at the last minute. Even his decisions to spend the weekend at the ranch are often withheld until very late, much to the irritation of White House correspondents who like to know whether they will be able to spend the weekend at home or on the move. In respect to appointments to high office, he is known to have canvassed as many as 300 names before settling on one. He once subjected his final choice to forty-six separate investigations before naming him.

It is inevitable that when there is so wide and thorough a canvass, names under consideration leak out and are published. Mr. Johnson considers such leaks an attempt to "hustle" him and shut off his options, and he does not hide his irritation. It is widely said that he has on occasion even reversed a choice because of premature publication, though the President emphatically denies it. Once when his plans for Vietnam were being projected, or guessed at, in the press, he told a news conference, "I sometimes wonder if General Eisenhower before the battle of Normandy had been confronted with all the —if the world had all the information concerning his plans that they seem to have concerning ours in Vietnam, what would have happened on that fateful day." His insistence on keeping all choices free until one is adopted is carried right down to the slightest of his plans. "I can never tell what he is going to do," his daughter Luci once said. "He can't either." Ideally, I suppose it would be best if the President took with quiet grace the occupational urge of the press to scoop him. But if there has to be an error in one direction or another in this highly inflammable world, it is probably best that he err on the side of excessive caution in protecting his freedom to decide.

The skill for which he is most famous appears in the next stage of executive action—after decisions are made and legislation is introduced—that is, the task of getting legislation passed by Congress. Johnson's success at this part of his work was phenomenal in his two "honeymoon" periods, the first after succeeding Kennedy in office and the second after his landslide election. Even after Congress, predictably, had dug in its heels, his record remained pretty good, as evinced by the few times he had to veto Congress's acts.

Like any highly distinctive feature, his ability to get legislation through has become easy to caricature and to describe in clichés. Unfortunately the clichés hide the truth. He gets his way, it is widely said, by twisting arms and by cajolery. These terms conjure up visions of legislators being conned into doing things they don't really want to do. In fact, the phrase that best describes his technique is simply: massive persuasion. He out-argues opponents, meets every objection, and gradually divests them of reasons for opposing.

Mr. Johnson relates that, when he first came to Washington, the average member of Congress saw the President little more than once a year, usually in the opening days of a session, after waiting in a long queue. Now in the Johnson years, members of Congress are repeatedly brought into the White House in groups and briefed at length by the President and his chief cabinet officers. They are prodded by the President to ask questions, and if they flag, the President himself assumes the role of interrogator to encourage his cabinet officers to bring out essential points.

This persuasion process continues while legislation is being debated. During the debates on civil rights legislation, Mr. Johnson stationed batteries of Justice Department lawyers just outside the Chamber to provide facts and rebuttals to arguments being made inside. The process even continues after legislation is passed. The high degree of compliance with rights laws is in part due to the fact that the President called in business and labor leaders from Southern states to lecture them on what would be lost if local and state officials failed to comply.

Another word is commonly used to describe the Johnson method, and that is *consensus*. The word implies that the President blurs issues or waters down legislation in order to win as broad support as possible. One would think that the President's stonily uncompromising stand on landmark civil rights acts, refusing to permit any weakening of them, would have banished this notion. But it persists to this day.

What, in fact, Mr. Johnson has done to win broad support is not to blur issues but rather to try to prove to interest groups that they may have a false conception of their own true interest. An example: though America is perhaps the most non-Marxist major nation on earth, the American mind is dominated by one Marxist concept. That is the tenacious belief that somehow the interests of management and those of labor are inevitably opposed; that if one gains, the other must lose. The truth, shown by the broad sweep of incomes over the years, is that their interests tend to move up or down together. The President hammered at this truth and helped dispel the legend of inevitable economic conflict.

The real meaning of the word *consensus* has been best grasped by the *Economist* of London. After watching Mr. Johnson at work for two years, that periodical wrote:

> The big thing to understand is that Johnson's consensus is in large measure a brilliant word play for an older concept, more controversial in a society where government is ritualistically distrusted; and that is leadership . . . the immediate political fact is that he is leading Congress and the American public as they have rarely been led before . . . that is the change: a change to positive government.

If the President has understood the strengths of his office as few Presidents have, he has also always been acutely aware of its weakness in a system of government made up of independent balancing branches. At the high tide of his success, he said, "I have watched Congress for forty years, and I have never seen a Congress that did not eventually take the measure of the

President it was dealing with." When he won his landslide election in 1964, he said to his Vice-President-elect, Senator Humphrey, "Hubert, I figure we have got about nine months to get our way in Congress, no more." Nine months and a few days later a bill he had put his heart into—home rule for Washington, D.C.—was defeated on the Hill. That evening, the President phoned Humphrey, who was on the Capitol Hill, and said, "I think we have had it." The honeymoon was over. But though no more miracles were wrought, Johnson continued to do passably well on the Hill.

Johnson's unprecedented success with legislation gave rise to the explanation among political writers—preconditioned to be skeptical—that he was a skilled "political mechanic" but had no larger vision to which he was committed. With this too I must quarrel. I have met few politicians who feel so strongly that, despite America's unmatched material resources, our nation is not fulfilling its whole promise and that some quite tangible things can be done about it.

The evils which prevent fulfillment, he has often said, are hard-core poverty, inadequate education for all, and racial discrimination. The President has attacked these ills with a vigor not paralleled before. He assaults pockets of poverty, a writer has said, as though they are personal enemies. Of education he has said, "I am going to use every rostrum to tell the people that we can no longer afford the great waste that comes from the neglect of a single child." When the landmark act of 1965 to give federal aid to education was passed, he said, "I will never do anything in my entire life that excites me more."

But his outstanding ingrained sentiment has been a hatred of racial bigotry in his inmost being. His proudest recollection of his father was a speech the elder Johnson made in the Texas State Legislature blasting the Ku Klux Klan—at a time when it was politically dangerous to do so. In my opinion, far the most effective speech President Johnson himself has ever made was his "We Shall Overcome" address to a joint session of Congress on March 15, 1965, when he asked for passage of a voting rights bill. Its high point was his description of the Mexican-American schoolchildren whom he taught as a young man:

> Somehow you never forget what poverty and hatred can do when you see its scars on the hopeful face of a young child. I never thought then, in 1928, that I would be standing here in 1965. It never even occurred to me in my fondest dreams that I might have the chance to help the sons and daughters of those students and to help people like them all over this country. But now I do have that chance—and I'll let you in on a secret—I mean to use it.

It is remarkable that only four major civil rights acts have been passed in Congress since 1875 and that Johnson was the key figure in each passage. Almost as impressive as his resolve to act has been his clear understanding that these acts are not enough. Passage of the Voting Rights Act of 1965, he said, "will still leave us on the side of the mountain below the peak."

I believe that time and perspective will be generous to this President. Long after we have forgotten the gossip about the disapproval of him by the backers of his predecessor, we will recall that John Kennedy said of him, "He really cares about this nation as I want a President to care."

Once Johnson said of the nation about which he cares, "Friendly cynics and fierce enemies alike often underestimate or ignore the strong thread of moral purpose which runs through the fabric of American history." In time, the same statement may be made, and universally accepted, of Johnson himself.

PART ONE

World Revolutions —And Our Own

Are We Relevant to the Future?

By Chester Bowles

American foreign policy in the postwar era can be divided into four periods or phases. The first covers the critically important period between the end of the war and the early 1950s; the second extends until 1960; the third from 1960 until the present; the fourth and probably most decisive period lies just ahead.

I do not suggest that the beginnings and ends of these periods can be determined with any degree of precision. Each flows into the other with significant overlaps. Nevertheless, they provide a convenient framework to consider the evolving world forces with which we have had to contend in the last twenty-three years, the adequacy of our response to these forces, and the challenges we are likely to face in the years ahead.

[I]

V–J Day, August 1945, ushered in the first of these four phases as a confident America faced a new kind of world. We had led the struggle in Asia against an imperialist Japan and in Europe against the Nazis. Our democratic institutions were the model for a dozen newly independent governments.

After a hundred years of isolationism, the United States emerged into the new postwar world with unchallenged power and influence, determined to carry its share of responsibilities.

The first challenge came in Europe where we responded promptly and vigorously. When Stalin's Russia, in the tradition of Czarist expansionism, launched its push toward the Mediterranean we threw our support behind Turkey and Greece. Tito split with his Russian comrades and the pressure was relieved.

When the Soviet Union sought to engulf Berlin by cutting all rail and road access to the Western sectors we again acted firmly. Within forty-eight hours American and British cargo planes were landing every ninety seconds at Tempelhof airfield to supply the embattled city. A few months later the Berlin blockade was lifted.

In June 1947, Secretary of State Marshall announced America's willingness to support a massive European economic recovery program, a plan "not directed against anyone, but against hunger, chaos and poverty." In 1948 the Organization of European Economic Cooperation was established joining seventeen European partners in the unprecedented and imaginative Marshall Plan.

At the same time, we organized a defense program to assure the military security of Western Europe. In 1949, the North Atlantic Treaty was signed by fourteen nations, and NATO came into being.

In this first postwar phase our record as a whole was one of imaginative concepts carried through vigorously and effectively. Yet in retrospect certain miscalculations are now evident.

It was logical and proper, for instance, that our immediate postwar concerns were focused on Europe. Europe represented a vast concentration of industrial resources; it controlled the approaches to the Atlantic and stood astride the most important routes of world commerce. Even more important, it was in Europe that our Western ideals of liberty and humanism were born.

Consequently it was not surprising that U.S. foreign policy during this critical period was in large measure an extension of the British policies which had helped maintain the peace of Europe between the Congress of Vienna in 1815 and World War I.

This called for a power balance in Europe which the British had skillfully maintained by opposing any power or combination of powers that sought to dominate the Continent.

There was, however, a fundamental difference: in the nineteenth century a peaceful Europe was the primary requirement for a peaceful world. The economic, political, and strategic decisions concerning Asia and Africa were not made in New Delhi, Hanoi, Leopoldville, or Batavia, but in the imperial capitals of London, Paris, Brussels, and The Hague.

What we failed adequately to take into account in this first postwar phase was the resulting surge which was rapidly demolishing the old colonial ties and enabling the new nations of Asia, Africa, and Latin America to begin to shape their own destinies.

We also wrongly assumed that in the developing continents the primary danger, as in Europe, would be Communist movements manipulated by Moscow and Peking. It was some years before we came to see that the revolutionary wave sweeping Africa and Asia was in fact generated by political and economic forces deeply rooted in Western concepts of nationalism, economic progress, and self-determination. We credited the Communists with having created a vast political wave which in fact they were only trying, often rather ineffectively, to ride—a wave which had been created by the indigenous forces to which I have referred.

Whatever influence the USSR and China exert today in Asia, Africa, and Latin America, and in some areas it is considerable, is not primarily because of their Communist ideology but because they are strategically placed major powers, highly sensitive to the social, political, and economic forces which are making history.

Under the impact of this wave of nationalism, the British withdrew with dignity from their far-flung empire. The Dutch left Indonesia; the Belgians pulled out of the Congo; and the French were driven out of Indochina and Algeria and finally withdrew from their remaining African possessions.

[II]

Our belated recognition of this massive political, economic, and social upheaval ushered in the second of the four postwar phases of American foreign policy. In dealing with these new global forces our conditioned reflex was an attempt to adopt our successful European experience to a totally different set of problems. A primary element of this effort was to draw nations which would agree to accept our leadership into military alliances, with few if any qualms about their political systems.

In Asia this approach limited our military-political relationships to a number of friendly, but relatively weak nations. With their inadequate support we set out to "contain" Communist China while the four largest non-Communist nations, Japan, India, Indonesia, and Pakistan, sat on the sidelines in various attitudes of neutrality.

This is not to ignore some notable accomplishments. Our effort to help build a stable, dynamic, friendly Japan was brilliantly successful. We rallied to the support of South Korea and led a massive UN effort to reestablish its independence. Indeed, in all parts of Asia, with the unhappy exception of French Indochina, our support for the new independence movements was unequivocal.

Similarly in Africa, despite our NATO ties with the then major colonial powers of Europe, we generally supported the anticolonial forces. In Latin America our acceptance of the forces of change, while often timid, was a major improvement over our prewar posture.

Also on the positive side of the ledger was our realization that the challenge posed by the developing nations had important economic and social dimensions. Out of this understanding came President Truman's Point Four, the World Bank, our support to the specialized agencies of the UN, and the

Economic Assistance Program, which was launched in India in 1952 during my first tour as Ambassador.

Yet on balance it is evident that during the 1950s the United States Government lacked a clear concept of developmental techniques and priorities. Instead of concentrating our economic assistance on those countries most willing and able to help themselves, our aid programs often came to be used to bolster pro-American leaders who lacked effective political roots among their people. In some cases political unrest led to military dictatorships supported by misguided American military assistance programs.

This misdirection of much of our early overseas developmental efforts was accompanied by our failure to educate the American people, press, and Congress in regard to the nature and dimensions of the new world challenge.

For instance, it has been generally assumed that our efforts to strengthen the nations of the developing world would be a relatively short-range affair similar to the reconstruction of Europe.

This was a serious misconception. In the case of the Marshall Plan we were dealing with long-established European nations with highly developed industrial skills, sophisticated concepts of government, modern technologies, and traditions of military organization and cooperation.

In much of Asia, Africa, and Latin America we were working with new nations, which with some notable exceptions had not yet generated the habits of thought, the codes of behavior, the literacy, education, and social integration essential for the establishment of free institutions and rapid economic progress.

It was also assumed that our economic assistance would automatically generate a feeling of warmth and gratitude toward the United States; consequently we expected those nations we had assisted to support our foreign policy objectives and to stand by our side in the United Nations. When they failed to do so we often scolded them for their "ingratitude."

These assumptions and reactions reflect our failure fully to understand either the political and psychological forces which have been shaping the developing countries or the limitations and purposes of economic assistance. After long years of colonial rule the people and leaders of the new nations are acutely sensitive to any action by a foreign government which appears to infringe on their sovereignty. Their posture on many foreign policy questions is determined by an overriding desire to prove that they are their own masters, regardless of how many American toes they may step on in the process, or how much they may be acting contrary to what we believe to be their nations' interests.

My experience in the developing countries has convinced me that there is only one realistic justification for providing foreign economic assistance: to make it possible for those developing nations which are prepared to adopt enlightened economic policies to become politically and economically viable and prepared to contribute their growing strength and influence toward the creation of a more stable world.

It is the task of the historians to strike a balance between the successes and failures of U.S. foreign policy in this second postwar stage. Our immediate concern is to consider the third phase, which was ushered in by the election of the Kennedy-Johnson Administration in January 1961.

[III]

With some, but by no means all, of the lessons of the 1950s in mind it may be said that we have made significant but by no means adequate progress.

On the plus side there are many highly important achievements. These include the transition, still incomplete, to a new, more realistic relationship with the nations of Western Europe, the launching of that exciting expression of youthful dedication, the Peace Corps, the Alliance for Progress, a more patient and realistic view of Africa, a new recognition of the overriding importance of improved relations with Eastern Europe and the USSR, the imaginative use of our vast capacity to produce food for export and an understanding of the urgent need to provide adequate development assistance to those nations which are genuinely prepared to help themselves.

On the positive side, too, there is now a much better understanding, achieved at a heavy cost in money, blood, and good will, of the limitations of military power and of the overriding importance of the forces generated by political and social change.

It is not within the scope of this article to discuss the pros and cons of our experience in Vietnam. However, it is fair to point out that much of the anguish which we have faced in that tragic area reflects our earlier failure fully to recognize the political and psychological forces at work in the underdeveloped continents.

The initial mistake occurred immediately following the war when we permitted the French to reestablish their colonial position in Vietnam. A few years later, when the Viet Minh rose in rebellion, we supported the colonial French with hundreds of millions of dollars worth of military supplies.

If the French had left Vietnam when the Dutch and the British withdrew from their empires in Asia and Africa, a half million American troops would never have been called upon to fight in Vietnam and the people of Southeast Asia would have been spared their tragic ordeal.

However, if the Vietnamese crisis has convinced our Congress, press, and people that political stability in Asia, Africa, and Latin America can be created only by the people themselves and that in the absence of such stability costly and unpredictable armed conflicts are inevitable, much will have been gained.

[IV]

As we move into the decisive fourth phase of our postwar foreign policy, it is essential that we keep these lessons firmly in mind. What we need to understand is not only our strengths, which are formidable, but our limitations which are also real, coupled with a more realistic set of national priorities.

We have been spending some $30 billion a year on an effort to establish a more politically stable Southeast Asia. Once this war is over will we be prepared to spend even one-third of this sum in preventing future Vietnams in South Asia, Africa, and Latin America?

Can the American people who spend tens of billions of dollars each year on cosmetics, nightclubs, cigarettes, and bubble gum be persuaded to support the enlightened policies which are required to build a world in which their children and the children of their contemporaries abroad can live in peace, comfort, and dignity?

Our answers to these and other relevant questions will constitute an acid test of American political leadership in the 1970s. In this context let us consider the choices we now face in Asia where a majority of mankind lives.

In the next few years I believe one of three developments will almost surely occur:

(1) A frustrated and embittered United States will withdraw from Asia allowing China and/or Russia to fill the vacuum,

(2) The United States will become engaged in a costly and impossible-to-win war with China, or

(3) A non-Communist, indigenous political consensus will gradually evolve in Asia solidly based on the areas of primary weight and influence. I refer to India, Japan, Australia, and Indonesia, which in cooperation with Pakistan, Thailand, New Zealand, the Philippines, Taiwan, Singapore, Malaysia, and South Korea are alone capable of providing the essential Asian counterweight to China.

Will we come to see that only through such an indigenous political-defense balance in Asia can we be relieved of the present heavy pressure on us—a question that is underscored by the decision early this year of the British Government to withdraw from practically all of its military commitments "east of Suez"? Will we understand that any such free Asian coalition, however anti-Communist, cannot accept American control and direction without losing the support of its own people? Will we also realize that its creation will take time, money, and infinite patience?

In this framework I believe that the emergence of a politically stable and economically viable India is of decisive importance. If the massive democratic experiment in India should fail, there is little hope for peace and stability in Asia. The reasons are clear.

—India's population is greater than that of Africa and Latin America combined. More than half of the non-Communist people of Asia live in India.

—India has survived twenty years of political freedom and has thus far maintained a genuine parliamentary democracy underscored by four general elections. When we remind ourselves that scarcely a dozen nations in all of Africa, Asia, and Latin America are still governed democratically, this in itself is a major accomplishment.

—If India's attempt to create a politically stable and economically viable society fails and this vast, complex, and often frustrating nation, with one-sixth of the human race, starts down the same slippery slope that China did a generation ago, all the blood and dollars which we have poured into our efforts to stabilize Southeast Asia will have been in vain.

But what of China itself? A non-Communist Asian coalition, anchored at the two ends by India and Japan, may for a decade or two provide an effective Asian counterweight to an embittered and irresponsible China. But for the long haul it is essential that China gradually be drawn into a rational relationship with the rest of mankind.

Although the door now appears to be closed we should seize whatever opportunities may arise to reestablish contacts of trade, culture, and diplomacy. By so doing we may hasten the day when that great and tragic people can again become a partner in the community of peaceful nations.

We must also recognize the decisive importance of our relations with the USSR, particularly in the next decade. In the USSR, as in America, we may assume that a political tug-of-war is in progress between advocates of international cooperation and understanding and those who are more at ease in a cold war setting. In the years immediately ahead, much will depend on the ability of American political leaders to establish a greater measure of cooperation and understanding with the Soviet Bloc provided, of course, that Soviet leaders are prepared to meet us halfway.

Here as elsewhere a flexible approach to world problems and pressures is of great importance. A notable aspect of international relationships in the last twenty years has been the often decisive impact of unpredicted developments. I refer to such events as the dramatic recovery of Japan and Germany, the break in Soviet-Chinese relations, the sudden collapse of European colonialism in Africa, and the like.

We must assume that the next ten years will be characterized by equally dramatic happenings which will surprise the most competent observers. This calls for a resiliency that combines a capacity to deal with current problems coupled with an ability to adapt quickly to brand new situations.

It should now be clear why I believe that the fourth postwar period, which is now in its beginning stages, will be decisive for generations to come. What is required of us is a capacity to understand how hundreds of millions of people—speaking different languages, worshiping different gods and living under different conditions—think and feel, and then to act effectively on this understanding.

There is nothing new about their poverty, illiteracy, slums, and ill health; what is new is the deep, worldwide, growing conviction among these masses of underprivileged rootless human beings that better answers must soon be found.

These awakening peoples want something more than schools, houses, and "things." Above all else they are seeking the sense of personal involvement and dignity which has thus far been denied them. Economic development experts who ignore these primary human goals and assume that an increase in gross national product automatically produces a similar increase in gross national stability are dangerously wrong.

It is understandable why so many of those with the greatest stake in the status quo view these vast political uncertainties with fear and confusion. But I believe history will determine that they reflect the churning of economic, social and political forces which hold enormous promise for all mankind.

For two decades fantastic new technologies have been literally tearing apart old societies, upsetting the traditional rhythm of individual lives, and generating new hopes among hundreds of millions of underprivileged people who have come to see poverty, ill health and slums as man-made evils which can and must be eliminated.

More than a century ago, the French student of democracy, Alexis de Tocqueville, described this process in the following words:

> Only great ingenuity can save a prince who undertakes to give relief to his subjects after long oppression. The sufferings that are endured patiently, as being inevitable, become intolerable the moment it appears that there might be an escape. Reform then only serves to reveal more clearly what still remains oppressive and now all the more unbearable; the suffering, it is true, has been reduced, but one's sensitivity has become more acute.

What was true in the more leisurely mid-nineteenth century is doubly true in our turbulent modern times. What is most uncertain is America's reaction to the challenge.

History is littered with examples of once-great empires whose leaders and peoples assumed that they could somehow exist and progress as islands of power and affluence in a sea of misery, envy, frustration, and violence. Thus one by one they failed the primary test of national survival; the capacity to recognize, understand and cope with political, social and economic change. After brief periods of prestige, power and glory, some were overwhelmed by their less fortunate but better adapted neighbors, while others were simply bypassed as irrelevant.

This leads us to the central, overriding question: Is our generation of Americans wise enough, courageous enough and above all sensitive enough to cope effectively with the new forces which are stirring mankind? In other words, are we Americans relevant to tomorrow's world?

Many members of the younger generation are openly skeptical; while our military power and our gross national product soar, our influence, they point out, continues to shrink. Tens of millions of Asians, Europeans, Africans and Latin Americans who revere the ideals of Jefferson, Jackson, Lincoln and Roosevelt as much as any American share their concern.

Acting in the framework of this new, turbulent but infinitely promising world, it is the task of the President, his envoys, his Administration and the Congress to disprove the doubters, to relate our policies and our actions to the values on which our nation is based, and thus to prove that modern America is in fact dramatically, dynamically, supremely relevant to the freedom, dignity, and progress of man in the latter decades of the twentieth century.

Lyndon B. Johnson

*"The first obligation of the community of man
is to provide food for all of its members . . ."*
The President recommends to Congress
steps in an international effort in the War against Hunger,
February 2, 1967.

[I]

Last February I proposed that all mankind join in a war against man's
oldest enemy: hunger.

Last March I proposed that the United States take part in an urgent international effort to help the Government of India stave off the threat of famine.

I address you today to report progress in organizing the war against
hunger and to seek your counsel on steps still to be taken. For again this
year, drought in India—as in other nations—underlines the cruel mathematics
of hunger and calls for action.

The problem is immense. It cannot be solved unless each country reaches
a considered judgment on the course to be pursued. The greatest power on
earth is the will of free peoples, expresssed through the deliberative processes

of their national assemblies. I ask you today to take the lead in a vital act of democratic affirmation.

India is not alone in facing the specter of near famine. One-half of the world's people confront this same problem.

India's plight reminds us that our generation can no longer evade the growing imbalance between food production and population growth. India's experience teaches that something more must be done about it.

From our own experience and that of our countries, we know that something can be done. We know that an agricultural revolution is within the capacity of modern science.

We know that land can be made to produce much more food—enough food for the world's population, if reasonable population policies are pursued. Without some type of voluntary population program, however, the nations of the world—no matter how generous—will not be able to keep up with the food problem.

We know, too, that failure to act—and to act now—will multiply the human suffering and political unrest, not only in our generation but in that of our children and their children.

The aim of the war against hunger is to help developing nations meet this challenge. It is the indispensable first step on the road to progress.

If we are to succeed, all nations—rich and poor alike—must join together and press the agricultural revolution with the same spirit, the same energy, and the same sense of urgency that they apply to their own national defense. Nothing less is consistent with the human values at stake.

Last year, many responded to India's emergency. Canada was particularly generous in sending food aid. Each member of the India Aid Consortium made a special effort to meet India's need. Nonmembers, Australia among others, also helped. The private contributions of the Italian and Dutch people were especially heartwarming. But the bleak facts require a sustained international effort on a greater scale. Today I propose that all nations make the new Indian emergency the occasion to start a continuing worldwide campaign against hunger.

[II]

The first obligation of the community of man is to provide food for all of its members. This obligation overrides political differences and differences in social systems.

No single nation or people can fulfill this common obligation. No nation should be expected to do so. Every country must participate to insure the future of all. Every country that makes a determined effort to achieve sufficiency in food will find our Government, our technical experts, and our people its enthusiastic partners. The United States is prepared to do its share.

In pursuing the War on Hunger, the world must face up to stark new facts about food in our times:

—*Food is scarce.* Nowhere is there a real surplus. Food aid must be allocated according to the same priorities that govern other development assistance.

—*Per capita food production in many parts of the less-developed world is not increasing.* In some cases, it is even declining. This grim fact reflects both a rising curve of population and a lagging curve of agricultural production.

—*There is no substitute for self-help.* The first responsibility of each nation is to supply the food its people needs. The war against hunger can only be won by the efforts of the developing nations themselves.

—*Food aid is a stop-gap, not a permanent cure.* It must be viewed as part of a nation's effort to achieve sufficiency in food, not as a substitute for it.

—*Agriculture must receive a much higher priority in development plans and programs.* The developing nations can no longer take food supplies for granted, while they concentrate on industrial development alone, or spend vitally needed resources on unnecessary military equipment.

—*Agricultural development must be planned as part of a nation's overall economic and social program.* Achieving a balance between population and resources is as important as achieving a balance between industrial and agricultural growth.

—*Fertilizer, seed, and pesticides must be provided in much greater quantities than ever before.* Their use increases food production and permanently changes the productive capability of farmers. A ton of fertilizer properly used this year can mean several tons of grain next year.

—*All advanced nations—including those which import food—must share the burden of feeding the hungry and building their capacity to feed themselves.*

—*The War on Hunger is too big for governments alone.* Victory cannot come unless businesssmen, universities, foundations, voluntary agencies, and cooperatives join the battle.

—*Developing nations with food deficits must put more of their resources into voluntary family planning programs.*

These are the facts your Government has been stressing throughout the world. Many of them are unpleasant. But our lives are pledged to the conviction that free people meet their responsibilities when they face the truth.

These facts draw into bold relief the two main thrusts in the offensive against hunger:

First, the hungry nations of the world must be helped to achieve the capacity to grow the food their people need or to buy what they cannot grow.

Second, until they can achieve this goal, the developed nations must help meet their needs by food shipments on generous terms.

The level of food aid will decline as self-help measures take hold. Until that point is reached, food aid is an inescapable duty of the world community.

[III]

During the past year the advanced nations have made progress in preparing the ground for the international War on Hunger.

First, the pattern of international cooperation has steadily improved.

Last July we were pleased to act as host to a high-level meeting of the Development Assistance Committee of the Organization for Economic Cooperation and Development which focused primarily on the world food problem.

We encouraged greater contributions to the World Food Program by increasing our pledge to that program and by offering to match with commodities contributions in both cash and commodities from other countries.

We cosponsored a resolution in the United Nations that launched a UN Food and Agriculture Organization study of whether and how to organize a multilateral food aid program of vastly larger proportions.

In the Kennedy Round of trade negotiations, we have advanced a proposal to make available from all sources ten million tons of food grains annually for food aid, to be supported by grain exporters and importers alike. This proposal is now being discussed in Geneva as part of an International Cereals Arrangement.

We are now participating in a study initiated by the Food and Agriculture

Organization—in cooperation with the World Bank, the UN, and the OECD—to examine how multilateral action might increase the availability and effective use of fertilizers and other materials needed to speed up agricultural production.

At the OECD Ministerial Meeting this fall, we advanced a proposal to develop an Agricultural Food Fund to encourage private investment in the basic agricultural industries of the developing countries.

Second, the United States encouraged a multilateral response to last year's emergency in India.

The worst drought of the century threatened millions with starvation and countless more with disease born of malnutrition. As a result, I recommended, and you in Congress approved, a program to send over eight million tons of food grain to India. In an unprecedented display of common concern, governments, private organizations, and individuals in forty-two other nations joined in providing $180 million in food and other commodities to meet the needs of that country. Over-all, India imported almost eleven million tons of grain and used several million tons from its own emergency food reserves.

The fact that India did not experience famine ranks among the proudest chapters in the history of international cooperation. But last year's effort—heartening as it was—was hasty and improvised. The world must organize its response to famine—both today and for the years ahead.

Third, this year's economic aid program makes agricultural development a primary objective.

The AID program which I will shortly send to the Congress, includes funds to finance imports of fertilizer, irrigation pumps, and other American equipment and know-how necessary to improve agriculture in the developing countries.

Fourth, I proposed and the Congress enacted far-reaching legislation which provides the strong foundation for the new Food for Freedom program.

The central theme of the program is self-help. The legislation authorized concessional sales of food to countries which prove their determination to expand their own food production.

[IV]

All of us know where the real battle is fought. Whatever the efforts in world capitals, the real tale is told on the land. It is the man behind the mule—or the bullock—or the water buffalo—who must be reached. Only his own government and his own people can reach him.

Thus, the most important progress of the past year has occurred in the developing countries themselves. And there is progress to report.

India—the largest consumer of food aid—perhaps provides the best example.

This has been a year of innovation in Indian agriculture. Agricultural development now has top priority in India's economic plan. Much remains to be done. But the evidence is unmistakable. India has started on the right path. India has:

—imposed a food rationing system to make efficient use of existing supplies;

—streamlined its transportation system to improve distribution;

—increased prices paid to the farmer, thus providing new incentives to use fertilizer, improved seeds, and other modern materials;

—begun large-scale operations with new varieties of rice introduced from Taiwan and with large quantities of high-yielding wheat seed imported from Mexico;

—approved plans to increase public investment in agriculture by more than 100 percent during the new Five Year Plan;

—started to expand rural credit, improve water supply, and accelerate the distribution of fertilizer to remote areas;

—stepped up family planning;

—negotiated an agreement for the first of several externally financed fertilizer plants to expand India's supply of home-produced fertilizers.

India is off to a good start. But it is only a start. As Indian officials have warned, hard work remains in reaching targets they have set and in improving coooperation among state governments. India's economic problems are enormous. But they can be solved.

What India has begun to do represents the growing realization in the developing world that long-term economic growth is dependent on growth in agriculture. Not every country has made an effort as great as India's. But in some countries, production has improved more rapidly.

Everywhere there is an air of change. No longer does industrial development alone attract the best minds and talents. Agriculture is now attracting the young and more enterprising economists, administrators, and entrepreneurs in the developing world.

This is the best measure of progress in the War on Hunger and the best assurance of success.

[V]

India's food problem requires a major commitment of our resources and those of other advanced countries. India's population is equal to that of sixty-six members of the United Nations.

Broad authority exists under our legislation for national action by Executive decision alone. But the issues presented here are of such moment, and on such a scale, as to make it important that we act together, as we do on other great issues, on the firm foundation of a Joint Resolution of Congress.

I ask you to support the broad approach we have proposed to the international community as a basic strategy for the War on Hunger. That strategy rests on three essential principles:

1. *Self-help.* The War on Hunger can be won only by the determined efforts of the developing nations themselves. International aid can help them. But it can only help if they pursue well-conceived and well-executed long-range plans of their own.

2. *Multilateral participation.* The assistance of the international community must be organized in a coalition of the advanced and the developing nations.

3. *Comprehensive planning.* The international community must develop a comprehensive plan to assist India to fulfill its program of achieving food sufficiency, not only during this year, but for the next few years as well.

Most of you are familiar with the events of the past year. Drought limited India's food grain production to seventy-two million tons in the 1965–66 crop year, compared with a record eighty-eight million tons the previous year. A massive international emergency program met the immediate crisis. But India had to use precious food reserves—that are thus not available to meet the shortages created by a second successive bad crop.

The weather since then has brought little relief. The general outlook is slightly improved, and overall production may reach seventy-nine million tons this year. But late last summer a severe drought hit heavily populated areas in northcentral India. Unless Indian production is supplemented by substantial imports—perhaps ten million tons by present estimates for calendar 1967—more than seventy million people will experience near famine.

The Government of India has already taken internal measures to move grain from its more fortunate areas to the drought areas. Imports of 2.3 million tons of grain are now in the pipeline to meet India's needs for the first two or three months of 1967. India has purchased some 200,000 tons of this grain with her own scarce foreign exchange. Canada with 185,000 tons, Australia with 150,000 tons and the Soviet Union with 200,000 tons have already joined the United States with its 1.6 million tons, in an impressive multilateral effort to help.

India's immediate problem—and the world's problem—is to fill the remaining gap for the balance of this year.

Because these facts bear heavily on the extent of U.S. food shipments, I have requested and received careful verification from our Ambassador in New Delhi, from the Secretary of Agriculture, and from members of Congress, who have recently been in India, including Senator McGee and Senator Moss.

I am particularly grateful to Representative Poage and Representative Dole and Senator Miller, who at my request made a special trip to India in December to assess the situation on the ground. Their careful and thorough analysis of the situation in India and their recommendations to me have been of great value.

During the last two weeks, the Undersecretary of State for Political Affairs and the Undersecretary of Agriculture have consulted in New Delhi and with most members of the World Bank's India Consortium.

The work of all these men and the diplomatic efforts of the Government of India have laid the foundation for the steps we must now take.

The United States cannot—and should not—approach this problem alone or on an improvised basis. We must support the Indian Government's efforts to enlist the aid of other nations in developing a systematic and international approach to the problems of Indian agriculture. Our long-term objective is to help India achieve its goal of virtual self-sufficiency in grain by the early 1970s. Meanwhile, as part of that effort, we must help India meet its immediate food needs.

[VI]

In line with policies established by the Congress, and after promising consultations with the Government of India and other governments involved, I recommend the following steps to achieve these objectives:

First: Our basic policy is to approach the problem of Indian food through the India Aid Consortium organized under the chairmanship of the World Bank. That Consortium has already developed a multilateral approach to economic assistance for India. Now, we propose to make food aid a part of that multilateral assistance program. We seek effective multilateral arrangements to integrate Indian food aid with broader programs of economic assistance and with capital and technical assistance for agricultural development.

In a preliminary way, we have consulted with the Government of India and with other members of the Consortium. There is substantial agreement among Consortium members on the major points of our proposal:

—Meeting food needs of India during this emergency should be accepted as an international responsibility in which each nation should share.

—Emergency food and food-related aid should be coordinated through the World Bank Consortium.

—This aid should not diminish the flow of resources for other development programs. It should be in addition to the targets for each country suggested by the World Bank.

Adding food aid to the responsibilities of the Consortium is sound economics and fair burden-sharing. The Consortium provides a proper channel for the food and food-related aid of donors who have not previously been involved in the food field. It will make clear that food provided from outside is as much a real contribution to Indian development as capital for specific projects or foreign exchange assistance for import programs.

Second: Should this program be established, we will support the Indian Consortium as it:

—undertakes a detailed projection of Indian food production and food aid requirements;

—prepares a program for non-food imports required to meet food production targets, as the basis for determining the equitable share of each donor;

—reviews India's self-help efforts, reports regularly on progress and identifies areas for future concentration of energies.

Third: We must take prompt action to help India meet its emergency food needs. Our best present estimate is that India needs deliveries of 10 million tons of food grains this year or roughly $725 million worth of food. 2.3 million tons, worth roughly $185 million, are already in the pipeline from a number of countries, including our own. To keep food in the pipeline, I am making an immediate allocation of 2 million tons, worth nearly $150 million, to tide India over while the Congress acts.

I recommend that Congress approve a commitment to share fully in the international effort to meet India's remaining food grain deficit of 5.7 million tons—worth about $400 million. To that end, I recommend a U.S. allocation of an additional amount of food grain, not to exceed 3 million tons, provided it is appropriately matched by other countries. I recommend that approximately $190 million available to the Commodity Credit Corporation in calendar 1967 be used for this purpose. These funds, if allotted, will have to be replenished by appropriation in fiscal 1968.

Fourth: I recommend your approval of an allocation of $25 million in food commodities for distribution by CARE and other American voluntary agencies, to assist the Government of India in an emergency feeding program in the drought areas of Bihar and Uttar Pradesh.

Fifth: We hope other donors will accelerate their exports of fertilizers to India.

Unless the application of chemical fertilizers rises sharply in India, she will not be able to meet her food grain targets. Those fertilizer targets are ambitious, yet they must be met and if possible, exceeded. Marshaling more fertilizer imports is as important to meeting India's emergency as gathering additional grain. India herself must take prompt steps to increase her fertilizer investment and production and improve its distribution.

Sixth: I propose for the longer run to continue encouraging U.S. private investors to participate in India's program to expand production of chemical fertilizers. We will urge other governments to encourage their own producers.

Seventh: We intend to pursue other initiatives in the broader context of world agricultural development:

—We shall continue to press for multilateral efforts in every international forum in which we participate, including the current negotiations to establish a food aid program as part of an International Cereals Arrangement.

—We shall continue our policy of encouraging private capital and technology to join the War on Hunger.

—We shall press for the creation of an investment guarantee fund by the OECD to encourage private investment in the agricultural industries of developing countries.

—We shall make available to food deficit nations the technology our scientists have now developed for producing fish protein concentrate.

—We shall look to the study by the President's Science Advisory Committee on the problems of food production to supply further and more definitive guidelines for near-term action and for long-range planning.

None of these steps can be as important as Indian resolve and Indian performance. The Indian Government is committed to a bold program of agricultural modernization. That program is the foundation for the entire international effort to help India. We believe that a self-reinforcing process of improvement is under way in India, affecting both agricultural techniques and government administration. On the basis of that conviction, we can move forward to do our share under the Food for Freedom Program of 1966.

[VII]

I believe these proposals are in our national interest. I believe that they reflect the deepest purposes of our national spirit.

I am asking the Congress, and the American people, to join with me in this effort and in an appeal to all the nations of the world that can help. I am asking the Congress to consider thoroughly my recommendations and to render its judgment. The Executive Branch, this Nation, and other nations will give full attention to the contributions that Congressional debate may produce.

There are many legitimate claims on our resources. Some may question why we devote a substantial portion to a distant country.

The history of this century is ample reply. We have never stood idly by while famine or pestilence raged among any part of the human family. America would cease to be America if we walked by on the other side when confronted by such catastrophe.

The great lesson of our time is the interdependence of man. My predecessors and I have recognized this fact. All that we and other nations have sought to accomplish in behalf of world peace and economic growth would be for naught if the advanced countries failed to help feed the hungry in their day of need.

"*Working with others, we are prepared to help build with you a modern Africa.*"

Remarks to Ambassadors from member states on the
Third Anniversary of the Organization of African Unity,
May 26, 1966.

The Charter signed on that day declares that "It is the inalienable right of all people to control their destiny," that "freedom, equality, justice and dignity are essential objectives . . . of the African peoples." It pledges to harness the natural and human resources of Africa for the total advancement of your peoples.

My country knows what those words mean. To us, as to you, they are not mere abstractions.

They are a living part of our experience as men and as nations.

They sum up the basic aspirations which your people and mine share in common: to secure the right of self-government; to build strong democratic institutions; and to improve the level of every citizen's well-being.

We have learned that these aspirations are indivisible. If it takes self-determination to become a free nation, it also takes a climate of regular growth to remain one. And that means the wise development of human and natural resources.

Whether nations are 5 years old or 190 years old, the striving for these goals never really ends. No nation ever completes the task of combining freedom with responsibility, liberty with order—and applying these principles, day after day, to our new problems.

Because these principles are imbedded in the hearts of Africans and Americans alike, I have asked you to come here today to join me in commemorating the founding of the Organization of African Unity.

It is a good occasion to reaffirm a unity of purpose that transcends two continents.

[I]

As your Charter and as our Declaration of Independence set forth, we believe that governments must derive their just powers from the consent of the governed.

This is the core of political freedom and the first principle of nation-building.

In the past fifteen years, belief in self-determination has fired the swift momentum of Africa toward full participation in the community of nations. It has been a truly remarkable era in which more than thirty nations have emerged from colonialism to independence.

The road has not been traveled without difficulty. Its end is not even yet in sight. There have been ups and downs—and of course there will be more. But as one of your distinguished ambassadors has pointed out, "What matters most about new nations is not that they have growing pains but that they are in fact growing."

There is in Africa today an increasing awareness that government must represent the true will of its citizens. Across the continent the majority of people prefer self-government with peril to subservience with serenity.

This makes all the more repugnant the narrow-minded, outmoded policy which in some parts of Africa permits the few to rule at the expense of the many.

The United States has learned from lamentable personal experience that domination of one race by another leads to waste and injustice. Just as we determined to remove the remnants of inequality from our midst, we are also with you—heart and soul—as you try to do the same.

We believe, as you do, that denial of a whole people's rights to shape their national future is morally wrong. We also know that it is politically and socially costly. A nation in the twentieth century cannot expect to achieve order and sustain growth unless it moves—not just steadily but rapidly—in the direction of full political rights for all of its peoples.

It has taken us time to learn this lesson. But having learned it, we must not forget it.

The Government of the United States cannot, therefore, condone the perpetuation of racial or political injustice anywhere in the world. We shall continue to provide our full share of assistance to refugees from social and political oppression.

As a basic part of our national tradition we support self-determination and an orderly transition to majority rule in every quarter of the globe. These principles have guided our American policy from India to the Philippines, from Vietnam to Pakistan. They guide our policy today toward Rhodesia.

We are giving every encouragement and support to the efforts of the United Kingdom and the United Nations to restore legitimate government in Rhodesia. Only when this is accomplished can steps be taken to open the full power and responsibility of nationhood to all the people of Rhodesia— not just 6 percent of them.

The disruptive effects of current sanctions fall heavily upon Zambia, adding a difficult burden to that young republic's efforts to strengthen its national life. I have informed President Kenneth Kaunda that we will work with him in trying to meet the economic pressures to which his country is being subjected.

The foreign policy of the United States is rooted in its life at home. We will not permit human rights to be restricted in our own country. And we will not support policies abroad which are based on the rule of minorities or the discredited notion that men are unequal before the law.

We will not live by a double standard—professing abroad what we do not practice at home, or venerating at home what we ignore abroad.

[II]

Our dreams and our vision are of a time when men of all races will collaborate as members of the same community, working with one another because their security is inseparable, and because it is right and because it is just.

This vision requires ever-increasing economic and social opportunity.

I know the enormous tasks that Africa faces in fulfilling its aspirations. I know how compelling is her need to apply modern science and technology to enrich the life of her people.

Much has been accomplished in the years since independence came to many members of your organization. You are proving what can be done when freedom and determination are joined with self-help and external assistance.

We have been particularly heartened by the impetus toward regional cooperation in Africa.

The world has now reached a stage where some of the most effective means of economic growth can best be achieved in large units commanding large resources and large markets. Most nation-states are too small, when acting alone, to assure the welfare of all of their people.

This does not mean the loss of hard-earned national independence. But it does mean that the accidents of national boundaries do not have to lead to hostility and conflict or serve as impossible obstacles to progress.

You have built new institutions to express a new sense of unity. Even as you grapple with the problems of early nationhood, you have sought out new possibilities of joint action—the OAU itself, the Economic Commission for Africa, the African Development Bank, and subregional groupings such as the Economic Community of Eastern Africa.

Growth in Africa must then follow the inspiration of African peoples. It must stem from the leadership of African governments. Assistance from others can provide the extra resources to help speed this growth.

Such assistance is already under way. In the last five years, aid from all external sources has amounted to over $8 billion. The United States of America has extended approximately $2 billion of that $8 billion.

But none of us can be content when we measure what is being done against what could be done.

We are anxious to work with you to fulfill your ambitions.

Working with others, we are prepared to help build with you a modern Africa.

I can think of many missions on which America and Africa can work together.

First, to strengthen the regional economic activities that you have already begun.

My country has offered the African Development Bank technical assistance funds to finance surveys of project possibilities, and loan funds for capital projects. We are ready to assist the regional economic communities through technical assistance and through the financing of capital projects. These will help to integrate the various economic regions.

Second, to increase the number of trained Africans.

We have been devoting a large part of our aid funds for Africa to education. This proportion will increase.

This year we are assisting in the development and the staffing of 24 colleges and universities. We are financing graduate and undergraduate training for over 2,000 African students in the United States. Altogether, almost 7,000 African students are studying with us now. We are helping some 40 secondary and vocational training institutions in Africa. We are aiding 21 teacher training institutions while also providing thousands of teachers, mostly through our Peace Corps.

But these efforts are not enough. One of the greatest needs is to overcome the frustration of many qualified students who are unable to obtain a higher education.

To help meet that problem, we propose:

—to assist your effort to make certain African universities regional centers of training and professional excellence;

—to explore with your governments an African Student Program for deserving students to attend African universities.

Third, to develop effective communications systems for Africa.

Africa is an immense continent embracing thirty-seven states with still more to emerge. Their communications links were formed in colonial times and tie them more to the outside world than to each other.

Africa's continental development needs a modern communications system to meet the regional requirements.

The United States has already financed several capital projects for communications facilities. We have provided technical assistance to communication services in a number of countries. I have authorized new surveys looking to the widening of existing telecommunications.

Communication satellites offer a striking opportunity to make even greater advances. To use these satellites effectively, ground stations must be built to bridge the continent. They would provide the essential links between the satellite and the conventional networks.

The United States is prepared to assist in the building of these stations. We will examine the need for additional ground links to enable Africa to secure greater benefits from these satellites.

These immediate actions illustrate some of the opportunities for cooperative effort. Other possibilities deserve early study.

Africa's great distances require more modern road, rail, and air links. The continent's great lakes and rivers could provide an enormous internal transport network.

The development of regional power grids offers an exciting possibility for regional cooperation and for national growth.

Opportunities for investment are still largely untapped despite the fact that African countries have welcomed private enterprise.

Africa's farm production does not meet the nutritional needs of its fast-growing population.

African territories may need special help in training their people and in strengthening their institutions as they move toward self-government.

So we want to explore these and other ways to respond to African needs. I have instructed the Secretary of State and other American officials to review our own development policies and programs in Africa. We shall be seeking new ideas and advice from American scholars, businessmen, and experts concerned with Africa's problems. Our Ambassador to Ethiopia, Ed Korry, will be working full time in the weeks ahead to follow through these initiatives. We wish to discuss these new cooperative approaches and ideas with African governments, as well as with other governments and international groups.

The United States wants to respond in any way that will be genuinely helpful—from the private American citizen to a combination of many nations, from a bilateral effort with a single African country to regional programs.

Above all, we wish to respond in ways that will be guided by the vision of Africa herself, so that the principles we share—the principles which underlie the OAU Charter—come to life in conformity with the culture and aspirations of the African peoples.

[III]

It once was said of Americans that "With nothing are we so generous as advice. . . . We prefer being with people we do things for to being with people who do things for us." But it is no longer a case of what we can do for or even with the people of Africa. We have come to recognize how much we have to learn from you.

As one of the great Africans—Dr. James Aggrey—wrote: "If you go to Africa expecting something from us, and give us a chance to do something for you, we will give you a surprise."

As we have deepened our relations with you, we have learned that Africa has never been as dark as our ignorance of it; that Africa is not one place and one people but a mosiac of places and peoples with different values and different traditions; that the people of Africa want to decide for themselves the kind of nations they wish to build.

We have learned not only about you but we have learned about ourselves. We have learned more about our debt to Africa and about the roots of so many of our American cultural values and traditions.

The human enterprise of which we are all a part has grown through contacts between men of different tribes, different states, and different nations. Through those contacts we have learned new ideas, new insights into ourselves, new ways of looking at the universe of nature, and—most importantly—new understanding of man's relation to his brothers.

It is this knowledge that endures.

It is this deepening appreciation and respect for the diversity of the world—each man and nation in it—that increases the possibilities for peace and order.

The Organization of African Unity has become an important organ for building that peace and order. On this third anniversary my countrymen join me in asking you to come here this afternoon, and join me in saluting you and the people that you so ably represent.

Thank you very much.

"The peaceful and progressive revolution
which is transforming Latin America
is one of the great inspirational movements of our time."
The President's Message to Congress
on the forthcoming Latin American Summit Meeting,
March 13, 1967.

In less than a month, the leaders of the American states will meet in Punta del Este in Uruguay.

It will be the first such meeting in a decade, and the second ever held, of the heads of the free nations of our hemispheric system.

This meeting represents another link in the bond of partnership which joins us with more than 230 million neighbors to the south.

The gathering is far more than a symbol of flourishing friendship. Its purpose is a review of the progress we have made together in a great adventure which unites the destinies of all of us. Beyond that it will include a

common commitment to the historic and humane next steps we plan to take together.

I look to this meeting with enthusiasm. The peaceful and progressive revolution which is transforming Latin America is one of the great inspirational movements of our time. Our participation in that revolution is a worthy enterprise blending our deepest national traditions with our most responsible concepts of hemispheric solidarity.

THE MEASURE OF PROGRESS

The cooperative spirit between the rest of the Americas and the United States has been building for decades.

The establishment of the Inter-American Development Bank in 1959, and the Act of Bogotá in 1960, under the leadership of President Eisenhower, helped turn that spirit to substance. In those historic compacts the American governments pledged their joint efforts to the development of programs to improve the lives of all the people of Latin America. They provided the impetus for an action taken in 1961 on which the history of the hemisphere has since turned. That action—the Alliance for Progress, which moved dramatically forward under President Kennedy—fused old dreams and fired new hopes. With its commitment of mutual assistance and self-help programs, it attacked evils as old as the condition of man—hunger, ignorance, and disease.

That Alliance is now six years old.

What can we say of it?

We can say that there is a clear record of progress. Per capita growth rates for Latin America show that more countries have broken the economic stagnation of earlier years. Reform and modernization are advancing as a new wave of managers and technicians apply their skills. There have been steady gains in private, national, and foreign investments. Inflation is easing. The struggle for social justice is proceeding.

These are all true. But the statements of progress are more meaningful, and they more realistically reflect the spirit of the Alliance, when they relate to the people for whose lives the Alliance itself was created. Since the Alliance began, and with the funds that we have contributed:

Men, women, and children are alive today who would otherwise have died.

—One hundred million people are being protected from malaria. In 10 countries, deaths caused by malaria dropped from 10,810 to 2,280 in three years' time. Smallpox cases declined almost as sharply.

—Twelve hundred health centers, including hospitals and mobile medical units, are in operation or soon will be.

For tens of thousands of families, the most fundamental conditions of life are improving.

—Three hundred and fifty housing units have been, or are now being, built.

—Two thousand rural wells and 1,170 portable water supply systems have been built to benefit some 20 million persons.

Children are going to school now who would not have gone before.

—Primary school enrollments have increased by 23 percent; secondary school enrollments by 50 percent; university enrollments by 39 percent.

—Twenty-eight thousand classrooms have been built.

—One hundred and sixty thousand teachers have been trained or given additional training.

—More than 14 million textbooks have been distributed.

—Thirteen million school children and 3 million preschoolers participate in school lunch programs.

Men whose fathers for generations have worked land owned by others now work it as their own.

—Sixteen countries have legislation dealing directly with land reform.

—With U.S. assistance, 1.1 million acres have been irrigated and 106,000 acres reclaimed.

—More than 700,000 agricultural loans have benefitted 3.5 million people.

—Fifteen thousand miles of road have been built or improved, many of them farm-to-market access roads.

All of these are heartening facts. But they are only the beginning of the story, and only part of it. Statistics can only suggest the deep human meaning of hope alive now where once none lived. Statistics cannot report the wonder of a child born into a world which will give him a chance to break through the tyranny of indifference which doomed generations before him to lives of bleakness and want and misery.

Nor can they reveal the revolution which has come about in the minds of tens of millions of people when they saw that their own efforts, combined with those of their governments and their friends abroad, could change their lives for the better.

Perhaps most important of all, statistics cannot adequately reflect the emergence of a vigorous, competent, and confident new generation of Latin American leaders. These men are determined to see realized in their own time a strong, modern Latin America, loyal to its own traditions and history. They are men who know that rhetoric and resolutions are no substitute for sustained hard work.

And statistics can never tell us what might have been. They cannot record the shots which might have rung out in the avenidas and plazas of a dozen Latin American cities, but did not—or the howls of angry crowds which might have formed, but did not. The full success of the Alliance for Progress must be sought not only in what has been accomplished but in what has been avoided as well.

Ferment gripped the hemisphere when the Alliance was born. In places throughout the world, terror with its bloodshed sought to redress ancient evils. And in some of these places—in Cuba and half a world away in Southeast Asia—even greater evil followed the thrust of violence. Through their own efforts under the Alliance for Progress, the Latin Americans have transformed the hemisphere into a region of determination and hope.

The United States participation in the Alliance was a bold affirmation of its belief that the true revolution which betters men's lives can be effected peacefully. The Alliance's six-year record of accomplishments is history's clear testament to the validity of that belief.

It is also a testament to the validity of the underlying principle of self-help. Our support has been vitally important to the successes so far achieved. But the commitments and dedication of the Latin American nations themselves to these tasks has been the keystone of that success.

THE TASK BEFORE US

The record of progress only illuminates the work which still must be done if life for the people of this hemisphere is truly to improve—not just for today, but for the changing years ahead.

Last August, in a statement on the fifth anniversary of the Alliance for Progress, I described the challenge in these terms:

"If present trends continue, the population of this hemisphere will be almost one billion by the year 2000. Two-thirds—some 625 million—will live in Latin America. Whatever may be done through programs to reduce the rate of population growth, Latin America faces a vast challenge.

"Farm production, for instance, should increase by 6 percent every year, and that will be double the present rate.

"At least 140 million new jobs will need to be created.

"Over a million new homes should be built each year.

"More than 175,000 new doctors need to be trained to meet the very minimum requirements.

"Hundreds of thousands of new classrooms should be constructed.

"And annual per capita growth rates should increase to the range of 4 to 6 percent.

"These requirements, added to the demands of the present, mean that new sights must be set, that new directions and renewed drive must be found if we are to meet the challenge, if we are to move forward."

It is with these sober problems confronting us that the leaders of the American states will meet at Punta del Este.

PILLARS OF PROGRESS

Our governments have been hard at work for months preparing for this meeting.

Our concern has centered on the question of how we can speed the development process in Latin America. We know that growth and trade are interacting forces. We know that they depend on the free movement of products, people, and capital. We know they depend on people who are healthy and educated. We know that these conditions contain the seeds of prosperity for all of us.

Further, based on our joint experience so far under the Alliance, we know that the future progress of the hemisphere must rest on four strong pillars:

1. *Elimination of Barriers to Trade*

Civilization in most of Latin America followed along the coastal rim of the continent. Today the centers of population are concentrated here. Vast inner frontiers lie remote and untouched, separated from each other by great rivers, mountains, forests, and deserts. Simon Bolívar saw these natural barriers as major obstacles to trade and communication and to his dream of a single great Latin American republic.

Because of them, Latin American countries for a century and a half tended to look outward for their markets to Europe and the United States.

Now they are looking inward as well. They see the same barriers, but they see them as less formidable. They are confident that with modern technology they can be overcome. Now with projects set in motion by the Alliance for Progress, men are beginning to carve roads along the slopes of the Andes, push bridges across the rushing rivers, connect power grids, extend pipelines, and link the overland national markets.

The barriers of nature symbolize obstructions every bit as restrictive as the artificial trade barriers that men erect. The work to remove them both must proceed together.

Latin American leaders have seen the very real threat of industrial stagnation in the high tariff barriers they have erected against their commerce with each other. They see economic integration as indispensible to their future industrial growth.

The Central American countries, stimulated by Alliance programs, have already achieved spectacular increases in trade and investment. The larger grouping of South American states and Mexico, however, has approached economic unity at a slower pace.

Now both groups together must systematically move toward a Latin American Common Market. When this is carried into effect, it will bring the most profound change in hemispheric relations since independence. The countries of Latin America have given clear and sure indication that they intend to join together to advance toward this goal.

2. *Improvement of Education*

The burden of illiteracy, which the masses of people in Latin America have borne for centuries, is beginning to lift. In other times, the pace might have been satisfactory. It cannot be considered so today.

The countries of Latin America hope and aim to be economically strong. Such nations will require trained people in an abundance far greater than their classrooms and laboratories provide. The scientists, the teachers, the skilled laborers, the administrators, and the planners on whom tomorrow depends must be trained before tomorrow arrives. Children must go to school in ever-increasing numbers. Adults who have never written their names must be raised to the level of literacy. University facilities must be expanded and scientific, technical, and vocational training must be provided of different kinds and in different fields.

All of this means more schools and an expansion of educational opportunities to reach more and more people with every passing month.

3. *Agriculture*

Half the people of Latin America live in rural areas.

Most of that rural life is still shackled by poverty and neglect. Agricultural productivity is still restricted by outdated methods and outmoded policies. Comprehensive programs and reforms must be accelerated to bring modern farming techniques to the campo.

We and our neighbors to the south envison a dynamic Latin American agriculture which will help raise the standards of rural life.

We envision a sufficient increase in the production of food to provide for their growing populations—and to help meet world needs as well.

We envision a modernization of farming policies and techniques which will lead to a healthy competitive climate for food production.

4. *Health*

Finally, we will strive harder than ever before to improve the health of all the people.

The battle against diseases that kill and cripple will be intensified.

Programs to make safe water supply and essential sanitation services available to all will be accelerated.

Nutrition levels for poor children and their parents will be advanced.

These are the problems we face together, and the promises we envision together, as we prepare for Punta del Este.

The problems are real. But the promises are also real. They are not empty visions. They are all within our reach. They will not be accomplished quickly or easily. But they are objectives worthy of the support of all our people.

INCREASED ASSISTANCE

In keeping with the spirit of our commitment under the Alliance for Progress and after a careful review of the objectives which our Latin American neighbors have set for themselves, I believe that we should pledge increased financial assistance in the years ahead.

The fundamental principle which has guided us in the past—demonstrated need and self-help—will continue to shape our actions in the future.

I recommend that Congress approve a commitment to increase our aid by up to $1.5 billion or about $300 million per year over the next five years.

It must not be at the expense of our efforts in other parts of this troubled world.

This amount will be in addition to the $1 billion we have been annually investing in the future of Latin American democracy, since the Alliance for Progress began six years ago. The total value of our economic assistance, even after the proposed increases, will still be only a fraction of the resources the Latin American nations are themselves investing.

The $1.5 billion increase I propose must be considered an approximate figure. Its precise determination will depend on steps which the Latin American nations themselves must take. But even so, we can project in a general way what will be necessary:

1. *Agriculture, Education, and Health*

Approximately $900 million of this increase should be used over the next five years to train teachers and build new laboratories and classrooms; to increase food production and combat the malnutrition which stunts the promise of young children; to fight disease and cure the ill.

One hundred million dollars of this amount has been included in the fiscal 1968 budget totals. I will request that it be added to the new obligational authority of $543 million already recommended for the Alliance for Progress.

For the next four fiscal years, the additional annual amount of some $200 million is within the $750 million authorization for the Alliance for Progress approved by Congress last year.

2. *A Latin American Common Market*

Approximately one-quarter to one-half billion dollars over a three to five year period, beginning about 1970, may be required to assist Latin America to move toward a common market.

Progress in this direction will require a period of transition. To help with this adjustment, assistance can be used to retrain workers, ease balance of payments problems, and stimulate intra-Latin American trade.

The members of the Alliance for Progress, including the United States, should be prepared to finance this assistance on an equitable matching basis.

I will ask Congress to authorize these funds only when the first essential steps toward a common market are taken.

3. *Multinational Projects—Communications, Roads, and River Systems*

Approximately $150 million over a three-year period should provide additional funds to the Inter-American Bank's Fund for Special Operations. These increased contributions can help finance preinvestment studies and a portion of the cost of new multinational projects:

—roads to link the nations and people of Latin America;

—modern communication networks to speed communications;

—bridges to carry the fruits of commerce over river barriers; dams to stem the ravages of flood;

—hydroelectric plants to provide a plentiful source of power for growth and prosperity.

We will request congressional authorization to provide this amount together with our regular $250 million annual contribution for each of the next three years to the Inter-American Bank's Fund for Special Operations.

We expect our partners in the Bank to increase their contributions on a proportional basis.

CONCLUSION

For the nations participating, Punta del Este will be a returning. It was there, six years ago in that city by the sea, that the American nations framed the charter of the Alliance which unites the hopes of this hemisphere.

We will be bringing with us the accumulated wisdom shaped by the experience gained in the years that have intervened.

We have learned much. Our sister countries know, and know well, that the burden of the task is theirs, the decisions are theirs, the initiative to build these new societies must be theirs. They know that the only road to progress is the road of self-help.

They know that our role can only be that of support, with our investment only a small portion of what they themselves contribute to their future.

This knowledge strengthens their own resolve, and their own commitment.

The people of the United States have learned over the six years since that first conference at Punta del Este, that the investment to which we pledged our support there is a good and honorable one.

It is an investment made in the spirit of our world view, so well described by a great American jurist, Learned Hand:

> Right knows no boundaries, and justice no frontiers; the brotherhood of man is not a domestic institution.

That view of the world provides us with the knowledge that service is mutually rewarding. We have learned in the span of a generation that when we help others in a truly meaningful way, we serve our own vital interests as well.

I could go to the summit meeting with the President's executive authority and reach understandings with our Latin American neighbors on behalf of this country. I believe it is much more in our democratic tradition if the Executive and the Congress work together as partners in this matter.

I am, therefore, going to you in the Congress not after a commitment has been made, but before making any commitment. I seek your guidance and your counsel. I have already met with some forty of your leaders.

I am asking the entire Congress and the American people to consider thoroughly my recommendations. I will look to their judgment and support as I prepare for our Nation's return to Punta del Este.

"Asia is now the crucial arena of man's striving for independence and order, and for life itself."

The President addresses the American Alumni Council, July 12, 1966.

. . . We have set out in this country to improve the quality of all American life. We are concerned with each man's opportunity to develop his talents. We are concerned with his environment—the cities and the farms where he lives, the air he breathes, the water he drinks. We seek to enrich the schools that educate him and, of course, to improve the governments that serve him.

We are at war against the poverty that deprives him, the unemployment that degrades him, and the prejudice that defies him.

As we look at other parts of the world, we see similar battles being fought in Asia, in Africa, and in Latin America. On every hand we see the thirst for independence, the struggle for progress—the almost frantic race that is taking place between education, on the one hand, and disaster on the other.

In all these regions we, too, have a very big stake.

Nowhere are the stakes higher than in Asia. So I want to talk to you tonight about Asia and about peace in Asia.

Asia is now the crucial arena of man's striving for independence and order, and for life itself.

This is true because three out of every five people in all this world live in Asia tonight.

This is true because hundreds of millions of them exist on less than 25 cents a day.

This is true because Communists in Asia tonight still believe in force in order to achieve their Communist goals.

So if enduring peace can ever come to Asia, all mankind will benefit. But if peace fails there, nowhere else will our achievements really be secure.

By peace in Asia I do not mean simply the absence of armed hostilities. For wherever men hunger and hate there can really be no peace.

I do not mean the peace of conquest. For humiliataion can be the seedbed of war.

I do not mean simply the peace of the conference table. For peace is not really written merely in the words of treaties, but peace is the day-by-day work of builders.

The peace we seek in Asia is a peace of conciliation between Communist states and their non-Communist neighbors; between rich nations and poor; between small nations and large; between men whose skins are brown and black and yellow and white; between Hindus and Moslems and Buddhists and Christians.

It is a peace that can only be sustained through the durable bonds of peace: through international trade; through the free flow of peoples and ideas; through full participation by all nations in an international community under law; and through a common dedication to the great tasks of human progress and economic development.

Is such a peace possible?

With all my heart I believe it is. We are not there yet. We have a long way to journey. But the foundations for such a peace in Asia are being laid tonight as never before. They must be built on these essentials:

[I]

First is the determination of the United States to meet our obligations in Asia as a Pacific power.

You have heard arguments the other way. They are built on the old belief that "East is East and West is West and never the twain shall meet":

—that we have no business but business interests in Asia;

—that Europe, not the Far East, is really our proper sphere of interest;

—that our commitments in Asia are not worth the resources they require;

—that the ocean is vast, the cultures alien, the languages strange, and the races different;

—that these really are not our kind of people.

But all of these arguments have been thoroughly tested. And all of them, I think, have really been found wanting.

They do not stand the test of geography—because we are bounded not by one, but by two oceans. And whether by aircraft or ship, by satellite or missile, the Pacific is as crossable as the Atlantic.

They do not stand the test of common sense. The economic network of this shrinking globe is too intertwined—the basic hopes of men are too inter-related—the possibility of common disaster is too real for us to ever ignore threats to peace in Asia.

They do not stand the test of human concern, either. The people of Asia do matter. We share with them many things in common. We are all persons. We are all human beings.

And they do not stand the test of reality, either. Asia is no longer sitting outside the door of the twentieth century. She is here, in the same world with all of us, to be either our partner or our problem.

Americans entered this century believing that our own security had no foundation outside our own continent. Twice we mistook our sheltered position for safety. Twice we were dead wrong.

And if we are wise now, we will not repeat our mistakes of the past. We will not retreat from the obligations of freedom and security in Asia.

[II]

The second essential for peace in Asia is this: to prove to aggressive nations that the use of force to conquer others is a losing game.

There is no more difficult task, really, in a world of revolutionary change— where the rewards of conquest tempt ambitious appetites.

As long as the leaders of North Vietnam really believe that they can take over the people of South Vietnam by force, we must not let them succeed.

We must stand across their path and say: "You will not prevail. But turn from the use of force and peace will follow."

Every American must know exactly what it is that we are trying to do in Vietnam. Our greatest resource, really, in this conflict—our greatest support for the men who are fighting out there—is your understanding. It is your willingness to carry—perhaps for a long time—the heavy burden of a confusing and costly war.

We are not trying to wipe out North Vietnam.

We are not trying to change their government.

We are not trying to establish permanent bases in South Vietnam.

And we are not trying to gain one inch of new territory for America.

Then, you say, "Why are we there?" Why?

Well, we are there because we are trying to make the Communists of North Vietnam stop shooting at their neighbors;

—because we are trying to make this Communist aggression unprofitable;

—because we are trying to demonstrate that guerrilla warfare, inspired by one nation against another nation, can never succeed. Once that lesson is learned, a shadow that hangs over all of Asia tonight will, I think, begin to recede.

"Well," you say, "when will that day come?" I am sorry, I cannot tell you. Only the men in Hanoi can give you that answer.

We are fighting a war of determination. It may last a long time. But we must keep on until the Communists in North Vietnam realize the price of aggression is too high—and either agree to a peaceful settlement or to stop their fighting.

However long it takes, I want the Communists in Hanoi to know where we stand.

First, victory for your armies is impossible. You cannot drive us from South Vietnam by your force. Do not mistake our firm stand for false optimism. As long as you persist in aggression, we are going to resist.

Second, the minute you realize that a military victory is out of the question and you turn from the use of force, you will find us ready and willing to reciprocate. We want to end the fighting. We want to bring our men back home. We want an honorable peace in Vietnam. In your hands is the key to that peace. You have only to turn it.

[III]

The third essential is the building of political and economic strength among the nations of free Asia.

For years they have been working at that task. And the untold story of 1966 is the story of what free Asians have done for themselves, and with the help of others, while South Vietnam and her allies have been busy holding aggression at bay.

Many of you can recall our faith in the future of Europe at the end of World War II when we began the Marshall Plan. We backed that faith with all the aid and compassion we could muster.

Well, our faith in Asia tonight is just as great. And that faith is backed by judgment and by reason. For if we stand firm in Vietnam against military conquest, we truly believe that the emerging order of hope and progress in Asia will continue to grow and to grow.

Our very able Secretary of State, Dean Rusk, has just returned from a trip through the Far East. He told me yesterday afternoon of many of the heartening signs he saw as the people of Asia continue to work toward common goals. And these are just some of them.

In the last year:

—Japan and Korea have settled their long-standing disputes and established normal relations with promise for closer cooperation.

—One country after another has achieved rates of economic growth that are far beyond the most optimistic hopes we had a few years ago.

—Indonesia and its more than 100 million people have already pulled back from the brink of communism and economic collapse.

—Our friends in India and Pakistan—600 million strong—have ended a tragic conflict and have returned to the immense work of peace.

—Japan has become a dramatic example of economic progress through political and social freedom and has begun to help others.

—Communist China's policy of aggression by proxy is failing.

—Nine Pacific nations—allies and neutrals, white and colored—came together on their own initiative to form an Asian and Pacific Council.

—New and constructive groupings for economic cooperation are under discussion in Southeast Asia.

—The billion dollar Asian Development Bank which I first mentioned in Baltimore in my televised speech a few months ago is already moving forward in Manila with the participation of more than thirty-one nations.

—And the development of the Lower Mekong River Basin is going forward despite the war.

Throughout free Asia you can hear the echo of progress. As one Malaysian leader said: "Whatever our ethical, cultural, or religious backgrounds, the nations and peoples of Southeast Asia must pull together in the same broad sweep of history. We must create with our own hands and minds a new perspective and a new framework. And we must do it ourselves."

For this is the new Asia, and this is the new spirit we see taking shape behind our defense of South Vietnam. Because we have been firm—because we have committed ourselves to the defense of one small country—other countries have taken new heart.

And I want to assure them tonight that we never intend to let you down. America's word will always be good.

[IV]

There is a fourth essential for peace in Asia which may seem the most difficult of all: reconciliation between nations that now call themselves enemies.

A peaceful mainland China is central to a peaceful Asia.

A hostile China must be discouraged from aggression.

A misguided China must be encouraged toward understanding of the outside world and toward policies of peaceful cooperation.

For lasting peace can never come to Asia as long as the 700 million people of mainland China are isolated by their rulers from the outside world.

We have learned in our relations with other such states that the weakness of neighbors is a temptation, and only firmness, backed by power, can really deter power that is backed by ambition. But we have also learned that the greatest force for opening closed minds and closed societies is the free flow of ideas and people and goods.

For many years, now, the United States has attempted in vain to persuade the Chinese Communists to agree to an exchange of newsmen as one of the first steps to increased understanding between our people.

More recently, we have taken steps to permit American scholars experts in medicine and public health, and other specialists to travel to Communist China. And only today we, here in the Government, cleared a passport for a leading American businessman to exchange knowledge with Chinese mainland leaders in Red China.

All of these initiatives, except the action today, have been rejected by Communist China.

We persist because we know that hunger and disease, ignorance and poverty, recognize no boundaries of either creed or class or country.

We persist because we believe that even the most rigid societies will one day awaken to the rich possibilities of a diverse world.

And we continue because we believe that cooperation, not hostility, is really the way of the future in the twentieth century.

That day is not yet here. It may be long in coming, but I tell you it is clearly on its way, because come it must.

Earlier this year the Foreign Minister of Singapore said that if the nations of the world could learn to build a truly world civilization in the Pacific through cooperation and peaceful competition, then—as our great President Theodore Roosevelt once remarked—this may be the greatest of all human eras—the Pacific era.

As a Pacific power, we must help achieve that outcome.

Because it is a goal worthy of our American dreams and it is a goal that is worthy of the deeds of our brave men who are dying for us tonight.

So I say to you and I pledge to all those who are counting on us: You can depend upon us, because all Americans will do their part.

Reforms Plus Results
Equal Revolutions

By David E. Lilienthal

On November 29, 1967, a ceremonial luncheon took place at the State Department that is a landmark of achievement in the history of American
cooperative assistance to the less developed countries. Heading the list of
guests were the Iranian Ambassador, Hushang Ansary, and Secretary of
State Rusk. The meeting was not to request additional economic aid but to
celebrate, with considerable satisfaction on both sides, that it was ending, because though Iran had benefited from that assistance it no longer needed it.

More than any single factor the "success story" of Iran's emergence is
the result of social and economic reforms instituted five years ago by the Shah
himself, in a platform calling for dramatic and comprehensive change in
that ancient land. These reforms were carried through under His Majesty's
leadership with speed and decisiveness. This took political and personal
courage. The Shah's "white revolution," as he called it, released the great
potential energies of the young educated men and women, the peasants, and
the industrial workers. As a consequence, economic and social development
came rapidly, until now Iran's new day is widely recognized.

It was not solely its great oil revenues, as some superficial commentators have said, that changed the face of Iran and the lives of many Iranians in these few years. Nor were American assistance and World Bank loans the chief factor, though these were of great consequence.

For the development of Iran or any other country the greatest asset is the energies and resolve of its people; it was the effect of these reforms upon *that* Iranian asset that brought this swift change, that created a new climate of life for the people of all classes. And it was the Shah's concern for people, made specific and credible by these social and economic reforms he sponsored, that was the underpinning of this program and of the transformation now under way.

Foreign aid is a very complex business. Sometimes it helps to look at one strand of the whole tapestry, over time.

To begin with, our great experiment in the 1930s, under Franklin D. Roosevelt, of the Tennessee Valley Authority had a tremendous impact on thinking abroad as well as at home. I remember talking with Vice-President Henry Wallace during the war. He was then making many speeches about postwar aims and ideals. I told him how important I felt it was that men in his position talk in concrete terms about *things*—about land, water, rivers, all over the earth, about electricity, gadgets, cattle—things that people everywhere could understand and that above all they wanted. I said it was desperately important that concrete substance of this sort be given to the inspiring general statements of purpose—"economic democracy," the Atlantic Charter, the Four Freedoms. I told him that basically the problems of developing the Tennessee Valley were strikingly similar to those of China and India and other places over the earth.

Then late in 1943 President Roosevelt met with Winston Churchill and Premier Stalin at Teheran, in part to plan postwar arrangements. FDR was a very observant man. He was concerned about ideals and about *things*—water, trees, soil, birds. He never forgot what he had seen on his trip to Iran. Some months later—on September 2, 1944—he wrote to the Shah:

My dear Shah Mohammed Reza:

Of course, I do not pretend to know Iran well on account of the short-ness of my visit, but may I write you about one of the impressions which I received on my air trip to Teheran?

It relates to the lack of trees on the mountain slopes and the general aridity of the country which lies above the plains.

All my life I have been very interested in reforestation and the increase of the water supply which goes with it.

May I express a hope that your Government will set aside a small amount for a few years to test out the possibility of growing trees or even shrubs on a few selected areas and to test out the possibility of trees which would hold the soil with their roots and, at the same time, hold back floods? We are doing something along this line in our western dry areas and, though it is a new experiment, it seems to be going well.

It is my thought that if your Government would try similar small ex-periments along this line it would be worthwhile for the future of Iran.

I do not need to tell you how much interested I am in that future, and the future of the people of Iran.

With my warm regards,

Cordially yours,
Franklin D. Roosevelt

The Shah replied that he was very interested, and would need help from Americans on the central problem of irrigation.

FDR was being modest when he referred to "doing something along this line in our western dry areas." Actually, through the Conservation Corps and other agencies he had led in the reforestation of hundreds of thousands of acres, especially in the West, but also in the TVA area. Roosevelt's interest in forestation and water resources was another link between him and LBJ, a young Texan growing up in a land needing water and trees. And by a nicety of history, this strand we are looking at finally connected Lyndon Johnson with Iran itself.

Concern for people and releasing their great potential should be, I think, the *basic building block* of economic advance everywhere. As exemplified in the person of Lyndon Johnson, this concern for people had far more to do with the Shah's resolve and therefore with the Iranian transformation than is generally known. We have this on no less authority than the Shah himself.

To understand how this came about one needs to have this background:

Five years ago Lyndon B. Johnson, then Vice-President, with Mrs. Johnson, paid a visit to Iran. He behaved in a way completely natural for a man who though the Vice-President of the United States has never forgotten his early struggles as a poor boy and young man, in an "underdeveloped" area of our own country. In Iran, instead of confining his visit to official functions, so often the practice of dignitaries, the then Vice-President went to the big bazaars, got out of his car and enthusiastically shook hands with peasants and poor townspeople, and exchanged greetings with them, to their obvious delight. What he did that day in Teheran is what comes naturally to Lyndon Johnson wherever he is. It is people he is interested in most of all.

One evening in August 1967 I was a guest at a White House State Dinner in honor of the Shah. In the historic East Room I saw the Shah look across that room to Lyndon Johnson, now President, and then glance down at the First Lady at the Shah's side. Then he made this statement as a part of an extemporaneous and moving talk:

"We have been inspired in so many ways by the Americans—in your humanitarian approach to the wonderful achievements of your people in every domain, also in many of your great leaders.

"If I may say so, the pleasure of meeting you, Mr. President, and Mrs. Johnson five years ago, *coincides, incidentally, with the reform that we have undertaken in our recent history.* [My italics.]

"What you represent, the morality that you represent—and trying to really uphold it in our world—the confidence that you have created that your word can be taken as the word of a man and a judgment, and so many other aspects of your great qualities are a real contribution to all of us.

"So I will always take this as a nice augury that your coming to our country coincided with our great effort to bring our country—even after 2,500 years of history—into the modern age."

By the inexplicable chemistry by which men of great influence find themselves drawn to each other, however great the difference of their background, the Shah of Iran and the Vice-President from Texas found they spoke the same language, the language of basic democracy.

As a prefatory note to that portion of this book dealing with speeches and declarations of President Johnson on economic cooperation to developing countries, I have chosen Persia as an example because it is a genuine case, now well recognized, of progress. But also because it falls within my own personal experience and observation. Thirteen years ago the Shah of Iran asked the private development company we had just established to devise a program and begin the management task of carrying it out for the development of a then bleak desert region, the Khuzistan, in southwestern Persia. Although neither American funds nor American governmental technical personnel were involved in this enterprise, we—Iranians and my American colleagues—did bring to our task the same lesson that Lyndon Johnson and his Administration exemplify: "Begin with the people." Build structures, yes; and this has been done in that region: one of the great dams of the world, irrigation canals, a sugar plantation and factory, and so on. But chiefly building the confidence and skills of the Iranians. And this too has been achieved, to a marked degree.

So Iran seems to me a good example as a preface to the declarations of the Johnson Administration in American economic cooperation. Many others might be cited, but about those I have less personal knowledge.

"International economic cooperation" with the less developed countries means quite different things to different people. To many it is primarily a field for broad geopolitical generalizations, econometric "models," studies, research, surveys. The gritty day-by-day work of making things happen in these countries is to them a matter of "managerial detail," without intellectual appeal.

To others economic development is finding out what is do-able in the here and now, and devising ways to get it done. This is essentially the outlook of the Johnson Administration in the area of economic assistance overseas.

Lyndon B. Johnson's public life has shown a preoccupation with getting things done. This is revealed in many ways. One is the question that he puts to many of his visitors: What do you think I should be *doing* that I'm not doing?

One cannot fully understand the policy declarations and speeches of this Administration in the area of economic development of less developed countries or any other field without reading between the lines, and noting the preoccupation with achieving results in the day-to-day lives of hard-pressed people. These are essentially the same kind of people young Lyndon Johnson knew in his earlier years. Their hardships and aspirations have colored his thinking throughout his career and shaped all the policies of his Administration.

Lyndon B. Johnson

"You have helped to turn the Peace Corps from an intriguing idea into an inspired operation."
The President speaks at the swearing-in
of Jack Hood Vaughn
on the fifth anniversary of the Peace Corps,
March 1, 1966.

Mr. Vice-president, Mr. Secretary of State, Your Excellencies, the Ambassadors and representatives of the forty-six countries where the Peace Corps is today operating, returned Peace Corps volunteers, members of the Peace Corps National Advisory Council, the first Peace Corps Director and the new Director, Members of Congress, all other members of our Government, all other members of the Peace Corps, ladies and gentlemen:

Happy birthday.

All of you have earned that greeting. Every person here, and many more who could not be here, helped to turn the Peace Corps from an intriguing idea into an inspired operation. You acted on faith:

—faith in the power of men and women to always translate their convictions into action;

—faith in the ability of our society to trust its citizens when they choose to be different;

—faith in the desire of other nations to welcome with patience and good will those who come to them offering not money or goods, but only themselves.

It was an act of faith on the part of that great President who established the Peace Corps by Executive order five years ago today. And it was faith on the part of the Congress of the United States that voted by increasingly overwhelming majorities to support this wonderful activity.

All of that faith, I think, has been vindicated. The constructive work of more than 20,000 people over five long years—the collaboration of the peoples with whom they have lived—is a real testament to the trust upon which the Peace Corps was founded.

In a world of violence, these volunteers have shown that there is really another way—the way of private dedication, the way of quiet courage working unheralded for ends that each has accepted as valuable and as vital.

In this way those of you in the Peace Corps have carried forward the real revolution of our day and time, the revolution of peaceful change. In this way you are really waging the only war that we in America want to wage— the war against the inhumanity of man to his neighbor and the injustice of nature to her children.

In Vietnam today there is another war. It is fueled by those who believe that they somehow might be able to accomplish their ends by means of terror and violence.

America's purpose there is to give peaceful change a real chance to succeed. In that struggle, soldiers are necessary not only to prevent but to halt aggression, and to provide security for those who are determined to protect themselves and to raise their families. So, too, are the other workers of peace necessary who must lay the foundation for economic and social progress in that land. Political freedom, no matter how dearly bought, can flourish only when men and women are free from want and free from despair.

We have already begun that important work in Vietnam. The day, I hope, will soon come when the Peace Corps will be there, too. It must somehow find the day and the time that it can go and make its contribution when peace is assured. The same spirit that the Peace Corps volunteers brought to thousands of villages and cities in forty-six countries should be carried to the hamlets of Vietnam.

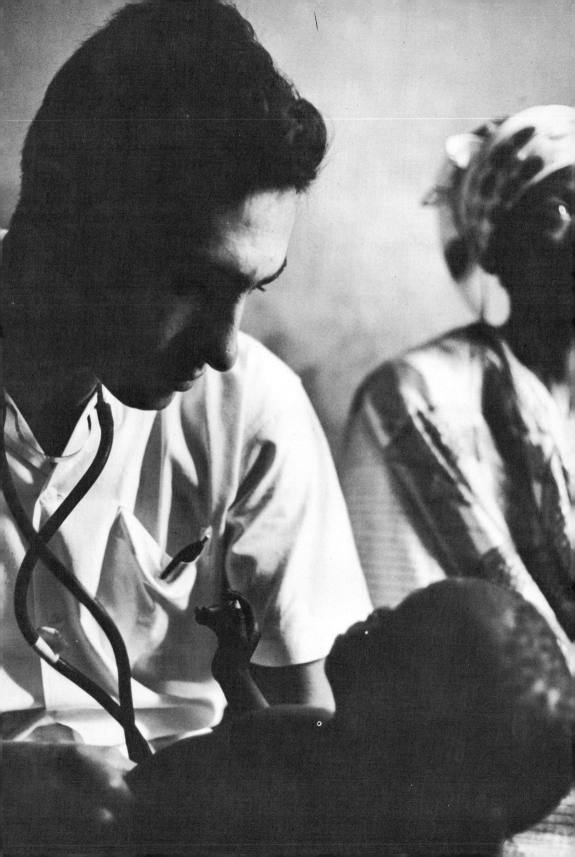

Yesterday, at the University of Michigan, your new Director, Mr. Vaughn, said, "All of the energy, the faith, the devotion which we in the Peace Corps bring to our service serves a single cause." I can only say, then, that no group, no organization, contributes more to the cause of peace, in my judgment, than the Peace Corps which we honor here today. You are fortunate. You are equipped with an idea whose time has really come.

It has come in Vietnam. We are there in order to restore peace and in order to let the works of peace serve the life of man.

So to the people of that land—North and South—we acknowledge that there are great differences between our people and our nations. But these gulfs of culture and tradition are spanned by a common humanity and shared needs of man—of food and shelter and education, a decent life for each family, the chance to build and to work and to till the soil free from fear and the arbitrary horrors of battle—and to walk in the dignity of those who have chosen their own destiny.

It is more than a shame; it is a crime—perhaps the greatest crime of man— that so much courage, and so much will, and so many dreams must be carelessly flung on the fires of death and war.

The long history of this conflict is filled with misunderstandings and invectives and passions. I think the time has come to strike off the chains of the past so that we may be free to shape anew the future. We should not permit endless and unrewarding argument over what has already happened to bar us from accomplishing what should happen.

Peace is within our grasp, if we will both reach for it together, and beyond peace are the wondrous gifts of peace, and beyond that a time when hope can reach unbounded for consummation.

There may be those who do not want peace, those whose ambitions stretch so far that war in Vietnam is but a welcome and a convenient episode in an immense and doomed design to subdue history to their will. But let them not suppose that our desire for peace springs either from weakness or from hesitation. Our desire for peace springs, rather, from a further recognition of our knowledge that the search for peace also always requires great skill and great courage.

If there are others, however, who do want peace, and if it is equally true that total victory is beyond expectation for them, as they must now know that it really is, then we think there is only one answer: Negotiate peace and let war stand aside while the people of Vietnam make their choice. For our part, here in America, we are eagerly willing to abide by the outcome.

We sincerely desire neither territory nor bases in Vietnam, neither economic domination nor military alliance. We fight for the principle that the people of South Vietnam should be able to choose their own course, free from the coercions of violence and terror and fear. We believe that the people of South Vietnam, through the process of elections, can select their own leaders and their own way of life.

That is the example we have set. That is the procedure we follow in our own land, and all the people of Vietnam can then freely express their will on the great questions of unification and national destiny.

Now, ladies and gentlemen, that is what your country wants for the people of South Vietnam. That is what the people of South Vietnam, we think, want. So together we seek the day when we can be as generous in peace as we must be determined in battle. We are ready when that day comes, ready to join in a massive effort of reconstruction and development that is open to all, including North Vietnam.

The Asian Bank, which we suggested in our speech in Baltimore, is only a beginning of what can be done when aggression ends and when men decide that peace and not war should be the testing ground of human experience. That measure has already passed the House and been reported in the Senate Foreign Relations Committee unanimously, and we hope it can be acted upon this week. It will be a great step forward.

The Peace Corps has already shown us what it can do. For the Peace Corps is a movement. It is a movement to place the vessel of peace in the hands of individual men and women who are driven by their own conscience to do something about healing this wounded world in which we live.

The man who, more than any other man, gave fire and gave purpose to your movement is stepping aside today on the fifth anniversary of the day that that movement began.

Is there any doubt of the enormous bequest that he is leaving?

For generations to come, as the harvests of his efforts are reaped time and time again, men will marvel at his contributions.

Of Sargent Shriver, it can be said that he is a man to whom excellence and public service are synonymous, one of those rare men of whom Virgil spoke when he said, "They can because they think they can."

Five years ago only a few thought he could.

There were moments, I am sure, at least from some of the cables I received from him when he was out in other parts of the world, when he, himself, doubted that he could. But he did.

He was, of course, inspired, so inspired that he ran off rather rudely, I thought, with one of my assistants back in 1961. In the last few months I have tried to pay him back. I have run off with several of his.

One of them is here today to succeed him.

Jack Vaughn I first met out in a little fishing village in Africa, but he, like Sargent Shriver, I observed on that first meeting, is a disciple of peace. His life has been spent in the service of the cause of peace. This is the third job that I have asked Jack Vaughn to take since I met him in that fishing village in 1961. Each of these jobs he has served with great distinction.

This is going to be the last time, though, that I make a request for him to take another job, because, frankly, I am tired of attending his swearing-in ceremonies!

Jack, I think you know that you are stepping into the shoes of a man who has done more for his country than his country really knows. His hands are going to be full with poverty and yours are going to be full with peace, and I hope that all of us will be the better for the work that both of you do.

In you two men I have the greatest confidence, and I have no doubt but what you will prove worthy of it.

Thank you very much.

"This is the only war in which we seek escalation."

The President speaks at the International Rice Research Institute, Los Baños, the Philippines, October 26, 1966.

We meet in a new Asia.

In this Asia the old barriers of distance, of indifference, and rivalry are slowly being overcome—and a new spirit of cooperation is taking shape.

Today, while our Asian friends still need a helping hand, they want to match it with their own efforts—aimed toward their own goals.

The International Rice Research Institute—here in Los Baños—is a product of intelligent assistance and massive self-help. Two American foundations have given invaluable support. One of the motive forces behind the creation of the Institute, I am proud to say, was the former president of the Rockefeller Foundation—Dean Rusk; the Institute's director today is a New Hampshire man, Robert Chandler. Yet the professional staff includes scientists of seven nationalities; about two-thirds of them are Asian.

In its short four years of existence this Institute has produced promising new strains of high-yield rice, which are now being planted in the soil of many countries. One strain developed here has been called the miracle rice— but it is not a miracle at all. Its development required countless efforts at crossbreeding, countless trials and errors. This strain—called IR–3—will be followed by better varieties still. But it has already given promise of multiplying rice yields here in the Philippines and elsewhere in Southeast Asia where they are now much too low.

I am glad to know that these seeds are going to be made available to all nations, whatever their politics and ideology. The need for food transcends all the divisions man has created for himself.

The work of this Institute symbolizes to me the progress that is being made in the other war in Asia.

At the Manila Conference we were deeply concerned with the military struggle in Vietnam.

But we were equally engrossed by the critical needs of the emerging societies of Asia—whatever their ideology.

Man's greatest problem is the fearful race between food and population. If we lose that race our hopes for the future will turn to ashes.

And the shocking truth is that as of this moment we are losing the war on hunger.

There are nations in the world with declining standards of living— where population growth is outrunning the supply of fundamental foodstocks.

At the same time the stocks of the surplus producing nations have rapidly declined.

There was, for example, in 1961 a grain surplus of 136 million tons. The figure for 1967 is 50 million.

A rice surplus of over a billion tons existed in 1956. It has dropped to a mere 300 million tons.

These are danger signals we can ignore only at our peril. For between now and 1980 we must prepare to feed one billion more people.

That may sound like a bloodless, economic abstraction.

But we must learn to hear what it says in human terms: one billion more people means one billion babies. And four out of five of these infants will be born in countries that cannot today feed their people from their own resources. That gap can be overcome.

And you at Los Baños are pointing the way toward overcoming it.

Drawing on your experiments, your new rice strains, the technical training you are giving in conjunction with the College of Agriculture of the University of the Philippines, we can escalate the war against hunger.

That is the only war in which we seek escalation.

We believe we can win it. Yet victory will not come easily. What it demands—within each country and on a cooperative basis among nations—is a higher level of social, economic, and political creativity than mankind has yet achieved.

Above all, it calls for the inspired dedication of the new generations of young people who are coming into maturity throughout the world. This is especially true in Asia where more than half of the population is less than twenty-five years old.

These young people believe—and they are right—that there is nothing natural or God-given about poverty, hunger, and disease.

Some of them react against an unjust fate by professing empty ideologies.

But some—and they are represented here at Los Baños—realize that only knowledge, skill, and hard work can provide fruitful avenues to a decent future.

In every country—but particularly in Asia, Latin America, and Africa—there is a desperate need for skilled men and women who can release their brothers from the *barrios* of poverty.

For if the world's need for food is to be met, it will be by scientists and economists who will discover better seeds, better methods of planting and marketing, better ways of distributing the harvest of the earth. It will not be by miracles, but by the qualities of mind and will that developed the new Los Baños rice strain.

If illiteracy and disease are to be conquered, it will be by armies of well-prepared teachers and doctors.

Pickets, pamphlets, angry shouting against the society—are all understandable among the young. But if that is all there is—if there is no equally vigorous determination to prepare for the long hard task of making a better life for one's people—it will not be enough.

There is an anger that cannot tolerate hunger, disease, illiteracy, and injustice in the world. And it becomes a divine anger when it is translated into the practical work of healing and teaching.

I know that there are healers and teachers in Asia—in the universities, among those fortunate enough to have escaped a life of poverty—and in the *barrios* and villages as well.

Asia's great task is to liberate their energies for her children's sake.

On her success our hopes for peace—and the conscience of all mankind—depend.

"'Dig deep and sow good seed. . . .'"

The President toasts
His Imperial Majesty Mohammed Reza Shah Pahlavi
at a dinner honoring the Shah,
the White House,
August 22, 1967.

Your Imperial Majesty, ladies and gentlemen:

The poet Emerson has said that "The ornament of a house is the friends who frequent it."

Our one regret this evening is that our warm friend and honored guest has not been able to ornament the occasion more—by bringing along his very beautiful and charming Empress. We miss her very much—because this Administration champions beauty in all its forms.

His Majesty's coronation will take place in October, after a reign of nearly twenty-six years. This gathering of friends offers you heartfelt good wishes and prayers for still brighter success.

To them I must add special congratulations on Your Majesty's superb sense of timing. You have had the foresight to schedule your coronation when your polls are up.

You also have the satisfaction of looking back on a most impressive record of very progressive leadership. You have taught Iran's people that they have in their own strength and imagination the power to solve their own problems and to realize their own dreams.

When I visited Iran with Mrs. Johnson—just five years ago next week—the land reform program, that we discussed until late in the evening, was just beginning. Tonight, 50 percent of Iran's rural families farm their own land. Some seven thousand or more rural cooperatives have already been established—and more than eight hundred extension corpsmen are out helping the farmers of that country to acquire new agricultural skills.

This promise of new progress and dignity beckons all the Middle East. The people of that region have just suffered a very great shock. But that shock should and must not obscure the vision of what they can do to solve their problems constructively, peacefully—by working together, by working with their neighbors.

We stand ready tonight, as before, to help those who ask our help—to strengthen the independence of all who seek it in purposeful partnership. Now, as always, America seeks no domination—by force of arms, by influence of wealth, by stealth or subversion.

We seek to build in brotherhood. We want to continue giving and learning—as we will again when Iranian and American scientists soon begin to study ways to exploit Iran's water resources, and to employ the exciting new technology of desalting. Our cooperation will continue to grow in this and many other ways.

We take great pride in having with us this evening Mr. David Lilienthal who has done so much to plan and develop our own land and who is now giving his talented energies to your country.

But turning the dreams we all share into a shared reality asks a long journey of both our countries. We take heart from the knowledge that the people of Iran, under Your Majesty's leadership, have the fortitude and vision to continue their advance, and to so inspire all who would follow in hope.

Ladies and gentlemen, I can conclude this statement in no better way than to recall for you the words of a great Persian poet:

Dig deep and sow good seed;
Repay the debt you owe your country's soil;
You need not then be beholden to any man.

Our distinguished guest this evening has truly sown good seed. I ask those of you who have come from throughout our land to join me in a toast to the architect of Iran's future, the distinguished sovereign and leader of the Iranian people, and our most valued and trusted friend, His Imperial Majesty, the Shah of Iran.

"Hunger poisons the mind.
It saps the body.
It destroys hope. . . .
I propose that the United States lead the world
in a war against hunger."
The President recommends to Congress
a Program for Food Aid and Food and Fiber Reserves,
February 10, 1966

Men first joined together for the necessities of life—food for their families, clothing to protect them, housing to give them shelter.

These are the essentials of peace and progress.

But in the world today, these needs are still largely unfulfilled.

When men and their families are hungry, poorly clad, and ill-housed, the world is restless—and civilization exists at best in troubled peace.

A War on Hunger

Hunger poisons the mind. It saps the body. It destroys hope. It is the natural enemy of every man on earth.

I propose that the United States lead the world in a war against hunger.

There can only be victors in this war. Since every nation will share in that victory, every nation should share in its costs. I urge all who can help to join us.

A Program for Mankind

The program I am submitting to Congress today, together with the proposals set forth in my message on foreign assistance, look to a world in which no man, woman, or child need suffer want of food or clothing.

The key to victory is self-help.

Aid must be accompanied by a major effort on the part of those who receive it. Unless it is, more harm than good can be the end result.

I propose:

1. *Expanded food shipments to countries where food needs are growing and self-help efforts are under way.*

Even with their maximum efforts abroad, our food aid will be needed for many years to come.

2. *Increased capital and technical assistance.*

Thus, self-help will bear fruit through increased farm production.

3. *Elimination of the "surplus" concept in food aid.*

Current farm programs are eliminating the surpluses in our warehouses. Fortunately the same programs are flexible enough to gear farm production to amounts that can be used constructively.

4. *Continued expansion of markets for American agricultural commodities.*

Increased purchasing power, among the hundreds of millions of consumers in developing countries, will help them become good customers of the American farmer.

5. *Increasing emphasis on nutrition, especially for the young.*

We will continue to encourage private industry, in cooperation with the Government, to produce and distribute foods to combat malnutrition.

6. *Provision for adequate reserves of essential food commodities.*

Our reserves must be large enough to serve as a stabilizing influence and to meet any emergency.

America's Past Efforts

This program keeps faith with policies this nation has followed since President Franklin D. Roosevelt proclaimed the Four Freedoms of mankind.

After World War II, we helped to make Europe free from want. We carried out on that continent massive programs of relief, reconstruction, and development.

This great effort—the Marshall Plan—was followed by President Truman's Point Four, President Eisenhower's Act of Bogotá, and its successor, President Kennedy's Alliance for Progress. Under these programs we have provided technical and capital assistance to the developing nations.

Our food aid programs have brought over 140 million tons of food to hungry people during the past decade.

Hunger, malnutrition and famine have been averted.

Schools and hospitals have been built.

Seventy million children now receive American food in school lunch and family and child feeding programs.

Nevertheless the problem of world hunger is more serious today than ever before.

A Balance Is Required

One new element in today's world is the threat of mass hunger and starvation. Populations are exploding under the impact of sharp cuts in the death rate. Successful public health measures have saved millions of lives. But these lives are now threatened by hunger because food production has not kept pace.

A balance between agricultural productivity and population is necessary to prevent the shadow of hunger from becoming a nightmare of famine. In my message on International Health and Education, I described our increased efforts to help deal with the population problem.

Improving Local Agriculture

Many of the developing countries urgently need to give a higher priority to improving and modernizing their own production and distribution of food. The overwhelming majority of those who till the soil still use the primitive methods of their ancestors. They produce little more than enough to meet their own needs, and remain outside of the market economy.

History has taught us that lack of agricultural development can cripple economic growth.

The developing countries must make basic improvements in their own agriculture.

They must bring the great majority of their people—now living in rural areas—into the market economy.

They must make the farmer a better customer of urban industry and thus accelerate the pace of economic development.

They must begin to provide all of their people with the food they need.

They must increase their exports, and earn the foreign exchange to purchase the foods and other goods which they themselves cannot produce efficiently.

In some developing countries, marked improvement is already taking place. Taiwan and Greece are raising their food output and becoming better cash customers for our food exports every year. Others have made a good beginning in improving agricultural production.

The Need for Self-Help

There is one characteristic common to all those who have increased the productivity of their farms: *a national will and determination to help themselves.*

We know what would happen if increased aid were dispensed without regard to measures of self-help. Economic incentives for higher production would disappear. Local agriculture would decline as dependence upon United States food increased.

Such a course would lead to disaster.

Disaster could be postponed for a decade or even two—but it could not be avoided. It could be postponed if the United States were to produce at full capacity and if we financed the massive shipments needed to fill an ever-growing deficit in the hungry nations.

But ultimately those nations would pay an exorbiant cost. They would pay it not only in money, but in years and lives wasted. If our food aid programs serve only as a crutch, they will encourage the developing nations to neglect improvements they must make in their own production of food.

For the sake of those we would aid, we must not take that course.

We shall not take that course.

But candor requires that I warn you *the time is not far off when all the combined production, on all of the acres, of all of the agriculturally productive nations, will not meet the food needs of the developing nations— unless present trends are changed.*

Dependence on American aid will not bring about such a change.

The program I present today is designed to bring about that change.

BETTER NUTRITION

Beyond simple hunger, there lies the problem of malnutrition.

We know that nutritional deficiencies are a major contributing cause to a death rate among infants and young children that is *thirty times higher in developing countries* than in advanced areas.

Protein and vitamin deficiencies during preschool years leave indelible scars.

Millions have died. Millions have been handicapped for life—physically or mentally.

Malnutrition saps a child's ability to learn. It weakens a nation's ability to progress. It can—and must—be attacked vigorously.

We are already increasing the nutritional content of our food aid contributions. We are working with private industry to produce and market nutritionally rich foods. We must encourage and assist the developing countries themselves to expand their production and use of such foods.

The wonders of modern science must also be directed to the fight against malnutrition. I have today directed the President's Science Advisory Committee to work with the very best talent in this nation to search out new ways to:

—Develop inexpensive, high-quality synthetic foods as dietary supplements. A promising start has already been made in isolating protein sources from fish, which are in plentiful supply throughout the world.

—Improve the quality and the nutritional content of food crops.

—Apply all of the resources of technology to increasing food production.

NEW DIRECTIONS FOR OUR ABUNDANCE

Our farm programs must reflect changing conditions in the United States and the world. Congress has provided:

—for American farmers, a continuing prospect of rising incomes;

—for American consumers, assurance of an abundance of high quality food at fair prices;

—for American taxpayers, less dollars spent to stockpile commodities in quantities greater than those needed for essential reserves.

Today—because of the world's needs, and because of the changing picture of U.S. agriculture—our food aid programs can no longer be governed by surpluses. The productive capacity of American agriculture can and should produce enough food and fiber to provide for:

1. domestic needs;
2. commercial exports;
3. food aid to those developing countries that are determined to help themselves;
4. reserves adequate to meet any emergency, and to stabilize prices.

To meet these needs, I am today directing the Secretary of Agriculture to:

1. *Increase the 1966 acreage allotment for rice by 10 percent.*

Unprecedented demands arising out of drought and war in Asia require us to increase our rice crop this year. I know that our farmers will respond to this need, and that the Congress will understand the emergency that requires this temporary response.

2. *Buy limited amounts of dairy products under the authority of the 1965 Act.*

We must have adequate supplies of dairy products for commercial markets, and to meet high priority domestic and foreign program needs. Milk from U.S. farms is the only milk available to millions of poor children abroad. The Secretary will use authority in the 1965 Act whenever necessary to meet our needs for dairy products.

3. *Take actions that will increase soybean production in 1966.*

The demand for soybeans has climbed each year since 1960. Despite record crops, we have virtually no reserve stocks. To assure adequate supplies at prices fair to farmers and consumers, the Secretary of Agriculture will use authority under the 1965 Act to encourage production of soybeans on acreage formerly planted to feed grains. Feed grain stocks are more than sufficient.

These actions supplement earlier decisions to increase this year's production of wheat and barley. Although our present reserves of wheat are adequate to meet all likely shipments, the Secretary of Agriculture has suspended programs for voluntary diversion of additional spring wheat plantings.

Our sixty million acres now diverted to conservation uses represent the major emergency reserve that could readily be called forth in the critical race between food and population. We will bring these acres back into production as needed—but not to produce unwanted surplus, and not to supplant the efforts of other countries to develop their own agricultural economies.

These actions illustrate how our domestic farm program will place the American farmer in the front ranks in the worldwide war on hunger.

Food for Freedom

I recommend a new Food for Freedom Act that retains the best provisions of Public Law 480, and that will
—make self-help an integral part of our food aid program;
—eliminate the "surplus" requirement for food aid;
—emphasize the development of markets for American farm products;
—authorize greater food aid shipments than the current rate;
—emphasize the building of cash markets and the shift toward financing food aid through long-term dollar credits rather than sales for foreign currencies. Except for U.S. requirements, we look to the completion of that shift by the end of five years;
—continue to finance the food aid program under the Commodity Credit Corporation;
—increase emphasis on combating malnutrition. The Act will authorize the CCC to finance the enrichment of foods;
—continue to work with voluntary agencies in people-to-people assistance programs;
—provide for better coordination of food aid with other economic assistance.

Food and Fiber Reserves

I recommend a program to establish the principle of the ever-normal granary by providing for food and fiber reserves.

This program supplements Food for Freedom.

It establishes a reserve policy that will protect the American people from unstable supplies of food and fiber, and from high prices in times of emergency.

The legislation I recommend to the Congress will enable us to draw strength from two great related assets:
—The productive genius of our farmers.
—The potential that lies in the sixty million acres now withdrawn from production.

In case of need, most of those acres could be brought back into productive farming within twelve to eighteen months. But because of the seasonal nature of farming, time would be needed to expand production even under the flexible provisions of the Agriculture Act of 1965. Therefore we need a reserve to bridge this gap.

We have been able to operate without a specific commodity reserve policy in recent years, because the surpluses built up in the 1950s exceeded our reserve needs. This condition has almost run its course.

Under present law, the Secretary of Agriculture must dispose of all stocks of agricultural commodities as rapidly as possible, consistent with orderly marketing procedures. As we continue to reduce our surpluses we need to amend the law to authorize the maintenance of reserve stocks.

The Act I recommend will do that.

It will authorize the Secretary of Agriculture to establish minimum reserve levels. Under the Act, he must take into account normal trade stocks, consumer and farm prices, domestic and export requirements, crop yield variations, and commitments under our domestic and foreign food programs.

The reserve would be used to meet priority needs, under prices and conditions to be determined within the broad guidelines established by existing law.

The Act could be implemented in the year ahead without any additional cost to the Government. We are still reducing our surpluses of most agricultural commodities. During the first year of the new program, it is not likely that we will have to purchase any commodity to build up a reserve.

Under the two acts I recommend today, with the farm legislation now on the statute books—and with the foreign assistance program I have recommended—we will be able to make maximum use of the productivity of our farms.

We can make our technology and skills powerful instruments for agricultural progress throughout the world—wherever men commit themselves to the task of feeding the hungry.

A Unified Effort

To strengthen these programs our food aid and economic assistance must be closely linked. Together they must relate to efforts in developing countries to improve their own agriculture. The Departments of State and Agriculture and the Agency for International Development will work together, even more closely than they have in the past in the planning and implementing of coordinated programs.

In the past few years AID has called upon the Department of Agriculture to assume increasing responsibilities through its International Agricultural Development Service. That policy will become even more important as we increase our emphasis on assisting developing nations to help themselves.

Under the Food for Freedom Act, the Secretary of Agriculture will continue to have authority to determine the commodities available. He will act only after consulting with the Secretary of State on the foreign policy aspects of food aid and with other interested agencies.

We must extend to world problems in food and agriculture the kind of cooperative relationships we have developed with the states, universities, farm organizations, and private industry.

An International Effort

It is not enough that we unify our own efforts. We cannot meet this problem alone.

Hunger is a world problem. It must be dealt with by the world.

We must encourage a truly international effort to combat hunger and modernize agriculture.

We shall work to strengthen the Food and Agriculture Organization of the United Nations. The efforts of the multilateral lending organizations, and of the United Nations Development Program should be expanded—particularly in food and agriculture.

We are prepared to increase our participation in regional as well as worldwide multilateral efforts, wherever they provide efficient technical assistance and make real contributions to increasing the food-growing capacities of the developing nations. For example, we will undertake a greatly increased effort to assist improvements in rice yields in the rice-eating less developed countries, as part of our cooperation with FAO during this International Rice Year.

For a World at Peace

The program I recommend today will raise a new standard of aid for the hungry, and for world agriculture.

It proclaims our commitment to a better world society—where every person can hope for life's essentials—and be able to find them in peace.

It proclaims the interdependence of mankind in its quest for food and clothing and shelter.

It is built on three universal truths:

—that agriculture is an essential pursuit of every nation;

—that an abundant harvest is not only a gift of God, but also the product of man's skill and determination and commitment;

—that hunger and want—anywhere—are the eternal enemies of all mankind.

I urge Congress to consider and debate these suggestions thoroughly and wisely in the hope and belief we can from them fashion a program that will keep free men free, and at the same time share our leadership and agricultural resources with our less blessed brothers throughout the world.

"Abroad, as at home, the true national interest
of the American people goes hand in hand
with their sense of freedom, justice, and compassion."
The President recommends to Congress
an updating of our foreign assistance programs,
February 9, 1967.

Twenty years ago, President Truman set forth the basic proposition underlying the foreign aid program when he told the Congress:

> I believe that we must assist free peoples to work out their own destinies in their own way. I believe that our help should be primarily through economic and financial aid which is essential to economic stability and orderly political processes.

This judgment was shared by Presidents Eisenhower and Kennedy and by every Congress since the Seventy-ninth in 1946. It is my judgment today. I believe it is the judgment of most Americans.

Our commitment to assist the economic growth and security of developing nations is grounded in the hard realities of the postwar world. We know that want is the enemy of peace and hopelessness the mother of violence.

We know that:

—in the long run, the wealthy nations cannot survive as islands of abundance in a world of hunger, sickness, and despair;

—the threat to our security posed by internal subversion and insurgency cannot be countered by withdrawal, isolation, or indifference;

—men—acting together—have the power to shape their destiny. Around the world, from Mexico to Greece to Taiwan, we have seen the energy and determination of the emerging peoples transform our aid into the seeds of prosperity;

—abroad, as at home, the true national interest of the American people goes hand in hand with their sense of freedom, justice, and compassion.

Precisely because foreign assistance programs are so vital to our national interest, they must reflect the circumstances of the late sixties, not those of the past. They must respond to the ideas which move men in the emerging nations today. They must draw upon the lessons of experience. They must take account of the growing wealth of other advanced countries.

The proposals in this message reflect the experience of our aid activities over two decades. They emphasize the six guiding principles on which our programs must be based:

1. *Self-help*—nations develop primarily through their own efforts. Our programs can only be supplements, not substitutes. This is the overriding principle.

2. *Multilateralism*—every advanced nation has a duty to contribute its share of the cost.

3. *Regionalism*—the future of many countries depends upon sound development of resources shared with their neighbors.

4. *Agriculture, health, and education*—these key sectors are the critical elements of advancement everywhere in the underdeveloped world.

5. *Balance of payments*—we cannot help others grow unless the American dollar is strong and stable.

6. *Efficient administration*—every American citizen is entitled to know that his tax dollar is spent wisely.

New Directions

To carry out these principles, I propose:

—*a new Foreign Assistance Act,* stating in clear language our objectives, our standards, and our program techniques;

—a statutory National Advisory Committee on Self-Help, to advise the Congress, the President, the Secretary of State, and the AID Administrator on how effectively recipient nations are mobilizing their own resources under the self-help criteria of the Act;

—a statutory objective that at least 85 percent of our development loan funds be spent in a regional or multilateral framework;

—more than $1 billion in programs to improve agriculture, education, and health, a 25 percent increase over last year;

—a shift in emphasis in our aid policy in Africa, to concentrate our help increasingly on regional and multinational projects;

—sympathetic consideration of a U.S. contribution to a new special fund of the African Development Bank;

—A $200 million U.S. contribution to new special funds of the Asian Development Bank, in accord with the recommendations of the Black mission, headed by Mr. Eugene Black, my Special Representative on Asian Development;

—a reorganization of the Agency for International Development, to better carry on the War on Hunger and to promote private investment and the growth of private enterprise in the less-developed world.

My proposals for programs authorized by the Foreign Assistance Act in fiscal 1968 will require total appropriations of slightly over $3.1 billion. Of this, some $2.5 billion will be devoted to economic aid. Almost $600 million will be for military assistance. Funds for the regional development banks would be authorized by separate legislation.

THE FOREIGN ASSISTANCE ACT OF 1967

Foreign aid now rests on a legislative foundation enacted in 1961. This pathfinding statute has served the nation well. But the experience we have gathered over the past several years should now be codified in a new law.

I propose the Foreign Assistance Act of 1967.

This Act will contain a clear statement of the philosophy which underlies our programs and the criteria to be used in this Administration. To provide the continuity needed for sound management, it will contain authorizations covering two years. Most important, it will provide a framework for each of the basic thrusts of our aid policy.

1. *Self-Help*

Self-help is the lifeblood of economic development. No sustained progress is possible without it. Aid provided as a substitute is aid wasted.

Waste is a luxury none of us can afford. The only obligation tied to our aid is the recipient's obligation to itself—to mobolize its own resources as efficiently as possible. I will not ask any American citizen to contribute his tax dollars to support any country which does not meet this test.

Accordingly, *the Act will make it clear that the development job is primarily the responsibility of the developing countries themselves.* In no case will the United States undertake to do for any country what it should do for itself. Nor will we assist in any venture which we believe has received less than full support from the recipient country. The United States will insist on the general economic policies necessary to make our aid effective.

We are now applying strict and effective self-help standards. The results are evident in the fact that, on the average, each citizen in the major aid-receiving countries is saving one of every eight dollars he earns. These savings become investments. For every dollar the United States and other donors provide, these local sources invest ten dollars.

Still, there is an urgent need for a permanent, nonpartisan, public body to evaluate self-help performance.

Thus, *the Act I propose will authorize the President to establish a National Advisory Committee on Self-Help.* This Committee will consist of members from both parties, from the business community, from labor, from universities, and from other walks of life. It will review and evaluate our aid programs in as many countries as it sees fit. It will examine our program to see whether the recipients are extending their best efforts and whether we are making the best possible use of our aid. Its findings will be available to the Congress.

2. *Multilateralism and Burden-Sharing*

Development is a world problem. No single country has all of the resources required. Equity demands that no single country be asked to carry the bulk of the load.

I propose that the Act set as an objective that 85 percent of our development loans be undertaken in a regional or multilateral framework.

This action fits the trend of recent years, as advanced nations have increasingly accepted the responsibilities associated with their growing wealth. The combined value of our economic and food aid is less than seven-tenths of one percent of our national income, only slightly more than the average for all advanced countries. We devote smaller shares to foreign assistance than such countries as France and Belgium.

But these figures do not tell the whole story. Our defense expenditures far exceed those of all other free nations combined and serve their common interest. This burden too must be counted in the balance.

Thus, we must redouble our efforts to get other donors to enlarge their commitments.

3. *Regionalism*

Resources know no national boundaries. Rivers flow through many countries, transportation and communication networks serve different peoples, sources of electric power must be shared by neighbors. Economic advance in every part of the world has required joint enterprises to develop shared sources of wealth.

These facts underlie the growing movement toward regional cooperation:

—The Alliance for Progress has transformed the inter-American system of institutions into a reliable and dynamic engine of change.

—Asian initiatives have created the framework for cooperation of all kinds. Such institutions as the Asian and Pacific Council and the Asian Development Bank are clear evidence of the new will to press forward.

I propose that the Act state that the United States will encourage regional economic development to the maximum extent consistent with the economic and poliical realities in each region.

I propose three steps to carry out this policy:

—First, in most African countries, we will gradually shift to cooperative projects which involve more than one donor or more than one recipient.

—Second, we will seek an appropriate means of responding to the recent request of the African Development Bank for U.S. participation in a special fund to finance worthy projects which are beyond the means of the Bank's ordinary capital.

—Third, we will respond favorably to the request for special funds for the Asian Development Bank. Preliminary explorations suggest a U.S. share of $200 million, to be contributed over a number of years with matching arrangements and balance of payments safeguards.

These proposals spring from a philosophy of pragmatic regionalism. They reflect the facts of economic life.

Political unity is neither required nor expected. But the resources available for development are too scarce to scatter among many countries when greater promise lies in joint action. We must take full advantage of the benefits of cooperation.

4. Agriculture, Health, and Education

The fundamentals of a decent life are sufficient food, freedom from disease, and an opportunity to absorb as much knowledge as individual capacities permit.

These are the first goals of all societies. They must be the first objects of our aid.

I propose that the Act establish agriculture, health, and education as our primary concerns and that investment in these areas be substantially expanded.

I propose that our investment in:

—agriculture rise from $504 million last year to $668 million in 1968;

—education rise from $166 million to $228 million;

—health rise from $192 million to $202 million.

In particular, we will wage War on Hunger. Together, the world must find ways to bring food production and population growth into balance. My proposals make clear our determination to help expand food supplies. We must be equally ready to assist countries which decide to undertake voluntarily population programs.

5. Balance of Payments

Our foreign assistance programs rest on the basic strength of the dollar and our balance of payments. This Administration will continue to see that our aid programs have the least possible adverse effect on our balance of payments.

Almost 90 percent of our economic assistance and over 95 percent of our military assistance is now spent in the United States. These programs serve to expand U.S. trade abroad. They help develop new trading patterns.

6. Efficient Administration

The Agency for International Development is a sound, well-run instrument of public policy. But, like all arms of government, AID can be improved. It can add further to its economy record—a record which includes $33 million in cost reduction last year alone, and a 20 percent cut in personnel—apart from Southeast Asia—since 1963.

I am establishing two new offices in AID:

—an Office of the War on Hunger to consolidate all AID activities relating to hunger, population problems, and nutrition;

—an Office of Private Resources to concentrate on marshaling private investment and the expansion of private sectors in the less-developed world—the best long-term route to rapid growth.

Both of these steps are consolidations—they will require no new appropriations or personnel. They will focus the attention and energy of the Agency directly upon two priority areas. They are significant steps forward.

ECONOMIC ASSISTANCE

LATIN AMERICA

For Latin America, I recommend an economic aid program of $624 million.

This amount is clearly justified by our own interests and the recent performance of our Latin American partners. The program I propose is lean and concentrated. Nearly 70 percent of it will be committed in four countries—Brazil, Colombia, Peru, and Chile. In each case, we will make certain that the amount actually spent is in accord with clear needs and meets the strict self-help criteria of the Act.

The outlook for a solid return from these expenditures is promising:

—*Brazil* shows greater economic dynamism than at any time in her recent history. She has forced inflation down from the 1964 high of 140 percent to 40 percent—still far too high, but an enormous improvement. Her balance of payments situation is well under control. Agricultural production has been increased. Per capita income is up. In general, the economic situation is more hopeful than the most favorable predictions of three years ago.

—*Peru* continues its steady economic climb. Per capita income last year was $378, compared to $325 five years before. The critical job now is to bring more people into the economic mainstream, while further stimulating the developed coastal areas. U.S. contributions will be heavy in the areas of agriculture and education.

—In *Chile*, the favorable copper market will make possible a reduction in our aid. We will concentrate our help in the crucial rural area to increase agricultural production and exports.

—In *Colombia*, economic trends are also encouraging. Our contributions will be made through a group of donors led by the World Bank. We will concentrate on agriculture and education.

—Our program for *Central America—Nicaragua, El Salvador, Guatemala, Costa Rica, and Honduras*—is tailored to support the Central American

Common Market. This Market is one of the most promising innovations in the developing world. The spirit it reflects has already increased trade within the Central American region by 400 percent over the past five years. We will make modest contributions to the Central American Integration Fund to continue and accelerate this pace.

—The balance of my request is largely for the *Dominican Republic* and *Panama*. It is essential that we maintain strong programs in these countries, although they will cost slightly less than in the past.

The vision and hard work of 450 million people in this hemisphere have made the Alliance for Progress into one of the great tools for human betterment. Its success is by no means assured. There will be disappointments as well as achievements along the way. But it is a vehicle for the hopes and energies of a continent. The program I propose will carry it forward.

Meetings among the governments of the Western Hemisphere during the year may produce further proposals, such as replenishment of the resources of the Inter-American Development Bank. Where these proposals merit our consideration and support and require action by the Congress. I will submit my recommendations to you at the appropriate time.

NEAR EAST—SOUTH ASIA

For the Near East–South Asia, I recommend a program of $758 million.

This region provides the harshest test of free institutions:

—Nowhere else in the free world are there so many people: as many as the combined populations of North and South America and Western Europe.

—Nowhere else do so many people live in such dire poverty: per capita income for nine out of every ten persons is under $100 per year.

—Nowhere else are divisive forces so poised to take advantage of any misstep.

Several advanced nations have banded together, under the leadership of the World Bank, to form an Aid Consortium for India and Pakistan. A similar group has been formed for Turkey, chaired by the Organization for Economic Cooperation and Development. These groups determine the share each member will contribute and provide a forum for continuing discussions with recipient countries. They have served the interests of all parties.

In my Message on Food for India, I proposed that food and related aid be added to the agenda of the consortium for India as an additional area of assistance in which all donors should join. We will exert the full extent of our influence to ensure that this consortium becomes the primary vehicle for all aspects of development aid to India—from grants of funds to evaluation of performance.

Despite the shadow of famine and the ever-present danger of renewed frictions, the situation in the three countries—India, Pakistan, and Turkey—which will receive 91 percent of our aid to the Near East—South Asia gives reason for hope:

—*India* is trying to regain the lead in the race between her expanding population and her food supply. She plans to double her outlays for agriculture in the next five years and to quadruple her voluntary population program. India has increased fertilizer purchases by 85 percent and has started crash programs in farmland development. She has begun campaigns to increase supplies of better seeds and pesticides. But Indian performance is not confined to agriculture. In early 1966 she liberalized her system of import controls and devalued her currency. All advanced nations must come to her aid if these hard-won opportunities are to be realized.

—*Pakistan* has an outstanding economic record. Her future is brighter still. From 1960 to 1965, her Gross National Product grew at an average annual rate of 5.8 percent compared to 2.5 percent previously; agricultural production grew at an average annual rate of 3.5 percent compared to 1.6 percent previously; local private investment grew by 54 percent; and total private investment was 63 percent over planned targets.

—*Turkey* also has a remarkable record. We and other Western nations are determined to help Turkey meet its goal of self-sustaining economic growth by 1973. She is already well on her way. In 1966, her Gross National Product grew by 8.3 percent, industry by 9.5 percent, agricultural production by 11 percent, and the use of fertilizer by 40 percent. The percentage of children of school age enrolled in primary schools increased to almost 80 percent.

If it cannot be demonstrated that hard work, coupled with relatively modest amounts of our aid, will produce better lives for the countless millions of this region, our cause will surely fail. The programs I propose will enable us to continue meeting this challenge.

AFRICA

For Africa, I recommend a program of $195 million.

Africa is undergoing the historic growing pains of attaining stable independence. Thirty-five of her thirty-nine nations have gained their freedom since World War II, many in the past five years. The inevitable strains are evident in the headlines of the world's newspapers.

The most hopeful sign of growing African maturity is the increased support for cooperative economic enterpries. With fourteen countries of less than five million people each, this attitude is essential for progress.

Our AID policy toward Africa will:

—encourage the African activities of the World Bank and its affiliates;

—direct a greater part of our resources into projects and programs which involve more than one African country;

—seek new breakthroughs in private investment in Africa, particularly the current efforts by private American banks and other financial institutions.

EAST ASIA

For East Asia, I recommend a program of $812 million.

Nearly 85 percent of our assistance to this region is directly or indirectly related to our effort to block Communist aggression.

My recent visit to Asia confirmed my deep conviction that foreign assistance funds for Vietnam and surrounding countries are just as important as military appropriations. They are vital to a successful war effort. They permit us to build for the future.

Most of these funds—about $650 million—will be used in Vietnam, Laos, and Thailand. The $550 million planned for Vietnam is indispensable to military success, economic stability, and continued political progress. It will stimulate and support measures to bind the people and government of South Vietnam together in a common cause. It will help to begin the task of reconstruction and development. It will relieve wartime suffering for millions of Vietnamese.

In Laos and Thailand, these funds will finance economic development and security which will assure that armed conflict will not engulf all of Southeast Asia.

Our assistance to Thailand will be channeled through a new consultative group of thirteen donors, chaired by the World Bank. In Laos, five other countries will join the U.S. with significant contributions.

Elsewhere in free Asia, the tide of history clearly favors progress:

—In *Korea*, the economy is now growing at the rapid annual rate of 8 percent. Industrial production is rising at a 14 percent rate annually, agricultural production at a 6 percent rate. In the few short years since the Korean

War, the Republic of South Korea has become strong enough not only to maintain its internal advance, but to help in the defense of freedom in Vietnam.

—In *Indonesia*, the new government has committed itself to a program of economic rehabilitation and recovery. We are joining with other European and Asian nations to provide urgently needed help to the stricken Indonesian economy. We are also participating in arrangements with other nations to reschedule Indonesian debts.

The road ahead in East Asia is long and dangerous. But these accomplishments are hopeful signs. We will encourage the vital and progressive spirit that has stimulated them.

MILITARY ASSISTANCE

For military assistance, I recommend appropriations of $596 million.

This is the smallest request since the program began in 1950. In part, this fact reflects transfer of appropriations for military assistance for Laos, Thailand, NATO Infrastructure, and international military headquarters to the budget of the Department of Defense.

But this request also represents a substantial reduction. Military assistance outside Southeast Asia is now only 45 percent of what it was in 1960.

For the *Near East–South Asia*, I recommend $234 million, down 50 percent from 1963. Virtually all this will be used in Greece, Turkey, and Iran, three countries which have shared the burden of mutual security for twenty years.

For *East Asia*, I recommend $282 million, almost entirely for Korea and Taiwan. We will use these funds to strengthen these outposts against further Communist expansion in Asia.

For *Latin America*, I recommend $45.5 million, largely for internal security and training.

For *Africa*, I recommend $31 million, heavily concentrated in countries where we have major interests and where there are problems of internal security.

It is not the policy of the United States to provide sophisticated arms to countries which could better use their resources for more productive purposes.

It is the policy of the United States to help:

—where we are asked,

—where the threat of invasion or subversion is real,

—where the proposal is militarily and economically sound,

—where it is consistent with our interests and our limited means.

This will continue to be our policy.

The Challenge Ahead

The programs I propose represent the minimum contribution to mutual security and international development which we can safely make.

There are some who say that even this request should be foregone in view of needs at home and the costs of the struggle in Vietnam.

Nothing could be more shortsighted and self-defeating. This country—the wealthiest in human history—can well afford to devote less than seven-tenths of one percent of its national income to reduce the chances of future Vietnams.

Some would have us renege on our commitments to the developing countries on the ground that "charity begins at home."

To them, let me emphasize that I have recommended no charity, nor have I suggested that we stray from home. The inescapable lesson of our century, inscribed in blood on a hundred beaches from Normandy to Vietnam, is that our home is this planet and our neighbors three billion strong.

Still others have grown weary of the long, hard struggle to bring the majority of the world's population out of the shadows of poverty and ignorance.

To them, let me say that we are dealing in decades with the residue of centuries. There is no shortcut. There is no easy way around. The only effective tools are ingenuity, capital, and, above all, the will to succeed.

All of us sometimes find ourselves sympathizing with these complaints. All of us are subject to the frustrations, disappointments and shattered hopes which accompany a supporting role in a task which must fundamentally be performed by others. But, in the cold light of reason, our responsibility to ourselves and our children reasserts itself and we return to the task with renewed vigor.

I am confident that the American people have not lost the will and the dedication which have made them the most powerful and responsible nation on earth.

I am confident that they will go forward into the new era of world progress for which their past efforts have prepared the way.

I am confident that their vision will transcend the narrow horizons of those who yearn for a simpler age.

The proposals I offer today are the practical requirements of that vision. To do less would endanger all we have accomplished in the past two decades.

I know that this test shall not find us wanting.

President Johnson's Foreign Policy

By Eugene V. Rostow

Our four Presidents since 1945 have faced a task completely new to our history—the necessity of taking a major part in world politics. Until 1914, our national security was protected by the exertions of others. Although most Americans would have been surprised—and outraged—if they realized it, our safety was based on a balance of world power maintained by the principal nations of Europe. The idea would have been particularly odious to most Americans at the time, for "the balance of power" is a reactionary phrase in the American language, evoking all that was evil in imperialism.

By 1945, the concert of Europe had gone the way of Humpty-Dumpty. It had prevented general war for a century before 1914. But the nations of Europe were exhausted by two wars, and by the tragedies and follies of the years between the wars. Vast new powers and new political forces were emerging in the world. Empire was gone, to be replaced by the struggling new nations, whose weakness tempted subversion and aggression. The Communist movement surged forward, as it did after 1917. The Soviet Union, China, Japan, and the United States were countries on a new scale. The nuclear weapon had been born. Time had transformed the problem of equilibrium. It was altogether beyond the reach of the old Entente.

As we lived through the successive shocks of the period since 1945, we came to understand but not quite to accept the fact that in the small, unstable nuclear world in which we have no choice but to live, the security of the United States depends on maintaining a tolerably stable balance of power not merely in the Western Atlantic, in Europe, and in the Hemisphere, but in the world as a whole. And we began to perceive as well that if the United States was to be protected, we were going to have do a major part of the job ourselves. There was no one else to lead in forming the coalitions of peace. In President Truman's phrase, "The buck stops here."

This fact has determined both the tasks we have had to undertake abroad since the war, and the recurrent spasms of domestic political conflict we have experienced in facing them.

[II]

When Lyndon B. Johnson became President in 1963, both foreign policy and public opinion were in transition. On the surface, the weather seemed relatively clear. But storms were brewing, and soon became manifest. In many respects, the last four years have been the most difficult yet faced by our postwar foreign policy. And our awareness of danger has revived latent American yearnings to escape into our isolationist past—the most powerful such wave of feeling since 1920, when we repudiated Wilson, and embraced Harding's empty promises.

In essence, the main positions of American foreign policy have been constant since the first hesitant months after the end of the Second World War. Together, they frame a program four Presidents and a bipartisan majority of the American people have found necessary to protect our security in the world as it is. The chief themes of that policy can be simply stated: containment and the steady pursuit of detente; support for the Atlantic Alliance, the European movement, and alliance with Japan; decolonization and aid to the developing nations; a liberal trade policy; international monetary cooperation in the interest of growth and full employment; arms limitation; the control of nuclear weapons.

But the continuity of these themes tends to conceal change. The view from President Johnson's window is not what it was in President Truman's time, nor even in President Kennedy's. Each of the four postwar Presidents has sought the same goal: to help build a reasonably stable and progressive system of world order—a world of wide horizons, in which we could live and breathe as a free society, not an autarchic enclave or a garrison state. In pursuing this goal, each President has had to deal with different combinations of men and events. Each has confronted a different stage of America's debate with its historical memory. And each has been a different human being—different in vision and will, differently endowed as a politician, different too in his luck.

For President Johnson, pressure has not been compressed into a single dramatic climax, but diffused through a series of simultaneous crises, some visible, others masked, on many interrelated fronts. All the streams of change in the world around us reached rip-tide together during the first few years of President Johnson's Presidency. And the nuclear stakes on the table have never been higher—more than enough to obliterate mankind.

In Asia, there has been an intensification of threat. The attack on South Vietnam has accelerated, and spread ominously to Laos, Thailand, Cambodia, and Burma. At the same time, the long-smoldering fire in the Near East, fueled by huge shipments of Soviet arms, exploded into hostilities, and has continued to blaze sporadically since June, 1967, menacing the security of Europe, Africa, and Asia, and the balance of world power. Castro's program of guerrilla warfare in South America has increased in scale and scope, raising the prospect of more revolutionary disorder for several struggling nations in this hemisphere.

Meanwhile, the process of European withdrawal from many areas of the world continued, producing new strains within the Atlantic Alliance, and new vacuums of power in scattered parts of the Third World. And Japan has not yet undertaken full participation in the processes of world politics.

In the developing world, the race between population and food supply continued, and some crucial programs of development faltered. At the same time, the developing countries adopted more and more realistic economic programs, and some made spectacular breakthroughs.

And in the background, nuclear scientists continued to perfect and manufacture their sinister weapons at an increasing pace, while Communist China became a nuclear power.

[III]

For many Americans, the international exertions we have had to undertake since 1945 have been accepted as temporary and transitional efforts. They tend to think the First World War was an aberration, and the Second a unique phenomenon caused by Hitler. If we did a good enough job with the Marshall Plan and aid programs, and fended off aggression in Berlin, Greece, and Korea, the Soviets and the Chinese would come to believe in the reasonableness of peaceful coexistence; Europe, the Middle East, and Asia would recover their capacity to defend themselves; then we could bring the boys home, and return to "normalcy."

The Presidency of Lyndon B. Johnson marks the end of these illusions. We see that the turmoil we have known since 1945 is not a temporary period of postwar disturbance, but our normal condition, at least until rules of peaceful coexistence can be accepted, and new groupings formed to guarantee them. And we realize now that it will take a long time and a great deal of patient, restrained effort to create a system that might effectively maintain order in a world that contains so many breeding grounds for hostility and violence.

This is the root of the revulsion of public opinion about Vietnam which President Johnson has had to confront. Other aspects of the war in Vietnam heighten the feeling of revulsion: the distaste for bombing as a form of warfare, and for any contest between a small country and a big one. But the decisive element in American concern about Vietnam is resistance to the bleak fact with which the President lives every day: the fact that the protection of our national security requires not a sprint, a one-shot effort, followed by the relief of a withdrawal, but a permanent involvement in the politics of every part of the globe, based on a strategy of peace that seeks to achieve order, and to make progress possible.

In one context after another, the American people have been caught up in this tension between history and the facts of life ever since President Wilson called on us to join the League of Nations in 1919. In times of stress, we yearn for the comfort and security of the nineteenth century. Then, we imagine, Americans lived in a Golden Age, when the country was more completely devoted to the austere virtues, and giants walked the earth.

With our minds, we understand that the nineteenth century is gone beyond recall, and indeed that our vision of the past is myth. But the outlook of those easy times is deep in our psyche. And our educational system does not give most Americans the feel for history which would equip them to understand the problem of power without a special effort. For these reasons, the debate has been protracted, and difficult to resolve. There are still respected and high-minded American leaders who contend that our main contribution to world order should be the power of our example as a model society at home.

Put in these terms, the debate heightens confusion by posing a choice between an effective foreign policy and social progress at home. The larger part of our people are committed to the ideal of social progress. They also understand the necessities of power which require us in our own interest to help safeguard the general peace. Between these goals, there need in fact be no choosing. The state of public opinion, and the strength of the nation, permit us to pursue both.

But the confusion has a deeper element than the question of choice. Nowadays, the goal of social improvement is to eliminate violence in social life, and to make progress towards social justice. As we slowly advance towards that ideal, after nearly one hundred and eighty years of effort, we confront an obligation to use or to threaten violence abroad on a much larger scale than ever before in our history, violence repugnant to all that is best in our aspiration for ourselves. No wonder troubled men ask themselves whether Revolutionary America has become an Imperial Power, taking over the role of the Redcoats, whether republican America must now support kings and dictators.

The argument between these two parts of the American mind has proceeded in stages. In the twenties, it focused on our membership in the League of Nations. Ten years later, it asked whether German and Japanese militarism really threatened our national safety. Twenty years ago, in the days of Henry Wallace and Senator Joseph McCarthy, it was directed to the Truman Doctrine, the Marshall Plan, and the hostilities in Korea. Today the nominal topic for debate is our involvement in Vietnam—whether that conflict genuinely concerns our national interests, and above all our national interest in the balance of power.

But every round of the debate has been in fact part of a more fundamental effort to free our minds of obsolete dogmas about ourselves and the world. The true issue at each stage has been the ultimate question: why do we have to be involved at all?

To that question, the facts permit only one answer: the alternative of isolation is not available to the American people, now or for the foreseeable future. And the patient, long-range campaigns of President Johnson's foreign policy are all addressed to this assessment of reality.

[IV]

When the President took office in late 1963, he faced an active agenda. Many items on the list were programs where success was readily available; others signified an array of trouble, arising from strain among the advanced countries, or tensions in the Third World persistently exacerbated and exploited by Soviet or Chinese efforts to extend their spheres of control. American policy since 1947 had interposed powerful arrangements of protection to deter such attempts, and had participated in regional and international programs of economic assistance. Much had been achieved by these efforts. Europe and Japan were flourishing. And many of the nonindustrialized countries had begun to succeed in their development efforts. All realized that success was possible.

In 1963, then, one could discern the possibilities of order in the world—the kind and degree of order required to assure our safety as a world power, equally involved in the Atlantic and the Pacific. But it was clear too that it was still a world of many risks. The European states, stripped of their empires, were withdrawing from Asia, Africa, and the Middle East. They had not yet succeeded in forming a political Europe, through which they could rejoin the United States as an equal partner in all the works of peace. And Japan, brilliantly successful in its postwar recovery, was only beginning her reentry into world politics as our colleague and ally.

At the same time the developing countries, not yet strong enough to withstand attack, generated conflicts of their own and tempted intervention by one sect or another of the Communist world.

It is absurd to imagine that all the trouble in the world is inspired by Communists. But it is equally absurd to suppose that Communists are not serious men, seriously committed to their creed. It is too much to expect that they will be more virtuous than other human beings in resisting temptation. It is no accident that in President Johnson's first four years the most acute problems of foreign policy have arisen in Southeast Asia and the Middle East, two areas where the end of empire has left weak states, vulnerable to direct or indirect takeover by Communist power.

Both these prolonged crises threaten the equilibrium of power in the world as a whole, and therefore create the risk of general war. Each involves not a local conflict among small quarreling neighbors, but, at one remove, the relationship between the United States and the Soviet Union, and, to a certain extent, that between both these powers and Communist China as well.

Some of our postwar confrontations with the Soviet Union have been visible and dramatic, like the several attempts to blockade Berlin, or the missile crisis in Cuba. These were open challenges, whose implications could not be hidden. The President's tests in Vietnam and the Near East are of a different order. They go on, month after month, taut and menacing. But they occur in circumstances which make comparative silence prudent. Their limits are determined by the clarity with which we define our essential purposes and prepare the way for peaceful settlement.

President Johnson's way in making foreign policy has a strongly marked style. Its dominant characteristic is perspective. Taken together, his programs have coherence. They reveal the architecture of a foreign policy which thrusts forward in the hope of shaping a more stable and progressive world. His foreign policy extends and applies that of his predecessors to changing circumstance. But on many fronts, his sense of strategy has carried policy beyond the past.

The essential idea of his foreign policy is to use the power of the United States as the magnetic center of several overlapping systems of international cooperation. Together, coalitions of this kind can counterbalance destructive tendencies, and provide a framework for stability and progress in the several regions of the world, and in the world as a whole.

President Johnson has given new meaning to the concept of regionalism. He has sought to apply in Asia, Africa, and Latin America the lessons of Europe's success in building an effective system of economic cooperation. In speeches and diplomatic conversations, and in the reorientation of our programs of aid and trade, he encourages the developing peoples to work with each other to create new institutions of cooperation and progress. In this way, more readily than in any other, they should be able to take command of their own destinies.

For the United States, the pattern of regional policy built by President Johnson promises a viable long-run alternative to the overwhelming involvement and responsibility of the early postwar years. Stable and cohesive regional systems, backed in differing combinations by the United States and other strong nations, offer high prospects of stability and progress. Nuclear questions aside, it is President Johnson's view that the United States could become in time the junior partner in the world's systems of regional cooperation.

The system of peace to which President Johnson aspires, and aspires with passion, is not a sterile program of order for its own sake, achieved by coercion, and maintained only by force. He wants to help build a world in which man could enjoy the blessings of liberty, and seek to overcome his burdens of hunger, ignorance, and ill health, through a process of political development towards self-government. That vision of the purpose of America in the world is fundamental to his nature.

But President Johnson is not engaged in an ideological crusade, either to extirpate one or another form of communism, or to remake the world in the image of America. The aim of his foreign policy is to protect our national interest in world stability. Of course the United States encourages the development of democratic institutions, and the pursuit of economic and social progress, wherever we can exert our influence to do so. That fact, however, is the consequence of our involvement, not its cause. The end President Johnson seeks is a tolerably stable system of peace in world politics, achieved in collaboration with other nations, and sustained with their consent and support: a system of diversity, in the spirit of the United Nations Charter, "based on respect for the principle of equal rights and self-determination of peoples"—above all, a system of peace.

This goal does not make us the world's gendarme, nor require us to intervene wherever there is trouble. It does, however, require us to act when aggression threatens the general equilibrium, and especially the balance between the Communist nations and the free world.

The process of world politics which faces the President is a race between fission and fusion, between the forces which tend to fragment the world and those which work toward harmony. The nations are drawn together by common interests, common values, and common fears. They are driven apart by pride, suspicion, ignorance of each other's motives, and the power of aggressive instincts. As Secretary Rusk has remarked, foreign ministers nowadays are accustomed to risk, and regard a 5 percent chance of success as favorable. President Johnson and his Secretary of State are not victims of false optimism. But they persevere, confident that in the end the strength and high purpose of American policy, and the sober second thoughts of the American people, will provide the margin of influence ultimately needed to achieve a system of peace.

The President's conduct of his office, in my experience, is dominated by two qualities of his mind and character: he takes long views; and his decisions are highly disciplined. In policy and in action, he achieves a stoic immunity from the pressure of criticism. Like every strong President since Wilson, President Johnson has been caught up in a round of the great American debate over foreign policy—a debate between our nostalgia for a simpler past, and our responsible understanding of the nature of the modern world. The President has refused to simplify the debate by arousing the force of national feeling, or by stirring alarm about Soviet or Chinese policy. Confident of the ultimate support of the American people, he subordinates passion to prudence, and politics to policy, as he pursues a steady course with formidable energy and imagination.

Lyndon B. Johnson

*"We cherish freedom—yes
. . . but the key to all we have done
is really our own security."*

The President speaks to the National Legislative Conference,
in San Antonio, Texas, on Vietnam,
September 29, 1967.

I deeply appreciate this opportunity to appear before an organization whose members contribute every day such important work to the public affairs of our state and of our country.

This evening I came here to speak to you about Vietnam.

I do not have to tell you that our people are profoundly concerned about that struggle.

There are passionate convictions about the wisest course for our Nation to follow. There are many sincere and patriotic Americans who harbor doubts about sustaining the commitment that three Presidents and a half a million of our young men have made.

Doubt and debate are enlarged because the problems of Vietnam are quite complex. They are a mixture of political turmoil—of poverty—of religious and factional strife—of ancient servitude and modern longing for freedom. Vietnam is all of these things.

Vietnam is also the scene of a powerful aggression that is spurred by an appetite for conquest.

It is the arena where Communist expansionism is most aggressively at work in the world today—where it is crossing international frontiers in violation of international agreements; where it is killing and kidnaping; where it is ruthlessly attempting to bend free people to its will.

Into this mixture of subversion and war, of terror and hope, America has entered—with its material power and with its moral commitment.

Why?

Why should three Presidents and the elected representatives of our people have chosen to defend this Asian nation more than 10,000 miles from American shores?

We cherish freedom—yes. We cherish self-determination for all people— yes. We abhor the political murder of any state by another, and the bodily murder of any people by gangsters of whatever ideology. And for twenty-seven years—since the days of lend-lease—we have sought to strengthen free people against domination by aggressive foreign powers.

But the key to all we have done is really our own security. At times of crisis—before asking Americans to fight and die to resist aggression in a foreign land—every American President has finally had to answer this question:

Is the aggression a threat—not only to the immediate victim—but to the United States of America and to the peace and security of the entire world of which we in America are a very vital part?

That is the question which Dwight Eisenhower and John Kennedy and Lyndon Johnson had to answer in facing the issue in Vietnam.

That is the question that the Senate of the United States answered by a vote of 82 to 1 when it ratified and approved the SEATO treaty in 1955, and to which the members of the United States Congress responded in a resolution that it passed in 1964 by a vote of 504 to 2, "the United States, is therefore, prepared, as the President determines, to take all necessary steps, including the use of armed force, to assist any member or protocol state of the Southeast Asia Collective Defense Treaty requesting assistance in defense of its freedom."

Those who tell us now that we should abandon our commitment—that securing South Vietnam from armed domination is not worth the price we are paying—must also answer this question. And the test they must meet is this: what would be the consequence of letting armed aggression against South Vietnam succeed? What would follow in the time ahead? What kind of world are they prepared to live in five months or five years from to-night?

For those who have borne the responsibility for decision during these past ten years, the stakes to us have seemed clear—and have seemed high.

President Dwight Eisenhower said in 1959:

"Strategically, South Vietnam's capture by the Communists would bring their power several hundred miles into a hitherto free region. The remaining countries in Southeast Asia would be menaced by a great flanking movement. The freedom of 12 million people would be lost immediately, and that of 150 million in adjacent lands would be seriously endangered. The loss of South Vietnam would set in motion a crumbling process that could, as it progressed, have grave consequences for us and for freedom. . . ."

And President John F. Kennedy said in 1962:

". . . Withdrawal in the case of Vietnam and the case of Thailand might mean a collapse of the entire area."

A year later, he reaffirmed that:

"We are not going to withdraw from that effort. In my opinion, for us to withdraw from that effort would mean a collapse not only of South Vietnam, but Southeast Asia. So we are going to stay there."

This is not simply an American viewpoint, I would have you legislative leaders know. I am going to call the roll now of those who live in that part of the world—in the great arc of Asian and Pacific nations—and who bear the responsibility for leading their people, and the responsibility for the fate of their people.

The President of the Philippines had this to say:

"Vietnam is the focus of attention now. . . . It may happen to Thailand or the Philippines, or anywhere, wherever there is misery, disease, ignorance. . . . For you to renounce your position of leadership in Asia is to allow the Red Chinese to gobble up all of Asia."

The Foreign Minister of Thailand said:

"[The American] decision will go down in history as the move that prevented the world from having to face another major conflagration."

The Prime Minister of Australia said:

"We are there because while Communist aggression persists the whole of Southeast Asia is threatened."

President Park of Korea said:

"For the first time in our history, we decided to dispatch our combat troops overseas . . . because in our belief any aggression against the Republic of Vietnam represented a direct and grave menace against the security and peace of free Asia, and therefore directly jeopardized the very security and freedom of our own people."

The Prime Minister of Malaysia warned his people that if the United States pulled out of South Vietnam, it would go to the Communists, and after that, it would be only a matter of time until they moved against neighboring states.

The Prime Minister of New Zealand said:

"We can thank God that America at least regards aggression in Asia with the same concern as it regards aggression in Europe—and is prepared to back up its concern with action."

The Prime Minister of Singapore said:

"I feel the fate of Asia—South and Southeast Asia—will be decided in the next few years by what happens out in Vietnam."

I cannot tell you tonight as your President—with certainty—that a Communist conquest of South Vietnam would be followed by a Communist conquest of Southeast Asia. But I do know there are North Vietnamese troops in Laos. I do know that there are North Vietnamese trained guerrillas tonight in northeast Thailand. I do know that there are Communist-supported guerrilla forces operating in Burma. And a Communist coup was barely averted in Indonesia, the fifth largest nation in the world.

So your American President cannot tell you—with certainty—that a Southeast Asia dominated by Communist power would bring a third world war much closer to terrible reality. One could hope that this would not be so.

But all that we have learned in this tragic century strongly suggests to me that it would be so. As President of the United States, I am not prepared to gamble on the chance that it is not so. I am not prepared to risk the security —indeed, the survival—of this American Nation on mere hope and wishful thinking. I am convinced that by seeing this struggle through now, we are greatly reducing the chances of a much larger war—perhaps a nuclear war. I would rather stand in Vietnam, in our time, and by meeting this danger now, and facing up to it, thereby reduce the danger for our children and for our grandchildren.

I want to turn now to the struggle in Vietnam itself.

There are questions about this difficult war that must trouble every really thoughtful person. I am going to put some of these questions. And I am going to give you the very best answers that I can give you.

First, are the Vietnamese—with our help, and that of their other allies— really making any progress? Is there a forward movement? The reports I see make it clear that there is. Certainly there is a positive movement toward constitutional government. Thus far the Vietnamese have met the political schedule that they laid down in January 1966.

The people wanted an elected, responsive government. They wanted it strongly enough to brave a vicious campaign of Communist terror and assassination to vote for it. It has been said that they killed more civilians in four weeks trying to keep them from voting before the election than our American bombers have killed in the big cities of North Vietnam in bombing military targets.

On November 1, subject to the action, of course, of the Constituent Assembly, an elected government will be inaugurated and an elected Senate and Legislature will be installed. Their responsibility is clear: to answer the desires of the South Vietnamese people for self-determination and for peace, for an attack on corruption, for economic development, and for social justice.

There is progress in the war itself, steady progress considering the war that we are fighting; rather dramatic progress considering the situation that actually prevailed when we sent our troops there in 1965; when we intervened to prevent the dismemberment of the country by the Vietcong and the North Vietnamese.

The campaigns of the last year drove the enemy from many of their major interior bases. The military victory almost within Hanoi's grasp in 1965 has now been denied them. The grip of the Vietcong on the people is being broken.

Since our commitment of major forces in July 1965 the proportion of the population living under Communist control has been reduced to well under 20 percent. Tonight the secure proportion of the population has grown from about 45 percent to 65 percent—and in the contested areas, the tide continues to run with us.

But the struggle remains hard. The South Vietnamese have suffered severely, as have we—particularly in the First Corps area in the north, where the enemy has mounted his heaviest attacks, and where his lines of communication to North Vietnam are shortest. Our casualties in the war have reached about 13,500 killed in action, and about 85,000 wounded. Of those 85,000 wounded, we thank God that 79,000 of the 85,000 have been returned, or will return to duty shortly. Thanks to our great American medical science and the helicopter.

I know there are other questions on your minds, and on the minds of many sincere, troubled Americans: "Why not negotiate now?" so many ask me. The answer is that we and our South Vietnamese allies are wholly prepared to negotiate tonight.

I am ready to talk with Ho Chi Minh, and other chiefs of state concerned, tomorrow.

I am ready to have Secretary Rusk meet with their Foreign Minister tomorrow.

I am ready to send a trusted representative of America to any spot on this earth to talk in public or private with a spokesman of Hanoi.

We have twice sought to have the issue of Vietnam dealt with by the United Nations—and twice Hanoi has refused.

Our desire to negotiate peace—through the United Nations or out—has been made very, very clear to Hanoi—directly and many times through third parties.

As we have told Hanoi time and time and time again, the heart of the matter really is this: the United States is willing to stop all aerial and naval bombardment of North Vietnam when this will lead promptly to productive discussions. We, of course, assume that while discussions proceed, North Vietnam would not take advantage of the bombing cessation or limitation.

But Hanoi has not accepted any of these proposals.

So it is by Hanoi's choice—and not ours, and not the rest of the world's—the war continues.

Why, in the face of military and political progress in the South, and the burden of our bombing in the North, do they insist and persist with the war?

From many sources the answer is the same. They still hope that the people of the United States will not see this struggle through to the very end. As one Western diplomat reported to me only this week—he had just been in Hanoi—"They believe their taxing power is greater than ours and that they can't lose." A visitor from a Communist capital had this to say: "They expect the war to be long, and that the Americans in the end will be defeated by a breakdown in morale, fatigue, and psychological factors." The Premier of North Vietnam said as far back as 1962: "Americans do not like long, inconclusive war. . . . Thus we are sure to win in the end."

Are the North Vietnamese right about us?

I think not. No. I think they are wrong. I think it is the common failing of totalitarian regimes, that they cannot really understand the nature of our democracy:

—They mistake dissent for disloyalty.

—They mistake restlessness for a rejection of policy.

—They mistake a few committees for a country.

—They misjudge individual speeches for public policy.

They are no better suited to judge the strength and perseverance of America than the Nazi and the Stalinist propagandists were able to judge it. It is a tragedy that they must discover these qualities in the American people, and discover them through a bloody war.

And, soon or late, they will discover them.

In the meantime, it shall be our policy to continue to seek negotiations—confident that reason will some day prevail; that Hanoi will realize that it just can never win; that it will turn away from fighting and start building for its own people.

Since World War II, this Nation has met and has mastered many challenges—challenges in Greece and Turkey, in Berlin, in Korea, in Cuba.

We met them because brave men were willing to risk their lives for their nation's security. And braver men have never lived than those who carry our colors in Vietnam at this very hour.

The price of these efforts, of course, has been heavy. But the price of not having made them at all, not having seen them through, in my judgment would have been vastly greater.

Our goal has been the same—in Europe, in Asia, in our own hemisphere. It has been—and it is now—peace.

And peace cannot be secured by wishes; peace cannot be preserved by noble words and pure intentions. "Enduring peace," Franklin D. Roosevelt said, "cannot be bought at the cost of other people's freedom."

The late President Kennedy put it precisely in November 1961, when he said: "We are neither warmongers nor appeasers, neither hard nor soft. We are Americans determined to defend the frontiers of freedom by an honorable peace if peace is possible but by arms if arms are used against us."

The true peace-keepers in the world tonight are not those who urge us to retire from the field in Vietnam—who tell us to try to find the quickest, cheapest exit from that tormented land, no matter what the consequences to us may be.

The true peace-keepers are those men who stand out there on the DMZ at this very hour, taking the worst that the enemy can give. The true peace-keepers are the soldiers who are breaking the terrorists' grip around the villages of Vietnam—the civilians who are bringing medical care and food and education to people who have already suffered a generation of war.

And so I report to you that we are going to continue to press forward. Two things we must do. Two things we shall do.

First, we must not mislead our enemy. Let him not think that debate and dissent will produce wavering and withdrawal. For I can assure you they won't. Let him not think that protests will produce surrender. Because they won't. Let him not think that he will wait us out. For he won't.

Second, we will provide all that our brave men require to do the job that must be done. And that job is going to be done.

These gallant men have our prayers—have our thanks—have our heart-felt praise—and our deepest gratitude.

Let the world know that the keepers of peace will endure through every trial—and that with the full backing of their countrymen, they are going to prevail.

*"History will look on this treaty
as a landmark in the effort
of mankind to avoid nuclear disaster. . . ."*
Statement by the President on submission of a draft treaty
to the Eighteen-Nation Disarmament Conference in Geneva;
Washington, D.C., January 18, 1968.

I am most heartened to learn that the Soviet Union will join the United States as Cochairman of the Eighteen-National Disarmament Committee, to submit a complete text of a treaty to stop the spread of nuclear weapons, and that this draft treaty will be submitted today to the Committee in Geneva. This revised text includes an agreed safeguards article and other revisions that will make the treaty widely acceptable.

We have worked long and hard in an effort to draft a text that reflects the views of other nations. I believe the draft presented today represents a major accomplishment in meeting these legitimate interests.

The text submitted today must now be considered further by all governments. Following its review by the conference in Geneva, it will be considered by the General Assembly in the spring. It is my fervent hope that I will be able to submit it to the Senate of the United States for its advice and consent this year.

The draft treaty text submitted today clearly demonstrates an important fact. In the face of the differences that exist in the world, the two nations which carry the heaviest responsibility for averting the catastrophe of nuclear war can, with sufficient patience and determination, move forward. They can move forward toward the goal which all men of good will seek—a reversal of the arms race and a more secure peace based on our many common interests on this one small planet.

I believe history will look on this treaty as a landmark in the effort of mankind to avoid nuclear disaster while ensuring that all will benefit from the peaceful uses of nuclear energy.

This treaty will be a testament of man's faith in the future. In that spirit I commend it to all.

"Uneasy is the peace that wears a nuclear crown."

The President speaks at the site
of the National Reactor Testing Station, Arco, Idaho,
August 26, 1966.

When Hernando Cortez returned to Spain after exploring the New World, he recommended to Charles I that a passage to India be opened by digging a canal across the Ithmus of Panama. Charles consulted his advisers and then rejected the recommendation because, as he later explained, "It would be a violation of the Biblical injunction: 'What God hath joined together, let no man put asunder.'"

I have often wondered what King Charles would have said if faced with the decision to split the atom. For in that act was not only the putting asunder a part of creation; it contained the potential for destroying creation itself.

We have come to a place today where hope was born that man would do more with his discovery than unleash destruction in its wake.

On this very spot the United States produced the world's first electricity from nuclear energy.

Only three years ago plans were announced for the first private nuclear power plant that would be competitive without any Government assistance. Since then, there have been more than twenty such installations announced by public and private utility companies. Orders have been placed for power reactors with a combined capacity of more than 15 million kilowatts—more than enough electric power for the homes of all the people of Idaho and seven other Western States.

By 1980, nuclear power units will have a capacity of more than 100 million kilowatts of electrical power—one-fifth of our national capacity at that time.

This energy is to propel the machines of progress; to light our cities and our towns; to fire our factories; to provide new sources of fresh water; and to really help us solve the mysteries of outer space as it brightens our life on this planet.

We have moved far to tame for peaceful uses the mighty forces unloosed when the atom was split. And we have only just begun. What happened here merely raised the curtain on a very promising drama in our long journey for a better life.

But there is another—and there is a darker—side of the nuclear age that we should never forget. And that is the danger of destruction by nuclear weapons.

It is true that these nuclear weapons have deterred war.

It is true that they have helped to check the spread of Communist expansion in much of the world.

It is true that they have permitted our friends to rebuild their nations in freedom.

But uneasy is the peace that wears a nuclear crown. And we cannot be satisfied with a situation in which the world is capable of extinction in a moment of error, or madness, or anger.

I can personally never escape, for very long at a time, the certain knowledge that such a moment might occur in a world where reason is often a martyr to pride and to ambition. Nor can I fail to remember that whatever the cause—by design or by chance—almost 300 million people would perish in a full-scale nuclear exchange between the East and the West.

This is why we have always been required to show restraint as well as to demonstrate resolve; to be firm but not to walk heavy footed along the brink of war.

This is why we also recognize that at the heart of our concern in the years ahead must be our relationship with the Soviet Union. Both of us possess unimaginable power; our responsibility to the world is heavier than that ever borne by any two nations at any other time in history. Our common interests demand that both of us exercise that responsibility and that we exercise it wisely in the years ahead.

Since 1945, we have opposed Communist efforts to bring about a Communist-dominated world. We did so because our convictions and our interests demanded it; and we shall continue to do so.

But we have never sought war or the destruction of the Soviet Union; indeed, we have sought instead to increase our knowledge and our understanding of the Russian people with whom we share a common feeling for life, a love of song and story, and a sense of the land's vast promises.

Our compelling task is this: to search for every possible area of agreement that might conceivably enlarge, no matter how slightly or how slowly, the prospect for cooperation between the United States and the Soviet Union. In the benefits of such cooperation, the whole world would share and so, I think, would both nations.

Common reasons for agreement have not eluded us in the past, and let no one forget that these agreements—arms control and others—have been essential to the overall peace in the world.

In 1963, we signed the limited test ban treaty that has now been joined by almost 100 other countries.

In 1959, the Antarctic Treaty—which restricted activity in this part of the world to peaceful purposes—was signed by the United States and the Soviet Union. It has now been joined by all countries interested in Antarctica.

In 1963, the United Nations unanimously passed a resolution prohibiting the placing in orbit of weapons of mass destruction.

When I first became President—almost my first act—I informed Premier

Khrushchev that we in the United States intended to reduce the level of our production of fissionable materials and we hoped that he and the Soviets would do likewise. Premier Khrushchev agreed.

I believe that the Soviets share a genuine desire to enlarge the area of agreement. This summer we have been negotiating with the Soviet Union and other nations, a treaty that would limit future activity on celestial bodies to peaceful purposes. This treaty would, for all time, ban weapons of mass destruction, not only on celestial bodies, but also in orbit around the earth.

Ambassador Arthur Goldberg, our Ambassador to the United Nations, has just informed me that much of the substance of this treaty has already been resolved. Negotiations were originally recessed on August 4 of this year, but the Soviet Government has now indicated its willingness to pursue them again as soon as possible. The Soviet Union has joined with us in requesting that all of the countries participating in the negotiations be prepared to resume discussions on the 12th day of next month. I am confident that with good will the remaining issues could be quickly resolved.

We are also seeking agreement on a treaty to prevent the spread of nuclear weapons.

This treaty would bind those who sign it in a pledge to limit the further spread of nuclear weapons and make it possible for all countries to refrain, without fear, from entering the nuclear arms race. It would not guarantee against a nuclear war; it would help to prevent a chain reaction that could consume the living of the earth. I believe that we can find acceptable compromise language on which reasonable men can agree. We just must move ahead, for we—all of us—have a great stake in building peace in this world in which we live.

In Southeast Asia the United States is today fighting to keep the North Vietnamese from taking over South Vietnam by force.

That conflict does not have to stop us from finding new ways of dealing with one another. Our objective in South Vietnam is local and it is limited: we are there trying to protect the independence of South Vietnam, to provide her people with a chance to decide for themselves where they are going and what they will become.

These objectives, I think, can be attained within the borders of Vietnam. They do not threaten the vital interests of the Soviet Union or the territory of any of her friends. We seek in Southeast Asia an order and security that we think would contribute to the peace of the entire world—and in that, we think, the Soviet Union has a very large stake.

It is the responsibility, then, of both of us to keep particular difficulties from becoming vehicles for much larger dangers.

For peace does not ever come suddenly or swiftly; only war carries that privilege. Peace will not dramatically appear from a single agreement or a single utterance or a single meeting.

It will be advanced by one small, perhaps imperceptible, gain after another, in which neither the pride nor the prestige of any large power is deemed more important than the fate of the world.

It will come by the gradual growth of common interests, by the increased awareness of shifting dangers and alignments, and by the development of confidence.

Confidence is not folly when both are strong. And we are both strong. The United States and the Soviet Union are both very strong, indeed.

So what is the practical step forward in this direction? I think it is to recognize that while differing principles and differing values may always divide us, they should not, and they must not, deter us from rational acts of common endeavor. The dogmas and the vocabularies of the Cold War were enough for one generation. The world must not now flounder in the backwaters of the old and stagnant passions. For our test really is not to prove which interpretation of man's past is correct. Our test is to secure man's future and our purpose is no longer only to avoid a nuclear war. Our purpose must be a consuming, determined desire to enlarge the peace for all peoples.

This does not mean that we have to become bedfellows. It does not mean that we have to cease competition. But it does mean that we must both want—and work for and long for—that day when "nation shall not lift up sword against nation, neither shall they learn war anymore."

I think those thousands of you who are here today at this most unusual event, at this most unusual place—the National Reactor Testing Center—know perhaps more than your other 190 million fellow-Americans just what a great force nuclear energy can be for peace, and just how much the liberty-, freedom-loving Americans have that as their number one objective. If we could have our one wish this morning, it would be that infiltration would cease, that bombs would stop falling, and that all men everywhere could live together without fear, in peace, under a government of their own choosing.

"By adding this treaty to the law of nations,
we are forging a permanent disarmament agreement
for outer space."

Remarks at a ceremony marking the entry
into force of the Outer Space Treaty,
October 10, 1967.

The Age of Space began just ten years ago last Wednesday. I am sure Ambassador Dobrynin does not have to be reminded of that date—nor do any of us.

The world will never forget the intelligence, the determination, and the courage that placed Sputnik into orbit, and launched man's great adventure into space.

That adventure has unfolded, during the past decade, with miraculous speed and scope. Man has probed the moon; he has reached out to other planets in the solar system. And he has done all of this in the spirit of peaceful exploration.

We are here today in the East Room to proclaim the intention of eighty-four nations that this exploration shall remain peaceful. By adding this treaty to the law of nations, we are forging a permanent disarmament agreement for outer space:

—It outlaws the weapons of mass destruction from man's newest frontier.

—It forbids military bases and fortifications on the moon and other celestial bodies.

—It prohibits the testing of weapons in space.

—It means that when man reaches the moon, he will land in a field of peace—not a new theater of war.

The spirit of international cooperation that has achieved this agreement is a beacon of hope for the future. It is a credit to all peoples. If we had sought for excuses to postpone agreement, we could have found them, I assure you, with the greatest of ease. Instead, we expended our efforts in achieving agreement—and we have succeeded.

The treaty was negotiated in less than six short months. For this, I gratefully thank our distinguished Ambassador Arthur Goldberg—who represented

our country—and all the wise and constructive statesmen of the other lands who shared in that accomplishment.

The Senate of the United States gave its unanimous consent—and I can assure all of our distinguished friends from abroad that this is not something that happens here every day.

That unanimous action testifies to the depth and sincerity of the American people's support for the purposes outlined in this treaty.

This unity is not new. As the Secretary of State remarked, it was nine years ago, when I was serving in the Senate, I appeared at the request of our very able then President, President Eisenhower, before the General Assembly of the United Nations. And upon that occasion, among other things, I had this to say:

"Until now our strivings toward peace have been heavily burdened by legacies of distrust and fear and ignorance and injury.

"Those legacies do not exist in space. They will not appear there unless we send them on ahead.

"To keep space as man has found it, and to harvest the yield of peace which it promises, we of the United States see one course—and only one—which the nations of earth may intelligently pursue. That is the course of full and complete and immediate cooperation to make the exploration of outer space a joint adventure."

That was our position nine years ago. It is our position now. I want to renew, therefore, today, America's offer to cooperate fully with any nation that may wish to join forces in this last—and greatest—journey of human exploration. Space is a frontier common to all mankind and it should be explored and conquered by humanity acting in concert.

We have urged cooperation:

—in exploring the planets, or any portion of the solar system;

—in the use of tracking facilities, so that our brave astronauts and cosmonauts may fly with much greater safety;

—in mapping the earth;

—in exchanging bioscientific information; and

—in international satellite communications.

We again renew these offers today. They are only the beginnings of what should be a long, cooperative endeavor in exploring the heavens together.

Whatever our disagreements here on earth, however long it may take to resolve our conflicts whose roots are buried centuries-deep in history, let us try to agree on this. Let us determine that the great space armadas of the future will go forth on voyages of peace—and will go forth in a spirit, not of national rivalry, but of peaceful cooperation and understanding.

The first decade of the Space Age has witnessed a kind of contest. We have been engaged in competitive spacemanship. We have accomplished much, but we have also wasted much energy and resources in duplicated or overlapping effort.

The next decade should increasingly become a partnership—not only between the Soviet Union and America, but among all nations under the sun and stars. I have directed the distinguished Secretary of State and the distinguished Director of NASA to bear this in mind every day in connection with their labors.

The hard business of foreign relations requires a certain optimism. One must be convinced that, in time, men and nations can direct their affairs toward constructive ends.

And it is with this optimism this morning that, here with you, I greet this treaty. I see it as a hopeful sign that mankind is learning, however slowly, that wars are not inevitable; that national rivalry is not a permanent barrier to international understanding; and that a world of hostility and hate need not be the abiding condition of mankind.

"We shall not unlearn the lesson of the thirties, when isolation and withdrawal were our share in the common disaster."

The President speaks on the Atlantic Alliance to the National Conference of Editorial Writers, New York City, October 7, 1966.

I remember some years ago Franklin Roosevelt addressed the Daughters of the American Revolution. His opening words were not "My friends," but "Fellow immigrants."

And he was right. Most of our fathers came from Europe—east or west, north or south. They settled in London, Kentucky; Paris, Idaho; and Rome, New York. Chicago, with Warsaw, is one of the great Polish cities of the world. And New York is the second capital of half the nations of Europe. That is the story of our country.

Americans and all Europeans share a connection which transcends political differences. We are a single civilization; we share a common destiny; our future is a common challenge.

Today two anniversaries especially remind us of the interdependence of Europe and America.

—On September 30, seventeen years ago, the Berlin airlift ended.

—On October 7, four years ago, the Nuclear Test Ban Treaty was ratified.

There is a healthy balance here. It is no accident. It reflects the balance the Atlantic allies have tried to maintain between strength and conciliation, between firmness and flexibility, between resolution and hope.

The Berlin airlift was an act of measured firmness. Without that firmness, the Marshall Plan and the recovery of Western Europe would have been impossible.

That hopeful and progressive achievement, the European Economic Community, could never have been born.

The winds of change which are blowing in Eastern Europe would not be felt today.

All these are the fruits of our determination.

The Test Ban Treaty is the fruit of our hope. With more than 100 other signers we have committed ourselves to advance from deterrence through terror toward a more cooperative international order. We must go forward to banish all nuclear weapons—and war itself.

A just peace remains our goal. But we know that the world is changing. Our policy must reflect the reality of today—not yesterday. In every part of the world, new forces are at the gates: new countries, new aspirations, new men. In this spirit, let us look ahead to the tasks that confront the Atlantic nations.

Europe has been at peace since 1945. But it is a restless peace—shadowed by the threat of violence.

Europe is partitioned. An unnatural line runs through the heart of a great and proud nation. History warns us that until this harsh division has been resolved, peace in Europe will not be secure.

We must turn to one of the great unfinished tasks of our generation: making Europe whole.

Our purpose is not to overturn other governments, but to help the people of Europe to achieve:

—a continent in which the peoples of Eastern and Western Europe work together for the common good;

—a continent in which alliances do not confront each other in bitter hostility, but provide a framework in which West and East can act together to assure the security of all.

In a restored Europe, Germany can and will be united.

This remains a vital purpose of American policy. It can only be accomplished through a growing reconciliation. There is no shortcut.

We must move ahead on three fronts:

—first, to modernize NATO and strengthen other Atlantic institutions;

—second, to further the integration of the Western European community;

—third, to quicken progress in East-West relations.

Let me speak to each in turn.

I. Our first concern is to keep NATO strong and abreast of the times.

The Atlantic Alliance has proved its vitality. Together, we have faced the threats to peace which have confronted us—and we shall meet those which may confront us in the future.

Let no one doubt the American commitment. We shall not unlearn the lesson of the thirties, when isolation and withdrawal were our share in the common disaster.

We are committed, and will remain firm.

But the Atlantic Alliance is a living organism. It must adapt to changing conditions.

Much is already being done to modernize its structures:

—We are streamlining NATO command arrangements.

—We are moving to establish a permanent nuclear planning committee.

—We are increasing the speed and certainty of supply across the Atlantic.

However, we must do more.

The Alliance must become a forum for increasingly close consultations. These should cover the full range of joint concerns—from East-West relations to crisis management.

The Atlantic Alliance is the central instrument of the Atlantic community.

But it is not the only one. Through other institutions the nations of the Atlantic are hard at work on constructive enterprise.

In the Kennedy Round, we are negotiating with the other free world nations to reduce tariffs everywhere. Our goal is to free the trade of the world from arbitrary and artificial constraints.

We are also engaged on the problem of international monetary reform.

We are exploring how best to develop science and technology as a common resource. Recently the Italian Government has suggested an approach to narrowing the gap in technology between the United States and Western Europe. That proposal deserves careful study. The United States is ready to cooperate with the European nations on all aspects of this problem.

Last—and perhaps most important—we are working together to accelerate the growth of the developing nations. It is our common business to help the millions in these nations improve their standards of life. The rich nations cannot live as an island of plenty in a sea of poverty.

Thus, while the institutions of the Atlantic community are growing, so are the tasks which face us.

II. Second among our tasks is the vigorous pursuit of further unity in the West.

To pursue that unity is neither to postpone nor neglect the search for peace. There are good reasons for this:

—A united Western Europe can be our equal partner in helping to build a peaceful and just world order.

—A united Western Europe can move more confidently in peaceful initiatives toward the East.

—Unity can provide a framework within which a unified Germany could be a full partner without arousing ancient fears.

We look forward to the expansion and further strengthening of the European Community. The obstacles are great. But perseverance has already reaped larger rewards than any of us dared hope twenty years ago.

The outlines of the new Europe are clearly discernible. It is a stronger, increasingly united but open Europe—with Great Britain a part of it—and with close ties to America.

III. One great goal of a united West is to heal the wound in Europe which now cuts East from West and brother from brother.

That division must be healed peacefully. It must be healed with the consent of Eastern European countries and the Soviet Union. This will happen only as East and West succeed in building a surer foundation of mutual trust.

Nothing is more important for peace. We must improve the East-West environment in order to achieve the unification of Germany in the context of a larger, peaceful, and prosperous Europe.

Our task is to achieve a reconciliation with the East—a shift from the narrow concept of coexistence to the broader vision of peaceful engagement.

Americans are prepared to do their part. Under the last four Presidents, our policy toward the Soviet Union has been the same. Where necessary, we shall defend freedom; where possible we shall work with the East to build a lasting peace.

We do not intend to let our differences on Vietnam or elsewhere prevent us from exploring all opportunities. We want the Soviet Union and the nations of Eastern Europe to know that we and our allies shall go step by step with them as far as they are willing to advance.

Let us—both Americans and Europeans—intensify our efforts.

We seek healthy economic and cultural relations with the Communist states:

—I am asking for early congressional action on the U.S.-Soviet consular agreement.

—We intend to press for legislative authority to negotiate trade agreements which could extend most-favored-nation tariff treatment to European Communist states.

And I am today announcing these new steps:

—We will reduce export controls on East-West trade with respect to hundreds of nonstrategic items.

—I have today signed a determination that will allow the Export-Import Bank to guarantee commercial credits to four additional Eastern European countries—Poland, Hungary, Bulgaria, and Czechoslovakia. This is good business. And it will help us build bridges to Eastern Europe.

—The Secretary of State is reviewing the possibility of easing the burden of Polish debts to the U.S. through expenditures of our Polish currency holdings which would be mutually beneficial to both countries.

—The Export-Import Bank is prepared to finance American exports for the Soviet-Italian FIAT auto plant.

—We are negotiating a civil air agreement with the Soviet Union. This will facilitate tourism in both directions.

—This summer the American Government took additional steps to liberalize travel to Communist countries in Europe and Asia. We intend to liberalize these rules still further.

—In these past weeks the Soviet Union and the United States have begun to exchange cloud photographs taken from weather satellites.

In these and many other ways, ties with the East will be strengthened— by the U.S. and by other Atlantic nations.

Agreement on a board policy to this end should be sought in existing Atlantic organs.

The principles which should govern East-West relations are now being discussed in the North Atlantic Council.

The OECD can also play an important part in trade and contacts with the East. The Western nations can there explore ways of inviting the Soviet Union and the Eastern European countries to cooperate in tasks of common interest and common benefit.

Hand in hand with these steps to increase East-West ties must go measures to remove territorial and border disputes as a source of friction in Europe. The Atlantic nations oppose the use of force to change existing frontiers.

The maintenance of old enmities is not in anyone's interest. Our aim is a true European reconciliation. We must make this clear to the East.

Further, it is our policy to avoid the spread of national nuclear programs— in Europe and elsewhere.

That is why we shall persevere in efforts to reach an agreement banning the proliferation of nuclear weapons.

We seek a stable military situation in Europe—one in which tensions can be lowered.

To this end, the United States will continue to play its part in effective Western deterrence. To weaken that deterrence might create temptations and endanger peace.

The Atlantic allies will continue together to study what strength NATO needs, in light of changing technology and the current threat.

Reduction of Soviet forces in Central Europe would, of course, affect the extent of the threat.

If changing circumstances should lead to a gradual and balanced revision in force levels on both sides, the revision could—together with the other steps that I have mentioned—help gradually to shape a new political environment.

The building of true peace and reconciliation in Europe will be a long process.

The bonds between the United States and its Atlantic partners provide the strength on which the world's security depends. Our interdependence is complete.

Our goal, in Europe and elsewhere, is a just and secure peace. It can most surely be achieved by common action. To this end, I pledge America's best efforts:

—to achieve new thrust for the Alliance;

—to support movement toward Western European unity;

—and to bring about a far-reaching improvement in relations between East and West.

Our object is to end the bitter legacy of World War II.

Success will bring the day closer when we have fully secured the peace in Europe, and in the world.

PART TWO

The Great Society Today

President Johnson and the Economy

By Walter W. Heller

The President's "economic situation room" is Room 314 in the Executive Office Building next to the White House, the office of the Chairman of the Council of Economic Advisers. Here the key data on the progress, prospects, and problems of the world's most powerful economy are sorted out, distilled, analyzed, interpreted in policy terms, and put at the President's disposal.

From this economic nerve center, President Johnson expects, gets, and—close President-watchers are agreed—*reads* no less than 250 memos a year.

Some 150 of them are the brief and pointed "Economic News Notes" that he gets three times a week (under a system set up at his request early in 1964) to keep him posted on the current and developing economic situation—more fully and systematically posted, I'm sure, than any other President in history.

Another 100 or so lie at the heart of the economic advisory process as it has developed in the Kennedy and Johnson administrations. In these, the Council interprets and analyzes economic events, alerts the President to emerging economic problems, and advises on policies to deal with them.

To elicit a Presidential response in situations where his decision or action may be needed, many a memo winds up with an action line reading "Yes_____. No_____. More information_____."

The writer of memos soon learns that what President Johnson demands as the price of admission to the "in" box of his office and to his mind is not brevity as such, but terseness, tight organization, and clarity. If these add up to brevity, as they usually do, so much the better. A President's time, as an economist above all should understand, is a resource in short supply and heavy demand.

President Johnson maximizes the effective supply of his time by converting every seemly opportunity—and now and then, an unseemly one—into an occasion for briefing, for probing, for cross-checking. Economic advisers are well advised to have their facts and judgments at the ready, not just in Cabinet meetings or sessions in the Oval Office, but in the midst of a White House reception, or as the President drives his guests over the back 2,000 at the LBJ Ranch, or at a family dinner, or at a luncheon for Chancellor Erhard, or in the helicopter from Andrews to the White House lawn. And in this electronic age a Presidential trip by car, plane, or ship is no signal to relax. Supplying an economic nugget or two for an airport arrival speech— even while Air Force One is in the approach pattern two thousand miles away—may be a singular, but not a unique, experience in Room 314.

The Commitment to Economic Expansion

What this reflects is not only the 24-hour-a-day Presidential personality of Lyndon Johnson, but the dawn of a new day in Presidential economics. The economic defenses of the country—against recession and unemployment, against sluggish growth, against spiraling costs and prices, against erosion of our international trade and payments position—have become a constant concern of Presidents. An economy mired in recession and slow growth or flushed with the fever of inflation lies directly athwart a President's domestic and international aspirations for America.

Against the background of the economic pressures of Vietnam and the prospect of more vigorous economic growth in the future, our attention has temporarily shifted to the problems of overexpansion and overheating. But in the first half of this decade, conditioned as we were by the three recessions and slow growth that immediately preceded it, our concern was understandably focused on the problem of expansion.

Presidents Kennedy and Johnson adopted the "new economics"—"new activism" is actually a better term, since the progress of the sixties has been in the *practice* rather than the *theory* of economics—not because they were carried away with the elegance of its analysis and the precision of its predictions, but because they found in it an instrument that could deliver the goods. Through the active use of tax, budget, and monetary changes, they could—and did—get the economy moving again and keep it moving in an expansion that is now well into its eighth consecutive year, having broken both the peacetime and all-time records for duration and strength.

So, in the sixties, political leaders in general and Presidents in particular have become aware of the vital importance of prosperity to their hopes for advancing the good society, for maintaining world leadership, and, not entirely incidentally, for getting reelected. An expanding economy enables the nation to declare social dividends out of growing output and income instead of having to wrench resources away from one group to give them to another, and thus enables Presidents to press ahead with a minimum of social tension and political dissent. Perhaps economics, as seen by Presidents, has not yet made the grade from the dismal science to the stuff that dreams are made of. But it's on the way.

Side by side with the growing Presidential commitment to the political economy of expansion, the 1960's have seen a growing acceptance of the "new economics" by the nation's business and financial leadership. (Labor leadership had largely entered the expansionary fold a good bit earlier.) It is more and more widely understood that:

—Positive Federal action to maintain high and rising levels of demand is a vital ingredient in high and rising sales volume, business investment, and profits and in a healthier environment for innovation and risk-taking.

—The measures to manage demand—cutting or boosting taxes, easing or tightening money, speeding up or slowing down Federal spending—are a form of Government intervention that does not undercut economic freedom, does not substitute Government for private economic decisions.

—The particular choice of policy weapons—for example, between tax cuts and spending hikes to boost the economy, between tighter money and fiscal restraint to tranquilize it, between heavier Federal spending and tax cuts as a means of distributing "fiscal dividends" once Vietnam is over—provides plenty of scope for expressing differences in economic and political philosophy.

Gradually, too, the citizen began to see his own self-interest in successful expansionary policy—his interest not only in the important ends of more jobs and rising incomes but in the pleasant means of tax cuts, easier money, and more generous Government programs. And he is finding that economic freedom and opportunity are growing, not shrinking, in the process.

PRESIDENTIAL PERSUASION AND EDUCATION

That the nation today begins to hold these economic truths to be self-evident is a tribute to the efforts of two Presidents to dispel the dense fog of economic ignorance, error, and suspicion that had long obscured the common need for a vigorous policy of growth and expansion. Few would dispute that Kennedy and Johnson will stand out in history as the first modern economists in the American Presidency. Their clear perception of the high stakes in economic policy; their bold use of the economic instruments of expansion; their casting aside of the myths that had crippled policy; their insatiable appetites for economic information, interpretation, and counsel—all these are unmatched in White House annals.

At first, to be sure, Kennedy was reluctant to tackle the false fiscal fears that had so recently been nourished by statements of high officials in the previous Administration denouncing deficits as synonymous with inflation, debt as an immoral burden on our grandchildren, Government spending as the primrose path to "hair-curling" depressions, and tax cuts—even in the 1958 and 1960 recessions—as fiscally unsound and irresponsible.

But by mid-1962, goaded by continued unemployment and economic slack and guided by the force of economic logic, Kennedy moved to the attack. In his landmark speech at Yale, he turned the withering fire of his wit and wisdom on the mistaken economic mythology that was holding us back. He put Presidential economic discourse on a wholly new plane in further speeches, press conferences, economic messages, White House statements, and particularly in his two nationwide telecasts on the tax cut. In economics, as in other fields, his policy declarations were ringing documents—frontal attacks full of challenge and call to arms.

There was no pause in the campaign for rational economic thinking and policy when Lyndon Johnson succeeded to the Presidency. Nor did the basic policy commitment change. But the approach to education and persuasion was distinctive in several respects.

First, in President Johnson's economic thinking, the test of actual *performance*—the hard evidence of *results* flowing from policy action—looms particularly large. He counts on those results not only to benefit the country but to educate it. Thus, he counted on the great tax cut of 1964 not only to bring us back at last to full employment but, by its success, to break the grip of the old fiscal fears and open the financial door to the Great Society. And he was right. Both the promises of economists and the hopes of Presidents were fulfilled when the tax cut dramatically stepped up consumer demand, business investment, and the pace of economic expansion—and, in the process, brought the Federal budget back into balance by the first half of 1965, just before escalation in Vietnam so rudely interrupted.

Second, Johnsonian policy messages tend to be low-key, treating new policy initiatives as natural, more or less self-evident, measures for a prospering and mature modern nation to take. Points of controversy and difference are muted. Viewing this process with some awe, the London *Economist* saw it "not so much as a new ideology as 'the end of ideology . . . an end of a vast amount of ritualistic response.' This perhaps is the great Johnson achievement—much of it the age-old political achievement of unleashing actions from the deadweight of cripplingly loaded words."

Third, President Johnson has used the White House meeting—both small and large—as a major instrument for acquainting hundreds of the nation's labor, business, agriculture, and education leaders with his economic policies and their rationale. Almost without exception, his listeners come away impressed by his mastery not only of the economic facts and figures, but of the economic issues and reasoning.

Why is it, people ask, that a President who is so effective in face-to-face persuasion, who has achieved breakthroughs in Federal support of education that surely merit the label of "education President" he so prizes, and who speaks with nostalgia and conviction (during a walk under the stars along the Pedernales) of returning to teaching one day—why is it that he does not go to the country more often to explain his policies and rally support for them?

One can only speculate. Like any President, he probably feels that a considerable part of the problem is not that the President isn't talking, but that the country isn't listening. Perhaps it is the knowledge of his greater effectiveness in give-and-take meetings with smaller groups—who do listen—coupled with the belief that the hundreds or even thousands who are exposed in depth to the President and his ideas will themselves become agents of his educational process.

How Durable Is Our Expansionary Commitment?

What might happen to the national commitment to economic expansion with a change in Administration? Given the critical importance of a prosperous and growing economy to the success of both domestic and foreign initiatives, I cannot imagine any future President forgoing the use of modern economics.

One can conjure up a nightmare of a conservative President heeding—as, indeed, the Republican candidate did in 1964—the counsel of a small school of conservative economists, the "monetarists," who believe that nothing but the money supply really counts in determining the level of economic activity. Following their precepts, he might persuade the Federal Reserve Board to set monetary policy on a rigid path of 3 to 4 percent annual increases in the money supply. Perhaps he would also try to persuade Congress to freeze tax policy into a rigid pattern of once-a-year tax cuts—as Senator Goldwater proposed in 1964.

With economic policy thus set on "automatic pilot," one can imagine what would happen when the economy hit the turbulence of recession, with its downdrafts in jobs, profits, and incomes. How long would even a conservative President stand idly by and deny himself—and the country—the proven tonic of tax cuts, spending step-ups, and easy money? Economic common sense and political sagacity would finally win out, I'm sure, over the rigid and static rules that so ill befit an ever-changing and dynamic economy.

But as a practical matter I don't expect the country to fall into the trap of lockstep economics. Even if the logic of modern economic policy were not persuasive, it is difficult to see how any future President could be immune to the record of the great expansion of the 1960's that is so closely associated with the "new economics":

—In sharp contrast with the ominous sequence of shorter and shorter expansions in the 1950's—which ended in recessions in 1954, after 45 months of expansion; in 1957, after 35 months; and in 1960, after 25 months—our Methuselah of expansions had already set a new peacetime record of 52 months by July 1965 when escalation began and has by now left the 80-month expansion record of the 1940's far behind.

Since the beginning of the advance in early 1961, 10 million new jobs have been created, more than twice as many as in the preceding seven years.

—The growth in real GNP since the first quarter of 1961 has averaged over 5 percent a year, more than double the feeble 2½ percent rate of advance from 1953 to 1960.

—The buying power of the average consumer—real disposable income per capita after taxes—has increased more in the 27 quarters beginning in the first quarter of 1961 than in the preceding eighteen.

—Corporate profits have enjoyed their longest sustained advance in history, more than doubling (after taxes).

—Yet, even with our Vietnam inflation, our consumer price index has risen far less than that of our trading partners—from 1960 to the end of 1967 our consumer price index was rising 14 percent at the same time that the price increase in our twenty partner countries in the OECD was averaging 33 percent.

But to say that the forces of reason and self-interest would induce any future President to use the tools of modern economics is not to suggest that the present Administration and some future conservative Administration would differ no more than Tweedledum and Tweedledee. Let me illustrate by raising three questions:

—First, would the unemployment objective be set at 4 percent or less, or would those who advise a Republican President counsel him—as some have in the past—that it ought to be set at 5 percent or more to "discipline labor" and prevent cost-push inflation?

—Second, what about the choice of policy weapons for economic stabilization? If recession threatens, would stimulus come primarily through tax cuts or expenditure step-ups? And would the longer-term preference be for tighter money and high interest rates with somewhat easier fiscal policy, or vice versa?

—And third, how would the bounties of economic growth be distributed? The normal advance in the American economy automatically pours over $10 billion a year of added revenue into the Federal coffers without any increase in tax rates. Would a conservative Administration declare most of its fiscal dividends in the form of tax cuts? Or would the battles against urban rot and blight, against poverty, and against pollution get a fair ration?

Vital issues, then, remain. And men of differing political persuasions and philosophies will provide decisively different answers.

WAR AND INFLATION

The effectiveness of fiscal-monetary measures in dealing with slack and recession has been tested under fire. The big tax cut was one case in point. Another was the use of expenditure speed-ups, tax changes, and monetary ease to avert recession in the winter of 1966–67. In the face of a housing slump of some $8 billion and a drop in inventory investment of some $18 billion—the latter, a classical recession trigger—the response of policy and the resiliency of the economy were impressively demonstrated. Quick easing of money, early restoration of tax incentives for investment, and the release of previously impounded funds for highways and housing kept final demand —the overall sales of goods and services—rising steadily. By his swift action, President Johnson bore out my earlier assurance that as long as he is in the White House, the economy won't have a recession—it wouldn't dare! By summer, the economy's case of indigestion was cured and it was again off to the races.

And there's the rub—the "new economics" has yet to demonstrate that it can deliver reasonable price stability side by side with full employment and vigorous expansion. This is a question we have been grappling with ever since escalation in Vietnam in mid-1965 began overheating and distorting the economy. To cope with the resulting pressure of excess demand, the "new economics"—coupled with the "old politics"—managed to produce two tax tightening measures in 1966, but did not deliver in either 1966 or 1967 the across-the-board income-tax boost that was clearly needed. The consequence was that we had to step too hard on the monetary brakes to check inflation. Housing, and to a lesser extent small business and state-local borrowing, bore the brunt of the resulting credit crunch.

Had the President called for—and been able to get—a surtax and suspension of investment tax incentives early in 1966, we could have eased inflationary pressures without such brutally tight money and the resulting jolt to housing. The economy would have maintained better balance.

Although the period of the Vietnam war is hardly economic policy's finest hour, one needs to be a bit measured in criticism of both policy and performance. Policy, after all, did deliver two tax bills in 1966, clamped a tight rein on credit, and did manage to hold inflation to an annual rate of about 3 percent even without drastic measures like wage and price controls. It responded swiftly and strongly to prevent the high-level stall in late 1966 from turning into a tailspin. And President Johnson's 10-percent surtax proposal was not only a responsible but a courageous reaction to the resurgence of the economy and the intensified threat of inflation in 1967–68.

The stubborn reluctance of Congress to act—even as the predicted rise in prices, interest rates, deficits, and imports was occurring—is more difficult to explain and defend. Some believe that the President could have gotten action last fall or winter by earlier expenditure cutbacks, or by simply appealing for the tax as necessary to finance the war.

I, for one, am glad that the President treated both Congress and the country as if they were mature enough to understand and respond to the rational rather than the emotional appeal for the surtax. I like to think that we have made a fair amount of progress since the day in 1951 when eighty-eight-year-old Chairman "Muley" Doughton of the Ways and Means Committee pointed a finger at me (when I was representing the Treasury Department before the Committee) and said, "Young man, if I thought that one dollar of this tax request of the President's was for these newfangled ideas of fighting inflation instead of financing the war in Korea, I'd vote against it."

Yet, one can see how far we still have to go when the Harris Poll late in 1967 finds only 22 percent of its respondents agreeing and 59 percent disagreeing with the statement that "one way to control inflation is to cut down consumer spending by raising taxes"—and this, after 59 percent had agreed and only 23 percent disagreed with the statement that "tax cuts can give people more money to spend, thus maintaining prosperity in slow times." The fiscal expansion lesson? Well-learned. The fiscal restraint lesson? Still to be taught.

Fortunately for the longer-run prospects of avoiding demand inflation, the human bias against tax increases and for inflation has a counter-force in the probable built-in bias against inflation in our Federal fiscal system. Nothing in our budget history prior to Vietnam suggests that spending increases will, on the average, absorb all of the $10-plus billion automatic annual growth in revenues associated with normal expansion of our economy. If this is true, we will be able—at least most of the time—to exercise fiscal restraint not by the painful process of raising taxes, but by the much more painless process of simply not declaring all of the $10 billion or more in such fiscal dividends as expenditure increases and tax cuts.

Even if we cope successfully with demand inflation, there remains the problem that vexes every advanced economy operating in the neighborhood of full employment. I refer, of course, to the tendency of strongly organized producer groups—both on the labor side and on the business side—to push costs and prices up in a never-ending spiral. Wage advances that outstrip productivity advances, coupled with price increases in some sectors not offset by price cuts in others, are bound to give an inflationary bias to a nation's economy. A rise of 1 percent to 1½ percent a year in price can be tolerated— a rise of 3 percent or 4 percent cannot, especially in a world in which we have to run a large trade surplus if we are to carry out our leadership responsibilities in finance, aid, and defense.

What instruments do we have to cope with this kind of cost-push inflation? Voluntary restraint in terms of standards crystallized in the wage-price guideposts worked well until they crumbled in 1966 under the pressure of excessive demand. Buttressed by President Johnson's intensive and effective efforts at persuasion—much of it in behind-the-scenes sessions with buiness executives and labor leaders—the guideposts were a helpful force for restraint. Perhaps with the aid of the new Cabinet Committee on Prices, and with the active participation of business and labor, they can be put back on their legs in more concrete form.

A LOOK TO THE FUTURE

As we look to the future, we can reflect on the directions that intelligent leadership in economic policy is likely to take. In viewing what is likely under an enlightened approach, I will inescapably be dealing also with what I would like.

Flexibility in Policy

First, we can look forward to an economic environment of both higher employment and more rapid rates of growth than anything we have known prior to the sixties. This implies—and is meant to—a prediction that interruptions of the steady upward march of the economy in the future will be shorter and milder than those of the past. But even though modern economic policy has helped stamp out old-fashioned business cycles, I don't mean to imply that one can rule out occasional slowdowns and recessions in an economy as vast, dynamic, and subject to external forces as ours. As President Johnson said in his 1965 Economic Report, we can head off recessions or at least moderate them greatly if we can act promptly. He suggested that if recession threatens, the Congress could help by "insuring that its procedures will permit rapid action on temporary income-tax cuts." Also, he saw promise in quick acceleration of existing public programs and advancing the effective dates of projected programs.

All this is to the good. But if economic policy is to be flexible enough to deal with the mistakes and surprises that do occur—to counteract unexpected turns in the private economy that will upset the best of forecasts—we will have to make our fiscal machinery more responsive than it is today.

One path is standby authority for the President, subject to Congressional veto, to make quick temporary cuts or increases in the basic individual income-tax rate to cope with recession or inflation. President Kennedy proposed such standby powers (for cuts only). As an alternative, perhaps Congress could be persuaded to hammer out ground rules, both for the structure of temporary tax cuts and boosts and for procedures of speedy enactment of such changes in response to Presidential requests.

Defenses against Cost Inflation

Second, since an active fiscal-monetary policy for full employment and vigorous growth constantly courts the danger of cost inflation, we need to strengthen our defenses on this front. As suggested above, President Johnson's call for voluntary restraint needs to be translated—through the cooperation of labor, business, and Government—into new and meaningful wage-price guideposts. The deeper defense of a more rapid rise in productivity—of rising output per unit of input, which is a basic source of "more to go around," i.e., of the wherewithal to satisfy rising wage and profit claims— needs to be constantly strengthened.

Our International Monetary Program

Third, one cannot speak of economic defenses without reference to President Johnson's program to protect our international financial flank. His measures to control the outflow of investment and loan funds and curb travel—distasteful and even distressing as they may be—make sense as a holding action in a world whose monetary system is still in the grip of gold and fixed exchange rates. One cannot break that grip overnight without running the risk of major disruption and autarchical responses in foreign trade and exchange policies. Seen in this light, the President's program is designed to buy time for

—a dignified demotion of gold by activating and expanding new monetary reserves not tied to gold, namely, the new Special Drawing Rights in the International Monetary Fund;

—restoring our foreign trade surplus to the lofty heights needed to "finance" our net outflow of funds for foreign investment, aid, and defense;

—bringing the war in Vietnam and both its direct and indirect drains on our balance of payments to an end.

Post-Vietnam Economic Planning

Fourth, to direct our economic thinking and planning to that blessed day when war in Vietnam does end, President Johnson in 1967 set up a government Post-Vietnam Policy Committee headed by the Chairman of the Council of Economic Advisers. Nine subgroups were set up to cope with the problems of economic slowdowns, readjustment, and redeployment of resources. In a word, their assignment is to convert economic problem into economic opportunity, primarily by having practical programs ready to redirect billions of dollars of released resources.

—to high-priority private uses through tax cuts, especially for low income groups;

—to high-priority public uses through expansion of the critically important programs that have had to wait their turn while war absorbed much of the energy and will that should have been theirs.

There, if it was not already plain, is the clear-cut answer to those who claim we need war as a prop to our economy. True, war's end can deliver full employment—the worst way. But the end of war will, I'm sure, show that we also know how to do it the best way—by helping our poor, by rehabilitating our cities, by cleansing our water and air and land, and by increasing the range of private pleasures and comforts.

But why wait till war's end? With a national product of $850 billion a year —less than $30 billion of it absorbed by Vietnam—the limit to our efforts is set not by lack of economic potential, but by our willingness to put the necessary resources at the disposal of government for these vital domestic purposes. In an economic sense, the President is dead right: the country *can* have both guns and butter when military outlays claim less than 10 percent of the country's huge annual output, a smaller proportion than in the peacetime years 1955–60.

History will surely say that the problem in 1968 was not whether we could afford to do what needed to be done, but whether we could afford *not* to do it. The severest domestic test of Presidents, Congress, and public alike is whether we will use our truly prodigious economic power and genius to keep the faith with the poor, the black, the ignorant, and the jobless—and, above all, with the humiliating home of all four, the urban ghetto.

Lyndon B. Johnson

*"You will win the race with time-tested
American business methods . . ."*

Remarks to members of the Business Council,
Washington, D.C.,
December 6, 1967.

If we wanted to celebrate the triumphs of our economy tonight, we would
have cause enough.

We are now in the eighty-second month of the American economic miracle.
This sustained prosperity is unparalleled in our history.

But it is not celebration which summons us.

We are here, rather, to look at the other side of the ledger—to assess some
of the challenges that now threaten our prosperity.

INTERNATIONAL MONETARY PROBLEMS

America's role in world trade and finance is crucial to our prosperity and
that of all free nations.

World trade has quadrupled since World War II. We have helped to
create that trade—and we have shared fully in its benefits.

In the world network of trade, America's role is doubly important. Our dollar stands at its center—the medium of exchange for most international transactions.

The recent devaluation of the British pound—with the tremors of uncertainty it stirred—makes it even more imperative that we maintain confidence in the dollar.

In the wake of devaluation, we witnessed a remarkable display of international financial cooperation. A speculative attack on the system was decisively repelled.

It was repelled because we stood firmly behind our pledge—which I reaffirm today—to convert the dollar to gold at $35 an ounce.

It was repelled because the leading governments of the Western World joined with us in that successful defense, at a relatively small cost in reserves.

But we cannot rest on this victory. We must look ahead. As world trade expands, so must the liquidity required to finance it. That liquidity need not rest on the uncertainties of gold production, consumption, and speculation. Nor can its supply be the responsibility of any one country.

So, even as we reaffirm our pledge to keep our dollar strong—and every ounce of our gold stock stands behind that pledge—we must look beyond gold.

We will press the case for other reserves which can strengthen the international monetary system of tomorrow.

We are joined with other nations in this venture.

Already we have laid out a blueprint. The agreement reached at the International Monetary Fund meeting in Rio is a first important step. It points the way to the creation of supplementary reserves backed by the full faith and credit of the participating nations.

Balance of Payments

A healthy balance of payments is essential to a sound dollar.

After a decade of deficits, our balance of payments problem still challenges the best efforts of government and business.

In recent years we have made some very real progress. But we find some of that progress offset by the cost of our defense efforts in Southeast Asia, and by events surrounding the devaluation of the pound.

This calls for special effort—by both government and business—to press even harder for progress.

Our investments in defense and foreign aid are vital to the security of every American. But, for our part in government, we are reducing to the barest minimum the drain of these essential activities on our balance of payments.

Business, too, has responded to the challenge.

In the voluntary balance of payments program, we have seen one of the finest examples of cooperative effort with government. Many firms have helped to reduce the deficit. They have borrowed funds overseas to finance foreign investments rather than borrow here and export our dollars abroad. Others have chosen to defer or scale down their investments.

We ask for even greater voluntary cooperation in 1968.

Before your dollars flow abroad to another industrial nation, ask yourself: Is this for an essential project? If it is, why can't you finance it overseas?

I know that borrowing overseas may cost an extra point or so in interest. But it is a necessary investment. It will strengthen the economy in which we all have a share.

EXPANDING OUR EXPORTS

The best way to strengthen our balance of payments is to expand our exports.

We used to talk of the world market in terms of billions of dollars—and more recently hundreds of billions. Now the economists tell us those measures no longer suffice.

The size of the economy outside the United States today exceeds $1 trillion.

American business has only begun to fight for this market.

I hope you will take this message back to the board rooms of America: Get going on exports.

We in government have helped you to promote and finance your sales to other markets abroad. We hope to do even more in the future.

But I ask business to remember this: trade must be a two-way street. Trade must be a fair and competitive race.

You cannot win this race confined by the quotas or high tariff walls the protectionists demand. Those walls have always been barriers to profits. You will win the race with time-tested American business methods—efficiency, better products, lower costs and prices.

Even though we know that a key to balance of payments is to export more, we also know this: if our prices rise faster than those of our overseas competitors, our exports will suffer and our imports will grow.

A growing export surplus demands that we maintain a higher degree of price stability than our competitors. We have done that over the past seven years.

THE RESPONSIBILITY OF BUSINESS AND LABOR

The challenge to business and labor is no less compelling than the challenge to Government.

We know that wage and price changes are inevitable—and desirable—in a free enterprise system.

But those changes must be restrained by a recognition of the fundamental national interest in maintaining a stable level of overall prices.

If strong labor unions insist on a wage rise twice the nationwide increase in output per man-hour—even where there is no real labor shortage—we are bound to have rising prices.

If members of an industry attempt to raise prices and profit margins— even when they clearly have excess capacity—we are bound to have rising prices.

Nobody benefits from a wage-price spiral. Labor knows that it does not. You know that business does not. And surely the American people do not.

Yet business says it is labor's responsibility to break the spiral, and labor says it is yours.

I say it is everyone's responsibility.

It is the responsibility of Government, of labor, and of business.

I intend to urge labor to restrain its demands for excessive wage increases.

I am urging business tonight to refrain from avoidable price increases, and to intensify its competitive efforts.

To both I say: It is your economy—your jobs and profits we need to protect it. It is your dollar whose strength we must maintain.

For the first time, America is fighting for freedom abroad without resorting to wage and price controls at home.

Voluntary restraint has made involuntary curbs unnecessary.

This is the way it should be done.

This is the way it can be done—if business and labor meet their responsibilities.

"The task of economic policy
is to create a prosperous America.
The unfinished task of prosperous Americans
is to build a great society."

The Economic Report of the President (excerpt),
January 28, 1965.

I am pleased to report:
 —that the state of our economy is excellent;
 —that the rising tide of our prosperity, drawing new strength from the
1964 tax cut, is about to enter its fifth consecutive year;
 —that, with sound policy measures, we can look forward to uninterrupted
and vigorous expansion in the year ahead.

Progress Toward Our Economic Goals

FULL EMPLOYMENT

In the year just ended, we have made notable progress toward the Employment Act's central goal of ". . . useful employment opportunities, including
self-employment, for those able, willing, and seeking to work, and . . .
maximum employment, production, and purchasing power."

But high levels of employment, production, and purchasing power cannot
rest on a sound base if we are plagued by slow growth, inflation, or a lack
of confidence in the dollar. Since 1946 therefore, we have come to recognize
that the mandate of the Employment Act implies a series of objectives closely
related to the goal of full employment:
 —*rapid growth,*
 —*price stability, and*
 —*equilibrium in our balance of payments.*

RAPID GROWTH

True prosperity means more than the full use of the productive powers available at any given time. It also means the rapid expansion of those powers. In
the long run, it is only a growth of overall productive capacity that can swell

individual incomes and raise living standards. Thus, *rapid economic growth* is clearly an added goal of economic policy.

—Our gain of $132 billion in GNP since the first quarter of 1961 represents an average growth rate (in constant prices) of 5 percent a year.

—This contrasts with the average growth rate of 2½ percent a year between 1953 and 1960.

Part of our faster gain in the last four years has narrowed the "gap" that had opened up between our actual output and our potential in the preceding years of slow expansion. But the growth of our potential is also speeding up. Estimated at 3½ percent a year during most of the 1950s, it is estimated at 4 percent in the years ahead; and sound policies can and should raise it above that, even while moving our actual performance closer to our potential.

PRICE STABILITY

I regard the goal of *overall price stability* as fully implied in the language of the Employment Act of 1946.

We can be proud of our recent record on prices:

—Wholesale prices are essentially unchanged from four years ago, and from a year ago.

—Consumer prices have inched upward at an average rate of 1.2 percent a year since early 1961, and 1.2 percent in the past 12 months. (Much of this increase probably reflects our inability fully to measure improvements in the quality of consumer goods and services.)

BALANCE OF PAYMENTS EQUILIBRIUM

The Employment Act requires that employment policy be "consistent" with "other essential considerations of national policy." Persistent balance of payments deficits in the 1950s reached an annual average of nearly $4 billion in 1958–60. Deficits of this size threatened to undermine confidence in the dollar abroad and limited our ability to pursue, simultaneously, our domestic and overseas objectives. As a result, *restoring and maintaining equilibrium in the U.S. balance of payments* has for some years been recognized as a vital goal of economic policy.

During the past your years:

—Our overall balance of payments position has improved, and the outflow of our gold has been greatly reduced.

—Our commercial exports have risen more than 25 percent since 1960, bringing our trade surplus to a new postwar record.

—The annual dollar outflow arising from our aid and defense commitments has been cut $1 billion, without impairing programs.

—Our means of financing the deficit have been strengthened, reducing the gold outflow and helping to build confidence in the dollar.

CONSISTENCY OF OUR GOALS

Thus, the record of our past four years has been one of simultaneous advance toward full employment, rapid growth, price stability, and international balance.

We have proved that with proper policies these goals are not mutually inconsistent. They can be mutually reinforcing.

The Role of Economic Policy

The unparalleled economic achievements of these past four years have been founded on the imagination, prudence, and skill of our businessmen, workers, investors, farmers, and consumers. In our basically private economy, gains can come in no other way.

But since 1960 a new factor has emerged to invigorate private efforts. *The vital margin of difference has come from Government policies which have sustained a steady, but noninflationary, growth of markets.*

I believe that 1964 will go down in our economic and political history as the "year of the tax cut."

It was not the first time that taxes were cut, of course, nor will it be the last time. But it *was* the first time our Nation cut taxes for the declared purpose of speeding the advance of the private economy toward "maximum employment, production, and purchasing power." And it was done in a period already prosperous by the standard tests of rising production and incomes. In short, *the tax cut was an expression of faith in the American economy:*

—It expressed confidence that our economy would translate higher after-tax incomes and stronger incentives into increased expenditures in our markets.

—It recognized the presence of untapped productive capacity. We cut taxes confident that the economy would respond to increased buying by producing more goods at stable prices rather than the same output at higher prices.

—It insisted on getting full performance from the American economy.

The promise of the tax cut for 1964 was fulfilled. Production, employment, and incomes jumped ahead. Unemployment was whittled down steadily.

Since 1960, the balance between budget expenditures and taxes has been boldly adjusted to the needs of economic growth. We have recognized as self-defeating the effort to balance our budget too quickly in an economy operating well below its potential. And we have recognized as fallacious the idea that economic stimulation can come only from a rapid expansion of Federal spending.

Monetary policy has supported fiscal measures. The supply of credit has been wisely tailored to the legitimate credit needs of a noninflationary expansion, while care has been taken to avoid the leakage of short-term funds in response to higher interest rates abroad.

Fiscal and monetary policies to build our prosperity have been buttressed by measures:

—to improve the education, skills, and mobility of our labor force;

—to stimulate investment in new and modern plants and machinery;

—to expand exports;

—to assist in rebuilding the economic base of communities and areas that have lagged behind;

—to strengthen our farm economy and support farm income;

—to conserve and develop our natural resources;

—to keep a sound flow of credit moving to home-buyers and small businesses;

—to redevelop decaying urban areas;

—to strengthen our transportation network; and

—to offer business and labor a guide for sound and noninflationary price and wage decisions.

Public policies to build a sound prosperity have found their response in equally constructive private efforts.

—Our businessmen have controlled their costs, increased their efficiency, and developed new markets at home and abroad.

—They have kept their inventories under tight control and have prudently geared their plant expansion to rising markets in an expanding economy.

—Consumers have used rising incomes and tax savings to lift their standards of living, while adding to their wealth to assure their future standards of living.

—Workers have realized that wage gains which justify employers' raising prices vanish when they take their pay envelopes into the stores—and cost them much when they draw on their savings.

—Workers and managers have cooperated to facilitate the adoption of new technology, while solving the human problems it sometimes creates.

As a result of public and private policies, we have come to our present state of prosperity without pressures or imbalances that would foretell an early end to our expansion. Instead, we look forward to another year of sustained and healthy economic growth.

The Unfinished Tasks

Our prosperity is widespread, but it is not complete. Our growth has been steady, but its permanence is not assured. Our achievements are great, but our tasks are unfinished.

1. Four years of steadily expanding job opportunities have not brought us to full employment. Some 3.7 million of our citizens want work but are unable to find it. Up to 1 million more—"the hidden unemployed"—would enter the labor force if the unemployment rate could be brought down just one percentage point.

In the next year, 1.3 million more potential workers will be added to our labor force, including a net increase of ½ million below the age of 20.

The more of these 6 million potential workers who find jobs in 1965:

—the faster our total output will grow;

—the greater will be the markets for the products of our factories and farms;

—the larger will be our Federal revenues;

—the greater will be the number of our citizens who know they are contributing to our society, not subsisting on the contributions of others;

—the smaller will be the number who know the pangs of insecurity, deprivation, even of hunger;

—the larger will be the number of teenagers who feel that society has a useful purpose for them.

The promise in the Employment Act of job opportunities for all those able and wanting to work has not yet been fulfilled. We cannot rest until it is.

2. Four years of vigorous efforts have not yet brought our external payments into balance. We need to complete that task—and we will.

The stability of the American dollar is central not only to progress at home but to all our objectives abroad. *There can be no question of our capacity and determination to maintain the gold value of the dollar at $35 an ounce. The full resources of this Nation are pledged to that end.*

Progress in key sectors of our international payments has been good, but not enough. Gains in trade and savings in Government overseas payments have been offset in large measure by larger capital outflows. As a result our deficit remains far too large. *We must and will reduce and eliminate it.*

In the process of restoring external balance we must continue—in concert with other nations of the free world—to build an international economic order:

—based on maximum freedom of trade and payments,

—in which imbalances in payments, whether surpluses or deficits, are soundly financed while being effectively eliminated,

—in which no major currency can be undermined by speculative runs, and

—in which the poorer nations are helped—through investment, trade, and aid—to raise progressively their living standards toward those of the developed world.

3. Ceaseless change is the hallmark of a progressive and dynamic economy. No planned economy can have the flexibility and adaptability that flow from the voluntary response of workers, consumers, and managements to the shifting financial incentives provided by free markets.

In those activities entrusted to governments—as in those where private profit provides the spur—the search for efficiency and economy must never cease.

The American economy is the most efficient and flexible in the world. *But the task of improving its efficiency and flexibility is never done.*

4. American prosperity is widely shared. But too many are still precluded from its benefits by discrimination; by handicaps of illness, disability, old age, or family circumstance; by unemployment or low productivity; by lack of mobility or bargaining power; by failure to receive the education and training from which they could benefit.

The war against poverty has begun; its prosecution is one of our most urgent tasks in the years ahead.

5. Our goals for individuals and our Nation extend far beyond mere affluence. The quality of American life remains a constant concern.

The task of economic policy is to create a prosperous America. *The unfinished task of prosperous Americans is to build a Great Society.*

Our accomplishments have been many; these tasks remain unfinished:

—to achieve full employment without inflation;

—to restore external equilibrium and defend the dollar;

—to enhance the efficiency and flexibility of our private and public economies;

—to widen the benefits of prosperity;

—to improve the quality of American life.

INTERNATIONAL ECONOMIC POLICIES

RESTORING BALANCE IN OUR EXTERNAL PAYMENTS

Continued cost and price stability is fundamental to correction of our balance of payments deficit—it is the foundation on which we must build our entire effort to achieve external equilibrium. In addition, we must continue and intensify more specific attacks on the problem:

—We are continuously reviewing our aid and defense programs to achieve the maximum savings in dollar expenditures abroad. Our aid programs must remain closely tied to exports of U.S. goods and services, until the balance of payments problem has been eliminated.

—We must continue and strengthen measures to promote U.S. exports.

—We will be alert to restrain any persistent outflow of short-term private funds in response to relatively high short-term interest rates in foreign countries.

—To increase our ability to attract foreign investment in U.S. securities, legislation will be proposed to improve the tax treatment of such investments.

More broadly, we need to reassess the adequacy of existing programs to deal with the balance of payments problem. The results of this reassessment will be set forth in a separate message to the Congress.

BUILDING A STRONGER WORLD ORDER

Through expanded trade: In the Kennedy Round of trade negotiations now underway at Geneva, we are working intensively for a broad liberalization of world trade in both industrial and agricultural products.

A successful outcome can be of crucial benefit not only to the industrialized countries but also to the developing countries of the world.

Through improved international monetary arrangements: We take pride in our leadership in the building of the postwar system of international monetary cooperation. We find reassurance in the wholehearted resolve of the industrialized countries of the free world to avoid repeating the costly mistakes of the 1920s and 1930s. The strength of international monetary cooperation was demonstrated dramatically in 1964 in repelling speculative attacks on the Italian lira and the British pound.

We will continue to pursue orderly growth at home and abroad:

—on the basis of stable convertible currencies and the fixed $35 price for gold;

—through a wide network of bilateral and multilateral credit arrangements; and

—through frequent consultation between countries.

But we still have more to learn about:

—how best to share the burden of making necessary mutual adjustments when countries run persistent deficits or surpluses in their balances of payments, and

—how best to meet the need of ensuring orderly growth in world liquidity to finance expanding world trade.

We will continue to seek agreement on these problems with other countries; we are confident that effective solutions will be found. We look toward early agreement on an increase in the resources of the International Monetary Fund, which will further strengthen the international monetary system.

Through helping to raise incomes in less developed countries: U.S. foreign assistance programs further three basic American aims. By helping to advance the economic growth of the less developed nations, they:

—create the kind of world in which peace and freedom are most likely to flourish;

—bring closer a world economic order in which all nations will be strong partners;

—simultaneously, give a major stimulus to U.S. exports both in the present through direct financing of U.S. goods and services and for the future by developing the recipient's ability to buy and his preference for American products.

OTHER ECONOMIC POLICIES FOR 1965 AND BEYOND

NATURAL RESOURCE DEVELOPMENT

America owes her greatness partly to the large public and private investments made to develop her abundant natural resources. Rapid growth and urbanization require intensified efforts to solve old problems and imaginative approaches to new challenges.

Especially requiring study and action are:

—The protection of our environment. We need to strengthen our attack on air, water, and soil pollution.

—Water resource programs. We must improve the efficiency, coordination, and comprehensiveness of our major water resource development programs. More realistic charges and user fees will improve equity and strengthen private incentives for efficient use.

—Research programs. We must find new and more efficient ways of utilizing available resources. I have recommended increased research efforts in several areas, including the desalting of sea water.

—Recreational resources. Urbanization, higher incomes, and expanded leisure time pose new demands for outdoor recreation. New and improved facilities are needed, particularly near metropolitan areas.

STRENGTHENING THE ECONOMIC BASE OF COMMUNITIES

In 1961, the Congress recognized the special needs of distressed areas by passing the Area Redevelopment Act. Since then, hundreds of urban and rural communities have been strengthened by grants, loans, technical assistance, and training programs to help to build or restore their economic base. This program has helped distressed areas to benefit more fully from sustained prosperity.

Redirection of this program can benefit from the experience of the last four years. Future assistance should be sufficient to make a significant impact on the economic growth of the communities assisted. Integrated development plans must be devised for larger economic areas with high promise of future viability, and communities must be helped to mobilize public and private leadership in an attack on local blight and depression.

I shall propose measures to achieve these goals, through an extension and strengthening of the Area Redevelopment Act.

I also urge the Congress to enact the special program to assist in redeveloping the Appalachian region.

CONSUMER INFORMATION

Informed consumer choice among increasingly varied and complex products requires frank, honest information concerning quantity, quality, and prices.

Truth-in-packaging will help to protect consumers against product misrepresentation. Truth-in-lending will help consumers more easily to compare the costs of alternative credit sources.

TRANSPORTATION

The technological revolution in transportation, and large public and private investments in our highways, railroads, airways, and waterways, have greatly altered the nature of our transportation system. Our national transportation policy should be revised to reflect these changes, particularly by placing greater emphasis on competition and private initiative in interstate transportation. Fair and adequate user fees for our inland waterways, our Federal airways, and our Federal-aid highways will improve equity and efficiency in the use of these public resources.

As part of a well-rounded system of moving goods and people, there is urgent need and opportunity for high-speed, comfortable, and economical passenger transportation on densely traveled routes, such as in the Northeast corridor.

I am recommending an enlarged program of research and demonstration projects to determine the best and cheapest way to meet this need.

INDUSTRIAL SCIENCE AND TECHNOLOGY

The Department of Commerce:

—has proposed a State Technical Services Program to enable states to join with universities and industry to create new jobs through wider application of advanced technology;

—is establishing a coordinated system for scientific and technical data, to reduce unnecessary duplication of research and lower the costs of obtaining scientific data.

My budget contains funds for these desirable programs.

AGRICULTURE

Americans owe much to the efficiency of our farmers. Their independent spirit and productive genius are the envy of the world. We must continue to assure them the opportunity to earn a fair reward for their efforts.

I will transmit to the Congress recommendations for improving the effectiveness of our expenditures on price and income supports.

Many small farmers cannot expect to earn good incomes from farming. But they—along with other rural Americans—will have an opportunity to share in the fruits of our society through faster economic growth, better education and training opportunities, and improved health and community facilities. We must extend the benefits of American prosperity to *all* our people, *including those in rural America.*

EDUCATION AND HEALTH

In my message on education I proposed a program to ensure an opportunity to every American child to develop to the full his mind and his skills.

In my message on health I proposed a massive new attack on diseases which afflict mankind.

We value education and health for their direct benefits to human understanding and happiness. But they also yield major economic benefits.

Investments in human resources are among our most profitable investments. Such investments raise individual productivity and incomes, with benefits to our whole society. They raise our rate of economic growth, increase our economy's efficiency and flexibility, and form the cornerstone of our attack on poverty.

I believe that the Congress will find economic as well as human reasons to support my proposals on education and health.

CONCLUSION

In our economic affairs, as in every other aspect of our lives, ceaseless change is the one constant.

Revolutionary changes in technology, in forms of economic organization, in commercial relations with our neighbors, in the structure and education of our labor force converge in our markets. Free choices in free markets—as always—accommodate these tides of change.

But the adjustments are sometimes slow or imperfect. And our standards for the performance of our economy are continually on the rise. No longer will we tolerate widespread involuntary idleness, unnecessary human hardship and misery, the impoverishment of whole areas, the spoiling of our natural heritage, the human and physical ugliness of our cities, the ravages of the business cycle, or the arbitrary redistribution of purchasing power through inflation.

But as our standards for the performance of our economy have risen, so has our ability to cope with our economic problems.

Economic policy has begun to liberate itself from the preconceptions of an earlier day, and from the bitterness of class or partisan division that becloud rational discussion and hamper rational action.

Our tools of economic policy are much better tools than existed a generation ago. We are able to proceed with much greater confidence and flexibility in seeking effective answers to the changing problems of our changing economy.

The accomplishments of the past four years are a measure of the constructive response that can be expected from workers, consumers, investors, managers, farmers, and merchants to effective public policies that strive to define and achieve the national interest in:

—full employment with stable prices;

—rapid economic growth;

—balance in our external relationships;

—maximum efficiency in our public and private economies.

These perennial challenges to economic policy are not fully mastered; but we are well on our way to their solution.

As increasingly we do master them, economic policy can more than ever become the servant of our quest to make American society not only prosperous but progressive, not only affluent but humane, offering not only higher incomes but wider opportunities, its people enjoying not only full employment but fuller lives.

"We have lived dangerously too long. . . .
We are going to put safety first."
Remarks on signing Bill to establish
the National Commission on Product Safety,
November 20, 1967.

We just counted the 200 millionth over at Secretary Trowbridge's department a few moments ago.

Actually, some time ago I appointed a commission to try to discover when that 200 millionth child was born and from the report that appears to have been leaked, he was born on June 21st in Seaton Hospital in Austin, Texas.

As those of you who are here this morning know, technology has brought us many blessings in this country. But many of them are booby trapped. Far too many of them cause us great tragedy and present great hazards to us in this twentieth century.

The homes that we live in can really be more dangerous than a booby-trapped mine field in the battle area:

—125,000 Americans are injured by faulty heating devices each year. Many of these victims of the faulty heating devices are the very young who cannot protect themselves, and the very old who are sometimes helpless.

I wonder about the marvels of this age when I recognize that 94 percent of our people have TV's, and I see how many are injured on the highway, and I see how many are wounded on the battlefield—although they didn't even stop to be hospitalized—that is presented to us on the screen.

I wonder if it wouldn't be good to remind ourselves of the 125,000 each year who are injured by faulty heating devices; or:

—the 100,000 who are hurt and maimed each year by faulty power mowers or faulty washing machines; or

—the 100,000 each year, mostly little children, who have their limbs crushed by the automatic clothes wringers; or

—the 40,000 each year who are gashed when they fall through a glass door; or

—the 30,000 who are shocked and burned by defective wall sockets and extension cords.

—And there are just so many other dozens of thousands that we don't know anything about because they either didn't know what did it or it wasn't reported.

So this summarizes the fact that we live each day and each hour surrounded by a great many hazards that we know nothing about. The most innocent product can sometimes bring great injury. The electric knife, for instance, that is going to carve our Thanksgiving turkey could injure a member of our family this Thanksgiving. The Christmas tree could flame and kill a whole family.

This adds up to saying that we have lived too dangerously too long. So we have come here this morning to try to accentuate and stress that we are going to put safety first.

We have acted to stop tragedy before that tragedy strikes. We are establishing a National Commission on Product Safety. That is the first commission of this type to ever be established in this country.

This Commission has primarily three vital jobs to do:

—first, to tell us which products are dangerous so we will know how to be on guard and how to protect ourselves;

—second, to tell us how good our present laws are—if they are good, or how bad they are—Federal, state, and local laws;

—third, to tell us what steps we should and what steps we must take to protect our children and our families from the hazards that occur in the home.

I want this Commission to make recommendations that are solid, that are solutions. I don't want just another statistical study group.

I want it to act in the national interest in the name of American consumers—in the name of American business, because business is threatened, too, by the hazard of unfair competition from unsafe products.

This happens to be the first major consumer law that I have signed this year. I don't want to blame anybody—and I am not going to call anybody's name—but it ought to be the twelfth consumer law. I hope that in due time we will be signing all twelve of them.

We have been here almost twelve months. We have observed all of our holidays. We worked hard on a lot of other legislation. But this is the first major consumer law that the Congress has passed this year, and that the President has signed. We need many others. We need them now. We ought to have had them already.

We need the strongest possible meat inspection bill. Nobody in this country ought to ever take a chance on eating filthy meat from filthy packinghouses—it doesn't make any difference how powerful the meat lobby is.

We need legislation to insure pipeline safety for people living in the areas where natural gas pipelines run. We don't want gas-filled pipes bursting in our homes and our streets, causing a major tragedy, before we wake up and pass a law that will protect us from that.

I know it is natural that the gas pipelines have some reservations in that field. But they will be the first ones begging after a terrible tragedy explodes upon them. So we ought to take the time now and pass that kind of legislation.

We need a truth-in-lending bill. It passed the Senate some time ago. Interest rates are going up every day. They will be going up more as a result of the financial crisis that has come about through the devaluation of the pound.

Although the Senate acted, and acted promptly, that legislation is still in committee. It ought to be reported and ought to be passed, because people in this country are paying usurious rates of interest, and the poor people pay the highest rates, usually. The poorer you are, the higher your money costs are.

We need to protect our families against fabrics that flame—burst into flames—without any warning—and without the family having any knowledge.

We need to crack down on the con man, the gyp who preys on the aged and who preys on the defenseless. Some of our parents save up all of their lives to buy a little home for retirement. Then some swindler comes along and gets hold of them. They wind up in a useless swamp with a piece of no-good land, or they wind up in a worthless shack.

We are producing the best social security bills this Nation has ever seen—the Senate is considering one now; I hope Congress passes the Senate bill; I hope it passes it today or tomorrow. I hope the conferees will get together and let no holidays or anything else come between us, so we can put that social security bill, as we recommended it and as the Senate has reported it, on the books.

There are millions of old people in this country sitting, waiting, and wondering what is going to happen. So I hope we can do this. All of these bills we need. We need them badly. I hope some time I can ask you to come back here to attend another signing ceremony. We don't raid the Treasury with any of them. Most of them cost very little and save very much. There is no field in this country that needs legislation more today than this one.

I am happy and proud that Miss Betty Furness and the women of this country are becoming aroused, and the Congress is awakening to its responsibility, and the Executive branch of the Government is trying to provide some leadership to give us desirable consumer legislation.

The delay of this legislation is bad. But we can pass it and we ought to. It is urgent. It is a magnificent opportunity now for responsible men and women of this country to look at these various measures and try to get behind them.

The legislation costs the taxpayers practically nothing, but the blessings will bring us safety of life, safety of limb, peace of mind, peace of heart. These are possessions beyond price for every family in this land. They await our answer. We are going to be graded on how well we do the job.

In a few months or a few years our people are going to look back at our meat inspection, our truth-in-lending, our gas safety, our flammable fabrics, and all of these things that are crying now for attention. They are going to take out a check card and say, "Where were we? How did we stand? What did we do?"

We can't use the argument that they cost too much because there is very little cost involved.

It gives me great pride to say to the Congress and to say to the people who sponsored this legislation, who helped bring it about, that I welcome it this morning and I will welcome the other 12 measures just as soon as we can get them.

"This is a consumer's administration . . .
still we have just begun
our program for the consumer."
Address to the Consumer Assembly,
Washington, D.C.,
November 2, 1967.

Someday your children and your grandchildren are going to be very proud to be able to say that you were here today at this conference. And I am very proud, myself, that you are here.

The idea that the consumer in America deserves protection is a relatively new American idea.

In the early days of our history, the only consumer law was "let the buyer beware." And a great many consumers thus were victimized by the fast-buck artists of those days. Our country was almost 100 years old before the first consumer protection law was passed in this country. And that law just prohibited the fraudulent use of the United States mails.

Some of the abuses that brought about that early legislation would insult our intelligence today. They were "American ingenuity"—at its very worst:

—For instance, there was a man who advertised that he would send you a steel engraving of George Washington if you sent him a dollar. When he got your dollar, safe and sound, he sent you a one-cent stamp.

—Another fellow asked for a dollar in return for a sure-fire method of exterminating potato bugs. For your dollar you received a slip of paper saying, "Catch the bug, put him between two boards, and mash him."

On the American frontier, the practice of medicine was equally haphazard at its best. People bought the cure-alls like "Kick-a-poo Indian Sagwa"—that promised you everything but the headache they produced.

At the turn of the century, there was no guarantee that the meat Americans ate was not diseased—or even that it came from the advertised animal. One newspaper wrapped up the problem in a short poem which read like this:

> Mary had a little lamb,
> And when she saw it sicken,
> She shipped it off to Packing-town,
> And now it's labeled chicken.

Foods were filled with very strange chemicals, whose effect nobody knew. It was 1909, the year after I was born, before President Theodore Roosevelt could say that America had finally awakened to the fact that "no man may poison the people for his private profit."

We take it for granted, today, that such outrageous practices are forbidden by the law of the land.

But without the indignation and without the action of an aroused public—without the Federal Government's very strong sense of responsibility to the consumers of America—the counters in our stores might still be filled with Kick-a-poo Indian Sagwa.

Without the great milestones of consumer legislation, we would still be playing Russian roulette every time we dealt in the marketplace:

—Our savings would be stolen by unscrupulous speculators.

—Our bodies would carry burn scars from clothing which ignited without warning.

—Our food would be tainted; our drugs would be unsafe.

—Our children would be maimed by the toys their parent brought home to them.

Consumer legislation is a continuing process of serving the changing times in which we live. Technology daily makes our present laws obsolete. Progress is never an unmixed blessing. It can bring countless unforeseen hazards.

Fortunately, these problems are usually resolved in our competitive market, by the engines of private enterprise and their energies.

But dangers must be predicted whenever possible. Standards must be set when necessary. Consumers must be safeguarded from the unreasonable risk.

In the modern marketplace, there are still plenty of traps for the ignorant and the unwary—plenty more subtle than those our grandfathers knew anything about, but they are no less dangerous than those that grandpa faced. The difference is that the confidence men who brew them up wear Brooks Brothers suits and have college degrees today:

—Every year, Americans pay millions of dollars for parched and worthless land.

—Every year, our citizens are lured, unsuspecting, into credit traps which drive them to desperation, and many to death.

—Every year, Americans eat, on the average, twenty-seven pounds of uninspected red meat—meat that may be mislabeled, tainted, or dangerously diseased.

—Every year American families furnish their homes with fabrics that are dangerously flammable.

This is a consumer's Administration, of which I am a part. I have sent three major messages to the Congress in the last four years—asking for strong laws to protect our people from those who would cheat them or those who would expose them to unreasonable hazards in pursuit of a cheap and easy dollar.

The Eighty-ninth Congress passsed several major pieces of legislation which materially helped the consumer to a better life:

—the Truth-in-Packaging Act, that would tell the buyer just what he is buying, how much it weighs, and, besides, who made it. The days of the "jumbo quart" and the "giant economy quart" are already over.

—the Child Protection Act, to guard our children against hazardous toys. Today there is a law that protects a child from poisoning if he puts one of his toys in his mouth—a law that protects him from being burned by firecrackers that look like candy.

—the Traffic and Highway Safety Acts, to protect our drivers from dangerous vehicles, and to train them to protect themselves from each other.

Still we have just begun our program for the consumer. There are currently on my recommendation twelve major actions before the Congress. There are some votes lost in every one of these major actions, but they are for the benefit of the American people. We are going to do right regardless of how popular it is.

At a time when economy is the byword of our Nation, these twelve measures should be among the first bills passed. The cost to the taxpayer is virtually nothing. The savings to the consumer are in untold grief as well as millions of dollars.

The Truth-in-Lending Bill—its great and distinguished author, Mrs. Sullivan, is on the platform today, and the chairman of the committee that is going to bring the bill out of the committee I hope very soon and pass it, Mr. Patman, is here with us—would require the moneylenders of our society to inform the citizen—to tell the parents who need to borrow for their children's education, or to pay medical bills, or to buy a car or a television set—just how much it will cost to borrow that money.

The lender knows to the very penny how much interest he is charging. We don't think it is too much to ask that he also tell the borrower.

We have proposed amendments to the Flammable Fabrics Act of 1953. As new materials are invented, new hazards occur. We don't want a repeat of the incident when young girls were incinerated by their own sweaters.

We want to see minimum safety standards set for the movement of natural gas by pipeline. These pipelines may run under your city streets and under your own bungalow. We don't want them to erupt; we don't want them to kill your townspeople.

As representatives of our 200 million consumers, these bills concern each of you directly. It has been said that the consumer lobby is the most widespread in our land, yet the least vociferous and the least powerful. I disagree.

You can only wield the power that you have if you are willing to make yourselves heard. You have the interest, you have the organization, you have the numbers, you have the horsepower.

And we have made sure that you have access to the highest councils of your own Government. The President's Committee on Consumer Interests, the Consumer Advisory Council, and my very talented Special Assistant for Consumer Affairs, Betty Furness, are all—I started to say available to you—available to consult with you.

They are willing to hear your ideas, take your suggestions, listen to your complaints, and then pass them along to me, if I can be helpful.

I don't want to have any monopoly on these complaints. Your Congressmen should hear from you, too—often, loud, and clear.

As I speak here, at this very moment, there are two specific issues which I think call for your attention. They threaten you consumers and they threaten your country.

The first is inflation. By keeping a close watch on our economy, we have managed for the past eighty-one months to keep our consumer price rise lower than that of any other nation in the industrial West. We have kept the housewife's dollar secure. We have even been able to lower taxes.

If the two tax bills that we repealed in the last two years were on the books today, they would bring in an additional $24 billion.

But now there are pressures on our economy which demand that we ask for a portion of that $24 billion back—in the form of a surcharge. It would be a penny out of every dollar.

We estimate that the 10 percent surcharge, so-called, would average one penny out of every dollar earned.

I realize that it is hard for you to ask the people that you represent for more taxes, but let me give you just two quick examples of what will happen, if we don't get that surcharge.

A family of four with an income of $5,000 would pay nothing under our tax proposal. They are exempt. But the chances are very great that they would pay $147 a year under the inaction inflation tax.

A family with an income of $10,000 will pay $285—or $174 more than some economists estimate it would pay if the surcharge is passed. So inaction will cost you an estimated $174, if you earn $10,000 a year.

You don't see the effects of inaction now, but you are going to see it next year when it is too late for you to correct your own errors.

The second issue you should know about is the threat of protectionism. Protectionism is rearing its head in the form of certain quota bills now before the Congress trying to take care of each Congressman's district. And when we begin to think more of our district than we think of the country, we are likely to get into trouble.

Those proposed quotas would invite massive retaliation from our trading partners throughout the world. Just the little publicity that has been spread around the globe has them all concerned and up in arms.

Prices would rise. Our world market would shrink. So would the range of goods which American consumers choose when they buy.

I think those protectionists' bills just must not become law. And they are not going to become law as long as I am President and can help it.

So I plead with you consumers. I plead with all Americans. I urge you to make yourselves heard, to exercise your rights, to fulfill your duties both as consumers and, more important, as citizens.

We have too much to preserve. We have reaped the harvest of a vigorous prosperity—a record prosperity that has lasted for eighty-one months—the longest in history. Our consumers now enjoy the highest standard of living in America that has ever been known to civilization. Yet one in every seven of our citizens—one out of every seven of our fellow human beings—exists below the poverty line. And every citizen faces unreasonable risks in the modern marketplace.

There are danger signs on the horizon now which should arrest the attention of each of you.

When all Americans enjoy the bounties of this rich land, when all Americans can live in dignity and security—then we can say we have done the consumer justice. This is the largest meeting of this kind that has ever been held, I am told, in this town for a cause like this. I hope you will not ever be satisfied with anything less than getting the consumer justice. I don't believe you will settle for anything less. And I promise you, as your President, that I will not settle for anything else.

"We are here to avoid tragedy."
Remarks on signing the Truth-in-Packaging Bill
and the Child Protection Bill,
November 3, 1966.

We have come here this evening to fulfill two obligations that we have to the American family:
   —We are here to defend truth.
   —We are here to avoid tragedy.

The two laws that I shall sign this evening will help the American housewife to save her pennies and dimes, and the American mother to save the lives of her children.

The first law is the Fair Packaging and Labeling Act. Its purpose is to uphold truth. Its target is labels that lie, packages that confuse, practices that too often deny the consumer a fair test and a clear choice in the shopping place.

This is a strong but simple law. It requires the manufacturer to tell the shopper clearly and understandably exactly what is in the package, who made it, how much it contains, and how much it costs.

The housewife should not need a scale or a yardstick or slide rule or computer when she shops. This law will eliminate that need. The housewife should not have to worry which is bigger—the full jumbo quart or the giant economy quart. This law will free her from that uncertainty and that problem. It will protect her from being shortchanged by slack filling where a box is made bigger than its contents.

This law is one weapon against high prices. It will mean that the American family will get full and fair value for every penny, dime, and dollar that that family spends.

The great majority of American manufacturers, I believe—and I hope—will welcome this law, because it protects the honest manufacturer against the dishonest competitors. It encourages fair competition, competition that is based on quality and value and price. It reflects our very strong belief that American producers can meet and want to meet the test of truth in what they produce and what they sell.

We are going to put this law to work right away. I have asked our able Secretary of Commerce, John Connor, to proceed immediately to call in those industries where the congressional hearings have shown protection to be most needed.

This Fair Packaging and Labeling Act will go a long way toward ending confusion and restoring truth in the marketplace.

The second law that I will sign today, the Child Protection Act, will do no less than protect the American family from needless tragedy.

It will ban the sale or use of toys and other children's articles that contain dangerous or deadly substances.

It will ban the sale of other household articles so hazardous that even labels cannot make them safe:

—Now there is a law that says the eyes of a doll will not be poisonous beans.

—Now there is a law that says what looks like candy will not be deadly firecracker balls.

—Now there is a law that says Johnny will not die because his toy truck was painted with a poison.

Both these laws offer sweeping new protection to the American family.

Both break new ground for the Federal Government. But both, I think, are very much in our American tradition. Thomas Jefferson said that the first object of government was the care of human life and happiness, and that is the single object of both of these laws.

They are based upon the principle of fair dealing which created the Pure Food and Drug Act, the Fiber Products Identification Act, and other humanitarian laws which have protected American mothers and fathers and children for generations.

The two really landmark laws that I will sign here this evening are fitting companions to the other safeguards enacted by the great Eighty-ninth Congress—the Traffic Safety Act and the Tire Safety Act.

These two laws confirm the historic record of compassion, wisdom, and achievement that has established this as the great Eighty-ninth Congress. They further establish that Congress in the hearts of the people.

We are very proud, particularly those members who have come here this evening, those of you who led and directed this fight. Also, we are very grateful to you, because we are fathers, mothers, and families, because we are wage earners, housewives, and consumers—because we are Americans.

We are better protected now by American laws, thanks to you. We will try to give them the best execution that is possible.

A great counselor of mine said to me, "You can take a good law and give it bad administration and it won't work. You can take a bad law and give it good administration and get by with it."

Now you have given us good laws. If you let us write them—if we just had one-man legislature down here—we think we could write better ones, but the wisdom of our Founding Fathers said that we are going to have our checks and balances.

We don't always see everything alike. You have given us good laws and we are going to do our best to give you good administration of those laws.

You don't know, really, how much satisfaction one in government gets.

You ought not to be in government if you don't want to serve humanity, if you don't want to do the greatest good for the greatest number. You ought to be somewhere else.

While this doesn't cover everything we were going to cover and we might have dotted an "i" here and crossed a "t" there that you didn't do, we nevertheless think that it is a great step forward. I am very proud to be associated with you. We will look back on it in the years to come and wonder, "How did this Congress do this much before October?"

"Each one of these waiting Americans
represents a potential victory
we have never been able to achieve . . . until now."
Message to Congress on a new program
to attack hard-core unemployment (excerpt),
January 23, 1968.

Twenty years ago, after a cycle of depression, recovery and war, America faced an historic question: could we launch what President Truman called "a positive attack upon the ever-recurring problems of mass unemployment and ruinous depression"?

That was the goal of the Employment Act of 1946. The answer was a long time in forming. But today there is no longer any doubt.

We can see the answer in the record of seven years of unbroken prosperity.

We can see it in this picture of America today: 75 million of our people are working—in jobs that are better paying and more secure than ever before.

Seven and a half million new jobs have been created in the last four years, more than 5,000 every day. This year will see that number increased by more than 1½ million.

In that same period, the unemployment rate has dropped from 5.7 percent to 3.8 percent—the lowest in more than a decade.

The question for our day is this: in an economy capable of sustaining high

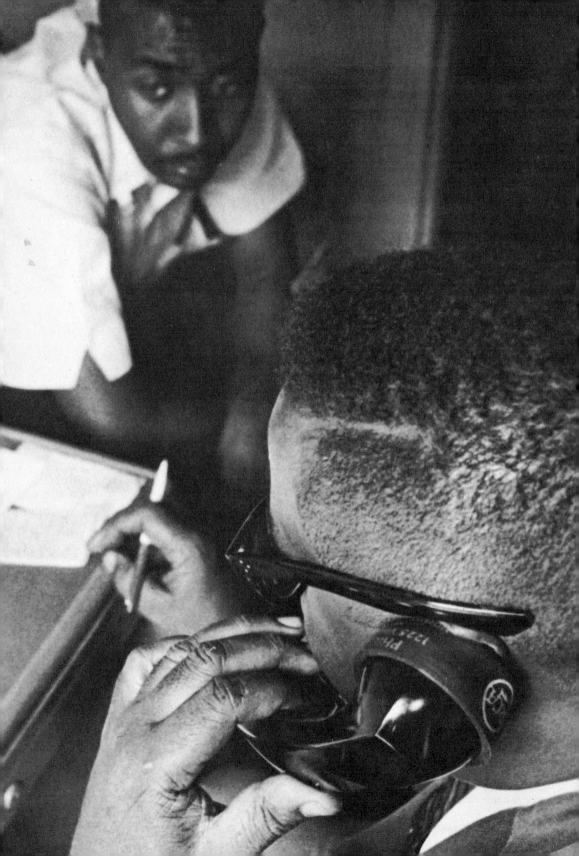

employment, how can we assure every American, who is willing to work, the right to earn a living?

We have always paid lip service to that right. But there are many Americans for whom the right has never been real:

—the boy who becomes a man without developing the ability to earn a living;

—the citizen who is barred from a job because of other men's prejudices;

—the worker who loses his job to a machine, and is told he is too old for anything else;

—the boy or girl from the slums whose summers are empty because there is nothing to do;

—the man and the woman blocked from productive employment by barriers rooted in poverty; lack of health, lack of education, lack of training, lack of motivation.

Their idleness is a tragic waste of the human spirit and of the economic resources of a great nation.

It is a waste that an enlightened nation should not tolerate.

It is a waste that a nation concerned by disorders in its city streets cannot tolerate.

This nation has already begun to attack that waste.

In the years that we have been building our unprecedented prosperity, we have also begun to build a network of manpower programs designed to meet individual opportunities.

OUR MANPOWER PROGRAM NETWORK

Until just a few years ago, our efforts consisted primarily of maintaining employment offices throughout the country and promoting apprenticeship training.

The Manpower Development Training Act, passed in 1962, was designed to equip the worker with new skills when his old skills were outdistanced by technology. That program was greatly strengthened and expanded in 1962, 1965, and again in 1966 to serve the disadvantaged as well. In fiscal 1969, it will help over 275,000 citizens.

Our manpower network grew as the nation launched its historic effort to conquer poverty:

—The Job Corps gives people from the poorest families education and training they need to prepare for lives as productive and self-supporting citizens. In fiscal 1969 the Job Corps will help almost 100,000 children of the poor.

—The Neighborhood Youth Corps enables poor youngsters to serve their community and themselves at the same time. Last year the Congress expanded the program to include adults as well. In fiscal 1969, The Neighborhood Youth Corps will help over 560,000 citizens.

Others, such as Work Experience, New Careers, Operation Mainstream, and the Work Incentive Program, are directed toward the employment problems of poor adults. In fiscal 1969, 150,000 Americans will receive the benefits of training through these programs.

These are pioneering efforts. They all work in different ways. Some provide for training alone. Others combine training with work. Some are full time. Others are part time.

One way to measure the scope of these programs is to consider how many men and women have been helped:

—In fiscal 1963, 75,000.

—In fiscal 1967, more than one million.

But the real meaning of these figures is found in the quiet accounts of lives that have been changed:

—In Oregon, a seasonal farm worker was struggling to sustain his eight children on $46 a week. Then he received on-the-job training as a welder. Now he can support his family on an income three times as high.

—In Pennsylvania, a truck driver lost his job, because of a physical disability and had to go on welfare. He learned a new skill. Now he is self-reliant again, working as a clerk with a city police department.

—In Kansas, a high school dropout was salvaged from what might have been an empty life. He learned a trade with the Job Corps. Now he has a decent job with an aircraft company.

Across America, examples such as these attest to the purpose and the success of our programs to give a new start to men and women who have the will to work for a better life.

These are good programs. They are contributing to the strength of America. And they must continue.

But they must reach even further.

I will ask the Congress to appropriate $2.1 billion for our manpower programs for fiscal 1969;

—This is the largest such program in the nation's history.

—It is a 25 percent increase over fiscal 1968.

—It will add $442 million to our manpower efforts.

In a vigorous, flourishing economy, this is a program for justice as well as for jobs.

These funds will enable us to continue and strengthen existing programs, and to advance to new ground as well.

With this program, we can reach 1.3 million Americans, including those who have rarely if ever been reached before—the hard-core unemployed.

THE CONCENTRATED EMPLOYMENT PROGRAM

Our past efforts, vital as they are, have not yet effectively reached the hard-core unemployed.

These hard-core are America's forgotten men and women. Many of them have not worked for a long time. Some have never worked at all. Some have held only odd jobs. Many have been so discouraged by life that they have lost their sense of purpose.

In the depression days of the 1930s, jobless men lined the streets of our cities seeking work. But today, the jobless are often hard to find. They are the invisible poor of our nation.

Last year I directed the Secretary of Labor to bring together in one unified effort all the various manpower and related programs which could help these people in the worst areas of some of our major cities and in the countryside.

The concentrated employment program was established for this purpose.

Its first task was to find the hard-core unemployed, to determine who they are, and where and how they live.

Now we have much of that information.

Five hundred thousand men and women who have never had jobs—or who face serious employment problems—are living in the slums of our fifty largest cities.

The first detailed profile we have ever had of these unemployed Americans reveals that substantial numbers:

—lack adequate education and job training;

—have other serious individual problems—such as physical handicaps—which impair their earning ability;

—are Negroes, Mexican-Americans, Puerto Ricans, or Indians;

—are teenagers, or men over 45.

As the unemployed were identified, the concentrated employment program set up procedures for seeking them out, counseling them, providing them with health and education services, training them, all with the purpose of directing them into jobs or into the pipeline to employment.

As part of the new manpower budget, I am recommending expansion of the concentrated employment program.

That program now serves 22 urban and rural areas. In a few months it will expand to 76. With the funds I am requesting, it can operate in 146.

JOB OPPORTUNITIES IN THE PRIVATE SECTOR

The ultimate challenge posed by the hard-core unemployed is to prepare rejected men and women for productive employment—for dignity, independence, and self-sufficiency.

In our thriving economy, where jobs in a rapidly growing private sector are widely available and the unemployment rate is low, the "make-work" programs of the 1930s are not the answer to today's problem.

The answer, I believe, is to train the hard-core unemployed for work in private industry:

—The jobs are there: Six out of every seven working Americans are employed in the private sector.

—Government-supported on the-the-job training is the most effective gateway to meaningful employment: Nine out of every ten of those who have received such training have gone on to good jobs.

—Industry knows how to train people for the jobs on which its profits depend.

That is why, late last year, we stepped up the effort to find jobs in private industry. With the help of American businessmen, we launched a $40 million test training program in five of our larger cities.

The program was built around three basic principles:

—to engage private industry fully in the problems of the hard-core unemployed;

—to pay with Government funds the extra costs of training the disadvantaged for steady employment;

—to simplify Government paperwork and make all Government services easily and readily available to the employer.

THE URGENT TASK

With that work, we prepared our blueprints. We have built the base for action.

Encouraged by our test program and by the progress that American industry has made in similar efforts, we should now move forward.

To press the attack on the problem of the jobless in our cities, I propose that we launch the Job Opportunities in Business Sector (JOBS) program— a new partnership between Government and private industry to train and hire the hard-core unemployed.

I propose that we devote $350 million to support this partnership—starting now with $106 million from funds available in our manpower programs for fiscal 1968, and increasing that amount to $244 million in fiscal 1969.

Our target is to put 100,000 men and women on the job by June 1969, and 500,000 by June 1971. To meet that target, we need prompt approval by the Congress of the request for funds for our manpower programs.

This is high-priority business for America.

The future of our cities is deeply involved. And so is the strength of our nation.

HOW THIS NEW PROGRAM WILL WORK

Our objective, in partnership with the business community, is to restore the jobless to useful lives through productive work.

There can be no rigid formulas in this program. For it breaks new ground.

The situation calls, above all, for flexibility and cooperation.

Essentially, the partnership will work this way:

The Government will identify and locate the unemployed.

The company will train them, and offer them jobs.

The company will bear the normal cost of training, as it would for any of its new employees.

But with the hard-core unemployed there will be extra costs.

These men will be less qualified than those the employer would normally hire. So additional training will often be necessary.

But even more than this will be needed. Some of these men and women will need transportation services. Many will have to be taught to read and write. They will have health problems to be corrected. They will have to be counseled on matters ranging from personal care to proficiency in work.

These are the kinds of extra costs that will be involved.

Where the company undertakes to provide these services, it is appropriate that the Government pay the extra costs as part of the national manpower program.

The concentrated employment program, in many areas, will provide manpower services to support the businessman's effort.

A NATIONAL ALLIANCE OF BUSINESSMEN

This is a tall order for American business. But the history of American business is the history of triumph over challenge.

And the special talents of American business can make this program work.

To launch this program, I have called on American industry to establish a National Alliance of Businessmen.

The Alliance will be headed by Mr. Henry Ford 2d.

Fifteen of the nation's top business leaders will serve on its executive board. Leading business executives from the nation's fifty largest cities will spearhead the effort in their own communities.

This Alliance will be a working group, concerned not only with the policy but with the operation of the program.

It will:

—Help put 500,000 hard-core unemployed into productive business and industrial jobs in the next three years.

—Give advice to the Secretaries of Labor and Commerce on how this program can work most effectively, and how we can cut Government "red tape."

The Alliance will also have another vital mission: to find productive jobs for 200,000 needy youth this summer—an experience that will lead them back to school in the fall, or on to other forms of education, training, or permanent employment.

The Alliance will work closely in this venture with the Vice-President. As chairman of the President's Council on Youth Opportunity he will soon meet with the Alliance and with the mayors of our fifty largest cities to advance this pressing work.

THE REWARDS OF ACTION

The rewards of action await us at every level.

To the individual, a paycheck is a passport to self-respect and self-sufficiency.

To the worker's family, a paycheck offers the promise of a fuller and better life—in material advantages and in new eductaional opportunities.

Our society as a whole will benefit when welfare recipients become taxpayers, and new job holders increase the nation's buying power.

These are dollars and cents advantages.

But there is no way to estimate the value of a decent job that replaces hostility and anger with hope and opportunity.

There is no way to estimate the respect of a boy or girl for his parent who has earned a place in our world.

There is no way to estimate the stirring of the American dream of learning, saving, and building a life of independence.

Finally, employment is one of the major weapons with which we will eventually conquer poverty in this country, and banish it forever from American life.

Our obligation is clear. We must intensify the work we have just begun. The new partnership I have proposed in this message will help reach that lost legion among us, and make them productive citizens.

It will not be easy.

But until the problem of joblessness is solved, these men and women will remain wasted Americans—each one a haunting reminder of our failure.

Each one of these waiting Americans represents a potential victory we have never been able to achieve in all the years of this nation.

Until now.

A STRENGTHENED MANPOWER ADMINISTRATION

The programs I have discussed are the visible evidence of a nation's commitment to provide a job for every citizen who wants it, and who will work for it.

Less visible is the machinery—the planning, the management and administration—which turns these programs into action and carries them to the people who need them.

I recently directed the Secretary of Labor to strengthen and streamline the manpower administration—the instrument within the Federal Government which manages almost 80 percent of our manpower programs.

That effort is now close to completion.

But we must have top administrators now—both here in Washington and in the eight regions across the country in which these manpower programs will operate.

As part of our new manpower budget, I am requesting the Congress to approve more than six hundred new positions for the manpower administration. These will include sixteen of the highest civil service grades.

The central fact about all our manpower programs is that they are local in nature. The jobs and opportunities exist in the cities and communities of this country. That is where the people who need them live. That is where the industries are—and the classrooms, the day care centers, and the health clinics.

What is required is a system to link Federal efforts with the resources at the state and local levels.

We already have the framework, the Cooperative Area Manpower Planning System (CAMPS) which we started last year.

Now I propose that we establish it for the long term.

CAMPS will operate at every level—Federal, regional, state, and local. At each level, it will pull together all the manpower services which bear on jobs.

But its greatest impact will be at the local level, where it will

—help the communities develop their own manpower blueprints;

—survey job needs;

—assure that all federal programs to help the job seeker are available.

As part of our manpower budget, I am requesting $11 million to fund the Cooperative Area Manpower Planning System in fiscal 1969.

OCCUPATIONAL SAFETY AND HEALTH

The programs outlined so far in this message will train the man out of work for a job, and help him find one.

To give the American worker the complete protection he needs, we must also safeguard him against hazards on the job.

Today, adequate protection does not exist.

It is to the shame of a modern industrial nation, which prides itself on the productivity of its workers, that each year:

—14,500 workers are killed on the job;

—2.2 million workers are injured;

—250 million man-days of productivity are wasted;

—$1.5 billion in wages are lost;

—The result: a loss of $5 billion to the economy.

This loss of life, limb, and sight must end. An attack must be launched at the source of the evil—against the conditions which cause hazards and invite accidents.

The reasons for these staggering losses are clear. Safety standards are narrow. Research lags behind. Enforcement programs are weak. Trained safety specialists fall far short of the need.

The Federal Government offers the worker today only a patchwork of obsolete and ineffective laws.

The major law—Walsh-Healey—was passed more than three decades ago. Its coverage is limited. It applies only to a worker performing a Government contract. Last year about half of the work force was covered, and then only part of the time.

It is more honored in the breach than observed. Last year, investigations revealed a disturbing number of violations in the plants of Government contractors.

Comprehensive protection under other Federal laws is restricted to about a million workers in specialized fields—longshoremen and miners, for example.

Only a few states have modern laws to protect the workers' health and safety. Most have no coverage, or laws that are weak and deficient.

The gap in worker protection is wide and glaring—and it must be closed by a strong and forceful new law.

It must be our goal to protect every one of America's 75 million workers while they are on the job.

I am submitting to the Congress the Occupational Safety and Health Act of 1968.

Here, in broad outline, is what this measure will do.

For more than 50 million workers involved in interstate commerce it will

—strengthen the authority and resources of the Secretary of Health, Education, and Welfare to conduct an extensive program of research. This will provide the needed information on which new standards can be developed;

—empower the Secretary of Labor to set and enforce those standards;

—impose strong sanctions, civil and criminal, on those who endanger the health and safety of the American working man.

For American workers in intrastate commerce, it will provide, for the first time, Federal help to the states to start and strengthen their own health and safety programs. These grants will assist the states to:
—develop plans to protect the worker;
—collect information on occupational injuries and diseases;
—set and enforce standards;
—train inspectors and other needed experts.

CONCLUSION

When Walt Whitman heard America singing a century ago, he heard that sound in workers at their jobs.

Today that sound rings from thousands of factories and mills, work benches and assembly lines, stronger than ever before.

Jobs are the measure of how far we have come.

But it is right to measure a nation's efforts not only by what it has done, but by what remains to be done.

In this message, I have outlined a series of proposals dealing with the task ahead—to give reality to the right to earn a living.

These proposals deal with jobs.

But their reach is far broader.

The demand for more jobs is central to the expression of all our concerns and our aspirations—about cities, poverty, civil rights, and the improvement of men's lives.

I urge the Congress to give prompt and favorable consideration to the proposals in this message.

The Myth of the
Flawed White Southerner

By Ralph Ellison

The question of how I regarded the President's statement that "Art is not a political weapon" was put to me by a group of young Negro writers during 1965, following President Johnson's sponsoring of a National Festival for the Arts at the White House. The Festival had been attacked by certain well-known writers, and these young men were seriously concerned with the proper relationship between the artist and government. I replied to their question by reading aloud from the President's address to the artists attending the Festival:

> Your art is not a political weapon, yet much of what you do is profoundly political, for you seek out the common pleasures and visions, the terrors and cruelties of man's day on this planet. And I would hope you would help dissolve the barriers of hatred and ignorance which are the source of so much of our pain and danger. . . .

a statement to which I was sympathetic, both as a foreshortened description and as the expression of a hope.

The young men then asked my opinion of the President's grasp of political reality, and I replied that I thought him far ahead of most of the intellectuals who were critical of him, "especially those northern liberals who have become, in the name of the highest motives, the new apologists for segregation," and I went on to say that "President Johnson's speech at Howard University spelled out the meaning of full integration for Negroes in a way that no one, no President, not Abraham Lincoln nor Franklin Roosevelt, no matter how much we loved and respected them, has ever done before. There was no hedging in it, no escape clauses."

My reference to the segregationist tendencies of certain intellectuals and northern liberals caused a few of my white colleagues to charge that I had "changed" or sold out to the "establishment," and I lost a few friends. The incident forced me to realize once again that for all the values that I shared, and still share, with my fellow intellectuals, there are nevertheless certain basic perspectives and attitudes toward art and politics, cultural affairs and politicians, which we are far from sharing, and I had to accept the fact that if I tried to adapt to their point of view I would not only be dishonest but would violate disastrously that sense of complexity, historical and cultural, political and personal, out of which it is my fate and privilege to write. My colleagues spoke out of their own interests, and properly so, but I found it irritating that they seemed to assume that *their* interests were automatically mine, and that, supposedly, I and those of my background possess no interest that they, my friends and colleagues, had any need to understand or respect.

Later, in thinking of this disagreement, I found myself recalling that during 1963 I was among those present at the White House for a celebration of the First Centennial of the Emancipation Proclamation given by President John F. Kennedy, an occasion of special significance for me, both as the grandson of slaves and as a writer and former student of Tuskegee Institute. For I was aware of the fact that in 1901, during the first month of his administration, Theodore Roosevelt had provoked a national scandal by inviting Booker T. Washington, Tuskegee's founder, to a White House dinner; a gesture taken by some as more menacing to the national security than an armed attack from a foreign nation. The invitation changed political alignments in the South, upset the structure of the Republican party, and caused President Roosevelt to advise Negro Americans to avoid careers in the professions and to subjugate their own political and social interests to those of antagonistic white Southerners.

As a novelist interested in that area of the national life where political power is institutionalized and translated into democratic ritual, and national style, I was impressed by the vividness with which a White House invitation had illuminated the emotional complexities and political dynamite underlying American social manners, and I welcomed the opportunity for closer observation that the occasion afforded. It seemed to me that one of the advantages that a novelist such as Henry James had over those of my generation was his familiarity with the movers and shakers of the nation, an advantage springing from his upper-class background and the easy availability of those who exercised political and social power. Artists who came later were likely to view such figures from a distance and thus have little opportunity to know at first hand the personalities who shaped the Nation's affairs. It is fortunate that with the Kennedy and Johnson Administrations this was no longer true.

At the celebration of the Emancipation Proclamation, some sixty-two years after the Washington incident, the majority of the four hundred or more White House guests were Negroes, and I was struck by how a cordial gesture once considered threatening to the national stability had with the passing of time become an accepted routine. Where Theodore Roosevelt had been put on the defensive and bowed before anti-Negro taboos, President Kennedy was free to celebrate the freeing of the slaves as an important step toward achieving a truer American democracy. So as I brooded over the Arts Festival controversy I asked myself if my memory of the Booker T. Washington incident had influenced the stand I took, and whether I had been so influenced by historical and racial considerations that I underevaluated the issues which so concerned my fellow intellectuals.

I concluded that perhaps I had. Nor was it simply that as a charter member of the National Council on the Arts I felt that governmental aid to the

American arts and artists was of a more abiding importance than my hopes that the Vietnam war would be brought to a swift conclusion. My response to the President's critics was shaped in fact by that personal and group history which had shaped my background and guided my consciousness, a history and background that marked a basic divergence between my own experience and that of the dissenting intellectuals. So for me the Festival was charged with meanings that went deeper than the issue of the Government's role in the arts or the issue of Vietnam; it had also to do with the President's own background, his accent of speech, and his values. And when I put the two social occasions into juxtaposition, the Emancipation celebration and the Festival for the Arts, I found it symbolic that my disagreement with my fellow intellectuals had been brought into focus around the figure of a President of Southern origin.

I say symbolic because historically speaking my presence at the Festival of the Arts was the long-range result of an act, in 1863, of an even more controversial holder of the Presidency, Abraham Lincoln. For it was Lincoln who, after a struggle involving much vacillation, procrastination, and rescissions, finally issued the Proclamation that allowed me to be born a relatively free American. Obviously, this was not so important a factor in my friends' conception of the nation's history, therefore it has not become a functioning factor in shaping their social and political awareness. Hence, while we may agree as to the importance of art in shaping the values of American society, we are apt to disagree as to the priorities in attacking social and political issues.

Some of the intellectuals in question spring from impoverished backgrounds, but for historical reasons none have ever been poor in the special ways that Negro Americans are poor. Some began to write, as did I, during the 1930s, but here again none came to writing careers from a background so barren of writers as mine. And to these racial and historical differences is added the fact that we spring from different regions of the land. I had come from a different part of the country and had been born of parents who were of this land far longer than many of theirs had been, and I had grown up under conditions far more explicitly difficult than they. Which outlines another important difference: I had come from a region adjacent to that from which the President emerged and where the American language was spoken—by whites at least—with an accent much like that with which he speaks. It is a region that has grown faster and in a more unplanned way than the East has grown, and it is a place where one must listen beneath the surface of what a man has to say, and where rhetorical style is far less important than the relationship between a man's statements and his conduct.

When I was growing up, a Negro Oklahoman always listened for a threat in the accent of a white Texan, but one learned to listen to the individual intonation, to *what* was said as well as to *how* it was said, to content and implication as well as to style. Black provincials cannot afford the luxury of being either snobbish or provincial. Nor can they ignore the evidence of concrete acts.

President Johnson's style and accent are said to be an important factor in his difficulties with many intellectuals, especially those of the literary camp. But perhaps what one listens for in the utterance of any President is very similar to what one listens for in a novel: the degree to which it contains what Henry James termed "felt life," which can here be translated to mean that quality conveyed by the speaker's knowledge and feeling for the regional, racial, religious, and class unities and differences within the land, and his awareness of the hopes and values of a diverse people struggling to achieve the American promise in their own time, in their own place, and with the means at hand.

It would seem that a few literary intellectuals would impose a different style and accent upon the President, but they forget that all individual American styles reflect a regional background, and this holds true for national leaders no less than others. Thus while a President's style and way with language are of national importance, still he cannot violate the integrity between his inherited idiom and his office without doing violence to his initial source of strength. For in fact his style and idiom form a connective linkage between his identity as representative of a particular group and region of people and his identity as President of *all* the people.

It is possible that much of the intellectuals' distrust of President Johnson springs from a false knowledge drawn from the shabby myths purveyed by Western movies. Perhaps they feel that a Texan intoning the values of humanism in an unreconstructed Texas accent is to be regarded as suspiciously as a Greek bearing gifts; thus they can listen to what he says with provincial ears and can ignore the President's concrete achievements here at home while staring blindly at the fires of a distant war.

Well, I too am concerned with the war in Vietnam and would like to see it ended, but the fact remains that I am also familiar with other costly wars of much longer duration right here at home, the war against poverty and the war for racial equality, and therefore I cannot so easily ignore the changes that the President has made in the condition of my people and still consider myself a responsible intellectual. My sense of priorities is of necessity different.

One thing is certain, I must look at the figure of the President from a slightly different angle, and although I try to approach people and events with something of that special alertness granted to those who give themselves over to the perceptive powers of the novel, I must dismiss any temptation to see President Johnson, or any living President, strictly in terms of his possibilities as a fictional character—which, I believe, is an impulse of many literary intellectuals when confronting the presidential role.

For example, when the image of President Lincoln is evoked by the resemblance between the 1960s and the 1860s—war, racial unrest, technological change, the inadequacies of established institutions and processes before the demand for broader economic and social freedom—the Lincoln who emerges is that figure released by the bullets fired at Ford's Theatre. It is not the backwoods politician who fought throughout the tragic years of the Civil War to keep the Nation whole, not the troubled man who rode the whirlwind of national chaos until released by death while watching the comedy, *Our American Cousin.*

Yet it was that unpopular, controversial Lincoln whose deeds, whose manipulation of power—political, rhetorical, and moral—who made possible the figure we create for ourselves whenever we think of the personification of democratic grandeur and political sainthood.

Lyndon B. Johnson is credited even by his enemies as being a political genius, but the phenomenon of a great politician becoming President confronts us with a dual figure, for even while entangled in the difficulties of his office he is identified by role with the achievements of the proven great who preceded him there. In our minds he is locked in a struggle with the illustrious dead even though he must be a man who manipulates power and involves himself in the muck and mire out of which great political parties are composed. He must be a man who initiates uneasy compromises and deals, who blends ideals and expediencies, who achieves what he can so as to give reality to his vision. He is a figure who knows better than most of us that politics is the art of the possible, but *only* of the possible, and that it is only by fighting against the limits of the politically possible that he can demonstrate his mastery and his worth.

But when such a figure is elevated to the Presidency an element of doubt soon enters the picture. Political action, his native mode, is tied to techniques—persuasion, eloquence, social pressure, compromises, and deals—all techniques that during our troubled times are increasingly confounded by the press and by the apparent clairvoyance of electronic data media which, as they seek to convert events into drama, work to undermine the mysteries of presidential power. The question of credibility is raised and we approach the Presidency with demands for a minute-to-minute knowledge of intricate events that is impossible even between the most devoted husband and wife. Little allowance is made for secrecy, for indecision, for interpersonal or international process. He is expected to be master not only of the present but of the future as well, and able to make decisions with the omniscience of a god and, most of all, he is expected to be an incarnation of Justice.

Part of the difficulty springs from the notion that great personalities are the results not of technical mastery but of some mysterious leap out of the past of race, class, family, onto a plateau from which an inherent mastery may be exercised with a superhuman facility. To this view great deeds are assumed to be the attributes of great personality. President Lincoln is taken to be the author of great deeds not because he was a great and persistent politician but because he possessed a great personality, very much as great poets are assumed to be great men because they compose great poems. And in the case of great Presidents now dead, the arrogance, the blind spots, the failures of will and vision are forgotten before the great transforming deeds that their deaths delineated as having marked their administrations.

Literary intellectuals make this mistake because they owe the formation of their functional personalities and their dreams to literature. Thus for them a great President is first of all a master of "style," a mythical figure born of all the great (and preferably eloquent) Presidents who preceded him. But having attained the Presidency he is paradoxically expected to have no further function as a politician. Indeed, he is expected to be above politics in a way virtually impossible if he is to exercise the powers and responsibilities of office.

But to my mind in these perpetually troubled United States a great President is one through whom the essential conflicts of democracy, the struggle between past and present, class and class, race and race, region and region, are brought into the most intense and creative focus. He is one who releases chaos as he creates order. He arouses hopes and expectations, even as he strives to modify the structures that have supported an unjust stability, in the interest of securing a broader social freedom. He is not necessarily a man possessing a new style of action or eloquence, but rather one who recognizes that the American is one whose basic problem is that of accepting the difficult demands of his essential newness in a world grown increasingly turbulent. He is one who knows instinctively, in the words of W. H. Auden, that for the American "it is not a question of the Old Man transforming himself into the New, but of the New Man becoming alive to the fact that he is new, that he has been transformed [by the land, by technology, by the break with the past, by the diversity of a pluralistic society] without his having realized it."

The great President is also a man possessed by his role and who becomes, to a painful extent, a prisoner of his role, and there is evidence that President Johnson is aware of this. "Every day," he has said,

> there come to this office new problems and new crises new difficulties demanding discussion and consultation and decision. I must deal with them, possessing no gift of prophecy, no special insight into history. Instead, I must depend, as my thirty-five predecesssors depended, on the best wisdom and judgment that can be summoned to the service of the Nation. This counsel must come from people who represent the diversity of America.

Nor is he unaware of the limitations of his power:

> A President must have a vision of the America and the world he wants to see. But the President does not put his purely personal stamp upon the future. His vision is compounded of the hopes and anxieties and values of the people he serves. The President can help guide them toward the highest and most noble of their desires. He cannot take them where they do not want to go. Nor can he hope to move ahead without the help of all those who share a common purpose. I believe the Presidency was conceived as an office of persuasion more than of sheer power. That is how I have tried to use the office since it was thrust upon me.

One of the most persistent criticisms of President Johnson is that he is arrogant (few who echo the charge bother to question its source or the sinister irony it expresses). But, although it is too early for final judgments, it is possible that what has been called the President's arrogance is actually an expression of a profound and dedicated humility before the demands and responsibilities of his office. Perhaps he is becoming possessed by the office in much the manner that Abraham Lincoln was possessed and is being consumed before our television-focused eyes by the role that he might well have expected, as politician, to have dominated.

As I see it, there is anguish here; an anguish born of strenuous efforts which turn endlessly into their opposites, of efforts to communicate which fail to get through, an anguish born of measures passed and projects set up only to be blocked, stalled, deprived of funds, and kept from functioning often by those who should in the Nation's broader interest render all assistance. His most successful measures have produced impatience and released forces and energies which obscure the full extent of his accomplishments. And they are great accomplishments. No one has initiated more legislation for education, for health, for racial justice, for the arts, for urban reform than he. Presently it is the fashion of many intellectuals to ignore these accomplishments, these promises of a broader freedom to come, but if those of other backgrounds and interests can afford to be blind to their existence, my own interests and background compel me to bear witness.

For I must be true to the hopes, dreams, and myths of my people. So perhaps I am motivated here by an old slave-born myth of the Negroes—not the myth of the "good white man," nor that of the "great white father," but the myth, secret and questioning, of the flawed white Southerner who while true to his Southern roots has confronted the injustices of the past and been redeemed. Such a man, the myth holds, will do the right thing however great the cost, whether he likes Negroes or not, and will move with tragic vulnerability toward the broader ideals of American democracy. The figure evoked by this myth is one who will grapple with complex situations that have evolved through history, and is a man who has so identified with his task that personal considerations have become secondary. Judge Waties J. Waring of South Carolina was such a man, and so—one hopes, one suspects —is Lyndon Baines Johnson. If this seems optimistic it is perhaps because I am of a hopeful people. Considering that he has changed inescapably the iconography of Federal power, from his military aides to the Cabinet, the Federal Reserve Board, to the Supreme Court, there appears to be ample reason for hope.

When all of the returns are in, perhaps President Johnson will have to settle for being recognized as the greatest American President for the poor and for the Negroes, but that, as I see it, is a very great honor indeed.

Lyndon B. Johnson

*"It is the glorious opportunity of this generation
to end the one huge wrong of the American Nation. . . ."*

Commencement Address at Howard University,
June 4, 1965.

I am delighted at the chance to speak at this important and this historic institution. Howard has long been an outstanding center for the education of Negro Americans. Its students are of every race and color and they come from many countries of the world. It is truly a working example of democratic excellence.

Our earth is the home of revolution. In every corner of every continent men charged with hope contend with ancient ways in the pursuit of justice. They reach for the newest of weapons to realize the oldest of dreams, that each may walk in freedom and pride, stretching his talents, enjoying the fruits of the earth.

Our enemies may occasionally seize the day of change, but it is the banner of our revolution they take. And our own future is linked to this process of swift and turbulent change in many lands in the world. But nothing in any country touches us more profoundly, and nothing is more freighted with meaning for our own destiny than the revolution of the Negro American.

In far too many ways American Negroes have been another nation: deprived of freedom, crippled by hatred, the doors of opportunity closed to hope.

In our time change has come to this Nation, too. The American Negro, acting with impressive restraint, has peacefully protested and marched, entered the courtrooms and the seats of government, demanding a justice that has long been denied. The voice of the Negro was the call to action. But it is a tribute to America that, once aroused, the courts and the Congress, the President and most of the people, have been the allies of progress.

LEGAL PROTECTION FOR HUMAN RIGHTS

Thus we have seen the high court of the country declare that discrimination based on race was repugnant to the Constitution, and therefore void. We have seen in 1957, and 1960, and again in 1964, the first civil rights legislation in this Nation in almost an entire century.

As majority leader of the United States Senate, I helped to guide two of these bills through the Senate. And, as your President, I was proud to sign the third. And now very soon we will have the fourth—a new law guaranteeing every American the right to vote.

No act of my entire administration will give me greater satisfaction than the day when my signature makes this bill, too, the law of this land.

The voting rights bill will be the latest, and among the most important, in a long series of victories. But this victory—as Winston Churchill said of another triumph for freedom—"is not the end. It is not even the beginning of the end. But it is, perhaps, the end of the beginning."

That beginning is freedom; and the barriers to that freedom are tumbling down. Freedom is the right to share, share fully and equally, in American society—to vote, to hold a job, to enter a public place, to go to school. It is the right to be treated in every part of our national life as a person equal in dignity and promise to all others.

FREEDOM IS NOT ENOUGH

But freedom is not enough. You do not wipe away the scars of centuries by saying: Now you are free to go where you want, and do as you desire, and choose the leaders you please.

You do not take a person who, for years, has been hobbled by chains and liberate him, bring him up to the starting line of a race and then say, "You are free to compete with all the others," and still justly believe that you have been completely fair.

Thus it is not enough just to open the gates of opportunity. All our citizens must have the ability to walk through those gates.

This is the next and the more profound stage of the battle for civil rights. We seek not just freedom but opportunity. We seek not just legal equity but human ability, not just equality as a right and a theory but equality as a fact and equality as a result.

For the task is to give 20 million Negroes the same chance as every other American to learn and grow, to work and share in society, to develop their abilities—physical, mental, and spiritual, and to pursue their individual happiness.

To this end equal opportunity is essential, but not enough, not enough. Men and women of all races are born with the same range of abilities. But ability is not just the product of birth. Ability is stretched or stunted by the family that you live with, and the neighborhood you live in—by the school you go to and the poverty or the richness of your surroundings. It is the product of a hundred unseen forces playing upon the little infant, the child, and finally the man.

PROGRESS FOR SOME

This graduating class at Howard University is witness to the indomitable determination of the Negro American to win his way in American life.

The number of Negroes in schools of higher learning has almost doubled in fifteen years. The number of nonwhite professional workers has more than doubled in ten years. The median income of Negro college women tonight exceeds that of white college women. And there are also the enormous accomplishments of distinguished individual Negroes—many of them graduates of this institution, and one of them the first lady ambassador in the history of the United States.

These are proud and impressive achievements. But they tell only the story of a growing middle-class minority, steadily narrowing the gap between them and their white counterparts.

A WIDENING GULF

But for the great majority of Negro Americans—the poor, the unemployed, the uprooted, and the dispossessed—there is a much grimmer story. They still, as we meet here tonight, are another nation. Despite the court orders and the laws, despite the legislative victories and the speeches, for them the walls are rising and the gulf is widening.

Here are some of the facts of this American failure.

Thirty-five years ago the rate of unemployment for Negroes and whites was about the same. Tonight the Negro rate is twice as high.

In 1948 the 8 percent unemployment rate for Negro teenage boys was actually less than that of whites. By last year that rate had grown to 23 percent, as against 13 percent for whites unemployed.

Between 1949 and 1959, the income of Negro men relative to white men declined in every section of this country. From 1952 to 1963 the median income of Negro families compared to white actually dropped from 57 percent to 53 percent.

In the years 1955 through 1957, 22 percent of experienced Negro workers were out of work at some time during the year. In 1961 through 1963 that proportion had soared to 29 percent.

Since 1947 the number of white families living in poverty has decreased 27 percent while the number of poorer nonwhite families decreased only 3 percent.

The infant mortality of nonwhites in 1940 was 70 percent greater than whites. Twenty-two years later it was 90 percent greater.

Moreover, the isolation of Negro from white communities is increasing, rather than decreasing as Negroes crowd into the central cities and become a city within a city.

Of course Negro Americans as well as white Americans have shared in our rising national abundance. But the harsh fact of the matter is that in the battle for true equality too many—far too many—are losing ground every day.

THE CAUSES OF INEQUALITY

We are not completely sure why this is. We know the causes are complex and subtle. But we do know the two broad basic reasons. And we do know that we have to act.

First, Negroes are trapped—as many whites are trapped—in inherited, gateless poverty. They lack training and skills. They are shut in, in slums, without decent medical care. Private and public poverty combine to cripple their capacities.

We are trying to attack these evils through our poverty program, through our education program, through our medical care and our other health programs, and a dozen more of the Great Society programs that are aimed at the root causes of this poverty.

We will increase, and we will accelerate, and we will broaden this attack in years to come until this most enduring of foes finally yields to our unyielding will.

But there is a second cause—much more difficult to explain, more deeply grounded, more desperate in its force. It is the devastating heritage of long years of slavery; and a century of oppression, hatred, and injustice.

SPECIAL NATURE OF NEGRO POVERTY

For Negro poverty is not white poverty. Many of its causes and many of its cures are the same. But there are differences—deep, corrosive, obstinate differences—radiating painful roots into the community, and into the family, and the nature of the individual.

These differences are not racial differences. They are solely and simply the consequence of ancient brutality, past injustice, and present prejudice. They are anguishing to observe. For the Negro they are a constant reminder of oppression. For the white they are a constant reminder of guilt. But they must be faced and they must be dealt with and they must be overcome, if we are ever to reach the time when the only difference between Negroes and whites is the color of their skin.

Nor can we find a complete answer in the experience of other American minorities. They made a valiant and a largely successful effort to emerge from poverty and prejudice.

The Negro, like these others, will have to rely mostly upon his own efforts. But he just can not do it alone. For they did not have the heritage of centuries to overcome, and they did not have a cultural tradition which had been twisted and battered by endless years of hatred and hopelessness, nor were they excluded—these others—because of race or color—a feeling whose dark intensity is matched by no other prejudice in our society.

Nor can these differences be understood as isolated infirmities. They are a seamless web. They cause each other. They result from each other. They reinforce each other.

Much of the Negro community is buried under a blanket of history and circumstance. It is not a lasting solution to lift just one corner of that blanket. We must stand on all sides and we must raise the entire cover if we are to liberate our fellow citizens.

THE ROOTS OF INJUSTICE

One of the differences is the increased concentration of Negroes in our cities. More than 73 percent of all Negroes live in urban areas compared with less than 70 percent of the whites. Most of these Negroes live in slums. Most of these Negroes live together—a separated people.

Men are shaped by their world. When it is a world of decay, ringed by an invisible wall, when escape is arduous and uncertain, and the saving pressures of a more hopeful society are unknown, it can cripple the youth and it can desolate the men.

There is also the burden that a dark skin can add to the search for a productive place in our society. Unemployment strikes most swiftly and broadly at the Negro, and this burden erodes hope. Blighted hope breeds despair. Despair brings indifferences to the learning which offers a way out. And despair, coupled with indifferences, is often the source of destructive rebellion against the fabric of society.

There is also the lacerating hurt of early collision with white hatred or prejudice, distaste, or condescension. Other groups have felt similar intolerance. But success and achievement could wipe it away. They do not change the color of a man's skin. I have seen this uncomprehending pain in the eyes of the little, young Mexican-American schoolchildren that I taught many years ago. But it can be overcome. But, for many, the wounds are always open.

FAMILY BREAKDOWN

Perhaps most important—its influence radiating to every part of life—is the breakdown of the Negro family structure. For this, most of all, white America must accept responsibility. It flows from centuries of oppression and persecution of the Negro man. It flows from the long years of degradation and discrimination, which have attacked his dignity and assaulted his ability to produce for his family.

This, too, is not pleasant to look upon. But it must be faced by those whose serious intent is to improve the life of all Americans.

Only a minority—less than half—of all Negro children reach the age of eighteen having lived all their lives with both of their parents. At this moment, tonight, little less than two-thirds are at home with both of their parents. Probably a majority of all Negro children receive Federally aided public assistance sometime during their childhood.

The family is the cornerstone of our society. More than any other force it shapes the attitude, the hopes, the ambitions, and the values of the child. And when the family collapses it is the children that are usually damaged. When it happens on a massive scale the community itself is crippled.

So, unless we work to strengthen the family, to create conditions under which most parents will stay together—all the rest: schools, and playgrounds, and public assistance, and private concern, will never be enough to cut completely the circle of despair and deprivation.

TO FULFILL THESE RIGHTS

There is no single easy answer to all of these problems.

Jobs are part of the answer. They bring the income which permits a man to provide for his family.

Decent homes in decent surroundings and a chance to learn—an equal chance to learn—are part of the answer.

Welfare and social programs better designed to hold families together are part of the answer.

Care for the sick is part of the answer.

An understanding heart by all Americans is another big part of the answer.

And to all of these fronts—and a dozen more—I will dedicate the expanding efforts of the Johnson Administration.

But there are other answers that are still to be found. Nor do we fully understand even all of the problems. Therefore, I want to announce tonight that this fall I intend to call a White House conference of scholars, and experts, and outstanding Negro leaders—men of both races—and officials of government at every level.

This White House conference's theme and title will be "To Fulfill These Rights."

Its object will be to help the American Negro fulfill the rights which, after the long time of injustice, he is finally about to secure.

To move beyond opportunity to achievement.

To shatter forever not only the barriers of law and public practice, but the walls which bound the condition of many by the color of his skin.

To dissolve, as best we can, the antique enmities of the heart which diminish the holder, divide the great democracy, and do wrong—great wrong—to the children of God.

And I pledge you tonight that this will be a chief goal of my Administration, and of my program next year, and in the years to come. And I hope, and I pray, and I believe, it will be a part of the program of all America.

WHAT IS JUSTICE?

For what is justice?

It is to fulfill the fair expectations of man.

Thus, American justice is a very special thing. For, from the first, this has been a land of towering expectations. It was to be a nation where each man could be ruled by the common consent of all—enshrined in law, given life by institutions, guided by men themselves subject to its rule. And all—all of every station and origin—would be touched equally in obligation and in liberty.

Beyond the law lay the land. It was a rich land, glowing with more abundant promise than man had ever seen. Here, unlike any place yet known, all were to share the harvest.

And beyond this was the diginity of man. Each could become whatever his qualities of mind and spirit would permit—to strive, to seek, and, if he could, to find his happiness.

This is American justice. We have pursued it faithfully to the edge of our imperfections, and we have failed to find it for the American Negro.

So, it is the glorious opportunity of this generation to end the one huge wrong of the American Nation and, in so doing, to find America for ourselves, with the same immense thrill of discovery which gripped those who first began to realize that here, at last, was a home for freedom.

All it will take is for all of us to understand what this country is and what this country must become.

The Scripture promises: "I shall light a candle of understanding in thine heart, which shall not be put out."

Together, and with millions more, we can light that candle of understanding in the heart of all America.

And, once lit, it will never again go out.

"We have made a good start. But . . . it is only a start."

Message to Congress setting forth
a seven-point civil rights program,
February 15, 1967.

Almost two centuries ago, the American people declared these truths to be self-evident: "That all men are created equal, that they are endowed by their Creator with certain inalienable rights, that among these are life, liberty and the pursuit of happiness."

Seventy-five years later, a savage war tested the foundations of their democratic faith. The issue of the struggle was, as Lincoln said, whether "we shall nobly save, or meanly lose, the last, best hope on earth."

Democracy triumphed in the field in 1865. But for the Negro American, emancipation from slavery was but the first engagement in a long campaign. He had still to endure the assaults of discrimination that denied him a decent home, refused his children a good education, closed the doors of economic progress against him, turned him away at the voting booth, the jury box, at places of public accommodation, seated him apart on buses and trains, and sometimes even threatened him with violence if he did not assent to these humiliations.

In 1948, President Truman ordered the defense establishment to accord equal treatment to servicemen of every race. That same year, the Supreme Court declared that state courts could not enforce racial covenants in the sale of houses. The Court later struck down racial discrimination in public transportation.

In 1954, segregated education was found to be inherently unequal and in violation of the Fourteenth Amendment.

In 1957, the first civil rights act in eighty-two years passed the Congress.

Three later acts were adopted within the next decade—in 1960, 1964, and 1965. Congress prohibited interference with the right to vote—to use any hotel, restaurant, or theater—to secure a job on the basis of merit. It barred the use of Federal funds to any agency that practiced racial discrimination.

Within these twenty years, the institutions of democratic government have begun to make the ancient, self-evident truths a reality for all Americans.

Though much of our task still lies before us, it is important to measure the progress we have made in the past few years.

Voting

Since the passage of the Voting Rights Act of 1965, the number of Negroes registered in the five states where voter discrimination was most severe has increased by 64 percent—from 715,099 to 1,174,569. The vast majority of the new voters—about 334,000—were registered by local officials, in voluntary compliance with the Act.

The remainder—some 125,000—were registered by Federal examiners in forty-seven counties of the five states. Federal observers were present in many counties during the 1966 primary and general elections to ensure that the newly registered voters were permitted to vote without interference.

In 1960, a Negro citizen complained that for ten years he had tried without success to register to vote. Not a single Negro had been registered in his county for sixty years. In 1966, he ran for a seat on the local school board—and won.

Today, twenty Negroes serve in Southern legislatures. Several important local offices, such as school boards and county commissions, now have Negro membership.

The electorate in these states has begun to change. The right to vote—the fundamental democratic right—is now exercised by men and women whose color served in years past to bar them from the polls. After centuries of silence, their voice is being heard. It will never again be stilled.

Schools

In the 1963–64 school year, ten years after the landmark *Brown* decision, one percent of the Negro students in the eleven Southern states were in schools also attended by white students.

Then came the 1964 Civil Rights Act and its prohibition against the use of Federal funds to support racial bias.

In September 1966, 12.5 percent of the Negro students in those same states

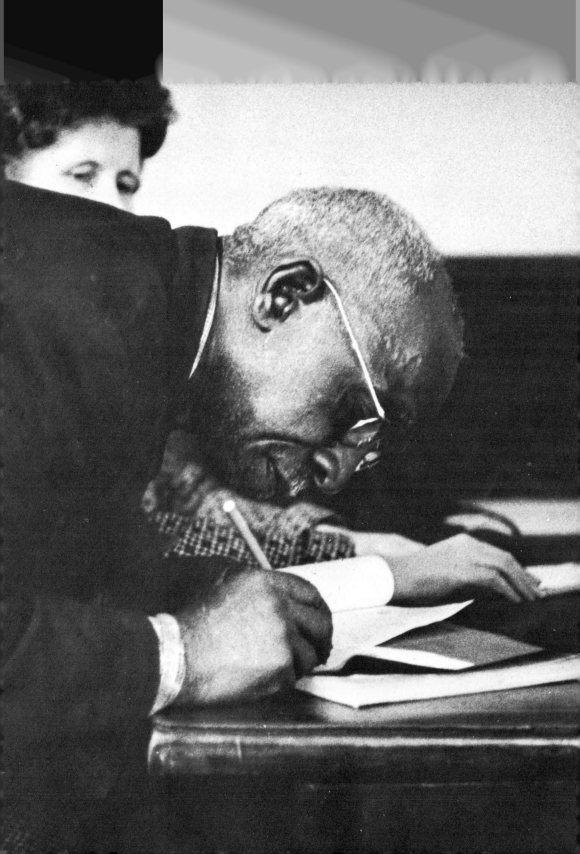

were enrolled in desegregated schools. We expect this figure to increase significantly next fall. We will proceed with the task of securing the rights of all our children.

Hospitals

This year, Negroes are being admitted to hospitals which barred them in the past. By January, 7,130 hospitals—more than 95 percent of the hospitals in the nation—had agreed to provide services without discrimination. More than 1,500 of those hospitals have had to change past policies to make that commitment.

Getting rid of discriminatory practices has benefited hospital systems, as well as the people they serve.

Last year, for example, half the beds in an all-white hospital were unoccupied. Yet Negroes in the community were sent to a completely segregated and overcrowded hospital. The half-empty hospital changed its policy to admit Negroes, and it now operates at full capacity. The formerly Negro hospital will be converted into a nursing home serving both races. The effect of the change was to provide better medical care for the entire community.

Public Accommodations

When the 1964 Civil Rights Act was passed, prohibiting racial discrimination in places of public accommodation, fears were expressed that this sharp change in established customs would bring about serious economic loss and perhaps even violence.

Yet from the start there has been widespread voluntary compliance with the law. Thousands of restaurants, motels, and hotels have been opened to Americans of all races and colors. What was thought to be laden with danger proved generally acceptable to both races.

Because all businesses of a similar type are covered, each businessman is free, for the first time, to operate on a nondiscriminatory basis without fear of suffering a competitive disadvantage.

Now Negro families traveling through most parts of their country do not need to suffer the inconvenience of searching for a place to rest or eat where they will be accepted or the humiliating indignity of being turned away.

PROGRAMS FOR SOCIAL JUSTICE

The struggle against today's discrimination is only part of the nation's commitment to equal justice for all Americans. The bigotry of the past has its effects in broken families, men without skills, children without learning, poor housing, and neighborhoods dominated by the fear of crime.

Because these effects are encrusted by generations of inferior opportunities and shattered hopes, they will not yield to laws against discrimination alone. Indeed there is no swift medicine, no matter how potent or massively applied, that can heal them at once. But we know some of the things we must do if the healing process is to begin—and we are doing them.

Education

Head Start has given deprived children a chance to learn in later years—instead of being merely exposed to school. Through this and other preschool programs, 2 million children have been offered better education and health care.

More than 7 million children in 70 percent of all school districts in the United States have participated in programs under Title I of the 1965 Education Act. These programs have a single aim: to improve the education of disadvantaged children. The better libraries, larger professional staffs, advanced instructional equipment, and other services they provide are investments in the future of children who need them most.

In my Message on America's Children and Youth, I asked the Congress to provide an additional $135 million to strengthen Head Start. With these funds, we will launch a Head Start Follow-Through Program in the early grades of elementary school to maintain the momentum the child has gained and we will extend the Head Start Program downward to cover more three-year-olds.

Extraordinary help at the start of life is necessary for all disadvantaged children. It is particularly necessary for the Negro child reared in poverty and encumbered by generations of deprivation.

Jobs and Training

Thousands of job opportunities for the young have been created by the Neighborhood Youth Corps and the Job Corps. The first, active in both urban and rural areas, has enabled many young people to earn enough to remain in school, and provided employment and remedial education for dropouts.

The Job Corps—also meant to help those between sixteen and twenty-one—has offered other thousands both a change of environment and the opportunity to acquire education and job training.

The Manpower Development and Training Act gives men without jobs or skills the chance to acquire both, by combining Government planning and resources with private industry. The Work Experience Program offers welfare recipients a means of obtaining the experience they need for gainful employment.

Today's strong economy, which last year put almost 3 million more Americans on the payrolls, is also of tremendous benefit to needy persons in search of dependable employment. But for the long term, and as demand for better qualified workers grows, training and remedial education will be of even greater importance to the disadvantaged. This is particularly true for those who leave the farm and move to urban areas in search of employment, without the skills an urban society requires.

During the last three years, our training programs have provided the means of self-sufficiency to almost a million men and women. The value of these programs to the Negro American is especially great.

The unemployment rate for Negroes is more than double that for whites. About 650,000 Americans, more than 20 percent of all unemployed, are nonwhite. About 213,000 of these are betwen fourteen and nineteen years of age. Job training is essential to enable them to get off the welfare rolls and to go on the tax rolls.

Our economy is also strengthened by these programs. If Negroes today had the same skills as other Americans, and if they were free from discrimination in employment, our Gross National Product could become $30 billion higher.

I will shortly submit recommendations to strengthen and expand these training programs. I am asking the Congress for an additional $135 million in appropriations for the Office of Economic Opportunity for a special program to open the doors of opportunity and meaningful employment to our most disadvantaged citizens.

I will call for the active assistance of private industry and organized labor to provide skills and jobs to those now confined to the welfare rolls and the slums.

THE NEED FOR PERSEVERANCE

There are those who believe this series of accomplishments is long enough. There are those who grow weary of supporting great social programs, impatient with the failures that attend them, and cynical about those they are intended to help. There are those who think "equal justice" is a rhetorical phrase, intended only as an admonition to judges, not as a guiding principle for national policy.

To them I can only say: Consider the consequences if the Nation—and I as the President—were to take what appears to be the easy way out, abandon the long, hard struggle for social and economic justice, and say that enough has been done:

—There would be little hope of strengthening the economy of the country through the improved earning power and productive capacity of Negro Americans.

—There would be little hope of avoiding massive welfare expenditures for people denied the training and jobs they need to become self-supporting.

—There would be little hope of ending the chain of personal tragedies that began with ancient bigotry and continues to this hour.

—*There would—above all—be little hope of achieving the self-respect that comes to a nation from doing what is right.*

Our task is far from over. The statistics demonstrate the magnitude of the effort required.

—The life expectancy of the Negro is five years shorter than that of his white contemporary and the infant mortality rate for Negroes is 40 percent higher.

—The adult white has had at least three more years of education—and has been educated in better schools—than the average adult Negro.

—The unemployment rate for nonwhites aged twenty-one—even in this time of near full employment—is double that of whites.

—Negroes are characteristically more densely housed in units only 56 percent of which meet health and safety standards.

—The income of the average Negro family is about 40 percent lower than that of the average white family.

The programs we have adopted in the past few years are only a beginning. We have made a good start.

But we must remember that it is only a start. We must realize that civil rights are also civil opportunities. Unless these rights are recognized as opportunities by Negro and white alike, they can achieve nothing. We must realize that training and education programs provide skills and opportunities. But only where there is both the will to seek the job and the willingness to hire the job applicant can these programs achieve their ultimate objectives.

The next steps are harder, but they are even more important. We shall need years of trial and error—years in which children can be strengthened to grow into responsible young adults, years of better training, better jobs, better health, and better housing—before the results of what we have done so far can be seen.

Perseverance, the willingness to abandon what does not work, and the courage to keep searching for better solutions—these are the virtues the times require.

CIVIL RIGHTS LEGISLATION

Last year I proposed the enactment of important civil rights legislation. I proposed that legislation because it was right and just.

The civil rights legislation of 1966 was passed by the House of Representatives, and brought to the floor of the Senate. Most of its features commanded a strong majority in both Houses. None of its features was defeated on the merits.

Yet it did not become law. It could not be brought to a final vote in the Senate.

Some observers felt that the riots which occurred in several cities last summer prevented the passage of the bill.

Public concern over the riots was great, as it should have been. Lawlessness cannot to be tolerated in a nation whose very existence depends upon respect for law. It cannot be permitted because it injures every American and tears at the very fabric of our democracy.

We want public order in America, and we shall have it. But a decent public order cannot be achieved solely at the end of a stick, nor by confining one race to self-perpetuating poverty.

Let us create the conditions for a public order based upon equal justice.

THE CIVIL RIGHTS ACT OF 1967

The Act I am proposing this year is substantially the same as last year's bill. Some revisions have been incorporated to take account of useful suggestions and perfecting amendments made by the Eighty-ninth Congress. I believe these revisions offer a basis for common action.

I recommend the adoption of a national policy against discrimination in housing on account of race, color, religion, or national origin. I propose the adoption of progressive steps to carry out this policy.

I recommend the clarification and strengthening of existing Federal criminal laws against interference with Federal rights.

I recommend requirements for the selection of juries in Federal courts to guard against discrimination and ensure that juries are properly representative of the community.

I recommend legislation to eliminate all forms of discrimination in the selection of state court juries.

I recommend that the Civil Rights Act of 1964 be amended to authorize the Equal Employment Opportunity Commission to issue judicially enforceable cease-and-desist orders.

I recommend the extension, for an additional five years, of the United States Commission on Civil Rights.

I recommend a 90 percent increase in appropriations for the Community Relations Service.

These measures are not new. I have recommended and supported them in the past. I urged the Congress to act favorably upon them because justice and human dignity demand these protections for each American citizen.

EQUAL JUSTICE IN HOUSING

For most Americans, the availability of housing depends upon one factor—their ability to pay.

For too many, however, there are other crucial factors—the color of their skin, their religion, or their national origin.

When a Negro seeks a decent home for himself and his family, he frequently finds that the door is closed. It remains closed—though the Negro may be a serviceman who has fought for freedom.

The result of countless individual acts of discrimination is the spawning of urban ghettoes, where housing is inferior, overcrowded, and too often overpriced.

Statistics tell a part of the story. Throughout the nation, almost twice as many nonwhites as whites occupy deteriorating or dilapidated housing. In Watts, 32.5 percent of all housing is overcrowded, compared with 11.5 percent for the Nation as a whole.

In Harlem, more than 237,000 people live in an area consisting of three and one-half square miles. This is a density of 105 people per acre. Ninety percent of the buildings in Harlem are more than thirty years old, and almost half were built before the end of the nineteenth century.

The environment of most urban ghettoes is the same: inferior public facilities and services—streets, lighting, parks; sanitation and police protection; inferior schools; and isolation from job opportunities. In every sphere of urban life the ghetto-dweller is short changed.

A child growing up in such an environment must overcome tremendous man-made obstacles to become a useful citizen. The misery we tolerate today multiplies the misery of tomorrow.

Many of our existing and proposed programs—though not directed simply at relieving the problems of any particular minority group—will relieve conditions found in their most acute form in the urban ghetto. These programs are necessary and they must be fully supported.

But money and assistance are not enough. Since the ratification of the Fourteenth Amendment to the Constitution, this Nation has been committed to accord every citizen the equal protection of its laws. We must strengthen that commitment as it relates to discrimination in housing—a problem that is national in scope.

The legislation I recommend would ultimately apply to all housing in the United States. It would go into effect by progressive stages.

The proposed legislation would direct the Secretary of Housing and Urban Development to carry out education and conciliation measures to seek an end to discrimination in housing. He would call conferences of leaders in the housing industry, consult with state and local officials, and work with private organizations.

The prohibition against discrimination in the sale or rental of housing would become effective progressively over a two-year period:

—immediately, to housing already covered by the presidential order on equal opportunities in housing;

—during 1968, to dwellings sold or rented by someone other than their occupant, and to dwellings for five or more families. Essentially, this stage would cover large apartment houses and real estate developments;

—in 1969, the Act would apply to all housing.

This Act would be aimed at commercial transactions, not at the privacy of the home. It would outlaw discriminatory practices in financing housing and in providing real-estate brokers' services. It would prohibit "block-busting," by which unscrupulous dealers seek to frighten homeowners into selling quickly, out of fear that the value of their homes will decline.

In every instance, the legislation would require the Secretary of Housing and Urban Development to try to achieve a voluntary solution. Only if such a settlement could not be reached would the Secretary be authorized to hold an administrative hearing. If, after an administrative hearing, a violation of the law were found, the Secretary would be authorized to issue a judicially enforceable cease-and-desist order.

The Secretary would work with state and municipal fair housing agencies that already exist. In appropriate cases he would be authorized to rely on their enforcement of the state and city laws.

The Attorney General would be empowered to support these enforcement efforts, when he had reason to believe that a general pattern or practice of discrimination exists.

Last year the legislation I proposed to ban discrimination in housing stirred great controversy. Although a majority of both Houses in the Congress favored that legislation, it was not enacted. Some of the problems raised by its adversaries were real; most involved myths and misinformation. The summer riots in our cities did as much damage to the chances of passing that legislation as the unfounded fears of many Americans and the opposition of special interest groups.

There should be no need for laws to require men to deal fairly and decently with their fellowman. There should be no need to enact a law prohibiting discrimination in housing—just as there should have been no need to send registrars to enforce voting rights, to issue guidelines to require desegregation of our schools, to bring suits in Federal courts to insure equal access to public accommodations, and to outlaw discrimination in employment.

But the Civil Rights Acts of 1957, 1960, and 1964 and the Voting Rights Act of 1965 were necessary and they have moved this country toward our goal of providing a decent life for each of our citizens.

I am proposing fair housing legislation again this year because it is decent and right. Injustice must be opposed, however difficult or unpopular the issue.

I believe that fair housing legislation must and will be enacted by the Congress of the United States. I was proud to be a member of the Congresses that enacted the Civil Rights Acts of 1957 and 1960 and as President to sign into law the 1964 and 1965 Acts. I believe that generations to come would look upon the enactment of this legislation by the Ninetieth Congress as one of its proudest achievements. I cannot urge too strongly that the Congress act promptly on this legislation.

Today the subject of fair housing is engulfed in a cloud of misinformation and unarticulated fear. Some believe the value of their homes must decline if their neighborhoods are integrated. They fear the conversion of their communities into unsightly slums, if a family of a different color moves into a house across the street. Neither of these events need occur. In an atmosphere of reason and justice, they would not occur. In the scores of cities and states that have such laws these events have not occurred.

The task of informing the minds and enlightening the consciences of those who are subject to these fears should begin at once. Churches can help perform this task with a unique competence—and they should. So should civic organizations, public officials, human relations commissions, labor unions, and private industries. It must be done. The sooner it is done, the nearer we will come to that just America it is our purpose to achieve.

INTERFERENCE WITH RIGHTS

Another basic test of equal justice is whether all men are free to exercise rights established by the Congress and the Constitution. A right has little meaning unless it can be freely exercised. This applies in particular to Negro Americans who seek to vote, attend school, and utilize public accommodations on an equal basis.

Negro children have been abused for attending previously segregated schools. Shots have been fired into the homes of their parents. Employers who practiced nondiscrimination have been harassed. Most shocking of all are the crimes which result in loss of life. Some of the victims have been Negroes; others were whites devoted to the cause of justice.

State and local officials are primarily responsible for preventing and punishing acts of violence. In many cases, however, these officials have not been able to detect or prosecute the perpetrators of the crimes. In some, unfortunately, they have not been willing to meet their obligations. For these reasons and because violence has too often been used to deny Federal rights, there is need for Federal legislation.

Present Federal statutes are inadequate in several respects. Maximum penalties are too low for crimes which cause death or serious injury. Only in some instances do the statutes reach misconduct by private persons not acting in concert with public officials. Existing laws do not spell out clearly the Federal rights which they protect.

To remedy these deficiencies, I recommend legislation to:

—specify the activities which are protected, including voting, purchasing a home, holding a job, attending a school, obtaining service in a restaurant or other place of public accommodation;

—prohibit acts or threats of violence, by private individuals acting alone or public officials, directed against Negroes or members of other minority groups because they are or have been participating in those activities;

—authorize victims of violence to bring civil actions for damages or injunctive relief.

The penalties prescribed are graduated, depending on the gravity of the offense. When physical injury results, the maximum penalty is $10,000 and ten years. When death occurs, the sentence may be imprisonment for any term of years or for life.

FEDERAL AND STATE JURIES

A fair jury is fundamental to our historic traditions of justice.

Fairness is most likely to result when the jury is selected from a broad cross section of the community. The exclusion of particular groups or classes from jury duty not only denies defendants their right to an impartial jury. It also denies members of the excluded group the opportunity to fulfill an important obligation of citizenship and to participate in the processes of their government.

On many occasions, I have emphasized the importance of respect for the law. Yet, creating respect for legal institutions becomes virtually impossible when parts of our judicial system operate unlawfully or give the appearance of unfairness.

Current methods of Federal court jury selection have sometimes resulted in the exclusion of Negroes and other minority groups. Often the cause lay in the method of selection.

I recommend legislation to:

—eliminate discrimination in the selection of juries in Federal courts;

—ensure that juries in Federal courts are uniformly drawn from a broad cross section of the community.

To reduce to a minimum the possibility of arbitrary exclusion of certain groups, the Act will spell out in detail the selection procedures to be followed in all Federal district courts. Names of prospective jurors would be obtained by random selection from voter lists—a broadly representative source in almost all parts of the country, now that the Voting Rights Act of

1965 is being implemented. Under the Bill only objective standards, including basic literacy requirements found in existing law, could be used to determine the qualifications of a prospective juror.

Legislation to deal with selection of state court juries is also needed. There has been persistent, intentional discrimination in juror selection in some localities. A recent case involved jury discrimination in a county whose population in 1960 was more than 70 percent Negro. Of the persons listed on the jury rolls between 1953 and 1965, less than 2 percent were Negro. No Negro had ever served as a member of a jury in that county.

Numerous criminal convictions obtained in state courts have been set aside on the ground that Negroes were excluded from the juries. Such court decisions may assure justice in a particular case. They cannot reform the jury selection systems.

The Fourteenth Amendment establishes equality before the law and charges the Congress with enforcing that requirement. Such flagrant persistent abuses as are revealed in many recent jury selection cases cannot be tolerated by a society which prides itself on the rule of law.

I recommend legislation to:

—prohibit discrimination on account of race, color, religion, national origin, sex, or economic status in the selection of state or local juries;

—authorize the Attorney General to sue state or local jury officials who exclude Negroes or members of other minority groups from juries;

—prescribe new remedies to make it easier to prove jury discrimination;

—authorize the courts to issue a variety of orders specially tailored to eliminate the most common methods by which jury discrimination is practiced.

EQUAL JUSTICE IN EMPLOYMENT

The Civil Rights Act of 1964 prohibited discrimination in hiring, promotion, and working conditions, as well as discrimination in the membership practices of labor organizations. The Equal Employment Opportunity Commission was created to carry out the congressional mandate.

The Commission was directed to eliminate discriminatory employment practices by informal methods of conciliation and persuasion. By the end of this fiscal year, the Commission will have completed over 2,000 investigations and more than 500 conciliation efforts. This is hard work, but when it succeeds, case by case it opens up new opportunities to:

—the minority group employees of an aircraft company, who no longer are confined to dead-end jobs but now have training opportunities in forty job classifications;

—the employees of a large ship construction firm which has improved the job rights of over 5,000 Negroes.

Unlike most other Federal regulatory agencies, the Equal Employment Opportunity Commission was not given enforcement powers. If efforts to conciliate or persuade are unsuccessful, the Commission itself is powerless. For the individual discriminated against, there remains only a time-consuming and expensive lawsuit.

In considering the proper role of the Equal Employment Opportunity Commission, it is important to bear in mind that nonwhite unemployment remains disproportionately high:

—In 1966, the unemployment rate was 3.3 percent for white persons. It was 7.3 percent for nonwhites.

—Nonwhite unemployment in 1965 was twice the rate for whites. In 1966, the ratio rose to 2.2 to 1.

—Among youth not attending school, the unemployment rate in 1966 was 8.5 percent for whites and 20.3 percent for nonwhites.

No single factor explains the differences in the unemployment rates of nonwhites and whites. But part of the disparity is clearly attributable to discrimination. For that reason, effective remedies against discrimination are essential.

I recommend legislation to give the Equal Employment Opportunity Commission authority to issue orders, after a fair hearing, to require the termination of discriminatory employment practices.

The cease-and-desist orders of the Commission would be enforceable in the Federal courts of appeal and subject to judicial review there. These powers are similar to those of other Federal regulatory agencies.

Enforcement power would harmonize the procedures of the Commission with the prevailing practice among states and cities that have had fair employment practices agencies for many years. It would reduce the burden on individual complainants and on the Federal courts. It would enhance the orderly implementation of this important national policy.

THE COMMISSION ON CIVIL RIGHTS

The United States Commission on Civil Rights has, since its creation in 1957, proved to be an exceptionally valuable agency. This bipartisan fact-finding agency has contributed substantially to our determined effort to assure the civil rights of all Americans. Its investigations and studies have contributed to important changes in the laws and policies of the Federal Government. Publications of the Commission—in the fields of voting, housing, employment, school segregation, and equality of opportunity in Government programs—have been helpful to other Government agencies and to private groups interested in equality of opportunity.

The Commission has also served as a clearinghouse for information on civil rights matters. It has provided information on Federal laws, programs, and services to assist communities and private organizations in dealing with civil rights issues and with economic and social problems affecting race relations.

Under existing law, the term of the Commission expires on January 31, 1968. But much more remains to be done.

I recommend that the life of the Commission be extended for an additional five years.

COMMUNITY RELATIONS SERVICE

The Civil Rights Act of 1964 recognized the importance of providing bridges of understanding for communities across the land struggling with problems of equal justice and discrimination. Last year, I recommended, and you in the Congress approved, the transfer of the Community Relations Service to the Department of Justice to make it a more effective instrument of national policy.

This year, I recommend that the funds for the work of the Community Relations Service be increased by 90 percent—from $1.4 million to $2.7 million.

In city after city and county after county, the men of the Community Relations Service have worked, quietly and effectively, behind the scenes, to conciliate disputes before they flared up in the courtrooms or on the streets.

I deeply believe that, under our democratic system, the work of conciliation can be brought to bear increasingly to remove many of the injustices, intentional and unintentional, which derive from prejudice. It is in this spirit and with this conviction that I request a substantial increase in the funds appropriated to the Community Relations Service.

EQUAL JUSTICE

We adopted a Constitution "to form a more perfect union, establish justice, insure the domestic tranquility," and "provide for the common defense."

In our wars Americans, Negro and white, have fought side by side to defend freedom. Negro soldiers—like white soldiers—have won every medal for bravery our country bestows. The bullets of our enemies do not discriminate between Negro Marines and white Marines. They kill and maim whomever they strike.

The American Negro has waited long for first-class citizenship—for his right of equal justice. But he has long accepted the full responsibilities of citizenship.

If there were any doubt, one need only look to the servicemen who man our defenses. In Vietnam, 10.2 percent of our soldiers are American Negroes bearing equal responsibilities in the fight for freedom—but at home, 11 percent of our people are American Negroes struggling for equal opportunities.

The bullets at the battlefront do not discriminate—but the landlords at home do. The pack of the Negro soldier is as heavy as the white soldier's—but the burden his family at home bears is far heavier. In war, the Negro American has given this nation his best—but this nation has not given him equal justice.

It is time that the Negro be given equal justice. In America, the rights of citizenship are conferred by birth—not by death in battle.

It is our duty—as well as our privilege—to stand before the world as a nation dedicated to equal justice. There may be doubts about some policies or programs, but there can be no doubt about the rights of each man to stand on equal ground before his Government and with his fellow man.

On June 4, 1965, at Howard University, I spoke about the challenge confronting this Nation—"to fulfill these rights." What I said then has even greater importance and meaning for every American today:

"Freedom is the right to share fully and equally in American society—to vote, to hold a job, to enter a public place, to go to school. It is the right to be treated in every part of our national life as a person equal in dignity and promise to all others.

"But freedom is not enough. You do not wipe away the scars of centuries by saying: Now you are free to go where you want, do as you desire, and choose the leaders you please.

"You do not take a person who, for years, has been hobbled by chains and liberate him, bring him up to the starting line of a race and then say, 'You are free to compete with all the others,' and still justly believe that you have been completely fair.

"Thus it is not enough just to open the gates of opportunity. All of our citizens must have the ability to walk through those gates.

"This is the next and more profound stage of the battle for civil rights. We seek not just freedom but opportunity—not just legal equity but human ability—not just equality as a right and a theory, but equality as a fact and as a result.

"For the task is to give 20 million Negroes the same chance as every other American to learn and grow, to work and share in society, to develop their abilities—physical, mental, and spiritual, and to pursue their individual happiness.

"There is no single easy answer to all of these problems.

"Jobs are part of the answer. They bring the income which permits a man to provide for his family.

"Decent homes in decent surroundings, and a chance to learn—an equal chance to learn—are part of the answer.

"Welfare and social programs better designed to hold families together are part of the answer.

"Care of the sick is part of the answer.

"An understanding heart by all Americans is also a large part of the answer.

"To all these fronts—and a dozen more—I will dedicate the expanding efforts of the Johnson Administration."

"Racism—under whatever guise
and whatever sponsorship—
cannot be reconciled with the American faith."
Message to Congress on civil rights (excerpts),
January 24, 1968.

In the State of the Union message last week I spoke of a spirit of restlessness in our land. This feeling of disquiet is more pronounced in race relations than in any other area of domestic concern.

Most Americans remain true to our goal: the development of a national society in which the color of a man's skin is as irrelevant as the color of his eyes.

In the context of our history, this goal will not be easily achieved. But unless we act in our time to fulfill our first creed—that "all men are created equal"—it will not be achieved at all.

Though the creed of equality has won acceptance among the great majority of our people, some continue to resist every constructive step to its achievement.

The air is filled with the voices of extremists on both sides:

—Those who use our very successes as an excuse to stop in our tracks, and who decry the awakening of new expectations in people who have found cause to hope.

—Those who catalogue only our failures, declare that our society is bankrupt, and promote violence and force as an alternative to orderly change.

These extremes represent, I believe, forms of escapism by a small minority of our people. The vast majority of Americans—Negro and white—have not lent their hearts or efforts to either form of extremism. They have continued to work forcefully—and lawfully—for the common good.

America is a multiracial nation. Racism—under whatever guise and whatever sponsorship—cannot be reconciled with the American faith.

EDUCATION FOR ALL

We confront this challenge squarely in the area of education.

Our Nation is committed to the best possible education for all our children. We are also committed to the constitutional mandate that prohibits segregated school systems.

Some maintain that integration is essential for better education. Others insist that massive new investments in facilities and teachers alone can achieve the results we desire.

We continue to seek both goals: better supported—and unsegregated—schools.

Thus far, we can claim only a qualified success for our efforts:

—We still seek better methods to teach disadvantaged youngsters—to awaken their curiosity, stimulate their interest, arouse their latent talent, and prepare them for the complexities of modern living.

—We still seek better methods to achieve meaningful integration in many of the various communities across our land—in urban ghettoes, in rural counties, in suburban districts.

But our lack of total success should spur our efforts, not discourage them.

In the last year many states, cities, communities, school boards and educators have experimented with new techniques of education, and new methods of achieving integration. We have learned much from these experiments. We shall learn much more.

We do know that progress in education cannot be designed in Washington, but must be generated by the energies of local school boards, teachers and parents. We know that there is no single or simple answer to the questions that perplex us. But our national goals are clear: desegregated schools and quality education. They must not be compromised.

THE URGENT NEED FOR LEGISLATIVE ACTION

The legacy of the American past is political democracy—and an economic system that has produced an abundance unknown in history.

Yet our forefathers also left their unsolved problems. The legacy of slavery —racial discrimination—is first among them.

We have come a long way since that August day in 1957 when the first civil rights bill in almost a century was passed by the Congress.

At our recommendation, the Congress passed major civil rights legislation —far stronger than the 1957 act—in 1964 and 1965. The 89th Congress passed groundbreaking legislation of enormous importance to disadvantaged Americans among us—in education, in health, in manpower training, in the war against poverty. The first session of the 90th Congress has continued these programs.

In this session, I appeal to the Congress to complete the task it has begun.

—To strengthen Federal criminal laws prohibiting violent interference with the exercise of civil rights.

—To give the Equal Employment Opportunity Commission the authority it needs to carry out its vital responsibilities.

—To assure that Federal and state juries are selected without discrimination.

—To make equal opportunity in housing a reality for all Americans.

PROTECTING THE EXERCISE OF CIVIL RIGHTS

A Negro parent is attacked because his child attends a desegregated public school. Can the Federal courts punish the assailant? The answer today is only "perhaps."

A Negro is beaten by private citizens after seeking service in a previously all-white restaurant. Can the Federal courts punish this act? Under existing law the answer is "no," unless that attack involved a conspiracy. Even there the answer is only "maybe."

Grown men force a group of Negro children from a public park. The question most Americans would ask is what punishment these hoodlums deserve. Instead, the question before the Federal court is whether it has jurisdiction.

The existing criminal laws are inadequate:

—The conduct they prohibit is not set out in clear, precise terms. This ambiguity encourages drawn-out litigation and disrespect for the rule of law.

—These laws have only limited applicability to private persons not acting in concert with public officials. As a result, blatant acts of violence go unpunished.

—Maximum penalties are inadequate to suit the gravity of the crime when injury or death result.

The bill reported by the Senate Judiciary Committee remedies each of these deficiencies. It would prohibit the use of force to prevent the exercise by minorities of rights most of us take for granted.

EMPLOYMENT

For most Americans, the nation's continuing prosperity has meant increased abundance. Nevertheless, as I noted earlier, the unemployment rate for non-whites has remained at least twice the rate for whites.

Part of the answer lies in job training to overcome educational deficiencies and to teach new skills. Yesterday I asked the Congress for a $2.1 billion man-power program to assist 1.3 million of our citizens. A special three-year effort will be made to reach 500,000 hard-core unemployed of all races and backgrounds in our major cities.

But we must assure our citizens that once they are qualified, they will be judged fairly on the basis of their capacities.

Even where the Negro, the Puerto Rican, and the Mexican-American possess education and skills, they are too often treated as less than equal in the eyes of those who have the power to hire, promote, and dismiss. The median income of college-trained nonwhites is only $6,000 a year. The median income of college-trained whites is over $9,000—more than 50 percent higher.

The law forbids discrimination in employment. And we have worked to enforce that law:

—More than 150 cases of employment discrimination are under investigation by the Department of Justice.

—Lawsuits have been filed to stop patterns and practices of discrimination by employers and unions in the North as well as the South.

But the Justice Department does not bear the major responsibility for enforcing equal employment opportunity. Congress created the Equal Employment Opportunity Commission in 1964 to receive and investigate individual complaints, and to attempt to eliminate unlawful employment practices by the informal methods of conference, conciliation, and persuasion.

This authority has yielded its fruits. Many employers and unions have complied through this process. We have gained valuable knowledge about discriminatory practices and employment patterns.

Yet even this stepped-up activity cannot reach those who will not agree voluntarily to end their discriminatory practices. As a result, only part of our economy is open to all workers on the basis of merit. Part remains closed because of bias.

The legislation that I submitted last year would empower the Equal Employment Opportunity Commission to issue, after an appropriate hearing, an order requiring an offending employer or union to cease its discriminatory practices and to take corrective action. If there is a refusal to comply with the order, the Government would be authorized to seek enforcement in Federal courts.

I urge the Congress to give the Commission the power it needs to fulfill its purpose.

FEDERAL JURIES

The Magna Carta of 1215—the great English charter of liberties—established a fundamental principle of our system of criminal justice: Trial by Jury. Our

Constitution guarantees this precious right and its principles require a composition of juries that fairly represents the community.

In some Federal judicial districts this goal has not been achieved, for methods of jury selection vary sharply:

—Some selective systems do not afford Negroes or members of other minorities an adequate opportunity to serve as jurors.

—Some obtain an excessively high proportion of their jurors from the more affluent members of the community, and thus discriminate against others.

In the first session of this Congress, I proposed, and the Judicial Conference supported, a Federal jury bill. The Senate passed a bill that would require each judicial district to adopt a jury selection plan relying upon random selection, voter lists, and objective standards.

This bill guarantees a fairly chosen and representative jury in every Federal court, while retaining flexibility to allow for differing conditions in judicial districts.

I urge the House of Representatives to pass it early in this session.

STATE JURIES

Our system of justice requires fairly selected juries in state as well as Federal courts.

But under our Federal system, the states themselves have the primary duty to regulate their own judicial systems. The role of the Federal Government is to ensure that every defendant in every court receives his constitutional right to a fairly selected jury.

The Federal courts have acted to secure this right by overturning convictions when the defendant established that his jury was improperly selected. But this process—of conviction, appeal, reversal, and retrial—is burdensome on our courts, tardy in protecting the right of the defendant whose case is involved, and ineffective in changing the underlying procedure for all defendants.

The legislation I have proposed would make it unlawful to discriminate on account of race, color, religion, sex, national origin, or economic status in qualifying or selecting jurors in any state court.

The National Housing Act of 1949 proclaimed a goal for the nation. "A decent home and a suitable living environment for every American family."

We have not achieved this goal.

This year I shall send to the Congress a message dealing with our cities—calling for $1 billion for the model cities program—and calling upon the Congress, industry, and labor to join with me in a ten-year campaign to build 6 million new decent housing units for low- and middle-income families.

FAIR HOUSING

But construction of new homes is not enough—unless every family is free to purchase and rent them. Every American who wishes to buy a home, and can afford it, should be free to do so.

Segregation in housing compounds the nation's social and economic problems. When those who have the means to move out of the central city are denied the chance to do so, the result is a compression of population in the center. In that crowded ghetto, human tragedies—and crime—increase and multiply. Unemployment and educational problems are compounded—because isolation in the central city prevents minority groups from reaching schools and available jobs in other areas.

The fair housing legislation I have recommended would prohibit discrimination in the sale or rental of all housing in the United States. It would take effect in three progressive stages:

—immediately, to housing presently covered by the executive order on equal opportunity in housing;

—then, to dwellings sold or rented by a nonoccupant, and to units for five or more families;

—and finally to all housing.

It would also:

—outlaw discriminatory practices in the financing of housing, and in the services of real-estate brokers;

—bar the cynical practice of "block-busting," and prohibit intimidation of persons seeking to enjoy the rights it grants and protects;

—give responsibility for enforcement to the Secretary of Housing and Urban Development and authorize the Attorney General to bring suits against patterns or practices of housing discrimination.

A fair housing law is not a cure-all for the nation's urban problems. But ending discrimination in the sale or rental of housing is essential for social justice and social progress.

For many members of minority groups, the past decade has brought meaningful advances. But for most minorities—locked in urban ghettoes or in rural areas—economic and social progress has come slowly.

CONCLUSION

When we speak of overcoming discrimination we speak in terms of groups—Indians, Mexican-Americans, Negroes, Puerto Ricans, and other minorities. We refer to statistics, percentages, and trends.

Now is the time to remind ourselves that these are problems of individual human beings—of individual Americans:

—Housing discrimination means the Negro veteran of Vietnam cannot live in an apartment which advertises vacancies.

—Employment statistics do not describe the feeling of a Puerto Rican father who cannot earn enough to feed his children.

—No essay on the problems of the slum can reveal the thoughts of a teen-ager who believes there is no opportunity for him as a law-abiding member of society.

Last summer our nation suffered the tragedy of urban riots. Lives were lost; property was destroyed; fear and distrust divided many communities.

The prime victims of such lawlessness—as of ordinary crime—are the people of the ghettoes.

No people need or want protection—the effective nondiscriminatory exercise of the police power—more than the law-abiding majority of slum-dwellers. Like better schools, housing, and job opportunities, improved police protection is necessary for better conditions of life in the central city today. It is a vital part of our agenda for urban America.

Lawlessness must be punished—sternly and promptly.

But the criminal conduct of some must not weaken our resolve to deal with the real grievances of all those who suffer discrimination. Nothing can justify the continued denial of equal justice and opportunity to every American.

Each forward step in the battle against discrimination benefits all Americans.

I ask the Congress to take another forward step this year—by adopting this legislation fundamental to the human rights and dignity of every American.

"We have taken the bitter years
that I talked about in the early 1930s
and . . . made them into better years."
Remarks on signing the Medicare Extension Bill,
San Antonio, Texas,
April 8, 1966.

First, I want to explain that the reason Henry [Rep. Henry Gonzalez] took so much time was because I asked him to. Henry said that he had a little statement of about 2½ minutes, and I told Henry this was my day off, that this was Good Friday, that I had come to San Antonio at my own invitation. Nobody had asked me to come here. I came because I wanted to. I wanted to because I get a great deal of pleasure out of returning to the scenes of my childhood—as you can observe by my frequent visits back to the Pedernales.

And then there are other reasons, too. I wanted to see Archbishop Lucey, and I wanted to be with him today, as he has been with me for almost thirty years now.

I remember what my father said to me about public service when I was a little boy walking around following him barefooted and standing there in the hot sand of Blanco County, and squeezing the dirt up between my toes. He used to say to me, "Son, if you are to speak for people, you must know them, and if you are to represent people, you must love them."

Sometimes among our more sophisticated, self-styled intellectuals—I say self-styled advisedly; the real intellectual I am not sure would ever feel this way—some of them are more concerned with appearance than they are with achievement. They are more concerned with style than they are with mortar, brick, and concrete. They are more concerned with the trivia and the superficial than they are with the things that have really built America.

I received a good deal of my political philosophy right here in San Antonio. Before I was born, my father was writing the bill—my grandfather wrote it because my father asked him to, as he wasn't a lawyer—my father was introducing a bill and speaking to the bill that saved the Alamo. It was being torn down and a hotel would have replaced the Alamo. He got a good lady to put up enough money long enough to hold the structure until the

Legislature could pass the bill to preserve the Alamo. That was in 1905. I was born in 1908, I believe.

Thirty-five years ago I took my first train trip out of Texas and it originated here in San Antonio. I went to Washington from San Antonio as an employee of the people of San Antonio, in this district—the first time I had ever crossed the boundary of this State in a train.

It took me three days to get there, and I had a chance to do some heavy thinking en route. Hitler was on the march. We were in the depths of the Depression. We knew nothing about old age assistance or Medicare or Social Security. People were starving. Farms were being foreclosed. The hungry and the unemployed lined our streets. Most of our political leaders seemed to be oblivious to what was happening.

I remember the first slum clearance housing bill that President Roosevelt signed. I was one of two Congressmen at that signing ceremony. I guess that is the reason I have always liked these signing ceremonies since.

I remember the first project under that bill came to Texas where people could have public housing, cheap housing, clean housing, decent housing, for their children to sleep in.

We had a three-bedroom home with a living room—dining room combination, a kitchen and a bath, for $14 a month. It was the cheapest constructed project in the United States and the cheapest rent.

Today I have great pride in it. That is why I am working so hard to get some more housing under our supplemental rent subsidy.

I remember Archbishop Lucey, and he wasn't nearly as respectable then as he is now—he was kind of a Bolshevik in the minds of a lot of people when he came down here—I remember his writing me and quarreling and fussing and just doing everything that he could do to try to help do something for these women that were picking pecans in San Antonio for 8 cents an hour, poor women working all day for 60 cents picking pecans, 8 cents an hour.

That is why I was one of three Congressmen from Texas that signed the petition back in the 1930s to force a vote to discharge a committee, to bring the wage and hour bill out, a bill that would guarantee not 8 cents an hour but the magnificent sum of 25 cents an hour. Only three Texans signed that petition and two of them got defeated at the next election. I just point that up, that was a 25-cent minimum wage bill, to show you how far we have come.

I have a recommendation before the Congress now for $1.60.

Maury Maverick voted for that 25 cents and W. D. McFarlane voted for it, and both of them got beaten in the next election.

I remember the Social Security Act that we are talking about today. When they called the roll on it, I believe it was in 1935, I remember a good friend of mine was worrying about whether he should vote for it or not. He said, "It is socialism. They are going to destroy our system of government."

I pled with him not for minutes but for hours in the Speaker's office, trying to convince him that it was a constructive and far-reaching measure.

I remember up here by the Maverick Cafeteria in downtown San Antonio, standing out there in 1935 and seeing little Mexican children go up to the garbage can outside of that cafeteria and take the grapefruit hulls out of that garbage can and try to get enough food in their body to sustain them by hulling the hulls. I saw that with my own eyes and I have not forgotten it.

I came back here again today to see how the people of San Antonio live, because I can't forget that you can't speak for them if you don't know them, and you can't represent them if you don't love them.

So I told Henry I wanted him to take whatever time he needed. If any of you want to leave you can leave. If any of you are in a hurry you can go on. I stay in a hurry all the time. I am back home now and I am not going to hurry. I am going to do what I like to do. This great city has meant a lot to me, not only in my political philosophy, but a good deal of other philosophy. Here is where I was married, and here is where I have been elected. I would never have been in the United States Senate except for the people of San Antonio. In the first primary I lost this county by 12,000 votes, and that is before they really realized how tough the election was on the West Side. In the second primary I carried it by 99, instead of losing it by 12,000. That gave me the great victory of 87 in the entire State of Texas. I remember that. I see a lot of the veterans of that campaign here.

I am so proud of San Antonio because of your interest in human beings, in humanity, and in good, constructive causes that advance the best interest of the people—p-e-e-p-u-l—the poor people of this country.

There is not one single Congressman in the House of Representatives of 435, including the Speaker, the Leader, and the Whip, that has a better record than Henry Gonzalez, and I am so proud of him. I am proud that I have had enough courage to come here before he was a Congressman, when he was a defeated candidate a time or two, and speak for him after President Eisenhower had come in ahead of me to speak on the other side, and to do what little I could to express my faith in Henry. He has justified it every month since.

For your own personal information, I will say he is one Congressman that has never had his arm twisted even the slightest. I have never called him on the telephone and asked for his vote or told him how I would like him to vote, and I have never allowed anybody else to do it, because it is a pure waste of time. Henry was born and grew up and learned how to vote before he ever came to Washington. When you get men like that, you don't have to call them.

We come here now to sign this bill today, and I come with both a pledge and a plea. My plea is that one and one-third million Americans that are over sixty-five years of age are not yet covered by Medicare. The pledge is to those citizens who missed the March 31st deadline, just past, and did not enroll in the Medicare, that now, under this legislation, they will have until May 31st to sign up because of what Henry, Senator Yarborough, and members of the House did in passing this bill we will sign this morning.

I want to ask each of you to make it your personal job not to come to me or to Henry a few years from now and say they just forgot to sign up, or they didn't hear about it, but for you to go out and have them sign up now while they have the time and while they can qualify.

The plea is that these citizens contact their local Social Security offices and consider signing up for the valuable protection that the Medicare law will give them.

I plead with every American to go and talk to your neighbors, because there are 1,300,000 of them that are going to miss the boat; there are 1,300,000 of them who should get their rights under the law now. In order to do that, they must sign up. So each good American should accept this personal challenge to ask every person they know over sixty-five, "Have you registered? If not, register at once."

There was a wise old Frenchman one time who said, "Growing older is no more than a bad habit which a busy man had no time to form." So this morning I urge every American to exercise his right to acquire this protection.

My friends here in this beautiful Victoria Plaza, you are a model for the rest of the citizens of this Nation. I think that those guests this morning should know that every single man and woman who lives here is already registered for Medicare.

Since I signed the Medicare and Social Security amendments last July in

Independence, Missouri, in the presence of that great Democratic President, and his wife, Harry S. Truman—you will remember that President Truman was the first President who actively urged this particular program—since that time, almost 17 million Americans, almost nine out of every ten of our older citizens, have already enrolled for medical insurance coverage. Getting 17 million to do something from July to now is a man-sized job, itself. But we still have 1,300,000 to go. And I am not going to let you forget it until we get every one of them signed up. Our work is not going to be completed until we are sure that everyone who can use the protection of this program has joined it. Every older American must have the opportunity to live out his life in security without the fear that serious illness will be accompanied by a financial ruin.

That is what Medicare is all about. What to do? How to live? Who will pay the doctor? Who will pay the hospital? Who will pay for the medicine? Who will pay the rent? Well, these are questions that older Americans that I have known all my life had dreaded to answer. Now Medicare is changing a lot of that.

There is hope because we respect the dignity of the individual. I thought that some of our sophisticated folks might say this morning that Henry was introducing too many people. That is why I told him to take all the time he wanted. But that just shows how he feels about human beings. He didn't want one single person to be neglected. He wanted to recognize the dignity of every person here because they might be pretty unimportant to a stranger but they are not unimportant to Henry or to me. They lead our people and provide for them.

So I think we must have hope and we must recognize that there is in the place of charity now dignity, and where the children, the kinfolks, the public agencies were the sole reliance just a few months ago, you now can have self-respect and realize that the machinery of government and the methods that we have evolved, the contributions of the individuals and the Government altogether—you can now have self-respect and still provide for your medical bills and your medicine, your nursing care, and things of that kind.

We have taken the bitter years that I talked about in the early 1930s and I think we have made them better years. In the doing, we have reclaimed, I think, a lot of lost pride and we have given a lot of new meaning to tomorrow.

As I sign this bill today, I am determined to do more. I don't think we must ever be satisfied in this growing, adventuresome country of America

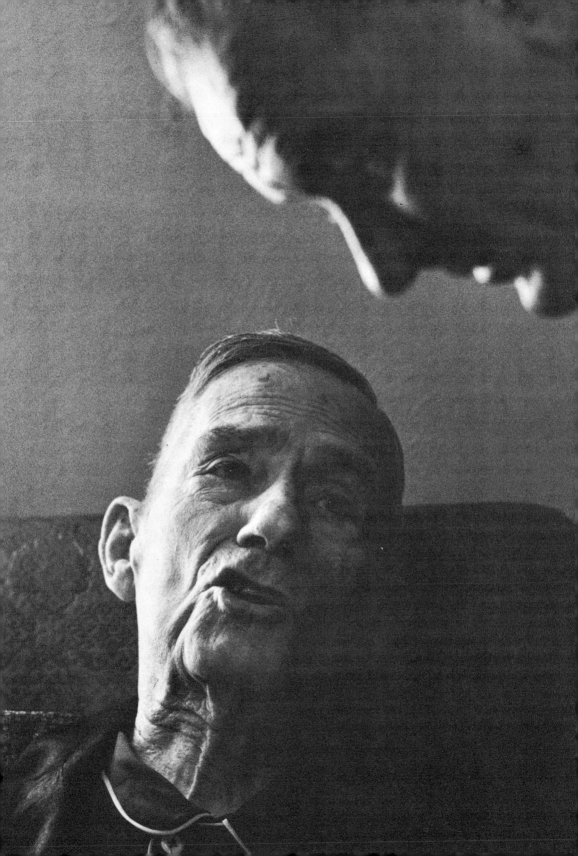

with the status quo. We must be determined to do more, because there is always going to be more that needs to be done.

Since I became President a little over two years ago, I have already signed and approved laws increasing Social Security benefits by more than $1½ billion; increases of more than $1½ billion, an increase of in the neighborhood of 7 percent. Yet too many of our older citizens are still trying to get along on income that is too small now to meet their needs, even though we have increased it 7 percent in two years.

So Social Security benefits which are the main source of their income still need to be increased, and they will be increased in the years ahead. Only by recognizing the facts of life can we really make it better for people that are over sixty-five.

Social Security protection must be improved for our disabled workers and their families. Several weeks ago I asked the Secretary of Health, Education and Welfare, Mr. John W. Gardner, to complete his study as soon as possible on improving the benefits and the financial structure of the Social Security program. I asked Secretary Gardner to develop sound and workable plans for these changes at as early a date as possible.

I will let you in on a secret: I intend to make these recommendations to the next session of Congress, and I expect you folks to have Henry back up there to help me get them passed.

I can't tell you about all the recommendations because we are now studying them. I want you to study them and let us hear from you. But this is what I would like to do: I would like to increase insurance benefits across the board for 21 million beneficiaries, the aged, the disabled, the widows, and the orphans, including an increase in the monthly minimum, the monthly maximum, and the total family benefits. That is what I would like to do.

We don't have a dictatorship, so no man can mash a button and get it done, but that is what I would like to do, what I hope to do, and with your help and with God's help, that is what we will do.

I would like to improve insurance protection for the widows and the orphans. I would like to keep our Social Security and public welfare programs up to date in relation to increased earnings. I would like for our individuals now on welfare rolls to be provided additional incentives for them to find work.

And Medicare need not just be for people over sixty-five. That is where we started.

Archbishop, you know, I have been wondering for some time now why we shouldn't bring our compassion and our concern to bear not just on people over sixty-five but upon our young children under six.

The President of an African country told me the other day—I had lunch with a bunch of their ambassadors yesterday and we discussed it again—in their country that one out of three babies born dies with measles, and the United States of America had come in with one of our most modern twentieth-century machines and had vaccinated 750,000 little children. The President of this African country said to me, "We men may not always like some of the things you in America do, but our women would never let us criticize them because since you vaccinated those 750,000 children we have not lost one from measles."

The satisfaction that I get from believing that we in America saved the lives of 250,000 little children is a satisfaction that never comes from a paycheck or a greenback.

I want to let you in on another secret: that is one of the reasons I asked John Gardner, because of my concern for these young folks—the Secretary of Health, Education and Welfare—to create new plans for a new program that you haven't heard before, to assist in financing dental services for children.

Luci spent all the way down here this morning fussing at me because I didn't say eye services for children. Luci was almost ready to get married before she found out she couldn't read very well, that she had had something wrong with her eyes since she was a child. When she corrected it, and found it out, it was reflected the next month in her grades, and I think in her looks. She not only couldn't see how to read well, but she couldn't see how to look well.

So we are going to have these new plans and we are going to have these new programs. We are going to someday point out that we started them right here at this scene this morning. We are never going to stop trying to find new ways to make Medicare sensitive to what our people need, and make it sensitive to what we ought to do to lift the quality of life in this land and this world.

I have three minutes to get to church and I want to conclude by saying this, because this is one of things that the church does, and does so well: I am not interested in building skyscrapers, or moving mountains, or pouring concrete. Those are all necessary in the modern world of communication and industrialization, and so forth. But since I have become President we have increased our expenditure for educating the mind from a little less than $5 billion to over $10 billion in two and a half years. We have more than doubled it.

We have increased our expenditures on health from a little under $5 billion—we were spending $1 billion when President Kennedy came into office —to a little over $10 billion this year. This is part of it here. It is more than double. So $10 billion extra this year goes into the mind and the body. Considering our loans, our grants, our aid, and our Public Law 480, and other things, we are spending additional billions on food.

So when everything else is gone and forgotten, I hope the people will remember that in this year of our Lord 1966, on Good Friday, we met here as neighbors and friends, and we concerned ourselves about human beings, and we dedicated whatever time is left for us, we dedicated our efforts and our talents to freeing the ignorant from the chains of ignorance and illiteracy, and teaching them to read and write, and to learn.

Whatever time is allotted us, we have tried to remove disease from the skins and the bodies of our people, and we have tried to find food to give them nourishment and to give them strength.

If I am ever to be remembered by any of you here, I want to be remembered as one who spent his whole life trying to get more people more to eat and more to wear, to live longer, to have medicine and have attention, nursing, hospitals and doctors' care when they need it, and to have their children have a chance to go to school and carry out really what the Declaration of Independence says: "All men are created equal."

But they are not equal if they don't have a chance to read and write, and they don't have a chance for a doctor to take care of their teeth or their eyes when they are little and their parents don't know about it.

So that is the purpose of our being here this morning. Sometime we are going to come back here and take stock, as the country merchant says, and see what progress we have made. There has been a revolution in this country and in the world in the last few years. I hope that the years of 1964, 1965, 1966, 1967, and 1968 will show that we moved ahead, that we made progress, that we weren't just concerned with what was in our platform, but we were concerned with what we did about it; that we just weren't concerned with style and appearance, we were concerned with achievement; that we weren't just concerned with talking about medical care for twenty years, we wanted to sign it and put it into effect; that we weren't interested in talking about people that didn't have homes and didn't have roofs over their heads, and all these eloquent phrases that get you elected to office, but what we are concerned about is what did you do about it after you were elected.

Well, here is what we did about it, just one little place; and here is what we are doing about it, just another little place.

We are going to continue to do it every day as long as we have the authority and this mission.

"The safety and security of its citizens is the first duty of Government."
Message to Congress on Crime and Law Enforcement, March 9, 1966.

Crime—the fact of crime and the fear of crime—marks the life of every American.

We know its unrelenting pace:

—a forcible rape every twenty-six minutes,

—a robbery every five minutes,

—an aggravated assault every three minutes,

—a car theft every minute,

— a burglary every twenty-eight seconds.

We know its cost in dollars—some $27 billion annually.

We know the cost it inflicts on thousands—in death, injury, suffering, and anguish.

We know the still more widespread cost it exacts from millions in fear:

—fear that can turn us into a nation of captives imprisoned nightly behind chained doors, double locks, barred windows;

—fear that can make us afraid to walk city streets by night or public parks by day.

These are costs a truly free people cannot tolerate.

The war against crime may be slowing its increase for the moment. The most recent report of the Federal Bureau of Investigation shows a 5 percent increase for 1965, compared to a 13 percent increase for 1964.

But we can take little comfort from such facts. We must not only slow, but stop—and ultimately reverse—the rate of crime increase.

The entire nation is united in concern over crime. The entire nation shares in the resolution to deal effectively with crime. But national concern is not enough. National resolution is not enough.

We must match our will with wisdom. We must match our determination with effective action.

The safety and security of its citizens is the first duty of government.

Today, therefore, I call on the Congress and the nation to join in a three-stage national strategy against crime, welding together the efforts of local, state, and Federal governments.

WHAT WE HAVE DONE

This Administration—with the support of this Congress—is committed to assist local authorities. For the first time in our history, an Administration has pledged to the American people that the growth of crime—local, state, and national—will be checked.

We are working in a creative Federal partnership to fulfill that pledge.

1. The Law Enforcement Assistance Act, passed last fall, provides a sound foundation upon which we can now build. Under its imaginative scope, we have already launched local and Federal action—generations overdue—to modernize not only police work but all aspects of the system of criminal justice.

2. The Prisoner Rehabilitation Act, passed last fall, is the most significant legislative reform in modern American penology. Hundreds of prisoners already are working in daytime jobs as they finish their sentences at night. They are learning job skills that will bring dignity to themselves and support to their families.

3. The National Crime Commission and the District of Columbia Crime Commission, established last year, have launched searching studies into the causes of crime and our present shortcomings in dealing with it.

4. The Federal Bureau of Investigation is expanding its National Academy sixfold. It will soon be able to train 1,200 rather than 200 law enforcement officials each year. It will provide special training for an additional 1,000 officers.

5. Federal efforts against organized crime have continued to increase. Racketeering indictments last year rose to a record 674, compared with 535 in 1964 and only 19 in 1960.

A Unified Attack

These programs are only initial steps on a long road. But they advance us far enough to see down that road more clearly.

And the plainest fact we can see is that piecemeal improvements will not be enough.

The need is not new. We have simply failed to meet it.

Despite the warnings of our law enforcement officials, years of public neglect have too often left the law enforcement system without necessary resources and public support.

Despite the devotion of our law enforcement officials, our law enforcement system does not deter enough of those who can be deterred. It does not detect and convict enough of those who cannot be deterred. It does not restore enough rehabilitated offenders into the law-abiding community.

Despite the dedication of our law enforcement officials, reforms too often defeat themselves because they do not go far enough.

There is a fundamental lesson we have too often ignored.

The problems of crime and law enforcement are closely interrelated.

One interlocking tie is within the very system of law enforcement.

Making police more effective is fruitless—if we continue to permit the overburdening of judges and the clogging of courts.

Increasing the number of judges is futile—if the number of competent prosecutors and defense attorneys remains inadequate.

An expanded judiciary cannot take advantage of modern thinking in sentencing—if new correctional facilities are not provided.

The best correctional programs will fail—if legitimate avenues of employment are forever closed to reformed offenders.

A second interlocking tie between all law enforcement problems is geographical.

Crime does not observe neat, jurisdictional lines between city, county, state, and Federal governments.

Failure of a correctional system in one state may have a decided impact on the crime rate in another.

Shortcomings in Federal or state law enforcement make more difficult the work of a city police department in its fight against racketeering.

Devoted police work in a city is of little consequence if it merely drives criminals to the adjacent county.

To improve in one field we must improve in all. To improve in one part of the country we must improve in all parts.

We must mobilize all of the resources of our creative Federal system if we are to repel the threat of crime to our common well-being. The problems of crime bring us together. We must make a common response. There is no other way.

Our National Strategy

Even as we join in common action, we know there can be no instant victory. We face an immense journey. Ancient evils do not yield to easy conquest. Modern criminology has yet to light many corridors.

We cannot limit our efforts to enemies we can see. We must, with equal resolve, seek out new knowledge, new techniques, and new understanding.

In the battle against crime, unity can give us strength. But strength can give us victory only if it is joined with a bold and clear plan for the future as well as the present.

I propose a three-stage national strategy.

The first stage is an agenda for immediate action. These are the legislative steps we already know are needed—steps that should be taken without hesitation or delay.

The second stage is development of a comprehensive agenda of direct steps based on experiment and assessment for the future.

The third stage is a still broader agenda, an attack not only against crime directly, but against the roots from which it springs.

These three stages involve varying resources and commitments. But we must proceed on each of them with equal force—and we must do so now.

FIRST: THE IMMEDIATE ATTACK

Each of the four aspects of law enforcement calls for reform. There are steps we can now take.

A. To Improve Crime Prevention and Detection

We must improve the quality of local law enforcement throughout the country.

The front-line soldier in the war on crime is the local law enforcement officer. Federal aid to law enforcement at the state and local level was made possible by the Law Enforcement Assistance Act of 1965. Police, court, correctional, and university authorities have responded to the newly created Office of Law Enforcement Assistance with hundreds of imaginative ideas and proposals.

A number of projects are now under way:

—The management methods of modern industry will be adapted to law enforcement problems in a new management institute for police chiefs.

—Several New England states are combining their efforts in police training by establishing the first regional leadership school in the nation.

—The first intensive national training institute for state directors of corrections will bring the advice of experts to all states in their efforts to break the cycle of criminal repeaters.

In support of these programs and the many others to follow, I am asking Congress to increase appropriations for the Law Enforcement Assistance Act from $7.2 to $13.7 million.

Even seeking the most imaginative reforms, however, underscores a fundamental truth: how well a job is done depends on the training and ability of the men who do it.

I have directed the Attorney General to:

—make grants to states, cities, and colleges and universities to elevate and intensify the training of law enforcement officers;

—provide grants for a management exchange program, enabling police officials to travel to other departments for on-the-spot studies of promising and effective approaches;

—provide grants to establish closed-circuit television training programs to teach basic police subjects. The first such program, involving over two hundred locations in a single state, is being launched now;

—establish an award program, in consultation with state and local officials, giving annual public recognition to outstanding police officers and others who make notable contributions to the field of law enforcement.

I recommend legislation to establish a program to send selected police officers to approved colleges and universities for a year of intensive professional study.

I recommend a loan forgiveness program under the National Defense Education Act for students who wish to enter the law enforcement profession.

If crime is to be controlled, we must control the weapons with which so many crimes are committed.

We must end the easy availability of deadly weapons to professional criminals, to delinquent youth, and to the disturbed and deranged.

We must stop the flow of firearms into dangerous hands.

It is not enough to say that gun control is a state responsibility. States with gun control laws now stand helplessly by while those laws are flouted daily by the unchecked sales of guns by mail.

Our Federal responsibility is clear. It is promptly to enact legislation, such as S. 1592, to regulate and control interstate traffic in dangerous firearms.

The front pages of our newspapers make us acutely aware of the human tragedies that flow daily from the unchecked purchase of firearms. Recent congressional hearings added abundant evidence of the gravity of his problem.

There is no need to curtail the right of citizens to keep arms for such traditional pastimes as hunting and marksmanship. But there is a pressing need to halt blind, unquestioned mail-order sales of guns, and over-the-counter sales to buyers from out of state whose credentials cannot be known.

Only the Federal Government can give the several states and cities their first real chance to enforce their own gun laws. We must do so without further delay. . . .

B. To Facilitate the Prosecution of Criminals

We must intensify our campaign against organized crime.

The most flagrant manifestation of crime in America is organized crime. It erodes our very system of justice—in all spheres of government.

It is bad enough for individuals to turn to crime because they are misguided or desperate.

It is intolerable that corporations of corruption should systematically flaunt our laws.

This concern already is deeply shared by Congress. Statutes enacted in recent years have greatly strengthened Federal authority to deal with racketeering. But another legislative tool is required.

Organized crime will stop at nothing to escape detection and prosecution. Torture and murder of witnesses, efforts to bribe prosecutors and jurors—these are not shocking exceptions. They are familiar racketeering techniques.

Such methods not only make it harder to prosecute racketeers—they poison the system of law enforcement itself. They require a strong antidote, and an important one is now pending in both Houses.

This legislation would expand the authority of the Department of Justice to immunize hostile but knowledgeable witnesses against prosecution and thereby enable them to testify without incriminating themselves.

Such immunity is already provided in laws covering a number of crimes. The pending legislation would extend it to such racketeering crimes as bribery, graft, bankruptcy fraud, jury-tampering, and other schemes for the obstruction of justice.

We Must Modernize Our Criminal Laws.

I propose the appointment of a commission to conduct a comprehensive review of all the Federal criminal laws and to recommend total revision by 1968.

A number of our criminal laws are obsolete. Many are inconsistent in their efforts to make the penalty fit the crime. Many—which treat essentially the same crimes—are scattered in a crazy-quilt patchwork throughout our criminal code.

The commission will be composed of outstanding Americans, including members of the Congress, officials of the Executive branch, jurists and members of the bar. This commission will bring to us the modern and rational criminal code.

We are a Nation dedicated to the precepts of justice, the rule of law, and the dignity of man. Our criminal code should be worthy of those ideals.

C. To Enhance Justice in Our Courts

We must reform our bail system.

The administration of criminal justice must be fair as well as effective.

Whether a person, released after arrest, is likely to flee before trial or endanger society is not determined by the wealth he commands. Yet all too often we imprison men for weeks, months, and even years—before we give them their day in court—solely because they cannot afford bail.

Effective law enforcement does not require such imprisonment.

To correct this injustice, I urge the Congress to complete action on the pending Federal Bail Reform Act and to give favorable consideration to the District of Columbia Bail Agency Bill.

These measures will ensure fairness. They will provide an enlightened model for those states and communities which have not already undertaken bail reform.

D. To Reclaim and Rehabilitate Lives in Our Prisons

We must establish a rational, coordinated correctional system.

No national strategy against crime can succeed if we do not restore more of our first offenders to productive society. The best law enforcement has little value if prison sentences are only temporary and embittering way stations for men whose release means a return to crime.

Today that situation is all too prevalent. In the Federal system, 30 percent of all parolees revert to crime. In most state systems the percentage is substantially higher. The task of breaking this cycle must be part of our program.

At present, we administer the prison, parole, and probation functions partly in the Executive branch and partly in the Judicial branch. I believe the effectiveness of our corrections programs depends on a rational, coordinated, and unified approach.

Consolidating Federal correctional efforts can reduce the number of repeaters.

It can strengthen the training and performance of correctional officials.

It can produce a career service of the highest professional order.

I recommend that the Federal prison, parole, and probation functions be unified within the Department of Justice to consolidate our presently fragmented correctional system.

We must capitalize on the beginning already made in rehabilitating prisoners.

The importance of up-to-date vocational training for inmates is clear. Chronic underemployment often goes hand in hand with crime. In our Federal prisons, one of every three prisoners worked less than six months of the two years before confinement.

I am, therefore, directing the Secretary of Labor to develop effective ways to provide correctional institutions with job information for "good risk" parolees.

I am also directing the Chairman of the Civil Service Commission to reexamine the policies of all Federal departments and agencies regarding the hiring of released "good risk" offenders. I am asking him to prepare progressive and effective policies to deal fairly and sensibly with them. I urge the states, local governments, and private industry to do the same.

We must deal realistically with drug addiction.

Drug addiction is a double curse. It saps life from the afflicted. It drives its victims to commit untold crimes to secure the means to support their addiction.

Drug addiction has been a matter of Federal concern for more than a half-century. The Bureau of Narcotics has pursued its enforcement duties energetically and effectively. Seizure of illegal narcotics and marijuana rose 62 percent from 1962 to 1965.

But our continued insistence on treating drug addicts, once apprehended, as criminals, is neither humane nor effective. It has neither curtailed addiction nor prevented crime.

Recognizing this, we have proposed legislation to authorize the civil commitment of certain addicts, while retaining full criminal sanctions against those who peddle and sell narcotics.

This measure can reclaim lives. It can begin to eliminate the driving hunger for drugs that leads so many into lives of crime and degradation.

I urge Congress to enact this legislation.

The Federal Government seeks to share its knowledge, its experience and its research in this area. I have already asked the Secretary of Treasury to develop materials which will enable local law enforcement organizations to train in far less time a far greater number of specialists in narcotics control.

I am today directing the Secretary of the Treasury to establish clinics in those cities where narcotics addition is most prevalent to help train local law enforcement officials.

By enacting the Drug Abuse Control Amendments of 1965, Congress has demonstrated its concern over the illegal flow of non-narcotic drugs. Traffic in these drugs offers a new source of income to the underworld and threatens our young people.

By these amendments, Congress has provided new weapons in the control of this traffic, and this Administration will use them with determination. *In my 1967 Budget, I propose to double the funds for this program.*

SECOND: A COMPREHENSIVE AGENDA

These various proposals are only beginning steps. If we knew today of measures to deal more effectively with crime, we would seek to adopt them. But we do not yet have the answers.

We must press forward for greater knowledge, better tools, and deeper insights. This is the task on which the National Crime Commisssion has already embarked. The Commission is composed of nineteen distinguished citizens, judges, law enforcement officers, and other experts.

It is engaged in some forty projects with state and local authorities.

It is drawing on the services of more than two hundred of the nation's leading police chiefs, judges, sociologists, and other specialists.

The Commission is

—surveying key American cities to learn where and when certain kinds of crime are committed, and which people are most likely to become victims. Such facts—now largely unknown—are essential to intelligent police work;

—consulting 2,200 law enforcement agencies to identify successful police methods developed by local initiative and imagination. Communities every-where should know about and benefit from these methods;

—seeking new ways to break the logjams in our criminal courts, where crowded calendars are a daily reminder that too often justice delayed is justice denied;

—analyzing alternatives to traditional, costly—and unsuccessful—prison sentences, in the effort to reclaim young first offenders and break the spiral of repeated crime;

—studying the sources of public respect and support for local police and police attitudes toward all segments of the community. Without mutual respect, effective law enforcement is not possible;

—exploring, in conjunction with the Law Enforcement Assistance Office, how to bring the remarkable advances of modern science to effective application in law enforcement.

The computer has revolutionized record keeping in modern industry. Surely it can do as much for criminal records.

Modern electronics has made it possible to summon a doctor from his seat at the opera. Surely it can do as much to make police instantly responsive to public needs.

And there may well be yet unimagined contributions which science can bring to the field of law enforcement.

The Commission's final report, due next year, can help provide specific blueprints for our national strategy. Its work will help replace the crutches of slogans, habits, and reflex with the firm support of knowledge and fact.

No matter how creative or detailed the blueprint we develop, we cannot succeed without parallel concentration by state and local authorities. They must undertake detailed planning of their own for reforms that take account of their own special strengths, needs, and traditions.

Some states and cities have already begun to do so. There is much for us to learn from them. But in many areas, there is no such broad planning, no recognition of the need for a unified attack on crime.

Therefore, I am asking the Attorney General to work with the governors of the fifty states to establish statewide committees on law enforcement and criminal justice.

Such state committees can assist—and be assisted by—the National Commission. They can stimulate the growth of public involvement and the development of a comprehensive anticrime agenda in every part of the country.

THIRD: ATTACKING CRIME AT THE ROOTS

A century ago, Thoreau wrote that "There are a thousand hacking at the branches of evil to one who is striking at the root." So it remains today.

The efforts I have described—more effective police action, more efficient courts, improved corrections, comprehensive planning for major reform—all are urgently needed.

And yet all of them together can permit us only to strike more quickly and surely at the branches. The roots of crime will remain.

An effective strategy against crime must also rest on a base of prevention. And that base can come only from action against the wellsprings of crime in our society.

Our commitment to ensuring social justice and personal dignity for all Americans does not flow from a desire to fight crime. We are committed to those goals because they are right.

But social conditions which foster a sense of injustice or exploitation also breed crime. More than thirty years ago, Clarence Darrow observed:

> It is very seldom that anyone is in prison for an ordinary crime unless early in life he entered a path that almost invariably led to the prison gate. Most of the inmates are the children of the poor. In many instances they are either orphans or half-orphans; their homes were the streets and byways of big cities, and their paths naturally and inevitably took them to their final fate.

The programs now under way to eliminate the degradation of poverty, the decay of our cities, the disgrace of racial discrimination, the despair of illiteracy—are all vitally important to crime prevention.

At the same time, even as we seek to fight crime by fighting injustice, the ways we deal with crime should not foster further injustice:

—Bail requirements need not add families to the welfare rolls.

—Court procedures need not increase a sense of unfair and differential treatment.

—Sentencing practices need not require that the poor go to jail while others pay fines.

—Imprisonment need not result in loss of job skills.

Social injustice is not the sole reason for crime. Social justice is not the sole cure.

Even the broadest social programs cannot be panaceas. The lives and attitudes of persons long neglected do not change upon command. The effects of even the most energetic programs may be long in coming. The vast majority of our citizens who suffer poverty and discrimination do not turn to crime.

But where legitimate opportunities are closed, illegitimate opportunities are seized.

Whatever opens opportunity and hope will help to prevent crime and foster responsibility.

Effective law enforcement and social justice must be pursued together, as the foundation of our efforts against crime.

The proposals I am making today will not solve the problem of crime in this country. The war on crime will be waged by our children and our children's children. But the difficulty and complexity of the problem cannot be permitted to lead us to despair. They must lead us rather to bring greater efforts, greater ingenuity, and greater determination to do battle.

*"Our task is to rise above the debate
between the rights of the individual
and the rights of the society,
by securing . . . the rights of both."*
The President signs the Bail Reform Act of 1966,
June 22, 1966.

Our Nation stands today at the threshold of a new era in our system of criminal justice. Those of you who have come here this morning—and scores of others like you throughout this great land of ours—are the mind and the force of this new era.

Today we join to recognize a major development in our entire system of criminal justice—the reform of the bail system.

This system has endured—archaic, unjust, and virtually unexamined—ever since the Judiciary Act of 1789.

Because of the bail system, the scales of justice have been weighted for almost two centuries not with fact, nor law, nor mercy. They have been weighted with money.

But now, because of the Bail Reform Act of 1966, which an understanding and just Congress has enacted and which I will shortly sign, we can begin to ensure that defendants are considered as individuals—and not as dollar signs.

The principal purpose of bail is to ensure that an accused person will return for trial, if he is released after arrest.

How is that purpose met under the present system? The defendant with means can afford to pay bail. He can afford to buy his freedom. But the poorer defendant cannot pay the price. He languishes in jail weeks, months, and perhaps even years before trial.

He does not stay in jail because he is guilty.

He does not stay in jail because any sentence has been passed.

He does not stay in jail because he is any more likely to flee before trial.

He stays in jail for one reason only—because he is poor.

There are hundreds, perhaps thousands, of illustrations of how the bail system has inflicted arbitrary cruelty:

—A man was jailed on a serious charge brought last Christmas Eve. He could not afford bail so he spent 101 days in jail until he could get a hearing. Then the complainant admitted that the charge was false.

—A man could not raise $300 for bail. He spent fifty-four days in jail waiting trial for a traffic offense for which he could have been sentenced to no more than five days.

—A man spent two months in jail before being acquitted. In that period, he lost his job, he lost his car, he lost his family—it was split up. He did not find another job, following that, for four months.

In addition to such injustices as I have pointed out, the present bail system has meant very high public costs that the taxpayer must bear for detaining prisoners prior to their trial.

What is most shocking about these costs—to both individuals and to the public—is that they are totally unnecessary.

First proof of that fact came because of really one man's outrage against injustice. I am talking now of Mr. Louis Schweitzer, who pioneered the development of a substitute for the money bail system by establishing the Vera Foundation and the Manhattan bail project.

The lesson of that project was simple. If a judge is given adequate information, he, the judge, can determine that many defendants can be released without any need for money bail. They will return faithfully for trial.

So this legislation, for the first time, requires that the decision to release a man prior to the trial be based on facts—like community and family ties and past record, and not on his bank account. In the words of the act, "A man, regardless of his financial status—shall not needlessly be detained . . . when detention serves neither the ends of justice nor the public interest."

And it specifies that he be released without money bond whenever that is justified by the facts. Under this act, judges would—for the first time—be required to use a flexible set of conditions, matching different types of releases to different risks.

These are steps that can be taken, we think, without harming law enforcement in any manner.

This measure does not require that every arrested person be released.

It does not restrict the power of the courts to detain dangerous persons in capital cases or after conviction.

What this measure does do is to eliminate needless, arbitrary cruelty.

What it does do, in my judgment, is to greatly enlarge justice in this land of ours.

So our task is to rise above the debate betwen the rights of the individual and the rights of the society, by securing and really protecting the rights of both.

I want to personally thank Senator Ervin, Congressman Celler, the Attorney General, the members of the Justice Department, and his predecessors who worked on this legislation. I also want to thank the able and distinguished leadership of all members of the Senate and the House Judiciary Committees, and the other members of those two bodies, for what I consider very fine work in making this legislation a reality.

I am proud now, as a major step forward, to sign the Bail Reform Act of 1966 into the law of the land.

"Ignorance, ill health, personality disorder —our Nation must rid itself of this bitter inheritance."

Message to Congress on America's children and youth, February 8, 1967.

In 1905, this Nation hummed with industrial growth—and Jane Addams discovered a boy of five working for a living by night in a cotton mill.

Thirteen percent of the laborers then in the cotton trade were child laborers. All across the Nation, in glass factories, in mines, in canneries, and on the streets, more than 2 million children under sixteen worked—full time.

Slowly, what Theodore Roosevelt called "public sentiment, with its corrective power" stirred and raised a cry for action.

"The interests of this nation," President Roosevelt declared to Congress in 1909, "are involved in the welfare of children no less than in our great national affairs."

By 1912, the Federal Children's Bureau was established. The long battle to end child labor moved toward victory. Congress had pledged its power to the care and protection of America's young people.

Upon that pledge, the Congress, the Executive Branch, and the states have built public policy—and public programs—ever since.

In the past three years, I have recommended and you in the Congress have enacted legislation that has done more for our young people than in any other period in history:

—Head Start and other preschool programs are providing learning and health care to more than 2 million children.

—The Elementary and Secondary Education Act is improving the education of more than 7 million poor children.

—Our Higher Education Programs support more than one million students in college—students who might otherwise not have been able to go.

—The Neighborhood Youth Corps, the Job Corps, and an expanded Manpower Development and Training Program are bringing skills to almost one million young Americans who only a few years ago would have been condemned to the ranks of the unemployed.

—The Medicaid program is now extending better medical service to millions of poor children.

In fiscal 1960, the Federal Government invested about $3.5 billion in America's children and youth. In fiscal 1965 that investment rose to $7.3 billion. In fiscal 1968 it will increase to over $11.5 billion—more than three times the amount the Government was spending eight years ago.

We are a young Nation. Nearly half our people are twenty-five or under—and much of the courage and vitality that bless this land are the gift of young citizens.

The Peace Corps volunteer in Bolivia, the Teachers Corps volunteer in a Chicago slum, the young Marine offering up his courage—and his life—in Vietnam: these are the Boy Scouts, the 4-H Club members, the high-school athletes of only a few years ago. What they are able to offer the world as citizens depends on what their Nation offered them as youngsters.

Knowing this, we seek to strengthen American families. We also seek to strengthen our alliance with state and local governments. The future of many of our children depends on the work of local public health services, school boards, the local child welfare agencies, and local community action agencies.

Recent studies confirm what we have long suspected. In education, in health, in all of human development, the early years are the critical years. Ignorance, ill health, personality disorder—these are disabilities often contracted in childhood: afflictions which linger to cripple the man and damage the next generation.

Our nation must rid itself of this bitter inheritance. Our goal must be clear—to give every child the chance to fulfill his promise.

Much remains to be done to move toward this goal. Today, no less than in the early years of this century, America has an urgent job to do for its young.

Even during these years of unparalleled prosperity:

—Five million and five hundred thousand children under six, and 9 million more under seventeen, live in families too poor to feed and house them adequately.

—This year one million babies, one in every four, will be born to mothers who receive little or no obstetric care.

—More than 4 million children will suffer physical handicaps and another 2 million will fall victim to preventable accidents or disease.

—One million young Americans, most of them from poor families, will drop out of school this year—many to join the unhappy legion of the unemployed.

—One in every six young men under eighteen will be taken to juvenile court for at least one offense this year.

Our nation can help to cure these social ills if once again, as in the past, we pledge our continuing stewardship of our greatest wealth—our young people.

I recommend a twelve-point program for the children and youth of America. With the help of the Congress, we can:

1. Preserve the hope and opportunity of Head Start by a "Follow-Through" program in the early grades.

2. Strengthen Head Start by extending its reach to younger children.

3. Begin a pilot lunch program to reach preschool children who now lack proper nourishment.

4. Create child and parent centers in areas of acute poverty to provide modern and comprehensive family and child development services.

5. Help the states train specialists—now in critically short supply—to deal with problems of children and youth.

6. Strengthen and modernize programs providing aid for children in poor families.

7. Increase Social Security payments for 3 million children, whose support has been cut off by the death, disability, or retirement of their parents.

8. Expand our programs for early diagnosis and treatment of children with handicaps.

9. Carry forward our attack on mental retardation, which afflicts more than 125,000 children each year.

10. Launch a new pilot program of dental care for children.

11. Help states and communities across the nation plan and operate programs to prevent juvenile delinquents from becoming adult delinquents.

12. Enrich the summer months for needy boys and girls.

STRENGTHENING HEAD START

Head Start—a preschool program for poor chidlren—has passed its first trials with flying colors. Tested in practice the past two years, it has proven worthy of its promise.

Through this program, hope has entered the lives of hundreds of thousands of children and their parents who need it the most.

The child whose only horizons were the crowded rooms of a tenement discovered new worlds of curiosity, of companionship, of creative effort. Volunteer workers gave thousands of hours to help launch poor children on the path toward self-discovery, stimulating them to enjoy books for the first time, watching them sense the excitement of learning.

Today Head Start reaches into three out of every four counties where poverty is heavily concentrated and into every one of the fifty states.

It is bringing more than education to children. Over half the youngsters are receiving needed dental and medical treatment. Hearing defects, poor vision, anemia, and damaged hearts are being discovered and treated.

In short, for poor children and their parents, Head Start has replaced the conviction of failure with the hope of success.

The achievements of Head Start must not be allowed to fade. For we have learned another truth which should have been self-evident—that poverty's handicaps cannot be easily erased or ignored when the door of first grade opens to the Head Start child.

Head Start occupies only part of a child's day and ends all too soon. He often returns home to conditions which breed despair. If these forces are not to engulf the child and wipe out the benefits of Head Start, more is required. Follow-through is essential.

To fulfill the rights of America's children to equal educational opportunity the benefits of Head Start must be carried through to the early grades.

We must make special efforts to overcome the handicap of poverty by more individual attention, by creative courses, by more teachers trained in child development. This will not be easy. It will require careful planning and the full support of our communities, our schools, and our teachers.

I am requesting appropriations to launch a "Follow-Through" program during the first schol grades for children in areas of acute poverty.

The present achievements of Head Start serve as a measure of the distance we must still go:

—Three out of four Head Start children participate only in a summer program. The summer months are far too brief to close the gap separating the disadvantaged child from his more fortunate classmate.

—Only a small number of three-year-olds are now being reached. The impact of Head Start will be far more beneficial if it is extended to the earlier years.

—Head Start has dramatically exposed the nutritional needs of poverty's children. More than 1.5 million preschoolers are not getting the nourishing food vital to strong and healthy bodies.

To build on the experience already gained through Head Start:

—I am requesting funds from the Congress and I am directing the Director of the Office of Economic Opportunity to:

   1. Strengthen the full year Head Start program.

   2. Enlarge the number of three-year-olds who participate in Head Start.

   3. Explore, through pilot programs, the effectiveness of this program on even younger children.

—I am recommending legislation to authorize a pilot program to provide school lunch benefits to needy preschoolers through Head Start and similar programs.

CHILD AND PARENT CENTERS

There is increasing evidence that a child's potential is shaped in infancy— and even during the prenatal period. Early in life, a child may acquire the scars that will damage his later years at great cost to himself and to society. No serious effort in child development can ignore this critical period.

In every community, we must attack the conditions that dim life's promise. Today, the Federal Government and the states support a wide range of services for needy children and their parents.

But we have fallen short. Many of these services are fragmented. Many do not provide imaginative and inventive programs to develop a child's full potential. Others fail to enlist the adults of the community in enriching the lives of children and thereby enriching their own lives as well.

The task is to marshal these services—to develop within our comprehensive neighborhood centers a single open door through which child and parent can enter to obtain the help they need.

I am instructing the Director of the Office of Economic Opportunity to begin a pilot program of child and parent centers through its community action program in areas of acute poverty.

I am also instructing the Secretaries of Health, Education, and Welfare, and Housing and Urban Development to support these centers with resources from related programs.

These child and parent centers would provide a wide range of benefits— as wide as the needs of the children and parents they must serve:
—health and welfare services;
—nutritious meals for needy preschoolers;
—counseling for parents in prenatal and infant care and instruction in household management, accident prevention, and nutrition;
—day care for children under three years old;
—a training base for specialists in child development.

A typical center might serve a slum neighborhood or a large housing project. Where possible, the centers would be affiliated with universities to provide greater research and experimentation in the fields of child development and education.

To Work with Children

A wealthy and abundant America lags behind other modern nations in training qualified persons to work with children.

These workers are badly needed—not only for poor children but for all children. We need experts and new professionals in child care. We need more preschool teachers, social workers, librarians, and nurses.

New training efforts must be supported—for day care counselors, parent-advisors, and health-visitors. We must train workers capable of helping children in neighborhood centers, in health clinics, in playgrounds, and in child welfare agencies. Others must be prepared to support the teacher in the school and the mother in the home.

These jobs promise excellent opportunities for high-school and grade-school graduates, and for citizens who are retired. They can provide meaningful employment for persons who are themselves economically deprived. In helping needy young children achieve their potential, they can also help to develop themselves.

Two OEO programs, Foster Grandparents and Home Health Aides, have already proved the value of such services.

To help provide the trained workers needed for America's children, I recommend legislation to increase to 75 percent the Federal matching funds for state child welfare personnel, including training programs.

I am also directing the Secretaries of Labor and Health Education, and Welfare, and the Director of the Office of Economic Opportunity, to emphasize through adult education, vocational rehabilitation and other programs, training for "new careers" in child care.

Only twenty-one states have taken advantage of a 1962 law, expiring this year, allowing children with unemployed parents to receive financial assistance. Only twelve states have community work and training programs for unemployed parents to give them the skills needed to protect their family and earn a decent living. A number of states discourage parents from working by arbitrarily reducing welfare payments when they earn their first dollar.

To remedy these deficiencies and give the poorest children of America a fair chance, I recommend legislation to:

—require each state to raise cash payments to the level the state itself sets as the minimum for subsistence, to bring these minimum standards up to date annually, and to maintain welfare standards at not less than two-thirds the level set for medical assistance;

—provide special Federal financial assistance to help poorer states meet these new requirements;

—make permanent the program for unemployed parents, which expires this year;

—require each state receiving assistance to cooperate in making community work and training available;

—require states to permit parents to earn $50 each month, with a maximum of $150 per family, without reduction in assistance payments.

Even well-established state welfare programs lack adequate services to protect children where there is physical abuse or neglect. There should be protection for the child, as well as help for the parent. Other state child welfare programs should expand day-care and homemaker services. New services must be tested, particularly for the mentally retarded, for the child requiring emergency shelter, and for the child in the urban slum.

I recommend legislation to authorize a program of project grants to encourage states and local communities to develop new forms of child services.

Child Health

Last year, nearly 400,000 needy mothers received care through maternal and child health nursing services. About 3 million children received public health nursing services, including almost 20 percent of all infants under one year of age.

But our public health record for children gives us little cause for complacency:

—At least ten other nations have lower infant mortality rates than the United States. Nearly 40,000 babies in America die each year who would be saved if our infant mortality rate were as low as Sweden's.

—Nearly one million pregnant women receive little or no prenatal care.

—More than 3.5 million poor children under five who need medical help do not receive it under public medical care programs.

Our whole society pays a toll for the unhealthy and crippled children who go without medical care: a total of incalculable human suffering, unemployment, rising rates of disabling disease, and expenditures for special education and institutions for the handicapped.

We have made hopeful beginnings toward reducing that toll.

Mental Retardation

Each year more than 125,000 infants are born mentally retarded.

This dread disability strikes rich families and poor. The tragedy of mental retardation affects the child, the parents, and the entire community.

In 1958, the late Congressman from Rhode Island, John E. Fogarty, introduced legislation which launched our attack on mental retardation.

For the past three years we have intensified that attack on all fronts—in prevention, treatment, rehabilitation, employment, recreation services.

But today, America still lacks trained workers and community facilities to carry on the fight.

I recommend legislation to:

—provide, for the first time, Federal support to assist the staffing of community mental retardation centers;

—extend Federal support for the construction of university and community centers for the mentally retarded.

SUMMER PROGRAMS FOR YOUNG AMERICANS

Last year, summer took on a new and brighter meaning for millions of needy young citizens:

—Head Start served 570,000 preschoolers.

—The Elementary and Secondary Education Act provided funds to bring remedial courses and day camps to two and a half million children.

—Upward Bound enabled 25,000 high-school students to live on college campuses and gain new learning experiences.

—The Youth Opportunity Campaign found more than a million jobs for sixteen-to-twenty-one-years-olds.

—The Neighborhood Youth Corps offered summer work to 210,000 young people.

—Community Action and other OEO programs, such as Operation Champ, offered recreation to nearly one million children.

This summer we can do more.

We can enable additional schools and playgrounds to remain open when vacation comes.

We can, with the help of public-spirited local organizations, bring fresh air and cool streams to the slum child who has known only a sweltering tenement and who must sleep on a crowded fire escape to get relief from the heat.

We can enlist the volunteer help of many citizens who want to give needy children a happy summer.

To further these purposes, I will:

—establish a cabinet-level Council headed by the Vice-President to promote Summer Youth Opportunities;

—direct this Council to make public facilities available to provide camping opportunities for additional needy children this summer;

—request the Council to call on public and private groups to sponsor and

operate these camps and to enlist college students and others to work in them;
—request the Council to call a national "Share Your Summer" conference
to encourage more-fortunate families to open their vacation homes to dis-
advantaged children for part of the summer.

In addition, I recommend legislation to provide funds for the construction
of summer camp facilities for at least 100,000 children in 1968. These camps
would be built only where there is an agreement with a private institution or
local government agency to operate and finance them.

I am directing every Federal agency to strengthen its programs which
provide summer employment, education, recreation, and health services.
These summer programs must become a permanent feature in the year round
effort to develop our children and teen-agers for responsible citizenship.

I call upon every city and local community to help make summers happy
and productive for the youth of America. It should not take an Act of Congress to turn on a fire hydrant sprinkler, to keep a swimming pool open a
little longer, or provide lights and supervision for a summer playground.

A New Priority

No ventures hold more promise than these: curing a sick child, helping a poor
child through Head Start, giving a slum child a summer of sunlight and
pleasure, encouraging a teen-ager to seek higher learning.

I believe that the Congress recognizes the urgency—and the great potential—of programs which open new opportunity to our children and young
people.

But beyond these beginnings, there is much to do.

We look toward the day when every child, no matter what his color or his
family's means, gets the medical care he needs, starts school on an equal
footing with his classmates, seeks as much education as he can absorb—in
short, goes as far as his talents will take him.

We make this commitment to our youth not merely at the bidding of our
conscience. It is practical wisdom. It is good economics. But, most important,
as Franklin D. Roosevelt said thirty years ago, because "the destiny of
American youth is the destiny of America."

We can shape that destiny if we act now and if we bring to this task the
energy and the vision it demands.

PART THREE

The Frontiers of Excellence

To Elevate the Life of the People

By Stewart L. Udall

By the next Presidential inauguration, the 1960s will almost have run their course. It is both presumptuous and premature to venture definitive judgments at this time about the international events of this crucial decade— but not, perhaps, on the domestic side, to express early opinions concerning the main lines of action, the thrust of national leadership, the new currents of thought.

At home, the economic performance of the "new economics," the resolution by the Eighty-ninth Congress of the unfinished business of the New Deal, and the new national goals espoused by President Lyndon B. Johnson should appear as milestones on the map of the sixties, and beyond. But these years also witnessed, at the pinnacle of our material success, an explosion of racial tensions that produced the most serious internal crisis since the Great Depression.

The urban uprisings revealed not only the sickness of our cities, the social costs of poverty and blight and racial strife. They also forced us, at long last, to question a group of interrelated and false assumptions that increasingly had led to the deterioration of American life: the assumption that the unmelted minorities would be content to remain servile, second-class citizens at the edge of our national being; the assumption that slums were an inevitable part of urban America; the assumption that the problems of the urban areas were "local" phenomena unworthy of national concern; and the assumption that any industrialized nation had to be an unclean country as well.

The domestic problems of the sixties derive from the disorder of our postwar priorities—priorities calculated to leave altogether uncorrected our long neglect of the cities, of the Negro, of the impoverished, and of our total environment.

At the heart of the crisis, too, was the partial paralysis of our politics. Rural control of state and national legislative bodies, and a Southern veto on social programs that only the Congress could pass, clogged the channels of creative change against effective postwar action in the areas of worst neglect.

When the pace of progress in these matters did not quicken in the 1950s, when bridges of racial amity were not built, the stage was set for the events and antagonism of the mid-sixties. President Eisenhower's neglect for six critical years to throw the moral force of his high office behind the Supreme Court's school decision cost us dearly, as did his opposition to Federal aid to education and his inaction with regard to the plight of the cities and the degradation of the American land.

The one great decision of the fifties—the school integration opinion, which altered the fabric and future of our institutions—was a manifestation of this political paralysis. It was not made by a President or the Congress but by the Supreme Court. Yet, our political system was so unresponsive it would take a full decade before the Congress would come to grips with a constitutional crisis and enact strong civil rights legislation.

At the turn of the decade, the uneasiness of the American people was evident: the reports of the Rockefeller Brothers' Fund sought to define new goals; *Life* magazine reached millions with a questioning seminar on the national purpose; and Dr. Galbraith, reminding us of the shortcomings of mere affluence, produced a best seller.

The exciting 1960 Presidential campaign also reflected the confusion over priorities and programs at home. The domestic debate concentrated on issues that had become political perennials: Medicare, the importance of the annual balanced budget, and Federal aid to education. The civil rights issue was played low key, and there was hardly a word about conservation and the American environment. The election itself was perhaps decided by such irrelevant and accidental issues or effects as the religious affiliation of Kennedy and (some even argued) the makeup man who ruined Richard Nixon's "image."

Kennedy was right on the big issue. The pace of change was much too slow. The Nation did, indeed, need to "get moving again," to abandon the belief that slow school integration would work, or that the ballot alone would speed up social change. (One of the angry ironies of the whole era lay in the contrast between the spacious and color-blind concept of the family of nations we hoped to nurture and our clear-cut intention of denying the Negro full fellowship in the American family.)

However, the hairline decision of the 1960 electorate made it plain the American people were not ready for rapid change. Such action would await the Eighty-ninth Congress, and the wide-ranging action proposals of President Johnson.

By the mid-sixties the full dimensions of our domestic predicament were apparent: decades of inaction had induced decay and discontent; Negro anger was rising; the cancerous fingers of pollution were reaching everywhere; the underfinanced cities were floundering; megalopolis was reaching ever outward; and a silent in-migration of the poor to the urban centers was underway. Then, for the first time, did we fully realize that our most urgent internal business concerned the creation of an equal opportunity society, the building of balanced cities, the renovation of the environment, and improving the quality of education.

Once again the Supreme Court acted. Its one-man, one-vote ruling set the stage for change. With 70 percent of the people living on just 1 percent of our land base, the urban areas would be able to achieve greater voice and increased freedom from rural domination.

At this point, the balance sheet was an embarrassing paradox: the United States led the world in manufactured wealth and machine power but in some respects also led in the degradation of the human habitat.

We enjoyed unmatched material progress but appeared ready to define and accept "progress" that meant the spoliation of our natural legacy and a diminution of the precious amenities of everyday living.

We had the most automobiles, but unsightly junkyards signaled the final resting place of an obsolescence that omitted any recycling of resources.

We were the most mobile people on earth—and we endured the most congestion.

We produced the most energy—and had the foulest air.

We had factories that turned out untold products for the marketplace and into the rivers poured unspeakable wastes.

We had the most goods to sell and the most unsightly signs to advertise their availability.

These ambiguous trends created dissatisfaction with the unevenness of our social growth and with the egregious forms of our affluence. They resulted, too, in an awareness that the aims of a great society and a growth society were markedly different. Various programs advanced by President Johnson were one answer to this challenge; they meant a high tide of acts to aid education and health; a frontal attack on the root causes of poverty; new proposals for urban betterment and conservation.

More important—for it would relate our proclivities to our potentialities— an Administration began to arouse discussion about upgrading the quality of American life: aid to the arts was instituted; the quality of education was emphasized; plans for model cities and new towns were presented.

A striking aspect of this Administration's approach to conservation and other problems has received far too little attention from the press and from scholars. This is the total, or "systems," approach. We have at last learned that deeply rooted problems—whether poverty in the city or blight in the country—cannot be solved by one-shot or piecemeal or scatter-gun or single-solution efforts. Such problems call for comprehensive, coordinated action along a wide front. The President understands the need for the total approach. Note, for example, some sentences from his February 8, 1965, message to Congress on natural beauty:

> The air we breathe, our water, our soil, and wildlife are being blighted by the poisons and chemicals which are the by-products of technology and industry. The skeletons of discarded cars litter the countryside. The same society which receives the rewards of technology *must as a cooperating whole* take responsibility for control.
>
> To deal with these new problems will require a new conservation. We must not only protect the countryside and save it from destruction, we must restore what has been destroyed and salvage the beauty and charm of our cities. *Our conservation must be not just the classic conservation of protection and development, but a creative conservation of restoration and innovation. Its concern is not with nature alone, but with the total relation between man and the world around him.* Its object is not just man's welfare, but the dignity of man's spirit.

I have italicized the above words because they bespeak the balanced, many-channeled approach of this Administration—the only approach, in my view, that can overcome the entrenched problems of the city and of the country. In the same speech the President went on to apply this approach to the goal of natural beauty for our countryside. "There is much the Federal Government can do, through a range of specific programs, and as a force for public education. But a beautiful America will require the effort of government at every level, of business, and of private groups. Above all it will require the concern and action of individual citizens. . . ."

Note that President Johnson's "total approach" is not a bland partnership of different interests and governments and persons, each "cooperating with" but also checking and even vetoing the others. He favors a driving, systematic effort by the Federal Government to mobilize all the talent, energies, and interests in the Nation and to lead these forces in a concerted attack on the problem.

Thus, there was a cascade of legislation to carry out the President's "new conservation" proposals: the Nation made a commitment to clean up its water and to cleanse the air; we achieved long-needed agreement on a national policy for wilderness preservation; we initiated a program to help finance the outdoor recreation and open space needs of the people; we added thirty-five new units to our National Park System, including a necklace of National Seashores; we expanded our refuge system for wildlife by nearly three-quarters of a million acres; and we have opened a halting campaign to convert our highways from neon nightmares into paths of aesthetic satisfaction. (And by the time this book appears in print, I predict a Redwoods National Park in California will be a reality, Congress will have established a new Scenic Rivers system for the Nation, and a magnificent National Park will be carved out in the North Cascades country of Washington.)

What did this mean? Simply this: there was a new era of conservation and its subject was to be man. The approach was no longer to be fragmented. We no longer would consider the elements of pollution but focus on man's elemental reliance upon water and air, the appeal of well-ordered cities, and the beauty of a well-kept countryside. We would cease our penchant for the conserving of parts of man's environment and for the first time concentrate on the whole.

A President is—and should be—judged by his vision of the future and by the vitality with which he guides the Nation along a wide arc of innovation and action. His public papers—no less than his public acts—are a national charter of ideals and concepts of growth.

It is the function of a President to elevate the life of the people; to arouse new expectations; to employ the Nation's resourcefulness, not merely its resources. These papers reflect the convictions of a President who believes we can enjoy the bounty of America in ways that will conserve and enhance its order and balance and beauty.

Lyndon B. Johnson

"The promise is clear rivers,
tall forests and clean air
—a sane environment for man."
Message to Congress,
February 23, 1966.

Albert Schweitzer said, "Man has lost the capacity to foresee and to forestall. He will end by destroying the earth."

The most affluent nation on earth may feel that it is immune from this indictment. A nation that offered its people—a century ago—uncharted forests, broad sparkling rivers, and prairies ripe for planting may have expected that bounty to endure forever.

But we do not live alone with wishful expectations.

We live with history. It tells us of a hundred proud civilizations that have decayed through careless neglect of the nature that fed them.

We live with the certain future of multiplying populations, whose demands on the resources of nature will equal their numbers.

We are not immune. We are not endowed—any more than were those perished nations of the past—with a limitless natural bounty.

Yet we are endowed with their experience. We are able to see the magnitude of the choice before us, and its consequences for every child born on our continent from this day forward.

Economists estimate that this generation has already suffered losses from pollution that run into billions of dollars each year. But the ultimate cost of pollution is incalculable.

We see that we can corrupt and destroy our lands, our rivers, our forests, and the atmosphere itself—all in the name of progress and necessity. Such a course leads to a barren America bereft of its beauty, and shorn of its sustenance.

We see that there is another course—more expensive today, more demanding. Down this course lies a natural America restored to her people. The promise is clear rivers, tall forests, and clean air—a sane environment for man.

I shall propose in this message one means to achieve that promise. It requires, first, an understanding of what has already happened to our waters.

"Pollution touches us all. We are at the same time pollutors and sufferers from pollution. Today, we are certain that pollution adversely affects the quality of our lives. In the future, it may affect their duration."

These are the words of the Environmental Pollution Panel of the President's Science Advisory Committee. They were written in November, 1965.

At that time, every river system in America suffered some degree of pollution.

At that time, discharges into our rivers and streams—both treated and untreated—equaled the raw sewage from almost 50 million people. Animal wastes and waste from our cities and towns were making water unfit for any use.

At that time, rivers, lakes, and estuaries were receiving great quantities of industrial chemicals—acids from mine runoff—detergents and minerals that would not "break down" in the ordinary life of the water. These pollutants were reentering domestic and industrial water supplies. They were killing fish. They posed hazards to both human and animal life.

By that time, on Lake Erie six of thirty-two public recreation and swimming areas had been closed down because the water was unsafe for human beings. The blue pike catch in the lake had fallen from 20 million pounds in

1937 to 7,000 pounds in 1960. The oxygen that fish need for life was being rapidly devoured by blooms of algae fed by pollutants.

At that time, in the lower Arkansas Red River Basin, oil-field development and irrigation were dumping salt into rivers. The result was an additional annual expense of $13 million to bring in fresh water.

I have placed these comments in the past tense not because they are no longer true. They are more tragically true today than they were four months ago.

I seek instead to make them a bench-mark in restoring America's precious heritage to her people.

I seek to make them that point in time when Americans determined to resist the flow of poison in their rivers and streams.

I seek to make them ancient history for the next generation.

And I believe the conditions they describe can become just that—if we begin now, together, to cleanse our rivers of the blight that burdens them. . . .

I propose that we begin now to clean and preserve entire river basins from their sources to their mouths.

I propose a new kind of partnership—built upon our creative Federal system—that will unite all the pollution control activities in a single river basin. Its task is to achieve high standards of water quality throughout the basin. . . .

SAVING OUR FORESTS

Since the century's beginning the national Government has labored to preserve the sublime legacy that is the American forest.

Time after time public intervention has prevented the destruction of irreplaceable forest lands.

Our national park and forest systems are America's principal trustee in the vital task of conservation. That task cannot be accomplished in a single stroke. It requires patient determination and careful planning to secure for our people the beauty that is justly theirs. It merits careful planning.

I propose that we plan now to complete our national park system by 1972—the one hundredth anniversary of Yellowstone, the world's first national park.

Substantial progress has been made during the last four years. Yet many scenic masterpieces remain unprotected and deserve early inclusion in the national park system.

A Redwood National Park

I propose the creation of a Redwood National Park in northern California.

It is possible to reclaim a river like the Potomac from the carelessness of man. But we cannot restore—once it is lost—the majesty of a forest whose trees soared upward 2,000 years ago. The Secretary of the Interior—after exhaustive consultations with preservationists, officials of the State of California, lumbermen, and others—has completed a study of the desirability of establishing a park of international significance.

I have reviewed his recommendations, and am submitting to the Congress legislation to establish such a park. This will be costly. But it is my recommendation that we move swiftly to save an area of immense significance before it is too late.

Other Outdoor Recreation Proposals

Other major outdoor recreation proposals which should be approved in 1966 are:

1. Cape Lookout National Seashore, North Carolina.
2. Sleeping Bear Dunes National Lakeshore, Michigan.
3. Indiana Dunes National Lakeshore, Indiana.
4. Oregon Dunes National Seashore, Oregon.
5. Great Basin National Park, Nevada.
6. Guadalupe Mountains National Park, Texas.
7. Bighorn Canyon National Recreation Area, Montana and Wyoming.
8. Flaming Gorge National Recreation Area, Utah and Wyoming.

For a region which now has no national park, I recommend the study of a Connecticut River National Recreation Area along New England's largest river, in the States of New Hampshire, Vermont, Massachusetts, and Connecticut.

I propose the early completion of studies and planning for two new parks —the Apostle Isles Seashore along Lake Superior and North Cascades in Washington State.

Nationwide Trail System

In my budget, I recommended legislation to extend Federal support to the Appalachian Trail, and to encourage the development of hiking trails accessible to the people throughout the country.

I am submitting legislation to foster the development by Federal, state, and local agencies of a nationwide system of trails and give special emphasis to the location of trails near metropolitan areas.

Preservation of Historic Sites

Historic preservation is the goal of citizen groups in every part of the country. To help preserve buildings and sites of historic significance, I will recommend a program of matching grants to states and to the National Trust for Historic Preservation.

Wild River System

I am encouraged by the response to my proposal for a national wild rivers system, and I urge the Congress to complete this pioneering conservation legislation this year.

Costs of Land Acquisition

The spiraling cost of land acquisitions by the Federal Government, particularly for water resource and recreational purposes, is a matter of increasing concern.

Landowners whose property is acquired by the Federal Government are, of course, entitled to just compensation as provided by the Constitution. At the same time, land for the use of the general public should not be burdened with the increased price resulting from speculative activities.

I have requested the Director of the Bureau of the Budget, together with the Attorney General, the Secretary of the Interior, and the heads of the other agencies principally concerned, to investigate procedures for protecting the Government against such artificial price spirals.

A Creed To Preserve Our Natural Heritage

To sustain an environment suitable for man, we must fight on a thousand battlegrounds. Despite all of our wealth and knowledge, we cannot create a redwood forest, a wild river, or a gleaming seashore.

But we can keep those we have.

The science that has increased our abundance can find ways to restore and renew an environment equal to our needs.

The time is ripe to set forth a creed to preserve our natural heritage—principles which men and women of good will will support in order to assure the beauty and bounty of their land. Conservation is ethically sound. It is rooted in our love of the land, our respect for the rights of others, our devotion to the rule of law.

Let us proclaim a creed to preserve our natural heritage with rights and the duties to respect those rights:

The right to clean water—and the duty not to pollute it.

The right to clean air—and the duty not to befoul it.

The right to surroundings reasonably free from manmade ugliness—and the duty not to blight.

The right of easy access to places of beauty and tranquillity where every family can find recreation and refreshment—and the duty to preserve such places clean and unspoiled.

The right to enjoy plants and animals in their natural habitats—and the duty not to eliminate them from the face of this earth. . . .

The work to achieve these rights will not be easy. It cannot be completed in a year or five years. But there will never be a better time to begin. . . .

"Either we stop poisoning our air
—or we become a Nation in gas masks. . . ."
Remarks on signing the Air Quality Act of 1967,
November 21, 1967.

I would like to begin this morning by reading you a little weather report.

". . . dirty water and black snow pour from the dismal air to . . . the putrid slush that waits for them below."

Now that is not a description of Boston, Chicago, New York, or even Washington, D.C. It is from Dante's "Inferno," a 600-year-old vision of damnation.

But doesn't it sound familiar?

Isn't it a forecast that fits almost any large American city today?

I think those like Secretary Gardner and Senator Muskie, all you members of the Congress and the Cabinet who have worked with this subject would agree with that.

Don't we really risk our own damnation every day by destroying the air that gives us life?

I think we do. We have done it with our science, our industry, our progress. Above all, we have really done it with our own carelessness—our own continued indifference and our own repeated negligence.

Contaminated air began in this country as a big-city problem. But in just a few years, the gray pall of pollution has spread throughout the Nation. Today its threat hangs everywhere—and it is still spreading.

Today we are pouring at least 130 million tons of poison into the air each year. That is two-thirds of a ton for every man, woman, and child that lives in America.

And tomorrow the picture looks even blacker. By 1980, we will have a third more people living in our cities than are living there today. We will have 40 percent more automobiles and trucks. And we will be burning half again as much fuel.

That leaves us, according to my evaluation, only one real choice. Either we stop poisoning our air—or we become a Nation in gas masks, groping our way through the dying cities and a wilderness of ghost towns that the people have evacuated.

We make our choice with the bill that we are going to sign very shortly. It is not the first clean air bill—but it is, I think, the best.

I am indebted to all of you who had a part in its fashioning.

Congress passed the Clean Air Act in 1963. I signed it to establish the Government's obligation and to establish the Government's authority to act forcefully against air pollution.

Two years later we amended that act. Standards were set in 1965 to control automobile pollution.

These were important steps. But they were really, as Senator Muskie has reminded us many times, just really baby steps. Today we grow up to our responsibilities. This new Air Quality Act lets us face up to our problem as we have never faced up before.

In the next three years, it will authorize more funds to combat air pollution—more funds in the next three years to combat air pollution—than we have spent on this subject in the entire Nation's history of 180 years.

It will give us scientific answers to our most baffling problem: how to get the sulphur out of our fuel—and how to keep it out of the air.

It will give Secretary Gardner new power to stop pollution before it chokes our children and before it strangles our elderly—before it drives us into the hospital bed.

It will help our states fight pollution in the only practical way—by regional "airshed" controls—by giving the Federal Government standby power to intervene if states rights do not always function efficiently.

It will help our states to control the number one source of pollution—our automobiles.

But for all that it will do, the Air Quality Act will never end pollution. It is a law—and not a magic wand to wave that will cleanse our skies. It is a law whose ultimate power and final effectiveness really rests out there with the people of this land—on our seeing the damnation that awaits us if the people do not act responsibly to avoid it and to curb it.

Last January, in asking Congress to pass this legislation. I had this to say:

"This situation does not exist because it was inevitable, nor because it cannot be controlled. Air pollution is the inevitable consequence of neglect. It can be controlled when that neglect is no longer tolerated.

"It will be controlled when the people of America, through their elected representatives, demand the right to air that they and their children can breathe without fear."

Let us then strengthen that demand from this moment on. Let us seize the new powers of this new law to end a long, dark night of neglect.

Let our children say, when they look back on this day, that it was here that a sleeping giant—it was here that their Nation awoke. It was here that America turned away from damnation, and found salvation in reclaiming God's blessings of fresh air and clean sky.

We are distressed at the condition that we cannot at the moment find the solution for—our men dying on the battlefields.

We are troubled with the economic international uncertainties and deficits here at home. There are many things that we can do and that we must do in the twentieth century that have not been done in the two centuries that have gone by.

I talked yesterday about some of the protections that this century requires for the consumers of this country. We have twelve measures that we have recommended and most of them are moving along. There is no reason why anyone in this country ought to be permitted to eat dirty, diseased, filthy meat and it is not going to bankrupt the Treasury to bring a stop to that.

There is no reason why anyone in his country should not know how much interest they are paying. So, we can have a truth-in-lending bill. The poorest people are paying the highest interest. We ought to act there. It is not going to bankrupt the Treasury.

There is no reason in the world why a baby ought to be put in a blanket and burned up. We ought to take some steps to protect them from all these casualties.

I feel the same way in this general field.

All the members of Congress whom I am looking at—I would call all your names if I had them—some of you tell me you are coming and don't make it —some of you say you won't come here and then you are here. So, when I start calling your names I am embarrassed.

However, I am indebted to everyone—beginning with the first man on the row and going down to attractive Edna Kelly, then, going over here and seeing the Cabinet members and Congressmen who worked on this—for what you are doing to keep our air clean and to keep our water pure, and to give our children a place where they can go and play without having their lungs filled with disease.

I sat with a great person, one of the greatest products of this land. I suffered with him not long ago because he could hardly utter a full sentence without coughing and choking because of the effects of what he had breathed and what had gone into his body from residence here in this town.

Senator Muskie has been shoving me as no other person has, all these years, to do something in the pollution field.

I remember an old man told me when I came to Washington, he said, "Son, you get ready. If you are going to live in this town you are either going to be shoving somebody or somebody is going to be shoving you."

When I see influential Senators, chairmen of committees like Senator Randolph and other members of Congress here this morning, I want to shove you.

It may not cost you $1 billion for the things we are shoving because we are going to have to watch those expenditures with the way things are developing. But we can purify the water. We can clean up our air. We can give protection to our babies and to our old folks.

We can mark how much we are paying on some of these things. We can clean up our diseased meats.

I think actually we will find it is pretty profitable if we deal with this question of disease. I expect we lose more from it than it would cost us to protect ourselves against it.

So, I appeal to you to try to do your best to get us those twelve consumer bills. If you can't pass them just exactly as we recommended, we will understand. Just give us 90 percent this year and we will come back next year—if we are all here—for the other 10 percent.

"I propose that we show how broad-based planning can inspire the people of rural America to unite the resources of their rural governments. . . ." Message to Congress, January 25, 1966.

Last year in my Message on Agriculture I described poverty's grip on rural America.

Nearly half of the poor in the United States live in rural areas.

Almost one in every two rural families has a cash income under $3,000.

One-fourth of rural non-farm homes are without running water.

Rural people lag almost two years behind urban residents in educational attainment.

Health facilities in rural areas are so inadequate that rural children receive one-third less medical attention than urban children.

These deficiencies persist in 1966. Their effect is as grievous on urban America—the recipient of millions of unskilled migrants from rural areas in the past two decades—as on the run-down farms and impoverished communities that still house 4.4 million poor rural families.

Last year, I directed:

—each department and agency administering a program that could benefit

rural people, to assure that its benefits were distributed equitably between urban and rural areas;

—the Secretary of Agriculture and the Director of the Budget to review the administrative obstacles that might stand in the way of such a distribution;

—the Secretary of Agriculture to put his field offices to the task of assisting other Federal agencies in making their programs effective in rural areas.

As a result, the Rural Community Development Service was created and charged with assuring that the Department made that assistance available.

This mission of the Department is now firmly established in practice. Its field personnel are active in informing rural people of their eligibility for Medicare, and of its requirements. They work with the Economic Development Administration in planning and encouraging new rural industrial developments. In several pilot counties, concerted projects are under way—joining the Departments of Labor, HEW, and Agriculture—in a common effort to bring social services to poor rural communities. The water and sewer facilities program has been simplified and made more responsive to the needs of small towns and communities.

The Office of Economic Opportunity has increased its efforts in rural areas. Community Action Programs are under way in a number of rural counties:

—supporting community action planning;

—providing remedial reading courses, vocational instruction, and adult education;

—and assisting small cooperatives to acquire farm machinery. These programs have inspired a new sense of hope among the rural Americans who have experienced them.

More—much more—needs to be done if their effects are to reach the dispersed but very real pockets of rural poverty throughout America.

Legislation enacted by the first session of this Congress, and in prior years, provides the means for a massive attack on poverty in America.

But—even with the help of these great new programs—too few rural communities are able to marshal sufficient physical, human, and financial resources to achieve a satisfactory level of social and economic development.

The central advantage of the city has been that a large and concentrated population can provide the leadership and technical capability, and can achieve economies of scale in operations, to provide adequate public services and facilities for its people.

On the other hand, it is difficult, if not impossible for every small hamlet to offer its own complete set of public services. Nor is it economic for the small city to try to achieve metropolitan standards of service, opportunity, and culture, without relation to its rural environs.

The related interests of each—the small city and its rural neighbors—need to be taken into account in planning for the public services and economic development of the wider community. In this way the benefits of creative Federalism can be brought to our rural citizens.

The base exists for such coordinated planning.

New communities are coming into being—stimulated by advanced means of travel and communications. Because of these it is possible to extend to people in the outlying rural areas a richer variety of public services, and of economic and cultural opportunities.

By combining resources and efforts in these larger and more functional groupings, rural and small urban communities—comprising a population base large enough to support a full range of efficient and high-quality public services and facilities—can achieve the conditions necessary for economic and social advance. . . .

I propose that we show how broad-based planning can inspire the people of rural America to unite the resources of their rural governments and small cities in improving the quality of life for the citizens of both.

I propose that we assist in the establishment of a number of community development districts to carry out, under local initiative, such comprehensive planning.

The boundaries of community development districts will correspond to the normal commuting or trading patterns of the rural and city residents. . . .

The efforts of five administrations have provided some relief for hundreds of thousands of poor families who remain on small farms in rural communities. Yet the old task remains undone: to end the travail of unemployed and underemployed men; to teach their children the skills they must have to prosper in a competitive society; to provide enough food, adequate shelter, and decent medical care for their families, and to help them achieve freedom from want and fear in their later years.

I do not believe we should stand idly by and permit our rural citizens to be ground into poverty—exposing them, unassisted and unencouraged, to the neglect of a changing society. Few other elements of our population are so treated by our humane and progressive people. . . .

Rural poverty has proved an almost intractable problem in past decades. Its abolition may require a journey of a thousand miles.

But the first step in that journey is the pooling of the common resources of rural Americans—joining them in a common planning effort that will magnify the resources of each.

In the program I propose, I ask the Congress to take that step with me today.

"We will not permit any part of this country
to be a prison where hopes are crushed. . . ."
Message to Congress,
March 25, 1965.

At a time of instant communication and swift transport, it is difficult to realize how varied are the regions of this country. Abundance and opportunity, progress and hope are, however, not evenly spread over the land. The same diversity of conditions which contributes to the richness of our society and culture, also bears with harsh inequality on those in stricken stretches of America. . . .

Opportunity should not be closed to any person because of the circumstances of the area in which he lives.

Moreover, the distress or underdevelopment of any part of the country holds back the progress of the entire Nation. This has been one of the great lessons of the last thirty years. Region after region from the deep South to the far West has been brought into the mainstream of our economic life. The consequence has been increased vitality and strength, not only in those areas whose resources had been previously underemployed, but for the Nation as a whole. Nonetheless, much remains to be done.

A growing Nation cannot afford to waste those resources, human and natural, which are now too often neglected and unused in distressed areas. We cannot afford the loss of buying power and of national growth which flow from widespread poverty. Above all, we cannot afford to shut out large numbers of our fellow citizens from the fulfillment of hope which is shared by the rest. For that would be the denial of the promise of America itself.

The troubles and the potentials of depressed areas which contain approximately 27 million people vary widely. They are scattered across almost every section of the country. But they share certain common characteristics.

Nearly always, their population growth is well below the national average, and often it is declining. Large areas in Illinois, Oklahoma, Arkansas, and elsewhere have lost more than 20 percent of their population in the last decade, while America as a whole was increasing its numbers by almost as much.

This pattern of decline is a symptom of economic distress. For in these areas employment and income are far below the national average. Unemployment rates of 10 to 15 percent are not uncommon. In dozens of counties more than 50 percent of all families have annual incomes of less than $2,000.

Worst of all, the distressed area is usually caught in a web of circumstances which block progress and lead to further decline.

Young people are forced to leave school earlier to help support their families, thus depriving themselves of needed skills and knowledge. Many young people must leave families and homes behind them in search of greater opportunity, stripping the area of badly needed skill and energy. Older men and women tend to stay on, clinging to the communities and friends which have been part of their lives and which enrich their existence.

As income goes down, these areas are less and less able to support schools, hospitals, and other public facilities needed to train their people and otherwise equip them to meet the demands of modern life. They are often too poor to provide the public structures—from roads to water—needed to attract new business and new jobs. The result is a steadily mounting toll in human poverty and retardation of the Nation's progress.

To break this downward spiral, to restore vitality and forward motion to America's distressed areas, I recommend a program of Area and Regional Economic Development—focused upon the economic needs of distressed areas and aimed at providing the conditions which can lead to growth. This program will be based primarily upon the experience of the Accelerated

Public Works Program, the Area Redevelopment Administration, and the Appalachian Regional Development Commission. . . .

Under the new program three basic principles will guide our action.

First, we will devote maximum effort to providing the conditions under which our private enterprise system can provide jobs and increased income. It is up to private business to take advantage of improved conditions for making profits by expanding present businesses or starting new ones, thereby increasing opportunity for the people of the region.

Second, no Federal plan or Federal project will be imposed on any regional, state, or local body. No area will be declared distressed by Federal decree. No economic development district will be designated unless the state and local people want it to be designated. No plan will be approved unless it also has the approval of state and local authorities. No programs or projects will be originated at the Federal level. The initiative, the ideas, and the request for assistance must all come to Washington, not from Washington.

Third, the Federal Government will seek full value from every dollar spent or loaned under this program. Every proposal will be tested to see if it offers substantial promise of increasing economic development commensurate with the Federal funds involved. Only if a project meets this test will it be approved. Over the years the increased economic activity stimulated by this program will return its cost many times to the Federal Treasury. . . .

There are three important things to remember about this program. First, it is designed to extend opportunity to those now deprived of a full chance to share in the blessings of American life. As such it has a call upon the moral conscience of every citizen.

Second, it will benefit all Americans. The experience of the last thirty years has shown conclusively that the increasing prosperity of any region of this country increases the prosperity of the Nation. We have truly become a national economy. Higher incomes for the people of Illinois or Arkansas mean increased markets for automobiles from Detroit and steel from Pittsburgh. Poverty in one area slows progress in other areas.

Third, the job can be done. We have the resources and the skill to extend American abundance to every citizen and every region of this land. This program will help give us the instruments to match our determination to eliminate poverty in America.

The conditions of our distressed areas today are among our most important economic problems. They hold back the progress of the Nation, and breed a despair and poverty which is inexcusable in the richest land on earth. We will not permit any part of this country to be a prison where hopes are crushed, human beings chained to misery, and the promise of America denied.

The conditions of our depressed areas can and must be righted. In this generation they will be righted.

"We know that cities can stimulate the best in man, and aggravate the worst."
Message to Congress
recommending a Demonstration Cities Program,
January 26, 1966.

Nineteen-sixty-six can be the year of rebirth for American cities.

This Congress, and this people, can set in motion forces of change in great urban areas that will make them the masterpieces of our civilization.

Fifty years from now our population will reach that of today's India. Our grandchildren will inhabit a world as different from ours, as ours is from the world of Jefferson.

None can predict the shape of their life with any certainty. Yet one thing is sure. It will be lived in cities. By the year 2000, four out of five Americans will live and work in a metropolitan area.

We are not strangers to an urban world.

We began our national life gathered in towns along the Atlantic seaboard. We built new commercial centers around the Great Lakes and in the Midwest, to serve our westward expansion.

Forty millions came from Europe to fuel our economy and enrich our community life. This century has seen the steady and rapid migration of farm families—seeking jobs and the promise of the city.

From this rich experience we have learned much.

We know that cities can stimulate the best in man, and aggravate the worst.

We know the convenience of city life, and its paralysis.

We know its promise, and its dark foreboding.

What we may only dimly perceive is the gravity of the choice before us.

Shall we make our cities livable for ourselves and our posterity? Or shall we by timidity and neglect damn them to fester and decay?

If we permit our cities to grow without rational design—

If we stand passively by, while the center of each city becomes a hive of deprivation, crime, and hopelessness—

If we devour the countryside as though it were limitless, while our ruins— millions of tenement apartments and dilapidated houses—go unredeemed—

If we become two people—the suburban affluent and the urban poor, each filled with mistrust and fear one for the other—

If this is our desire and policy as a people, then we shall effectively cripple each generation to come.

We shall as well condemn our own generation to a bitter paradox: an educated, wealthy, progressive people, who would not give their thoughts, their resources, or their wills to provide for their common well-being.

I do not believe that such a fate is either necessary or inevitable. But I believe this will come to pass—unless we commit ourselves now to the planning, the building, the teaching, and the caring that alone can forestall it.

That is why I am recommending today a massive Demonstration Cities Program. I recommend that both the public and private sectors of our economy join to build in our cities and towns an environment for man equal to the dignity of his aspirations.

I recommend an effort larger in scope, more comprehensive, more concentrated—than any that has gone before.

The Work of the Past

I know the work of the past three decades. I have shared in the forging of our Federal housing and renewal programs. I know what they have done for millions of urban Americans:

Eight million single family dwellings assisted by the Federal Housing Administration.

An additional 6.7 million assisted by the Veterans Administration.

One and one-tenth million multiple units created.

Six hundred and five thousand families moved out of decayed and unsanitary dwellings into decent public housing.

Three hundred thousand dwelling units supported under urban renewal.

Without these programs, the goal I recommend today would be impossible to achieve. Because Federal sponsorship is so effective a part of our system of home-building, we can conceive a far larger purpose than it has yet fulfilled. We must make use of every established housing program—and of social, educational, and economic instruments as well—if the Demonstration Cities Program is to succeed.

THE PROBLEM TODAY

Our housing programs have built a platform, from which we may see how far away is the reborn city we desire. For there still remains:

—some 4 million urban families living in homes of such disrepair as to violate decent housing standards;

—the need to provide over 30 percent more housing annually than we are currently building;

—our chronic inability to provide sufficient low- and moderate-income housing, of adequate quality, at a reasonable price;

—the special problem of the poor and the Negro, unable to move freely from their ghettoes, exploited in the quest for the necessities of life;

—increasing pressures on municipal budgets, with large city per capita expenditures rising 36 percent in the three years after 1960;

—the high human costs: crime, delinquency, welfare loads, disease, and health hazards. This is man's fate in those broken neighborhoods where he can "feel the enclosure of the flaking walls and see through the window the blackened reflection of the tenement across the street that blocks out the world beyond";

—the tragic waste and, indeed, the chaos that threatens where children are born into the stifling air of overcrowded rooms, destined for a poor diet, inadequate schools, streets of fear and sordid temptation, joblessness, and the gray anxiety of the ill-prepared;

—and the flight to the suburbs of more fortunate men and women, who might have provided the leadership and the means for reversing this human decline.

THE INADEQUATE RESPONSE

Since 1949, the urban renewal program has been our chief instrument in the struggle for a decent urban environment.

Over 800 cities are participating in urban renewal programs. Undertaken and designed by the cities themselves, these efforts have had an increasing influence on the use of urban land. Last year the Congress wisely extended the authorization for urban renewal, at a higher level than before.

Years of experience with urban renewal have taught us much about its strengths and weaknesses.

Since 1961 we have made major alterations in its administration. We have made it more responsive to human needs. We have more vigorously enforced the requirement of a workable program for the entire community. Within the limits of current law, we have achieved conisderable progress toward these goals.

Nevertheless the social and psychological effects of relocating the poor have not always been treated as what they are. They are the unavoidable consequences of slum clearance, demanding as much concern as physical redevelopment.

The size and scale of urban assistance has been too small, and too widely dispersed.

Present programs are often prisoners of archaic and wasteful building practices. They have inhibited the use of modern technology. They have inflated the cost of rebuilding.

The benefits and efficiencies that can come from metropolitan planning are still unrealized in most urban regions.

Insufficient resources cause extensive delays in many projects. The result is growing blight and overcrowding that thwart our best efforts to resist them.

The goals of major Federal programs have often lacked cohesiveness. Some work for the revitalization of the central city. Some accelerate suburban growth. Some unite urban communities. Some disrupt them.

URBAN DILEMMAS

Virtually every forward step we have taken has had its severe limitations. Each of those steps has involved a public choice, and created a public dilemma:

—major clearance and reconstruction, with its attendant hardships of relocation;

—relieving traffic congestion, thereby widening the gulf between the affluence of suburbia and the poverty of the city;

—involving urban residents in redeveloping their own areas, hence lengthening the time and increasing the cost of the job;

—preserving the autonomy of local agencies, thus crippling our efforts to attack regional problems on a regional basis.

These dilemmas cannot be completely resolved by any single program, no matter how well designed. The prize—cities of spacious beauty and lively promise, where men are truly free to determine how they will live—is too rich to be lost because the problems are complex.

Let there be debate over means and priorities.

Let there be experiment with a dozen approaches, or a hundred.

But let there be commitment to that goal.

WHAT IS REQUIRED

From the experience of three decades, it is clear to me that American cities require a program that will:

—concentrate our available resources—in planning tools, in housing construction, in job training, in health facilities, in recreation, in welfare programs, in education—to improve the conditions of life in urban areas;

—join together all available talent and skills in a coordinated effort;

—mobilize local leadership and private initiative, so that local citizens will determine the shape of their new city—freed from the constraints that have handicapped their past efforts and inflated their costs.

A DEMONSTRATION CITIES PROGRAM

I propose a Demonstration Cities Program that will offer qualifying cities of all sizes the promise of a new life for their people.

I propose that we make massive additions to the supply of low- and moderate-cost housing.

I propose that we combine physical reconstruction and rehabilitation with effective social programs throughout the rebuilding process.

I propose that we achieve new flexibility in administrative procedures.

I propose that we focus all the techniques and talents within our society on the crisis of the American City.

It will not be simple to qualify for such a program. We have neither the means nor the desire to invest public funds in an expensive program whose net effects will be marginal, wasteful, or visible only after protracted delay.

We intend to help only those cities who help themselves.

I propose these guidelines for determining a city's qualifications for the benefits—and achievements—of this program.

1. The demonstration should be of sufficient magnitude both in its physical and social dimensions to arrest blight and decay in entire neighborhoods. It must make a substantial impact within the coming few years on the development of the entire city.

2. The demonstration should bring about a change in the total environment of the area affected. It must provide schools, parks, playgrounds, community centers, and access to all necessary community facilities.

3. The demonstration—from its beginning—should make use of every available social program. The human cost of reconstruction and relocation must be reduced. New opportunities for work and training must be offered.

4. The demonstration should contribute to narrowing the housing gap between the deprived and the rest of the community. Major additions must be made to the supply of sound dwellings. Equal opportunity in the choice of housing must be assured to every race.

5. The demonstration should offer maximum occasions for employing residents of the demonstration area in all phases of the program.

6. The demonstration should foster the development of local and private initiative and widespread citizen participation—especially from the demonstration area—in the planning and execution of the program.

7. The demonstration should take advantage of modern cost-reducing technologies without reducing the quality of the work. Neither the structure of real-estate taxation, cumbersome building codes, nor inefficient building practices should deter rehabilitation or inflate project costs.

8. The demonstration should make major improvements in the quality of the environment. There must be a high quality of design in new buildings, and attention to man's need for open spaces and attractive landscaping.

9. The demonstration should make relocation housing available at costs commensurate with the incomes of those displaced by the project. Counseling services, moving expenses, and small business loans should be provided, together with assistance in job placement and retraining.

10. The demonstration should be managed in each demonstration city

by a single authority with adequate powers to carry out and coordinate all phases of the program. There must be a serious commitment to the project on the part of local, and where appropriate, state authorities. Where required to carry out the plan, agreements should be reached with neighboring communities.

11. The demonstration proposal should offer proof that adequate municipal appropriations and services are available and will be sustained throughout the demonstration period.

12. The demonstration should maintain or establish a residential character in the area.

13. The demonstration should be consistent with existing development plans for the metropolitan areas involved. Transportation plans should coordinate every appropriate mode of city and regional transportation.

14. The demonstration should extend for an initial six-year period. It should maintain a schedule for the expeditious completion of the project.

These guidelines will demand the full cooperation of government at every level and of private citizens in each area. I believe our Federal system is creative enough to inspire that cooperative effort. I know it must be so creative if it is to prosper and flourish. . . .

METROPOLITAN PLANNING

The success of each demonstration will depend on the quality of its planning, and the degree of cooperation it elicits from the various governmental bodies concerned, as well as from private interests.

Most metropolitan areas conduct some degree of metropolitan planning now. The Federal Government has made funds available throughout the country so that state and local planning agencies might devise—many for the first time—comprehensive plans for metropolitan areas.

I recommend improvements and extensions of this program. The Congress enacted them recognizing that the problems of growth, transportation, housing, and public services cannot be considered by one entity of government alone.

The absence of cooperation between contiguous areas is wasteful. It is also blind to the reality of urban life. What happens in the central city, or the suburb, is certain to affect the quality of life in the other.

The widespread demand for these funds has resulted in their being spread thinly across the fifty states. Thus, the benefits of a truly coordinated attack on metropolitan problems have not generally been realized. . . .

DEMONSTRATIONS OF EFFECTIVE PLANNING

I propose that a series of demonstrations in effective metropolitan planning be undertaken promptly.

Metropolitan areas would be selected to return the broadest possible data and experience to Federal, state, and local governments. They should therefore be of varying size and environment, in widely separated locations. They would be selected to assure that their benefits reach small communities surrounding the large cities.

Advanced techniques and approaches should be employed. There must be
—balanced consideration of physical and human development programs;
—coordinated treatment of the regional transportation network;
—technical innovations, such as metropolitan data banks and systems analysis;
—new educational and training programs;
—new arrangements for coordinating decisions of the various local governments involved.

I estimate the cost of the demonstrations at $6,500,000.

I shall impose on the new Department of Housing and Urban Development the continuing responsibility to stimulate effective planning. If local governments do not plan cooperatively and sufficiently in advance of inevitable urban growth, even adequate funds and an aggressive determination to improve our cities cannot succeed.

HOUSING FOR ALL

The programs I have proposed—in rebuilding large areas of our cities, and in metropolitan planning—are essential for the rebirth of urban America.

Yet at the center of the cities' housing problem lies racial discrimination. Crowded miles of inadequate dwellings—poorly maintained and frequently overpriced—is the lot of most Negro Americans in many of our cities. Their avenue of escape to a more attractive neighborhood is often closed, because of their color.

The Negro suffers from this, as do his children. So does the community at large. Where housing is poor, schools are generally poor. Unemployment is widespread. Family life is threatened. The community's welfare burden is steadily magnified. These are the links in the chain of racial discrimination.

This Administration is working to break that chain—through aid to education, medical care, community action programs, job training, and the maintenance of a vigorous economy.

The time has come when we should break one of its strongest links—the often subtle, but always effective force of housing discrimination. The impacted racial ghetto will become a thing of the past only when the Negro American can move his family wherever he can afford to do so.

I shall, therefore, present to the Congress at an early date legislation to bar racial discrimination in the sale or rental of housing.

NEW COMMUNITIES

Our existing urban centers, however revitalized, cannot accommodate all the urban Americans of the next generation.

Three million new residents are added each year to our present urban population. The growth of new communities is inevitable. Unless they are to be casual parts of a general urban sprawl, a new approach to their design is required.

We must:

—enlarge the entire scale of the building process;

—make possible new efficiencies in construction, land development, and municipal services;

—relieve population densities;

—offer a variety of homes to a wide range of incomes.

These communities must also provide an environment harmonious to man's needs.

They must offer adequate transportation systems, attractive community buildings, and open spaces free from pollution. They must retain much of the natural beauty of the landscape.

The private sector must continue its prominent role in the new community development. As I recommended to the Congress last year, mortgage insurance should be made available for sites and community facilities for entire new communities.

It is apparent that new communities will spring into being near an increasing number of major metropolitan areas. Some, already in existence, promise dramatic efficiencies through size and new construction techniques, without sacrificing beauty. Obviously such a development should be encouraged. I recommend that the Congress provide the means of doing so.

THE NEW DEPARTMENT

No Federal program can be effective unless the agency that administers it is efficient. This is even more crucial for programs that call for comprehensive approaches at both the Federal and local level.

Progress was made after 1961 toward unifying the Housing and Home Finance Agency. But the very nature of that agency limited the extent to which its several parts could be welded into a truly unified whole. Its administrator lacked the statutory basis for gaining full control over partially independent agencies.

With this in mind, I requested—and you enacted—legislation to create a Department of Housing and Urban Development.

As a result, the Secretary of the new Department now has the authority and the machinery for implementing the new programs I have asked for.

I see five ways by which he can do this:

1. He can organize the Department so that its emphasis will be upon meeting modern urban needs—rather than fitting new programs into old and outworn patterns.

2. He can strengthen the regional structure so that more decisions can be made in the field.

3. He can assert effective leadership throughout the Department.

4. He can mesh together all our social and physical efforts to improve urban living.

5. He can assume leadership among intergovernmental agencies dealing with urban problems.

Such a Department, and such leadership, will be worthy of the program I recommend you adopt.

A YEAR OF REBIRTH

The evidence is all about us that to be complacent about the American city is to invite, at best, inconvenience; at worst, a divided nation.

The programs I have proposed in this message will require a determined commitment of our energy and a substantial commitment of our funds.

Yet these programs are well within our resources. Nor do they compare in cost with the ugliness, hostility, and hopelessness of unlivable cities.

What would it mean to begin now, and to bring about the rebirth of our cities?

It would mean:

—a more tolerable and a more hopeful life for millions of Americans;

—the possibility of retaining middle-income families in the city, and even attracting some to return;

—improving the cities' tax base, at a time of heavy strain on city budgets;

—ultimately reducing welfare costs;

—avoiding the unnecessary waste of human resources;

—giving to both urban and suburban families the freedom to choose where they will live;

—a clean room and a patch of sky for every person, a chance to live near an open space, and to reach it on a safe street.

As Thomas Wolfe wrote, "To every man his chance—to every man, regardless of his birth, his shining, golden opportunity—to every man the right to live, to work, to be himself, and to become whatever thing his manhood and his vision can combine to make him—this . . . is the promise of America."

I believe these are among the most profound aspirations of our people. I want to make them part of our destiny.

I urge the Congress promptly to adopt the Demonstration Cities Act of 1966. If we begin now the planning from which action will flow, the hopes of the twentieth century will become the realities of the twenty-first.

"Vital as it is,
mammoth and complex as it has become,
the American transportation system
is not good enough."

Message to Congress,
March 2, 1966.

Two centuries ago the American Nation came into being. Thirteen sparsely populated colonies, strung out along the Atlantic seaboard for 1,300 miles, joined their separate wills in a common endeavor.

Three bonds united them.

There was the cultural bond of a single language.

There was the moral bond of a thirst for liberty and democratic government.

There was the physical bond of a few roads and rivers, by which the citizens of the colonies engaged in peaceful commerce.

Two centuries later the language is the same. The thirst for liberty and democracy endures.

The physical bond—that tenuous skein of rough trails and primitive roads —has become a powerful network on which the prosperity and convenience of our society depend.

In a Nation that spans a continent, transportation is the web of union.

The Growth of Our Transportation System

It is not necessary to look back to the 1760s to chronicle the astonishing growth of American transportation.

Twenty years ago there were 31 million motor vehicles in the United States. Today there are 90 million. By 1975 there will be nearly 120 million.

Twenty years ago there were 1.5 million miles of paved roads and streets in the United States. Today this figure has almost doubled.

Twenty years ago there were 38,000 private and commercial aircraft. Today there are more than 97,000.

Twenty years ago commercial airlines flew 209 million miles. Last year they flew one billion miles.

Twenty-five years ago American transportation moved 619 billion ton miles of cargo. In 1964, 1.5 trillion ton miles were moved.

The manufacturing of transportation equipment has kept pace. It has tripled since 1947. Last year $4.5 billion was spent for new transportation plant and equipment.

Transportation is one of America's largest employers. There are

—737,000 railroad employees,

—270,000 local and interurban workers,

—230,000 in air transport,

—almost a million men and women in motor transport and storage.

Together with pipeline and water transportation employees, the total number of men and women who earn their livelihoods by moving people and goods is well over two and one-half million.

The Federal Government supports or regulates almost every means of transportation. Last year alone more than $5 billion in Federal funds were invested in transportation—in highway construction, in river and harbor development, in airway operation and airport construction, in maritime subsidies. The Government owns 1,500 of the Nation's 2,500 ocean-going cargo vessels.

Our transportation system—the descendant of the horse-drawn coaches and sailing ships of colonial times—accounts for one in every five dollars in the American economy. In 1965, that amounted to $120 billion—a sum greater than the Gross National Product of this Nation in 1940.

Shortcomings of Our System

Vital as it is, mammoth and complex as it has become, the American transportation system is not good enough.

It is not good enough when it offers nearly a mile of street or road for every square mile of land—and yet provides no relief from time-consuming, frustrating, and wasteful congestion.

It is not good enough when it produces sleek and efficient jet aircraft—and yet cannot move passengers to and from airports in the time it takes those aircraft to fly hundreds of miles.

It is not good enough when it builds superhighways for supercharged automobiles—and yet cannot find a way to prevent 50,000 highway deaths this year.

It is not good enough when public and private investors pour $15 million into a large, high-speed ship—only to watch it remain idle in port for days before it is loaded.

It is not good enough when it lays out new freeways to serve new cities and suburbs—and carelessly scars the irreplaceable countryside.

It is not good enough when it adheres to custom for its own sake—and ignores opportunities to serve our people more economically and efficiently.

It is not good enough if it responds to the needs of an earlier America—and does not help us expand our trade and distribute the fruits of our land throughout the world.

Why We Have Fallen Short

Our transportation system has not emerged from a single drawing board, on which the needs and capacities of our economy were all charted. It could not have done so, for it grew along with the country itself—now rest-lessly expanding, now consolidating, as opportunity grew bright or dim.

Thus investment and service innovations responded to special needs. Re-search and development were sporadic, sometimes inconsistent, and largely oriented towards the promotion of a particular means of transportation.

As a result, America today lacks a coordinated transportation system that permits travelers and goods to move conveniently and efficiently from one means of transportation to another, using the best characteristics of each.

Both people and goods are compelled to conform to the system as it is, despite the inconvenience and expense of:

—aging and often obsolete transportation plant and equipment;

—networks chiefly designed to serve a rural society;

—services long outstripped by our growing economy and population, by changes in land use, by new concepts in industrial plant location, warehous-ing, and distribution;

—the failure to take full advantage of new technologies developed else-where in the economy;

—programs and policies which impede private initiative and dull incen-tives for innovation.

The result is waste—of human and economic resources—and of the tax-payers' dollar.

We have abided this waste too long.

We must not permit it to continue.

We have too much at stake in the quality and economy of our transporta-tion system. If the growth of our transport industries merely keeps pace with our current national economic growth, the demand for transportation will more than double in the next twenty years.

But even that is too conservative an estimate. Passenger transportation is growing much faster than our Gross National Product—reflecting the desires of an affluent people with ever-increasing incomes.

Private and Public Responsibility

The United States is the only major nation in the world that relies primarily upon privately owned and operated transportation.

That national policy has served us well. It must be continued.

But private ownership has been made feasible only by the use of publicly granted authority and the investment of public resources:

—by the construction of locks, dams, and channels on our rivers and inland waterways;

—by the development of a vast highway network;

—by the construction and operation of airports and airways;

—by the development of ports and harbors;

—by direct financial support to the Merchant Marine;

—by grants of eminent domain authority;

—by capital equipment grants and demonstration projects for mass transit;

—in years past, by grants of public land to assist the railroads.

Enlightened government has served as a full partner with private enterprise in meeting America's urgent need for mobility.

That partnership must now be strengthened with all the means that creative Federalism can provide. The costs of a transportation paralysis in the years ahead are too severe. The rewards of an efficient system are too great. We cannot afford the luxury of drift—or proceed with "business as usual."

We must secure for all our travelers and shippers the full advantages of modern science and technology.

We must acquire the reliable information we need for intelligent decisions.

We must clear away the institutional and political barriers which impede adaptation and change.

We must promote the efforts of private industry to give the American consumer more and better service for his transportation dollar.

We must coordinate the executive functions of our transportation agencies in a single coherent instrument of government. Thus policy guidance and support for each means of transportation will strengthen the national economy as a whole.

A DEPARTMENT OF TRANSPORTATION

I urge the Congress to establish a cabinet-level Department of Transportation.

I recommend that this Department bring together almost 100,000 employees and almost $6 billion of Federal funds now devoted to transportation.

I urge the creation of such a Department to serve the growing demands of this great Nation, to satisfy the needs of our expanding industry, and to fulfill the right of our taxpayers to maximum efficiency and frugality in Government operations.

In so doing, I follow the recommendations of many outstanding Americans.

In 1936, a Select Committee of the United States Senate recommended a Department of Transportation, or in the alternative, the consolidation of all transportation programs in the Department of Commerce.

In 1949, the Hoover Commission Task Force on Transportation recommended a Department of Transportation.

In 1961 President Eisenhower recommended such a Department in his Budget Message.

In 1961 a Special Study Group of the Senate Committee on Commerce recommended that all promotional and safety programs of the Federal Government be concentrated in a Department of Transportation.

Many distinguished members of Congress have offered bills to create the Department. Private citizens, the Nation's leading experts in the field, have made the same recommendation to me.

It is time to act on these recommendations.

SCOPE OF THE DEPARTMENT

I propose that the following agencies and functions be consolidated in the Department of Transportation.

1. *The Office of the Undersecretary of Commerce for Transportation,* and its Policy, Program, Emergency Transportation, and Research staffs.

2. *The Bureau of Public Roads and the Federal-aid Highway Program it administers.*

3. *The Federal Aviation Agency.* The key agency, with its functions in aviation safety, promotion, and investment, will be transferred in its entirety to the new Department. It will continue to carry out these functions in the new Department.

4. *The Coast Guard,* whose principal peacetime activities relate to transportation and marine safety. The Coast Guard will be transferred as a unit from the Treasury Department. As in the past, the Coast Guard will operate as part of the Navy in time of war.

5. *The Maritime Administration,* with its construction and operating subsidy programs.

6. *The safety functions of the Civil Aeronautics Board,* the responsibility

for investigating and determining the probable cause of aircraft accidents and its appellate functions related to safety.

7. *The safety functions and car service functions of the Interstate Commerce Commission,* principally the inspection and enforcement of safety regulations for railroads, motor carriers, and pipelines, and the distribution of rail car supply in times of shortage.

8. *The Great Lakes Pilotage Administration, the St. Lawrence Seaway Development Corporation, the Alaska Railroad, and certain minor transportation-related activities of other agencies.*

As this list indicates, I am recommending the consolidation into the Department of those Federal agencies whose primary functions are transportation promotion and safety.

NATIONAL TRANSPORTATION SAFETY BOARD

No function of the new Department—no responsibility of its Secretary—will be more important than safety. We must ensure the safety of our citizens as they travel on our land, in our skies, and over our waters.

I recommend that there be created under the Secretary of Transportation a National Transportation Safety Board independent of the operating units of the department.

The sole function of this Board will be the safety of our travelers. It will review investigations of accidents to seek their causes. It will determine compliance with safety standards. It will examine the adequacy of the safety standards themselves. It will assume safety functions transferred from the ICC and the CAB.

I consider the functions of this Board so important that I am requesting authority from the Congress to name five presidential appointees as its members.

RELATION TO OTHER GOVERNMENT ACTIVITIES

The activities of several departments and agencies affect transportation promotion and safety. Sound management requires that an appropriate and intimate relationship be established between those activities and the new Department of Transportation.

1. *The subsidy functions of the Civil Aeronautics Board.* Aviation subsidies—now provided only for local airline service—clearly promote our

domestic transportation system. But subsidy awards are an integral part of the process of authorizing air carrier service. This is a regulatory function.

Therefore the airline subsidy program should remain in the Civil Aeronautics Board. The Secretary of Transportation, however, will develop principles and criteria which the Board will take into consideration in its proceedings. In this way the subsidy program will be coordinated with overall national transportation policy.

2. *The navigation program of the Corps of Engineers.* The Corps of Engineers—through its construction of locks and harbor facilities and its channel deepening and river bank protection work—makes a major contribution to water transportation. The Department of Transportation should not assume the responsibility for that construction, but its Secretary should be involved in the planning of water transportation projects.

With the approval of the President, the Secretary of Transportation should also issue standards and criteria for the economic evaluation of Federal transportation investments generally. In the case of transportataion features of multipurpose water projects, he should do so after consulting with the Water Resources Council.

3. *International aviation.* The Secretary of Transportation should provide leadership within the Executive branch in formulating long-range policy for international aviation. While foreign policy aspects of international aviation are the responsibility of the Secretary of State, the Secretary of Transportation should ensure that our international aviation policies are consistent with overall national transportation policy.

Subject to policy determinations by the President, the Civil Aeronautics Board regulates international aviation routes and fares as they affect the United States. This function has far-reaching effects on our foreign policy, our balance of payments, and the vitality of American aviation. The Secretary of Transportation should participate in Civil Aeronautics Board proceedings that involve international aviation policy.

4. *Urban transportation.* The Departments of Transportation and Housing and Urban Development must cooperate in decisions affecting urban transportation.

The future of urban transportation—the safety, convenience, and indeed the livelihood of its users—depends upon wide-scale, rational planning. If the Federal Government is to contribute to that planning, it must speak with a coherent voice.

The Department of Housing and Urban Development bears the principal responsibility for a unified Federal approach to urban problems. Yet it cannot perform this task without the counsel, support, and cooperation of the Department of Transportation.

I shall ask the two Secretaries to recommend to me, within a year after the creation of the new Department, the means and procedures by which this cooperation can best be achieved—not only in principle, but in practical effect.

ROLE OF THE DEPARTMENT

The Department of Transportation will

—coordinate the principal existing programs that promote transportation in America;

—bring new technology to a total transportation system, by promoting research and development in cooperation with private industry;

—improve safety in every means of transportation;

—encourage private enterprise to take full and prompt advantage of new technological opportunities;

—encourage high-quality, low-cost service to the public;

—conduct systems analyses and planning, to strengthen the weakest parts of today's system;

—develop investment criteria and standards, and analytical techniques to assist all levels of government and industry in their transportation investments.

THE INTERSTATE COMMERCE COMMISSION

The cabinet-level Department I recommend will not alter the economic regulatory functions of the Interstate Commerce Commission, the Civil Aeronautics Board, or the Federal Maritime Commission.

I do recommend, however, a change in the manner of selecting the Chairman of the Interstate Commerce Commission.

Today, the Chairman of this vital Commission—alone among the Federal regulatory agencies—is selected, not by the President, but by annual rotation among the eleven commissioners.

This is not sound management practice in an agency whose influence on our rail, highway, waterway, and pipeline industries is so far reaching.

The ICC bears the demanding and challenging responsibility to keep

Federal regulation attuned to the needs and opportunities of a dynamic industry. Its jurisdiction extends to 18,000 transport companies. It handles 7,000 cases each year. No priviate corporation of such size and importance would change its chief executive officer once each year.

I shall shortly submit to the Congress a reorganization plan to give the President authority to designate the Chairman of the Interstate Commerce Commission from among its members, and to strengthen his executive functions.

SAFETY

One hundred and five thousand Americans died in accidents last year.

More than half were killed in transportation, or in recreation accidents related to transportation.

49,000 deaths involved motor vehicles.

1,300 involved aircraft.

1,500 involved ships and boats.

2,300 involved railroads.

Millions of Americans were injured in transportation accidents—the overwhelming majority involving automobiles.

Each means of transportation has developed safety programs of varying effectiveness. Yet we lack a comprehensive program keyed to a total transportation system.

Proven safety techniques in one means have not always been adapted in others.

Last year the highway death toll set a new record. The prediction for this year is that more than 50,000 persons will die on our streets and highways— more than 50,000 useful and promising lives will be lost, and as many families stung by grief.

The toll of Americans killed in this way since the introduction of the automobile is truly unbelievable. It is 1.5 million—more than all the combat deaths suffered in all our wars.

No other necessity of modern life has brought more convenience to the American people—or more tragedy—than the automobile.

WHY WE ARE FAILING

The carnage on the highways must be arrested.

As I said some weeks ago, we must replace suicide with sanity and anarchy with safety.

The weaknesses of our present highway safety program must be corrected:

—Our knowledge of causes is grossly inadequate. Expert opinion is frequently contradictory and confusing.

—Existing safety programs are widely dispersed. Government and private efforts proceed separately, without effective coordination.

—There is no clear assignment of responsibility at the Federal level.

—The allocation of our resources to highway safety is inadequate.

—Neither private industry nor government officials concerned with automotive transportation have made safety first among their priorities. Yet we know that expensive freeways, powerful engines, and smooth exteriors will not stop the massacre on our roads.

WHAT CAN BE DONE

State and local resources are insufficient to bring about swift reductions in the highway death rate. The Federal Government must provide additional resources. Existing programs must be expanded. Pioneer work must begin in neglected areas.

Federal highway safety responsibilities should be incorporated into the Department of Transportation, in a total transportation safety program.

I have already set in motion a number of steps under existing law:

1. *To strengthen the Federal role,* I am assigning responsibilty for coordinating Federal highway safety programs to the Secretary of Commerce. I am directing the Secretary to establish a major highway safety unit within his Department. This unit will ultimately be transferred to the Department of Transportation. The President's Committee on Traffic Safety will be reorganized, strengthened and supported entirely by Federal funds. The Interdepartmental Highway Safety Board will be reconstituted and the Secretary's role strengthened.

2. *To give greater support to our safety programs,* I am requesting increased funds for research, accident data collection, improved emergency medical service, driver education and testing, and traffic control technology.

I have also asked the Secretary of Commerce to evaluate systematically the resources allocated to traffic safety, to ensure that we are receiving the maximum benefits from our present efforts.

3. *To improve driving conditions,* I have ordered that high priority be given to our efforts to build safety features into the Federal-aid highway network.

4. *To save those who are injured,* I have directed the Secretary of Health, Education, and Welfare, in cooperation with the Secretary of Commerce, immediately to initiate projects to demonstrate techniques for more effective emergency care and transportation. He will work in full cooperation with state, local, and private officials.

5. *To help us better understand the causes of highway accidents,* I have asked the Secretary of Commerce to establish accident investigation teams, who will bring us new understanding of highway accidents and their causes.

6. *To make Government vehicles safer,* I have asked the Administrator of General Services, in cooperation with the Secretary of Commerce, to begin a detailed study of the additional vehicle safety features that should be added to the Federal fleet.

THE TRAFFIC SAFETY ACT OF 1966

More—much more—remains to be done. The people of America deserve an aggressive highway safety program.

I believe that the Congress—the same Congress which last year gave the Secretary of Commerce broad authority to set uniform standards for state highway safety programs—will join in our efforts to bring that program into being.

I urge the Congress to enact the Traffic Safety Act of 1966.

I urge greater support for state highway safety programs.

I urge the creation of a National Highway Research and Test Facility.

To begin, I recommend a $700 million, six-year program.

The three components of this program are as critically important as the problems they address.

First, Federal grants to the states for highway safety will be increased. With these funds, a comprehensive highway safety program can be developed by each state under standards approved by the Secretary of Commerce. Included will be measures such as driver education and licensing—advanced traffic control techniques—regular vehicle safety inspections—police and emergency medical services.

Second, automobile safety performance will be improved. Proper design and engineering can make our cars safer. Vehicles sold in interstate commerce must be designed and equipped for maximum safety. Safe performance design standards must be met in tomorrow's cars.

I recommend that the Secretary of Commerce be given authority to deter-

mine the necessary safety performance criteria for all vehicles and their components.

If, after a two-year period, the Secretary finds that adequate voluntary standards are not satisfactory, he would be authorized to prescribe nation-wide mandatory safety standards. He would be also authorized to prohibit the sale in interstate commerce of new vehicles, and their components, which failed to meet those standards.

Third, the Federal Government's highway safety research efforts will be expanded.

I recommend construction of a national highway safety research and test center.

Funds are needed to support research and testing in many disciplines related to highway safety. The public interest demands a better under-standing of the human, highway, and vehicle factors which cause death and injury. We must develop more effective countermeasures and objective standards to guide our national programs. Special accident teams should be organized—accurate data collection should be enlarged on a national basis—fellowship grants and research support should be made available to attract the best minds and talents of our Nation to this urgent work.

This new highway safety program would be transferred to the Secretary of Transportation upon the creation of the new Department.

Congress has not hesitated to establish rigorous safety standards for other means of transportation when circumstances demanded them.

Today's highway death toll calls for an equally vigorous and effective expression of concern for our millions of car-owning families. For unless we avert this slaughter, one out of every two Americans will one day be killed or seriously injured on our highways.

SAFETY STANDARDS FOR MOTOR VEHICLE TIRES

I urge the Congress to act speedily and favorable on S. 2669, a bill establish-ing safety standards for motor vehicle tires sold or shipped in interstate commerce.

Most tires sold to American drivers are produced and properly tested by reputable companies. Nevertheless, evidence has shown that increasing numbers of inferior tires are being sold to unwitting customers throughout the country. The dangers such tires hold for high-speed automobiles and their occupants is obvious.

S. 2669 provides that the Secretary of Commerce shall establish, and publish in the Federal Register, interim minimum safety standards for tires. The Secretary would be required to review these standards two years from the enactment of the bill, and to revise them where necessary. A research and development program under his direction would improve the minimum standards for new tires, and develop such standards for retreaded tires.

Our driving public deserves the prompt passage of S. 2669, and the protection it will afford them from accidents caused by tire failures.

SAFETY AT SEA

Last year ninety men and women lost their lives when the cruise ship *Yarmouth Castle* burned and sank in the calm waters of the Caribbean.

The *Yarmouth Castle* was exempt from United States safety standards—partially because of its "grandfather rights" under law. It was built before 1937.

We cannot allow the lives of our citizens to depend upon the year in which a ship was built.

The Coast Guard is presently completing its investigation of the *Yarmouth Castle* disaster. The Maritime Administration has already finished its investigation of financial responsibility.

Later in this session—when our inquiries are accomplished and our findings reported—*we will submit to the Congress legislation to improve safety measures and guarantees of financial responsibility on the part of owners and operators of passenger-carrying vessels sailing from our ports.*

AIR ACCIDENT COMPENSATION

The United States has declared its intention to withdraw from the Warsaw Convention. Under this pact, the financial liability of a member nation's airline is limited to $8,300 for a passenger's death.

Discussions are under way in the International Civil Aviation Organization to increase this liability for passengers flying anywhere in the world. We have expressed our opinion that the limit of liability should be raised to $100,000.

RESEARCH AND DEVELOPMENT

Today the United States ranks as the world's leader in technology.

Despite this—and despite the importance of transportation in the competition for international trade—exclusive of national security and space, the Federal Government spends less than one percent of its total research and development budget for transportation.

Under our system of government, private enterprise bears the primary responsibility for research and development in the transportation field.

But the Government can help. It can plan and fashion research and development for a total transportation system which is beyond the responsibility or capability of private industry.

Through government-sponsored research and development we can:

—fully understand the complex relationships among the components of a total transportation system;

—provide comprehensive and reliable data for both private and public decisions;

—identify areas of transportation which can be exploited by private industry to provide safer and more efficient services to the public;

—build the basis for a more efficient use of public resources;

—provide the technological base needed to assure adequate domestic and international transportation in times of emergency;

—help make significant advances in every phase of transport—in aircraft, in ocean-going ships, in swifter rail service, in safer vehicles.

The Department of Transportation—working with private industry and other Government agencies—will provide a coordinated program of research and development to move the Nation toward our transportation goals. The Department can help translate scientific discovery into industrial practice.

SUPERSONIC TRANSPORT AIRCRAFT

The United States is preeminent in the field of aircraft design and manufacture.

We intend to maintain that leadership.

As I said in my State of the Union Message, I am proposing a program to construct and flight test a new 2,000-mile-per-hour supersonic aircraft.

Our supersonic transport must be reliable and safe for the passenger.

It must be profitable for both the airlines and the manufacturers.

Its operating performance must be superior to any comparable aircraft.

It must be introduced into the market in a timely manner.

We have under way an intensive research and design program on the supersonic transport, supported by appropriations of $231 million.

The design competition for this aircraft and its engines is intense and resourceful.

I am requesting $200 million in fiscal year 1967 appropriations to initiate the prototype phase of the supersonic transport. My request includes funds for the completion of design competition, expanded economic and sonic boom studies, and the start of prototype construction.

We hope to conduct first flight tests of the supersonic transport by 1970, and to introduce it into commercial service by 1974.

AIRCRAFT NOISE

The jet age has brought progress and prosperity to our air transportation system. Modern jets can carry passengers and freight across a continent at speeds close to that of sound.

Yet this progress has created special problems of its own. Aircraft noise is a growing source of annoyance and concern to the thousands of citizens who live near many our large airports. As more of our airports begin to accommodate jets and as the volume of air travel expands, the problem will take on added dimension.

There are no simple or swift solutions. But it is clear that we must embark now on a concerted effort to alleviate the problems of aircraft noise. To this end, I am today directing the President's Science Advisor to work with the Administrators of the Federal Aviation Agency and of the National Aeronautics and Space Administration, and the Secretaries of Commerce, and of Housing and Urban Development, to frame an action program to attack this problem.

I am asking this group to:

—study the development of noise standards and the compatible uses of land near airports,

—consult with local communities and industry,

—recommend legislative or administrative actions needed to move ahead in this area.

ADVANCED OCEAN VESSEL CONCEPTS

After years of United States leadership, maritime technology in other countries has caught up with and, in some instances, surpassed our own.

The U.S. Merchant Marine suffers in world competition because it bears much higher costs than its competitors. This can be offset in some measure by technological improvements.

The Department of Defense recently launched the Fast Deployment Logistics Ship program. This concept introduces to the maritime field the same systems approach that has proven so successful in other Defense and Aerospace programs.

To achieve comparable improvements throughout the maritime industry I am directing the Secretary of Commerce, with the Secretary of Defense, the President's Scientific Advisor, and the Atomic Energy Commission, to conduct a study of advanced vessel concepts.

The work of this team will include:

—research, development, and planning of high speed, large capacity ships, devoted primarily to transporting preloaded containers of varying types between the major ports in the world;

—research on an ocean-going Surface Effects Vessel capable of skimming over the water at speeds of more than 100 knots;

—continued exploration of the application of nuclear propulsion to merchant marine ships.

Our private shipyards should continue to serve the needs of the country. They can become more productive and competitive through research and development and through standardization of ship construction. With a new Department of Transportation, we will increase our efforts to bring a modern, efficient merchant marine fleet to this Nation.

ADVANCED LAND TRANSPORT

Last year Congress took a long step toward advanced land transportation by enacting the High-Speed Ground Transportation Research and Development program. This program will be continued at the most rapid pace consistent with sound management of the research effort.

Similar vision and imagination can be applied to highway transport.

Segments of the Interstate Highway network already in operation are the most efficient, productive roads ever built anywhere in the world. Motor vehicles move at higher rates of speed, more safely, and in greater number per lane than on conventional roads. Transportation costs are reduced, and less land area is needed for this volume of traffic.

With the network about half completed after ten years, it is apparent that interstate highways, as well as other roads and streets, can become even more productive and safe.

Accordingly, I am directing the Secretary of Commerce to:

—investigate means for providing guidance and control mechanisms to increase the capacity and improve the safety of our highway network;

—conduct research into the means of improving traffic flow—particularly in our cities—so we can make better use of our existing roads and streets;

—investigate the potential of separate roadways for various classes of vehicles, with emphasis on improving mass transportation service.

SYSTEMS RESEARCH

Some of our brightest opportunities in research and development lie in the less obvious and often neglected parts of our transportation system.

We spend billions for constructing new highways, but comparatively little for traffic control devices.

We spend millions for fast jet aircraft—but little on the traveler's problem of getting to and from the airport.

We have mounted a sizable government-industry program to expand exports, yet we allow a mountain of red tape paperwork to negate our efforts. Worldwide, a total of 810 forms are required to cover all types of cargo imported and exported. In this country alone, as many as 43 separate forms are used in one export shipment. Eighty separate forms may be needed to process some imports. This is paperwork run wild.

I am directing the Secretaries of Treasury and Commerce and the Attorney General to attack these problems, through the use of effective systems research programs. And I have directed them to eliminate immediately every unnecessary element of red tape that inhibits our import and export programs.

TRANSPORTATION FOR AMERICA

The Founding Fathers rode by stage to Philadelphia to take part in the Constitutional Convention. They could not have anticipated the immense complexity—or the problems—of transportation in our day.

Yet they, too, recognized the vital national interest in commerce between the states. The early Congresses expressed that interest even more directly, by supporting the development of road and waterway systems.

Most important, the Founding Fathers gave us a flexible system of government. Cities, states, and the Federal Government can join together—and in many cases work with private enterprise—in partnerships of creative Federalism to solve our most complex problems.

For the very size of our transportation requirements—rising step-by-step with the growth of our population and industry—demands that we respond with new institutions, new programs of research, new efforts to make our vehicles safe, as well as swift.

Modern transportation can be the rapid conduit of economic growth—or a bottleneck.

It can bring jobs and loved ones and recreation closer to every family—or it can bring instead sudden and purposeless death.

It can improve every man's standard of living—or multiply the cost of all he buys.

It can be a convenience, a pleasure, the passport to new horizons of the mind and spirit—or it can frustrate and impede and delay.

The choice is ours to make.

We build the cars, the trains, the planes, the ships, the roads, and the airports. We can, if we will, plan their safe and efficient use in the decades ahead to improve the quality of life for all Americans.

The program I have outlined in this message is the first step toward that goal.

I urge its prompt enactment by the Congress.

"To those who believe that we are backing off,
I say, no—we are not backing off.
We are staying for the long pull."
Remarks to Conference on Women in the War on Poverty,
May 8, 1967.

Those of you who have been listening to speeches all day, I know you would not wish me to detain you long.

But I do want to share a few thoughts with you about the struggle that we have been waging with increasing intensity against poverty in this land that we all love.

Long before there was an official Federal "war on poverty"—long before the New Deal, the Fair Deal, and the New Frontier, the women's groups were fighting poverty in the neighborhoods and in the legislative halls. Many of the early victories in the struggle against poverty were won because the women cared enough to work, to plan, and to make their influence felt. The battles for compulsory education, the battles against child labor, are two that come most readily to my mind that the women carried on and the women won.

Now you have organized a new program, using new methods and new resources. But this program—like all of those that have gone before—will succeed only if you make the same commitment that women have made over the generations past. That commitment is

—to teach,

—to heal,

—to awaken the conscience of this great Nation.

I would like to speak realistically this afternoon about the job that remains to be done—by all of us.

We have heard a great deal of contrary talk about poverty during the past few weeks.

Some people say we are spending too much, or we are wasting too much, on a losing battle to help poor Americans.

Others say that we are spending too little, that we backed away from our commitment to this war because of our commitment to the other war—in Vietnam.

Both views are earnestly held. But both, unfortunately, I believe, are wide of the mark.

To those who believe that we are backing off, I say, no—we are not backing off. We are staying for the long pull.

Let the figures speak to you—not because they can tell the whole story, but because they represent a conscious and deliberate commitment of the American people over the past six years.

The figures show that in this fiscal year, the amount of Federal funds going to help the poor in America—through all of our social programs—is a little over $22 billion.

If Congress passes the 1968 budget that has been recommended, that it is now considering, this $22 billion will be increased to $25 billion 600 million, or plus $3 billion 600 million.

That is 2½ times as much as this Government was spending in 1960.

So it is clear to me, at least, that we are not backing off from our commitments to fight poverty. Nor will we—so long as I have anything to say about it. We are really just beginning.

To those of you who believe we are spending too much, I want to address a very special word:

You—and I—are both against crime in the streets.

We are against violence and delinquency.

We are against the dulling effects of dependence on welfare that continues from generation to generation.

We want our fellow men to be productive. We want them to be responsible citizens—not dropouts from our society.

I would like to suggest that we cannot logically oppose the effects of poverty and the efforts to relieve them. We cannot abhor the disease and then fight the cure—not if we want this to be a healthy Nation. And poverty, I believe, is curable, I have seen it cured.

More than thirty years ago in my home State of Texas, when I was only twenty-seven years old, I served as the administrator for the National Youth Administration. That program was started by a great President with vision, President Franklin Delano Roosevelt. It was in many ways similar to the program that we have today in the Job Corps, in the Neighborhood Youth Corps, and Upward Bound.

It was a depression version of the War on Poverty, and it was quite a success. In all, we had then some 33,000 young Texans involved in the NYA program. Some learned trades. Some were provided part-time jobs so they could stay in school. Many got full-time jobs.

You who are here this afternoon who are not familiar with those days may not know it, but the first beautification expert in the Johnson family was me—not Lady Bird. The NYA youth in Texas, under a great governor, Jimmy Allred, built more than 100 roadside parks that are still in existence today and are the pride of our state. They worked on hundreds of other projects that helped that state, but most of all helped themselves.

So don't think the NYA and the other programs didn't have their critics—just as the War on Poverty has its today. But for all the criticisms, most of the programs went on—and more importantly, they helped millions of Americans to survive, and ultimately to prosper.

I was on a Job Corps platform down in my state not long ago. I was speaking. As I looked down the list I saw a governor that had been on NYA. I saw a congressman that had been on NYA. I saw the chairman of the state Board of Regents who had been on NYA. So that is what happens. I see a congressman today who was in the NYA over here. I am not going to look much more. It would take too much time from my speech.

But today, when I go through that state, I meet the people who were helped by NYA more than thirty years ago. Most of them are now in their late forties or fifties. Most are responsible and productive citizens. They are doctors, businessmen, teachers, and skilled craftsmen. And it will be hard for their children to understand what poverty is like. That is one of the information gaps of our time; many of our middle-class Americans cannot grasp the elementary facts of life for the poor people of this country:

—Many of us wake up in the morning to gentle music of a clock radio. A poor person in America may wake up because there is no heat or because a rat is running across his bed.

That is no exaggeration. In one poor neighborhood 40 percent of the four-year-old children identified a picture of a teddy bear as the only animal they knew—a rat.

—Middle-class Americans may complain about how hard it is to arrange a house call from a doctor. But a poor person in America may go without a doctor altogether—because there are few doctors' offices located in our slums. The poor in America do not know what the phrase "family doctor" really means. They take their medicine—when they can—usually from the emergency room of a public hospital. And they do not see the same doctor twice.

One doctor summed up the relation between illness and poverty very clearly. He said, "The poor get sicker. The sick get poorer."

—Middle-class Americans may settle most of their legal problems with ease. But when a poor person reports a violation of the housing code, he and his family may be evicted by the landlord. He cannot afford a lawyer to fight the eviction.

Poverty means all of these things—not one by one, but all at once. Each compounds the other.

Poverty wears different masks in different places. We think of it as a city disease. But almost half of American poverty is found in our rural areas. We sometimes may think of it as a Negro affliction, but seven in ten poor people are white. Poverty afflicts the old man and it affects the young child.

Poverty is found on an Indian reservation, in the hollows of West Virginia, in the migrant camps of Oregon, and here, in Washington, D.C., as well as throughout my state.

These dimensions of poverty are not new. What is new is the all-out American effort to break their grip on millions of our fellow citizens.

I believe under the very able, imaginative, and inspiring direction of Sargent Shriver we are making great progress.

The tide of progress is clear. Let me share with you a letter from a mother in Peoria, Illinois: "You literally saved my boy's life. Before he entered the Job Corps, he used to say that the only way he could ever have anything was to steal it. He could have ended up in prison—or worse. Now he has a job at the Caterpillar Tractor Company and makes $2.96 an hour, and he has a chance to advance as he becomes more experienced."

The only thing the Government gave this young man was the chance—the chance to help himself. If that is a giveaway program then I am for it. I am for more of them.

The Job Corps will not eliminate poverty—or the effects of poverty—in the United States. Neither will the Neighborhood Youth Corps, nor a hundred retraining programs. Neither will the massive education programs that are now pumping over a billion dollars a year into education for the disadvantaged children; nor will the medical centers or the legal centers, the VISTA program, or Head Start. Urban renewal alone will not eliminate poverty, nor will the new model cities program. The Teacher Corps will not eliminate poverty, nor will an increase in Social Security.

I wish I could say that all of the programs together—all $25 billion worth—would eliminate poverty and its effects in America during this decade.

But they won't.

For the War on Poverty is not fought on any single, simple battlefield, and it will not be won in a generation. There are too many enemies: lack of jobs, bad housing, poor schools, lack of skills, discrimination—and each aspect of poverty relates to, and intensifies, the others. That is the vicious circle that you must break.

We have spent well over $100 billion in the past six years in that effort. Those dollars have not brought us total victory. But they have brought partial victory. They have helped many millions of Americans take their first steps toward full and meaningful participation in this society.

We can see that as we look out at the faces of young people from the

Job Corps—many of them now wearing the uniform of their country. We can see it in the Head Start classroom—although we may not be able to measure its results for a generation.

We can see it as fully 20 percent of the young people from households in poverty are now going on to college, and break forever their own bondage to the vicious circle. We can see it in the hollows of Appalachia, where a job is again becoming a common occurrence, instead of a rarity.

Perhaps most importantly we can see progress in the fact that bitterness is being rejected as the solution to poverty in the United States. The seeds of aspiration—of the will to succeed—have been planted in the slums and the ghettoes and the hollows of America.

As they grow, there grows with them a new and restless spirit that seeks a constructive change and seeks a voice and participation in our society. That spirit, I believe, is going to build for us a better America. Bitterness and strife and separatism will not and cannot build anything; those things just destroy. And that fact, I believe, is understood among all but a very small minority today.

We may never live to see an America without poverty.

But we may see an America:

—where a life time of poverty is not the inevitable fate of a child born into it;

—where there is a genuine opportunity for every child and young person to live in decency and security;

—where the means of liberation and the understanding of how to use them are available to all of us.

If we reach that America it will be because we did not grow tired. It will be because we gave Americans a chance to help themselves.

That is in the finest and oldest American tradition: the same tradition that established the land grant colleges and public education, and the GI bill of rights; the same tradition that passed the Homestead Act; the same tradition that established the NYA more than thirty years ago.

It is also the tradition out of which you have come.

I was looking at some figures as I flew up on the plane today. I looked back a little over three years ago when I considered my first budget.

Then we were spending a little over $4 billion a year on educating our people. This year, we have more than $12 billion in our budget for education.

Three years ago we were spending about $4 billion a year on our health

programs for all of our people. This year we are spending more than $12 billion.

So on health and education we are spending about $24 billion 800 million on those two subjects.

Now, can you think of a better place in the world to spend your money than to invest it in the bodies and the minds of our children?

You have given hope to so many of us. We think better lives are going to be the result.

We thank you for coming here to this meeting. We enlist your approval. We ask for your assistance. We urge your support.

May you never grow weary of the blessed work that you do. In the years to come, you can look back on this meeting here in Washington today and say, "I was one. We came, we saw, and we conquered."

At least we are going to try.

Thank you very much.

Revolutions, Present and Future

By McGeorge Bundy

The mid-winter of 1968 is not an easy time for assessment of the achievements of our society and its government in the large fields of education and communication. Viewed in the short-range focus of the 1969 budget, our position can seem extremely difficult and the immediate judgment may be that we are not doing all that we should. This is a judgment I share; I would feel better both for the country and for an Administration I admire if the President had chosen to seek larger sums for education this year and some more explicit decisions in certain questions of communication policy. Yet I remain confident that the President has asked for all that he thought he could get, and I respect his right to prefer this practical calculus to the less tangible advantages of keeping the national targets high.

I begin with this short-range difference for the double purpose of stating it candidly and putting it aside. On the larger canvas of history I think it will be clear that the first full term of Lyndon Johnson has been a time of extraordinary and even decisive change in the role of the national government as a constructive force in American education. In this field the country has truly turned a corner since 1964. And in the still larger field of our communications systems as a whole, while no corner has been turned, at least the lights have been turned on.

EDUCATION

In the messages and speeches that follow, the reader will find a variety of statistical measures of achievement and a number of striking examples of good new things that have been made possible by a dozen new laws and billions of new dollars. President Johnson shares with his predecessors a penchant for statistics and illustrations that tell us no more than they tell us. In the case of Federal aid to education, however, both the stories and the statistics are somehow less than the underlying achievement.

I could not prove that all this new money has been well spent; it needs no expert to see that in the scores of titles of the new laws of the 1960s there may be breeding grounds for some waste and much confusion. In that respect, indeed, there may be a considerable silver lining to the cloud of financial stalemate that hangs over the Office of Education as I write. A pause for regrouping can be healthy. Still, I have been an educational administrator and I know from painful memory how heavily the budget for the coming year fills the horizon for that league of harassed men.

But above and beyond the statistics of Presidents, the growing pains of new programs, and the temporary stalemate of budgets, there is a double claim for educational revolution in the Johnson years. First, it was in this Administration that the President and the Congress together got past the national hang-up on the question of church and state and aid to schools. To me, as one who was then preoccupied with foreign affairs, there will always be some mystery in the process by which this great change was achieved between 1963 and 1965. That there was a practical bargain, worked out below the level of the President, seems likely. That readiness for such a bargain was somehow increased in the aftermath of the tragic death of our first Catholic President seems more likely still. That roles of particular importance were played by a great professional educator and a political reporter turned political operator seems necessary, given the positions of Francis Keppel as

Commissioner of Education and Douglass Cater in the White House. But that such a change could have occurred without the presiding political guidance of the President of the United States does not seem plausible at all.

The executive and the legislative branches are not all of government, and in early 1968 it appears likely that there will be a series of court tests of the new laws of the 1960s, against the Establishment Clause of the First Amendment. This is as it should be, and in my judgment the courts have some distance to go now to reach the common sense views of the Administration and the Congress. On the historical record it is reasonable to expect that there will be more than one bump in the path to judicial progress, but on the historical record also it seems reasonably likely that the court will follow the country. If this optimism is not misplaced, then the Johnson Administration will surely be remembered for its role in leading us all from an irrelevant and outdated bitterness and mistrust toward cooperation and understanding—all in response to the Nation's educational need.

If the breakdown of mutual mistrust on the church-state issue is one of the larger achievements of these years, surely the second is precisely the new recognition of the need for national action in education. Educators described this need in the late 1950s, and President Kennedy described it even more clearly and eloquently in the opening of the 1960s. But it is only in the Johnson years that the people as a whole have reached this same decision. Much more important than the size of a given budget or the shape of a particular law is the achievement of national recognition—in every region and in every party except at the fringes—that national action for American education is now a permanent necessity.

In the years in which a country is changing its major premises, the surrounding rhetoric is not always precise, and some of our greatest political leaders have helped to move the nation across a great divide while protesting their loyalty to existing traditions. Overtones of this Lincolnian technique are not lacking in President Johnson's remarks on education, but what comes through both in the speeches and in the actions of the man is the happy congruence between this new national necessity and Lyndon Johnson's own sense of human priorities. As a retired educator, indeed, I sometimes think the President expects too much of education; I think freedom from ignorance is a long way off—and I consider it no more than a way station to the good life in any case. But for a President in the 1960s this error is on the right side. It has enabled this President to add personal passion to political skill in leading a revolution that will not be undone. Laws will be amended and procedures will be revised; budgets will face competition from other necessities; and those who care for education have a long way to go before they can expect the unquestioning budgetary support that is accorded to the national defense. But if we compare the position today with the position of 1958—the year of the *National Defense* Education Act—the very language of that early law tells the distance we have come. Among the makers of this revolution, President Johnson must stand first.

COMMUNICATIONS POLICY

The revolution in communications policy is still ahead, but the drums of the advance guard can be heard in two of the documents that follow—the President's remarks as he signed the Public Broadcast Act of 1967 and his message on Communications and Technology to the Congress, sent in the August just preceding. At this writing the Public Television Corporation still has no money, and the President's Task Force on Communications Policy has made no report. But the existence of the Act and the Task Force is eloquent testimony to the fact that the President has understood what most of the rest of us have not—that we are faced with a revolution in our communications that will require a revolution in the way we manage them. The President's own remarks sufficiently sketch the breathtaking possibilities of a whole set of new technologies and they also sufficiently suggest the complexities, both internal and international, that beset this enormous field. Moreover, the slow progress of the Public Broadcasting Corporation reminds us of the special difficulty that surrounds any effort in this country to provide public funds for a cultural and informational undertaking in ways that are insulated from crude political pressure. I have to confess my own regret in this case that the hard priorities of tax legislation have again led the President to call for further study instead of action. But regret alone cannot remake the House Ways and Means Committee.

In the long range again, what deserves attention is not the immediate fact of delay but the larger reality that the President sees the issues. In education the revolution is a fact, while in communications we stand at the threshold. The man who is President as we cross into the 1970s must lead in this still larger revolution. It is a pleasure to record my own conviction that on the record as a whole this President can do that job of leadership.

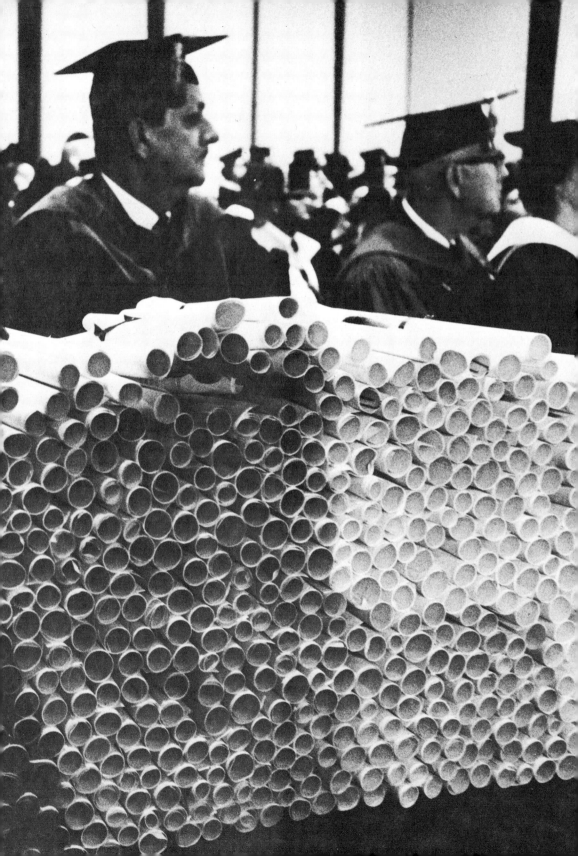

Lyndon B. Johnson

"To fulfill the individual . . ."

Message to Congress on Education and Health in America,
February 28, 1967.

In Edmonds, Washington, three new evening classes today are helping 150
high-school dropouts finish school and gain new job skills.

In Detroit, a month ago, 52,000 children were immunized against measles,
during a campaign assisted by Federal funds.

In twenty-five states, Federal funds are helping improve medical care for
6.4 million citizens who get public assistance.

Over 8 million poor children are now getting a better education because
of funds provided under Title I of the Elementary and Secondary Education Act. Nineteen million older citizens enjoy the protection of Medicare.

Three years ago, not one of these programs existed.

Today, they are flourishing—because a concerned people and the creative
Eighty-ninth Congress acted. They are the result of twenty-four new health
laws and eighteen new education laws.

But even the best new programs are not enough.

Today, we face major challenges of organization and evaluation. If our new projects are to be effective, we must have the people to run them, and the facilities to support them. We must encourage states and localities to plan more effectively and comprehensively for their growing needs and to measure their progress towards meeting those needs.

Above all, each community, each state, must generate a spirit of creative change: a willingness to experiment.

In this, my fourth message to Congress on health and education, I do not recommend more of the same—but more that is better: to solve old problems, to create new institutions, to fulfill the potential of each individual in our land.

Nothing is more fundamental to all we seek than our programs in health and education:

Education—because it not only overcomes ignorance, but arms the citizen against the other evils which afflict him.

Health—because disease is the cruelest enemy of individual promise and because medical progress makes less and less tolerable that illness still should blight so many lives.

I. Education

I believe that future historians, when they point to the extraordinary changes which have marked the 1960s, will identify a major movement forward in American education.

This movement, spurred by the laws of the last three years, seeks to provide equality of educational opportunity to all Americans—to give every child education of the highest quality, no matter how poor his family, how great his handicap, what color his skin, or where he lives.

We cannot yet fully measure the results of this great movement in American education. Our progress can be traced partially by listing some of the extraordinary bills I have signed into law:

—The Higher Education Act of 1965.

—The Elementary and Secondary Education Act of 1965.

—The Higher Education Facilities Act of 1963.

—The Vocational Education Act of 1963.

The scale of our efforts can be partially measured by the fact that today appropriations for the Office of Education are nearly seven times greater than four years ago. Today we can point to at least one million college students who might not be in college except for government loans, grants and work-study programs, and to more than 17,500 school districts helping disadvantaged children under the Elementary and Secondary Education Act.

This breakthrough is not the work of Washington alone. The ideas for these programs come from educational leaders all over the country. Many different communities must supply the energy to make these programs work. Yet they are national programs, shaped by national needs. Congress has played a vital role in reviewing these needs and setting these priorities.

The new Federal role in education is, in reality, a new alliance with America's states and local communities. In this alliance, the Federal Government continues to be a junior partner:

—Local school districts will submit, and state governments will approve, the plans for spending more than one billion dollars this year to improve the education of poor children.

—Federal funds for vocational education are administered through state plans controlled by state, not Federal, officials.

—The recommendations of the states have been sought and followed in more than 95 percent of the projects for centers and services which are founded by the U.S. Office of Education.

The education programs I recommend this year have three major aims:

—to strengthen the foundations we have laid in recent years, by revising, improving, and consolidating existing programs;

—to provide special help to those groups in our society with special needs: the poor, the handicapped, victims of discrimination or neglect;

—to build for the future by exploiting the new opportunities presented by science, technology, and the world beyond our borders.

The budget proposals I am making for 1968 will carry forward our efforts at a new level. The total Federal dollar expenditures for educational purposes, including health training, which I have proposed for fiscal 1968 will amount to $11 billion—an increase of $1 billion, or 10 percent, over 1967 and $7 billion, or 175 percent, over 1963.

STRENGTHENING EDUCATION PROGRAMS

State and community education leaders have shouldered heavy new burdens as a result of recent increases in Federal programs. If these officials are to develop wise and long-range plans for education, they must have more help.

The Elementary and Secondary Education Act has provided funds to strengthen state departments of education. But additional funds are needed— money to improve community, state, and regional educational planning. Nothing can do more to ensure the effective use of Federal dollars.

I recommend legislation authorizing $15 million to help state and local governments evaluate their education programs and plan for the future.

A Better Education Timetable

One condition which severely hampers educational planning is the congressional schedule for authorizations and appropriations. When Congress enacts and funds programs near the end of a session, the Nation's schools and colleges must plan their programs without knowing what Federal resources will be available to them to meet their needs. As so many governors have said, the Federal legislative calendar often proves incompatible with the academic calendar.

I urge that the Congress enact education appropriations early enough to allow the Nation's schools and colleges to plan effectively. I have directed the Secretary of Health, Education, and Welfare to work with the Congress toward this end.

Another way to ease this problem is to seek the earliest practical renewal of authorization for major education measures.

I recommend that Congress this year extend three major education measures now scheduled to expire in June 1968:

—*The National Defense Education Act of 1958.*

—*The Higher Education Act of 1965.*

—*The National Vocational Student Loan Insurance Act of 1965.*

Improving Program Evaluation

Most of our education programs have been operating too short a time to provide conclusive judgments about their effectiveness. But we should be heartened by the evaluations so far.

Recently, the National Advisory Council on the Education of Disadvantaged Children reported:

> The morale of teachers and administrators in schools with many poor children—their will to succeed and their belief in the possibility of succeeding—is perceptibly on the rise in many of the schools visited. More teachers than ever are involved in an active search for paths to success. The paths are not all clearly visible as yet, but decidedly the search has taken on a new vigor.

The Council did identify problems and weaknesses in the school districts. Our efforts to identify shortcomings and to assess our progress can never be fully effective until we provide sufficient resources for program evaluation.

I have requested $2.5 million to assure careful analysis of new programs so that we can provide a full accounting to the Congress and the American people of our successes and shortcomings.

The Education Professions Act of 1967

Our work to enrich education finds its focus in a single person: the class-room teacher, who inspires each student to achieve his best.

Next year, more than 170,000 new teachers will be needed to replace un-certified teachers, to fill vacancies, and to meet rising student enrollments. Moreover:

—There are severe shortages of English, mathematics, science, and ele-mentary school teachers.

—More teachers are needed for our colleges and junior colleges.

—Well-trained administrators at all levels are critically needed.

—New kinds of school personnel—such as teacher aides—are needed to help in the schools.

—By 1975, the Nation's schools will need nearly 2 million more new teachers.

To help meet this growing demand, the Federal Government has sponsored a number of programs to train and improve teachers.

These programs, though they have been effective, have been too frag-mented to achieve their full potential and too limited to reach many essential sectors of the teaching profession. Teacher aides and school administrators have not been eligible to participate.

We must develop a broader approach to training for the education profes-sions. At the state and local level, education authorities must have greater flexibility to plan for their educational manpower needs.

I recommend the Education Professions Act of 1967 to:

—combine and expand many of the scattered statutory authorities for teacher training assistance;

—provide new authority for the training of school administrators, teacher aides, and other education workers for schools and colleges.

Improving Student Loan Programs

In the Higher Education Act of 1965, Congress authorized a program to support state guarantees for student loans made by banks and other lending institutions. For students of modest means, the Federal Government also subsidizes the interest cost.

The program has become an example of creative cooperation between the Federal Government, the states, private financial institutions, and the academic community.

Though it began in a time of tight credit, the program is off to a promising start. This year, it is expected that loans totalling $400 million will be made to nearly 480,000 students. By 1972, outstanding loans are expected to total $6.5 billion.

I have asked all of the Government officials concerned with the program— the Secretary of Health, Education, and Welfare; the Secretary of the Treasury; the Director of the Budget; and the Chairman of the Council of Economic Advisors—to review its operations in consultation with state and private organizations concerned.

If administrative changes in the program are necessary, we will make them. If any amendments to the legislation are in order, we will submit appropriate recommendations to the Congress.

SPECIAL PROGRAMS FOR SPECIAL NEEDS

Educating Poor Children

Over the past two years, we have invested more than $2.6 billion in improving educational opportunities for more than 10 million poor children. This has been an ambitious venture, for no textbook offers precise methods for dealing with the disadvantaged. It has also been rewarding: we have generated new energy, gained new workers and developed new skills in our effort to help the least fortunate.

Dollars alone cannot do the job—but the job cannot be done without dollars.

So let us continue the programs we have begun under Head Start and the Elementary and Secondary Education Act.

Let us begin new efforts—like the Head Start Follow Through program which can carry forward into the early grades the gains made under Head Start.

The Teacher Corps

Young as it is, the Teacher Corps has become a symbol of new hope for America's poor children and their parents—and for hard-pressed school administrators.

More than 1,200 interns and veteran teachers have volunteered for demanding assignments in city and rural slums. Teacher Corps volunteers are at work in 275 schools throughout the country: helping children in twenty of our twenty-five largest cities, in Appalachia, in the Ozarks, in Spanish-speaking communities.

The impact of these specialists goes far beyond their number. For they represent an important idea: that the schools in our Nation's slums deserve a fair share of our Nation's best teachers.

Mayors and school officials across the country cite the competence, the energy, and the devotion which Teacher Corps members are bringing to these tasks.

Perhaps the best measure of the vitality of the Teacher Corps is the demand by school districts for volunteers and the number of young Americans who want to join. Requests from local schools exceed by far the number of volunteers we can now train. Ten times as many young Americans as we can presently accept—among them, some of our brightest college graduates—have applied for Teacher Corps service.

The Teacher Corps, which I recommended and which the Eighty-ninth Congress established, deserves the strong support of the Ninetieth Congress.

I recommend that the Teacher Corps be expanded to a total of 5,500 volunteers by the school year beginning in September 1968.

I propose amendments to enhance the role of the states in training and assigning Teacher Corps members.

Finally, to finance the next summer's training program, I strongly recommend early action on a supplemental appropriation request of $12.5 million for the Teacher Corps in fiscal year 1967.

Educating the Handicapped

One child in ten in our country is afflicted with a handicap which, if left untreated, severely cripples his chance to become a productive adult.

In my Message on Children and Youth, I proposed measures to bring better health care to these children—the mentally retarded, the crippled, the chronically ill.

We must also give attention to their special educational needs. We must more precisely identify the techniques that will be effective in helping handicapped children to learn.

We need many more teachers who have the training essential to help these children. There are now only 70,000 specially trained teachers of the handicapped—a small fraction of the number the Nation requires. In the next decade, five times that number must be trained and put to work.

I recommend legislation to:

—establish regional resource centers to identify the educational needs of handicapped children and help their parents and teachers meet those needs;

—recruit more men and women for careers in educating the handicapped;

—extend the service providing captioned films and other instructional materials for the deaf to all handicapped people.

Ending Discrimination

Giving every American an equal chance for education requires that we put an end once and for all to racial segregation in our schools.

In the Civil Rights Act of 1964, this Nation committed itself to eliminating segregation. Yet patterns of discrimination are still entrenched in many communities, North and South, East and West.

If equal opportunity is to be more than a slogan in our society, every state and community must be encouraged to face up to this legal and moral responsibility.

I have requested $30 million—nearly a fourfold increase over this year's appropriation—to provide the needed resources under Title IV of the Civil Rights Act to help states and communities face the problems of school desegregation.

Education for the World of Work

Three out of ten students in America drop out before completing high school. Only two out of ten of our Nation's young men and women receive college degrees.

Too few of these young people get the training and guadance they need to find good jobs.

I recommend legislation to aid secondary schools and colleges to develop new programs in vocational education, to make work part of the learning experience and to provide career-counseling for their students.

A number of our colleges have highly successful programs of cooperative education which permits students to vary periods of study with periods of employment. This is an important educational innovation that has demonstrated its effectiveness. It should be applied more widely in our schools and universities.

*I recommend an amendment of the College Work-Study Program which
will for the first time permit us to support cooperative education projects.*

*I am also requesting the Director of the Office of Economic Opportunity
and the Secretary of Labor to use Neighborhood Youth Corps funds at the
high-school level for this purpose.*

Combating Adult Illiteracy

At least 3 million adults in America cannot read or write. Another 13
million have less than an eighth-grade education. Many of these citizens lack
the basic learning to cope with the routine business of daily life.

This is a national tragedy and an economic loss for which each one of us
must pay.

The Adult Education Act, enacted last year, is our pledge to help eliminate
this needless loss of human talent.

*This year, I am requesting $44 million—an increase of nearly 50 percent—
for adult basic education programs.*

These funds will help new projects, sponsored by both public agencies
and nonprofit private groups, to train volunteers for work in adult literacy
programs and to establish neighborhood education programs reaching
beyond the formal classroom.

BUILDING FOR TOMORROW

Public Television

In 1951, the Federal Communications Commission set aside the first 242
television channels for noncommercial broadcasting, declaring: "The public
interest will be clearly served if these stations contribute significantly to the
educational process of the Nation."

The first educational television station went on the air in May 1953. Today,
there are 178 noncommercial television stations on the air or under construction. Since 1963 the Federal Government has provided $32 million under
the Educational Television Facilities Act to help build towers, transmitters,
and other facilities. These funds have helped stations with an estimated
potential audience of close to 150 million citizens.

Yet we have only begun to grasp the great promise of this medium, which,
in the words of one critic, has the power to "arouse our dreams, satisfy our
hunger for beauty, take us on journeys, enable us to participate in events,

present great drama and music, explore the sea and the sky and the winds and the hills."

Noncommercial television can bring its audience the excitement of excellence in every field. I am convinced that a vital and self-sufficient noncommercial television system will not only instruct, but inspire and uplift our people.

Practically all noncommercial stations have serious shortages of the facilities, equipment, money, and staff they need to present programs of high quality. There are not enough stations. Interconnections between stations are inadequate and seldom permit the timely scheduling of current programs.

Noncommercial television today is reaching only a fraction of its potential audience—and achieving only a fraction of its potential worth.

Clearly, the time has come to build on the experience of the past fourteen years, the important studies that have been made, and the beginnings we have made.

I recommend that Congress enact the Public Television Act of 1967 to:

—increase Federal funds for television and radio facility construction to $10.5 million in fiscal 1968, more than three times this year's appropriations;

—create a Corporation for Public Television authorized to provide support to noncommercial television and radio;

—provide $9 million in fiscal 1968 as initial funding for the Corporation.

Next year, after careful review, I will make further proposals for the Corporation's long-term financing.

Noncommercial television and radio in America, even though supported by Federal funds, must be absolutely free from any Federal Government interference over programming. As I said in the State of the Union Message, "We should insist that the public interest be fully served through the public's airwaves."

The board of directors of the Corporation for Public Television should include American leaders in education, communications, and the creative arts. I recommend that the board be comprised of fifteen members, appointed by the President and confirmed by the Senate.

The Corporation would provide support to establish production centers and to help local stations improve their proficiency. It would be authorized to accept funds from other sources, public and private.

The strength of public television should lie in its diversity. Every region and every community should be challenged to contribute its best.

Other opportunities for the Corporation exist to support vocational training for young people who desire careers in public television, to foster research and development, and to explore new ways to serve the viewing public.

One of the Corporation's first tasks should be to study the practicality and the economic advantages of using communication satellites to establish an educational television and radio network. To assist the Corporation, I am directing the Administrator of the National Aeronautics and Space Administration and the Secretary of Health, Education, and Welfare to conduct experiments on the requirements for such a system, and for instructional television, in cooperation with other interested agencies of the Government and the private sector.

Formulation of long-range policies concerning the future of satellite communications requires the most detailed and comprehensive study by the Executive branch and the Congress. I anticipate that the appropriate committees of Congress will hold hearings to consider these complex issues of public policy. The Executive branch will carefully study these hearings as we shape our recommendations.

Instructional Television

I recommend legislation to authorize the Secretary of Health, Education, and Welfare to launch a major study of the value and the promise of instructional television which is being used more and more widely in our classrooms, but whose potential has not been fully developed.

Computers in Education

In my 1968 budget, I propose that the National Science Foundation be given new resources to advance man's knowledge and serve the Nation. Its endeavors will help our scholars better to understand the atmosphere, exploit the ocean's riches, probe the behavior and the nature of man.

The Foundation will also step up its pioneer work to develop new teaching materials for our schools and colleges. The "new math" and the "new science" are only the first fruits of this innovative work.

One educational resource holds exciting promise for America's classrooms: the electronic computer. Computers are already at work in educational institutions, primarily to assist the most advanced research. The computer can serve other educational purposes—if we find ways to employ it effectively and economically and if we develop practical courses to teach students how to use it.

I have directed the National Science Foundation working with the U.S. Office of Education to establish an experimental program for developing the potential of computers in education.

Enriching the Arts and the Humanities

Our progress will not be limited to scientific advances. The National Foundation on the Arts and the Humanities, established in 1965, has already begun to bring new cultural and scholarly spirit to our schools and communities. State arts councils, museums, theaters, and orchestras have received not only new funds but new energy and enthusiasm through the National Endowment for the Arts.

The National Endowment for the Humanities has made grants to support new historical studies of our Nation's heritage, to encourage creative teaching in our colleges, to offer outstanding young scholars opportunities for advancement.

I recommend that Congress appropriate for the National Foundation on the Arts and Humanities $16 million—an increase of nearly one-third.

Higher Education for International Understanding

For many years, America's colleges and universities have prepared men and women for careers involving travel, trade, and service abroad. Today, when our world responsibilities are greater than ever before, our domestic institutions of higher learning need more support for their programs of international studies.

The Eighty-ninth Congress, in its closing days, passed the International Education Act—an historic measure recognizing this Nation's enduring belief that learning must transcend geographic boundaries. Through a program of grants under the Act, America's schools, colleges, and universities can add a world dimension to their students' learning experience.

I urge the Congress to approve promptly my forthcoming request for a supplemental appropriation of $350,000 for the International Education Act, to permit necessary planning for next year's program, as well as an appropriation of $20 million for fiscal 1968.

II. HEALTH

No great age of discovery in history can match our own time. Today, our wealth, our knowledge, our scientific genius give us the power to prolong man's life—and to prevent the erosion of life by illness.

In 1900, an American could expect to live only forty-nine years. Today, his life expectancy has been increased to seventy years.

These advances are the result of spectacular progress in research, in public health, in the medical arts. We have developed:

—sufficient knowledge to end nearly all of the hazards of childbirth and pregnancy;

—modern nutrition to wipe out such ailments as rickets, goiter, and pellagra;

—vaccines, antibiotics, and modern drugs to control many of the killers and cripplers of yesterday: polio, diphtheria, pneumonia;

—new medical and surgical techniques to combat cancer and cardiovascular disease;

—life-saving devices: plastic heart valves, and artificial artery transplants.

In 1967, to pursue this vital work, the Federal Government is investing more than $440 million in the construction of health facilities, $620 million for health manpower education and training, $1.3 billion in biomedical research, $7.8 billion to provide medical care.

But each gain, each victory, should focus our attention more sharply on the unfinished business facing this Nation in the field of health:

—Infant mortality is far higher than it need be.

—Handicaps afflicting many children are discovered too late or left untreated.

—Grave deficiencies remain in health care for the poor, the handicapped, and the chronically ill.

—American men between the ages of forty-five and fifty-four—which should be the most productive years of their lives—have a death rate twice that of men of the same age in a number of advanced countries.

—We still search in vain for ways to prevent and treat many forms of cancer.

—Many types of mental illness, retardation, arthritis, and heart disease are still largely beyond our control.

Our national resources for health have grown, but our national aspirations have grown faster. Today we expect what yesterday we could not have envisioned—adequate medical care for every citizen.

My health proposals to the Ninetieth Congress have four basic aims:

—to expand our knowledge of disease and our research and development of better ways to deliver health care to every American;

—to build our health resources, by stepped-up training of health workers and by improved planning of health facilities;

—to remove barriers to good medical care for those who most need care;

—to strengthen our Partnership for Health by encouraging regional, state, and local efforts—public and private—to develop comprehensive programs serving all our citizens.

HEALTH RESEARCH AND DEVELOPMENT:

THE FOUNDATION OF OUR EFFORTS

Supporting Biomedical Research

Our progress in health grows out of a research effort unparalleled anywhere in the world. The scientists of the National Institutes of Health have shaped an alliance throughout the nation to find the causes and the cures of disease.

We must build on the strong base of past research achievements, exchange ideas with scholars and students from all parts of the world, and apply our knowledge more swiftly and effectively.

We must take advantage of our progress in targeted research as we have done in our vaccine development program, in the heart drug study, in artificial kidney and kidney transplant research, and in the treatment of specific types of cancer.

In the 1968 budget, I am recommending an increase of $65 million—to an annual total of almost $1.5 billion—to support biomedical research.

I am seeking funds to establish an International Center for Advanced Study in the Health Sciences and to provide scholarships and fellowships in the Center.

I am directing the Secretary of Health, Education, and Welfare to appoint immediately a lung cancer task force, to supplement the continuing work of existing task forces on leukemia, cancer, chemotherapy, uterine cancer, solid tumor and breast cancer.

Health Services Research and Development

America's annual spending for health and medical care is more than $43 billion. But despite this investment, our system of providing health services is not operating as efficiently and effectively as it should.

—In some U.S. counties infant mortality rates, one yardstick of health care, are 300 percent higher than the national average.

—Seventy percent of automobile accident deaths occur in communities of less than 2,500 people, where medical facilities are often poorest.

—Even though we have good techniques for detecting and curing cervical cancer, 8,000 women die each year for lack of proper care.

—Emergency rooms in U.S. hospitals are seriously overcrowded, not with actual emergency cases, but with people who cannot find normal outpatient care anywhere else.

Research and development could help eliminate these conditions by pointing the way to better delivery of health care. Yet the Government-wide total investment in health service research amounts to less than one-tenth of one percent of our total annual investment in health care.

We have done very little to mobilize American universities, industry, private practitioners, and research institutions to seek new ways of providing medical services.

There have been few experiments in applying advanced methods—systems analysis and automation, for example—to problems of health care.

Our superior research techniques have brought us new knowledge in health and medicine. These same techniques must now be put to work in the effort to bring low-cost, quality health care to our citizens.

We must marshal the Nation's best minds to:

—Design hospitals, nursing homes, and group practice facilities which provide effective care with the most efficient use of funds and manpower;

—Develop new ways of assisting doctors to reach more people with good health services;

—Devise new patterns of health services.

To begin this effort, I have directed the Secretary of Health, Education, and Welfare to establish a National Center for Health Services Research and Development.

I recommend legislation to expand health services research and make possible the fullest use of Federal hospitals as research centers to improve health care.

I also recommend an appropriation of $20 million to the Department of Health, Education, and Welfare in 1968, for research and development in health services—nearly twice as much as in 1967.

DEVELOPING MANPOWER AND FACILITIES FOR HEALTH

Health Manpower

The United States is facing a serious shortage of health manpower. Within the next decade this nation will need one million more health workers. If we are to meet this need, we must develop new skills and new types of health workers. We need short-term training programs for medical aides and other health workers; we need programs to develop physicians' assistants, and speed the training of health professions. We also need to make effective use of the thousands of medical corpsmen trained in the Armed Forces who return to civilian life each year.

Last May, I appointed a National Advisory Commission on Health Manpower to recommend how we can:

—speed the education of doctors and other health personnel without sacrificing the quality of training;

—improve the use of health manpower both in and outside the Government.

Meanwhile, I directed members of my Cabinet to intensify their efforts to relieve health manpower shortages through Federal programs. This week they reported to me that Federally supported programs in 1967 will train 224,000 health workers—an increase of nearly 100,000 over 1966. Thirty thousand previously inactive nurses and technicians will be given refresher training this year.

Through the teamwork of Federal and state agencies, professional organizations and educational institutions, we have launched a major effort to provide facilities and teachers for this immense training mission.

To maintain this stepped-up training already started in fiscal year 1967, I am recommending expenditures of $763 million—a 22 percent increase for fiscal year 1968—to expand our health manpower resources.

Planning for Future Health Facilities

Over the past two decades, the Hill-Burton program has assisted more than 3,400 communities to build hospitals, nursing homes, and other health care centers. Hill-Burton funds have helped to provide 350,000 hospital and nursing home beds, and to bring modern medical services to millions of Americans. The authorization for this program expires on June 30, 1969. The contribution of the Federal Government in financing construction of health facilities has changed, especially with the beginning of Medicare, Medicaid, and other new programs. It is timely, therefore, that we take a fresh look at this area.

I am appointing a National Advisory Commission on Health Facilities to study our needs for the total system of health facilities—hospitals, extended care facilities, nursing homes, long-term care institutions, and clinics. In addition to considering the future of the Hill-Burton Program, the Commission will make recommendations for financing the construction and modernization of health facilities.

ELIMINATING BARRIERS TO HEALTH CARE

In previous messages to Congress this year, I have made recommendations to:

—extend Medicare to 1.5 million seriously disabled Americans under age sixty-five;

—establish new health services through broader maternal and child health programs; a strengthened crippled children's program, and new projects in child health and dental care;

—improve medical services for the needy under Medicaid;

—combat mental retardation by supporting construction of university and community centers for the mentally retarded, and for the first time, helping to staff the community centers;

—guarantee the safety of medical devices and laboratory tests by requiring Food and Drug Administration pre-clearance of devices, and by requiring licensing of clinical laboratories in interstate commerce.

We must act in other ways to overcome barriers to health care.

The Office of Economic Opportunity has developed a program of Neighborhood Health Centers which not only bring modern medical care to the poor but also train citizens for jobs in the health field.

Last year, Congress endorsed this new approach and authorized funds for twenty-four such centers. More are needed.

I am requesting the Director of the Office of Economic Opportunity to encourage communities to establish additional centers. Our goal will be to double the number of centers in fiscal 1968.

In the past four years, we have launched a new program to attack mental illness through community mental health centers. This program is now well under way. More centers are needed, and we must strengthen and expand existing services.

I recommend legislation to extend and improve the Community Mental Health Centers Act.

Among the most tragically neglected of our citizens are those who are both deaf and blind. More than 3,000 Americans today face life unable to see and hear.

To help reach the deaf-blind with the best programs our experts can devise, I recommend legislation to establish a National Center for the Deaf and Blind.

Ending Hospital Discrimination

With the launching of the Medicare program last July, the Nation took a major step toward ending racial segregation in hospitals.

More than 95 percent of the Nation's hospitals have already complied with the antidiscrimination requirements of the Medicare legislation. They are guaranteeing that there will be no "second-class patients" in our health care institutions; that all citizens can enter the same door, enjoy the same facilities and the same quality of treatment.

We will continue to work for progress in this field—until equality of treatment is the rule not in some, but in all of our hospitals and other health facilities.

Rising Medical Costs

In 1950, the average cost per patient per day in a hospital was $14.40. In 1965, this cost more than tripled to over $45. Other health costs have also risen sharply in recent years.

Last August, I asked the Secretary of Health, Education, and Welfare to initiate a study of medical costs. This study, now completed, indicates that medical costs will almost certainly continue to rise. It emphasizes the absolute necessity of using medical resources more efficiently if we are to moderate this increase in the cost of health care.

This is a job for everyone who plays a part in providing or financing medical care—the medical profession, the hospital industry, insurance carriers, state and local governments, and many other private and public groups. Federal programs must also play a role in promoting cost consciousness in medical care.

The new National Center for Health Services Research and Development will develop ways to make our medical systems more efficient. The Center's first assignment will be to develop new ways to improve the use of professional and auxiliary health workers—a key factor in reducing hospital costs.

We can take other steps.

I am directing Secretary John Gardner to convene at the Department of Health, Education, and Welfare a National Conference on Medical Costs.

This conference will bring together leaders of the medical community and members of the public to discuss how we can lower the costs of medical services without impairing the quality.

In the weeks and months ahead, the Secretary of Health, Education, and Welfare will consult with representatives of the medical profession, universities, business, and labor to:

—find practical incentives for the effective operation of hospitals and other health facilities;

—reduce the costs of construction and speed the modernization of hospitals, nursing homes, and extended care facilities;

—support those innovations in medical education which will lead to better training programs and promote the efficient practice of medicine.

OUR PARTNERSHIP FOR HEALTH

The Partnership for Health legislation, enacted by the Eighty-ninth Congress, is designed to strengthen state and local programs and to encourage broad-gauge planning in health. It gives the states new flexibility to use Federal funds by freeing them from tightly compartmentalized grant programs. It also allows the states to attack special health problems which have special regional or local impact.

I recommend that Congress extend the Partnership for Health legislation for four years; provide supplemental appropriations for planning in fiscal 1967 and total appropriations of $161 million—an increase of $41 million—in fiscal 1968.

Our regional medical programs for heart disease, cancer, and stroke depend on a second partnership, involving doctors, medical schools, hospitals, and state and local health departments. These programs will bring to every citizen the fruits of our Nation's research into the killer diseases. They will also promote the continuing education of the Nation's doctors, nurses, and other health workers.

To sustain these nationwide programs, I recommend an appropriation of $64 million for fiscal 1968—an increase of $19 million over 1967.

Occupational Health and Safety

Occupational health and safety is another area in which we need to strengthen our partnership with labor, industry, medicine, and government.

In 1965, more than 14,000 job-connected deaths and 2 million disabling work injuries caused untold misery and privation to workers, 230 million lost mandays of production, and billions of dollars in lost income.

We must learn more about the nature of job-connected injuries, so we can set effective safety standards and develop better protective measures.

I am recommending in the 1968 budget an appropriation for the Department of Health, Education, and Welfare of $8.1 million—a 25 percent increase over this year—to expand research and training programs in occupational health, and to strengthen state and local public health programs in this field.

I am directing the Secretary of Labor to improve and strengthen health protection and safety standards for workers through cooperative Federal-state programs.

III. To Fulfill the Individual

As a people, we have wanted many things, achieved many things. We have become the richest, the mightiest, the most productive nation in the world.

Yet a nation may accumulate dollars, grow in power, pile stone on stone—and still fall short of greatness. The measure of a people is not how much they achieve—but what they achieve.

Which of our pursuits is most worthy of our devotion? If we were required to choose, I believe we would place one item at the top of the list: fulfillment of the individual.

If that is what we seek, mere wealth and power cannot help us. We must also act—in definable and practical ways—to liberate each individual from conditions which stunt his growth, assault his dignity, diminish his spirit. Those enemies we know; ignorance, illness, want, squalor, tyranny, injustice.

To fulfill the individual—this is the purpose of my proposals. They present an opportunity—and an obligation—to the Ninetieth Congress.

I hope and believe this Congress will live up to the high expectations of a progressive and humanitarian America.

" 'I'll gamble with you, I'll take a chance' . . ."

Remarks at the memorial service for Carl Sandburg,
at the Lincoln Memorial,
September 17, 1967.

I am both honored and saddened by the opportunity to join today with Carl Sandburg's friends in celebrating that vital, exuberant, wise, and generous man.

This is the right place for thinking about Carl Sandburg. To him—and to me—Abraham Lincoln was the embodiment of our national aspirations, the nearest that any man has come to summing up the American experience in himself.

Sandburg loved to come here, to what he once called "the fog-swept Lincoln Memorial, white as a blond woman's arm."

I have no pretensions as a literary critic, but I think Carl Sandburg belongs in a very special category among poets, along with Walt Whitman.

Whitman wrote: "The United States themselves are essentially the greatest poem. . . . Here at last is something in the doings of man that corresponds with the broadest doings of the day and night."

And like Whitman, Sandburg seemed to have his finger on the American pulse. He seemed able to give voice to the whole range of America's hopes and America's hates. He seemed able to communicate, above all, the restless energy that has vitalized, stimulated, and—on occasion—degraded the history of our Nation.

He could give you the savage emotions of a lynch mob. He could just as well express, with affection and insight, the courage, and the impatience, even the braggadocio, that spurred our amazing development.

He said in "Good Morning America":

> We are afraid;
> What are we afraid of?
> We are afraid of nothing much, nothing at all, nothing
>   in the shape of god, man or beast.
> We can eat any ashes offered us,

> We can step out before the fact of the Fact of Death
>   and look it in the eye and laugh, "You are the begin-
>   ning or the end of something,
>   I'll gamble with you, I'll take a chance."

And only those of us who have spent almost a lifetime in the pressure chamber of politics could possibly appreciate the humor and the insight of his "Money, Politics, Love and Glory."

> Who put up that cage?
> Who hung it up with bars, doors?
> Why do those on the inside want to get out?
> Why do those outside want to get in?
> What is this crying inside and out all the time?
> What is this endless, useless beating of baffled wings
>   at these bars, doors, this cage?

At the end of a long day, with the phones all ringing and the world in disarray, those words have a very special impact for some of us.

Well, Carl Sandburg is gone. He is part of the earth that he celebrated in Illinois and Kentucky and North Carolina. He is part of the American earth.

What will live forever is his faith in the individual human beings whom we impersonally call "Americans."

He knew that always in America, "the strong men keep coming on."

So let us respect his wishes and "ring no bell at all" to mourn his death. But surely we must, as he asked us, "sing one song" in memory of this strong singer of ours.

I will miss him; we will all miss him. There will not be one like him again.

"The future of this new technology stirs our imagination."

Message to Congress on the alliance of space exploration
and communications,
August 14, 1967.

Man's greatest hope for world peace lies in understanding his fellow man. Nations, like individuals, fear that which is strange and unfamiliar. The more we see and hear of those things which are common to all people, the less likely we are to fight over those issues which set us apart.

So the challenge is to communicate.

No technological advance offers a greater opportunity for meeting this challenge than the alliance of space exploration and communications. Since the advent of the communications satellite, the linking of one nation to another is no longer dependent on telephone lines, microwaves, or cables under the sea. Just as man has orbited the earth to explore the universe beyond, we can orbit satellites to send our voices or televise our activities to all peoples of this globe.

Satellite communications has already meant much in terms of human understanding.

—When President Lincoln was assassinated, it took twelve days for the news to reach London. Britons watched and grieved with us at the funeral of John F. Kennedy.

—Europeans watched Pope Paul speak to the United Nations in New York—and Americans saw his pilgrimage to Fatima.

—The peoples of three continents witnessed the meeting of an American President and a Soviet Premier in Glassboro.

The future of this new technology stirs our imagination.

In business and commerce:

—Commercial telephone calls will be carried routinely by satellite to every part of the globe.

—Rapid and universal exchange of data through satellite-linked computers will encourage international commerce.

—Productive machinery can be operated at great distances and business records can be transmitted instantaneously.

In education and health:

—Schools in all lands can be connected by television—so that the children of each nation can see and hear their contemporaries throughout the world.

—The world community of scholars can be brought together across great distances for face-to-face discussions via satellite.

—Global consultations, with voice and pictures, can bring great specialists to the bedsides of patients in every continent.

—The art, culture, history, literature, and medical science of all nations can be transmitted by satellite to every nation.

Who can measure the impact of this live, direct contact between nations and their people? Who can assess the value of our new-found ability to witness the history-making events of this age? This much we know: because communication satellites exist, we are already much closer to each other than we have ever been before.

But this new technology—exciting as it is—does not mean that all our surface communications facilities have become obsolete. Indeed, one of the challenges before us is to integrate satellites into a balanced communications system which will meet the needs of a dynamic and expanding world society. *The United States must review its past activities in this field and formulate a national communications policy.*

U.S. ACTIVITIES TO DATE

The Communications Act of 1934 has provided the blueprint for Federal involvement in the communications field. That Act, and the Federal Communications Commission it created, have served our national interest well during one-third of a century of rapid communications progress.

The Communications Satellite Act of 1962 established a framework for our Nation's participation in satellite communications systems. Congress weighed with care the relative merits of public and private ownership of commercial satellite facilities. The Act authorized creation of the Communications Satellite Corporation (ComSat)—a private corporation with public responsibilities—to establish a commercial satellite system.

In 1964 we joined with ten other countries in the formation of the International Telecommunications Satellite Consortium (INTELSAT). Fifty-eight nations are now members. Each member contributes investment capital and shares in the use of the system. ComSat, the U.S. representative, is the Consortium manager and now contributes 54 percent of the total investment. All satellites managed by ComSat are owned by INTELSAT—so that commercial satellite communications has from its beginning been a product of international cooperation.

Progress has been rapid. Early Bird was launched in 1965. Now the INTELSAT II series serves both the Atlantic and the Pacific. Twelve ground stations—the vital links for sending and receiving messages—have been constructed all over the world. Forty-six are anticipated by the end of 1969.

Today, just five years after the passage of the Communications Satellite Act and three years after the INTELSAT agreement, developments have exceeded our expectations:

—The synchronous satellite, which rotates with our globe and thus maintains a stationary position in orbit, has been developed well ahead of schedule.

—Those responsible for U.S. international communications—with ownership divided among a number of surface carriers and ComSat—now look forward to an integrated system which will utilize satellite technology.

—Proposals are being discussed for the establishment of a domestic communications satellite—either limited to TV transmission or servicing a variety of domestic communications uses.

Because we have been the leaders in the development and use of satellite communications, other countries are deeply interested in our country's position on the continuation of INTELSAT, and in the importance we assign to international cooperation in the field of satellite communications.

On February 28, 1967, I declared in a message to Congress:

"Formulation of long-range policies concerning the future of satellite communications requires the most detailed and comprehensive study by the Executive branch and the Congress. I anticipate that the appropriate committees of Congress will hold hearings to consider these complex issues of public policy. The Executive branch will carefully study these hearings as we shape our recommendations."

A number of important communications issues are presently before the Federal Communications Commission for consideration. Some of them have been discussed in the Senate and House Commerce Committee hearings on the Public Television Act of 1967. ComSat and the State Department have opened discussion of the international questions with our foreign partners and their governments.

In order to place this important policy area in perspective, I want the views of the President to be clear. This message includes a report of the past, a recommendation for the present, and a challenge for the future.

GLOBAL COMMUNICATIONS SYSTEM

Our country is firmly committed to the concept of a global system for commercial communications. The Declaration of Policy and Purpose of the Communications Satellite Act of 1962 set forth Congressional intent:

"The Congress hereby declares that it is the policy of the United States to establish, in conjunction and in cooperation with other countries, as expeditiously as practicable a commercial communications satellite system, as part of an improved global communications network, which will be responsive to public needs and national objectives, which will serve the communications needs of the United States and other countries, and which will contribute to world peace and understanding."

The INTELSAT Agreement of 1964—to which fifty-eight nations have now adhered—left no doubt as to its purpose. Its preamble expressed the desire "to establish a single global commercial communications satellite system as part of an improved global communications network which will provide expanded telecommunications services to all areas of the world and which will contribute to world peace and understanding."

Of course, these agreements do not preclude the development and operation of satellite systems to meet unique national needs. The United States is developing a defense system—as will others. But INTELSAT members did pledge that commercial communications between nations would be a product of international cooperation.

Today I reaffirm the commitments made in 1962 and 1964. We support the development of a global system of communications satellites to make modern communications available to all nations. A global system eliminates the need for duplication in the space segment of communications facilities, reduces the cost to individual nations, and provides the most efficient use of the electromagnetic frequency spectrum through which these communications must travel.

A global system is particularly important for less developed nations which

do not receive the benefits of speedy, direct international communications. Instead, the present system of communications:

—encourages indirect routing through major nations to the developing countries,

—forces the developing nations to remain dependent on larger countries for their links with the rest of the world, and

—makes international communications service to these developing nations more expensive and of lower quality.

A telephone call from Rangoon to Djakarta must still go through Tokyo. A call from Dakar, Senegal, to Lagos, Nigeria, is routed through Paris and London. A call from American Samoa to Tahiti goes by way of Oakland, California. During the recent Punta del Este conference, I discovered that it usually cost Latin American journalists more than their American colleagues to phone in their stories because most of the calls had to be routed through New York.

Such an archaic system of international communications is no longer necessary. The communications satellite knows no geographical boundary, is dependent on no cable, owes allegiance to no single language or political philosophy. Man now has it within his power to speak directly to his fellow man in all nations.

We support a global system of commercial satellite communications which is available to all nations—large and small, developed and developing—on a nondiscriminatory basis.

To have access to a satellite in the sky, a nation must have access to a ground station to transmit and receive its messages. There is a danger that smaller nations, unable to finance or utilize expensive ground stations, may become orphans of this technological advance.

We believe that satellite ground stations should be an essential part of the infrastructure of developing nations. Smaller nations may consider joint planning for a ground station to serve the communications needs of more than one nation in the same geographical area. *We will consider technical assistance that will assist their planning effort.*

Developing nations should be encouraged to commence construction of an efficient system of ground stations as soon as possible. When other financing is not available, *we will consider financial assistance to emerging nations to build the facilities that will permit them to share in the benefits of a global communications satellite system.*

CONTINUATION OF INTELSAT

The 1964 INTELSAT agreement provides only interim arrangements—subject to renegotiation in 1969. Our representatives to the Consortium will soon begin discussions for a permanent arrangement.

We support the continuation of INTELSAT. Each nation or its representative contributes to its expenses and benefits from its revenues in accordance with its anticipated use of the system. The fiifty-eight members include representatives from the major nations who traditionally have been most active in international communications. It has been a successful vehicle for international cooperation in the ownership and operation of a complex communications system.

We will urge the continuation of the Consortium in 1969. The present arrangements offer a firm foundation on which a permanent structure can be built.

Some nations may feel that the United States has too large a voice in the Consortium. As heavy users of international communications, our investment in such an international undertaking is exceptionally large. The early development of satellite technology in the United States and the size of our investment has made it logical that ComSat serve as Consortium manager.

We seek no domination of satellite communications to the exclusion of any other nation—or any group of nations. Rather, we welcome increased participation in international communications by all INTELSAT members. We shall approach the 1969 negotiations determined to seek the best possible permanent organizational framework:

—We will consider ceilings on the voting power of any single nation—including the United States—so that the organization will maintain its international character.

—We will support the creation of a formal assembly of all INTELSAT members—so that all may share in the consideration of policy.

—We favor efforts to make the services of personnel of other nations available to ComSat as it carries out its management responsibilities.

—We will continue the exchange of technical information, share technological advances, and promote a wider distribution of procurement contracts among members of the Consortium.

It is our earnest hope that every member nation will join with us in finding an equitable formula for a permanent INTELSAT organization. . . .

"Today we rededicate a part of the airwaves . . . to all the people."
Remarks on signing the bill establishing
the Corporation for Public Broadcasting,
November 7, 1967.

It was in 1844 that Congress authorized $30,000 for the first telegraph line between Washington and Baltimore. Soon afterward, Samuel Morse sent a stream of dots and dashes over that line to a friend who was waiting. His message was brief and prophetic and it read:
"What hath God wrought?"
Every one of us should feel that same awe and wonderment today.
For today, miracles in communication are our daily routine. Every minute, billions of telegraph messages chatter around the world. Some are intercepted on ships. They interrupt law enforcement conferences and discussions of morality. Billions of signals rush over the ocean floor and fly above the clouds. Radio and television fill the air with sound. Satellites hurl messages thousands of miles in a matter of seconds.
Today our problem is not making miracles—but managing miracles. We might well ponder a different question: What hath man wrought—and how will man use his inventions?
The law that I will sign shortly offers one answer to that question.
It announces to the world that our Nation wants more than just material wealth; our Nation wants more than a "chicken in every pot." We in America have an appetite for excellence, too.
While we work every day to produce new goods and to create new wealth, we want most of all to enrich man's spirit.
That is the purpose of this act.
It will give a wider and, I think, stronger voice to educational radio and television by providing new funds for broadcast facilities.
It will launch a major study of television's use in the Nation's classrooms and their potential use throughout the world.
Finally—and most important—it builds a new institution: the Corporation of Public Broadcasting.

This Corporation will assist stations and producers who aim for the best in broadcasting good music, in broadcasting exciting plays, and in broadcasting reports on the whole fascinating range of human activity. It will try to prove that what educates can also be exciting.

It will get part of its support from our Government. But it will be carefully guarded from Government or from party control. It will be free, and it will be independent—and it will belong to all the people.

Television is still a young invention. But we have learned already that it has immense—even revolutionary—power to change, to change our lives.

I hope that those who lead the Corporation will direct that power toward the great and not the trivial purposes.

At its best, public television would help make our Nation a replica of the old Greek marketplace, where public affairs took place in view of all the citizens.

But in weak or even in irresponsible hands, it could generate controversy without understanding; it could mislead as well as teach; it could appeal to passions rather than to reason.

If public television is to fulfill our hopes, then the Corporation must be representative, it must be responsible—and it must be long on enlightened leadership.

I intend to search this Nation to find men who I can nominate, men and women of outstanding ability, to this board of directors.

As a beginning, this morning I have called on Dr. Milton Eisenhower from the Johns Hopkins University and Dr. James Killian of MIT to serve as members of this board.

Dr. Eisenhower, as you will remember, was chairman of the first citizens committee which sought allocation of airwaves for educational purposes.

Dr. Killian served as chairman of the Carnegie Commission which proposed the act that we are signing today.

What hath man wrought? And how will man use his miracles?

The answer just begins with public broadcasting.

In 1862, the Morrill Act set aside lands in every state—lands which belonged to the people—and it set them aside in order to build the land grant colleges of the Nation.

So today we rededicate a part of the airwaves—which belong to all the people—and we dedicate them for the enlightenment of all the people.

I believe the time has come to stake another claim in the name of all the people, stake a claim based upon the combined resources of communications. I believe the time has come to enlist the computer and the satellite, as well as television and radio and to enlist them in the cause of education.

If we are up to the obligations of the next century and if we are to be proud of the next century as we are of the past two centuries, we have got to quit talking so much about what has happened in the past two centuries and start talking about what is going to happen in the next century beginning with 1967.

So I think we must consider new ways to build a great network for knowledge—not just a broadcast system, but one that employs every means of sending and of storing information that the individual can use.

Think of the lives that this would change:

—The student in a small college could tap the resources of a great university.

Dr. Killian has just given me an exciting report of his contacts in Latin America as a result of some of the declarations of the presidents at Punta del Este that he has followed through on and how these presidents are now envisioning the day when they can dedicate 20 or 25 or a larger percent of their total resources for one thing alone—education and knowledge.

Yes, the student in a small college tapping the resources of the greatest university in the hemisphere:

—the country doctor getting help from a distant laboratory or a teaching hospital;

—a scholar in Atlanta might draw instantly on a library in New York;

—a famous teacher could reach with ideas and inspirations into some far-off classroom, so that no child need be neglected.

Eventually, I think this electronic knowledge bank could be as valuable as the Federal Reserve Bank.

And such a system could involve other nations, too—it could involve them in a partnership to share knowledge and to thus enrich all mankind.

A wild and visionary idea? Not at all. Yesterday's strangest dreams are today's headlines and change is getting swifter every moment.

I have already asked my advisers to begin to explore the possibility of a network for knowledge—and then to draw up a suggested blueprint for it.

In 1844, when Henry Thoreau heard about Mr. Morse's telegraph, he made his sour comment about the race for faster communication. "Perchance," he warned, "the first news which will leak through into the broad, flapping American ear will be that the Princess Adelaide has the whooping cough."

We do have skeptic comments on occasions. But I don't want you to be that skeptic. I do believe that we have important things to say to one another—and we have the wisdom to match our technical genius.

In that spirit this morning, I have asked you to come here and be participants with me in this great movement for the next century, the Public Broadcasting Act of 1967. . . .

"The arts and the humanities belong to the people."
Remarks on signing the Arts and Humanities Bill,
September 29, 1965.

In the long history of man, countless empires and nations have come and gone. Those which created no lasting works of art are reduced today to short footnotes in history's catalog.

Art is a nation's most precious heritage. For it is in our works of art that we reveal to ourselves, and to others, the inner vision which guides us as a Nation. And where there is no vision, the people perish.

We in America have not always been kind to the artists and the scholars who are the creators and the keepers of our vision. Somehow, the scientists always seem to get the penthouse, while the arts and humanities get the basement.

Last year, for the first time in our history, we passed legislation to start changing that situation. We created the National Council on the Arts.

The talented and the distinguished members of that Council have worked very hard. They have worked creatively. They have dreamed dreams and they have developed ideas.

This new bill, creating the National Foundation for the Arts and the Humanities, gives us the power to turn some of those dreams and ideas into reality.

We would not have that bill but for the hard and the thorough and the

dedicated work of some great legislators in both houses of the Congress. . . . And now we have it. Let me tell you what we are going to *do* with it. Working together with the state and the local governments, and with many private organizations in the arts:

—We will create a national theater to bring ancient and modern classics of the theater to audiences all over America.

—We will support a national opera company and a national ballet company.

—We will create an American film institute, bringing together leading artists of the film industry, outstanding educators, and young men and women who wish to pursue the twentieth century art form as their life's work.

—We will commission new works of music by American composers.

—We will support our symphony orchestras.

—We will bring more great artists to our schools and universities by creating grants for their time in residence. . . .

It is in the neighborhoods of each community that a nation's art is born. In countless American towns there live thousands of obscure and unknown talents.

What this bill really does is to bring active support to this great national asset, to make fresher the winds of art in this great land of ours.

The arts and the humanities belong to the people, for it is, after all, the people who create them.

"The exercise of power in this century has meant for the United States not arrogance but agony."

Remarks upon dedicating Woodrow Wilson Hall,
the Woodrow Wilson School of Public and International Affairs,
Princeton University,
May 11, 1966.

I am happy that I could come with Secretary Gardner to help celebrate Princeton's continued growth. It is good that one of the Nation's oldest universities is still young enough to grow.

This commitment to the increase of higher learning has deep roots in our country. Our forefathers had founded more than fifty colleges before the Republic was half a century old.

With a sure sense that the pursuit of knowledge must be part and parcel of the pursuit of life, liberty, and happiness, they set in motion two irreversible forces which have helped to shape our land.

The first was that learning must erect no barriers of class or creed. The university was to nourish an elite to which all could aspire. Soon after our first colleges came the first scholarships for worthy students who could not pay their own way.

The second idea was that the university would not stand as a lonely citadel isolated from the rest of the community. Its mission would be to search for truth and to serve mankind. As Woodrow Wilson later said: "It is the object of learning not only to satisfy the curiosity and perfect the spirits of individual men, but also to advance civilization."

THE VITAL FLOW

We who work in Washington know the need for the vital flow of men and ideas between the halls of learning and the places of power. Each time my Cabinet meets, I can call the roll of former professors—Humphrey and Rusk, McNamara and Wirtz, Katzenbach (another distinguished Princetonian), Gardner and Weaver. The 371 major appointments I have made in the last

2½ years, collectively hold 758 advanced degrees. And so many are the consultants called from behind the ivy that a university friend of mine recently said: "At any given moment a third of the faculties of the United States are on a plane going somewhere to advise—even if not always to consent."

While learning has long been the ally of democracy, the intellectual has not always been the partner of government. As recently as the early years of this century the scholar stood outside the pale of policy, with government usually indifferent to him.

That has changed.

The intellectual today is very much an inside man. Since the 1930s our Government has put into effect major policies which men of learning helped to fashion.

More recently, the Eighty-ninth Congress passed bill after bill suggested by scholars from all over the country in the task forces I appointed in 1964.

In almost every field of governmental concern, from economics to national security, the academic community has become a central instrument of public policy.

The Affluence of Power

This affluence of power for an intellectual community that once walked on the barren fringes of authority has not been won without some pain. An uneasy conscience is the price any concerned man pays, whether politician or professor, for a share of power in the nuclear age.

More than one scholar, thus, has learned how deeply frustrating it is to try to bring purist approaches to a highly impure problem.

They have come to recognize how imperfect are the realities which must be wrestled with in a complicated world.

They have learned that criticism is one thing, diplomacy another.

They have learned to fear dogmatism in the classroom as well as in the Capital—and to reject the notion that expertise acquired in a lifetime of study in one discipline brings expertise in all other subjects as well.

They have learned, too, that strident emotionalism in the pursuit of truth, no matter how disguised in the language of wisdom, is harmful to public policy—just as harmful as self-righteousness in the application of power. For as Macaulay said: "The proof of virtue"—and, we might add, of wisdom—"is to possess boundless power without abusing it."

The responsible intellectual who moves between his campus and Washington knows, above all, that his task is, in the language of the current generation, to "cool it"—to bring what my generation called "not heat but light" to public affairs.

The man for whom this school is named always believed that to be the scope of scholarship. He never doubted the interdependence of the intellectual community and the community of public service. "The school," he said, "must be of the Nation."

A Worthy Calling

So we dedicate this building not only to the man, but to his faith that knowledge must be the underpinning of power—and that the public life is a calling worthy of the scholar as well as the politician.

There was once a time when knowledge seemed less essential to the processes of good government. Andrew Jackson held the opinion that the duties of all public offices were "so plain and simple" that any man of average intelligence could perform them.

We are no longer so sanguine about our public service. The public servant today moves along paths of adventure where he is helpless without the tools of advanced learning.

He seeks to chart the exploration of space, combining a thousand disciplines in an effort whose slightest miscalculation could have fatal consequences.

He has embarked on this planet on missions no less filled with risk and no less dependent on knowledge.

He seeks to rebuild our cities and to reclaim the beauty of our countryside. He seeks to promote justice beyond our courtrooms, making education and health and opportunity the common birthright for every citizen. And he seeks to build peace based on man's hopes rather than his fears.

These goals will be the work of many men and of many years. They will call for enormous new drafts of trained manpower into the public service.

Over the next four years, the Federal Government will need 30,000 more scientists and engineers and 6,000 more specialists in health, technology, and education.

By 1970, our state governments must grow by more than 600,000 to keep pace with the times. Employment for state and local government will exceed 10 million persons. Each year over the next decade, our Nation will need 200,000 new public school teachers to keep up with the growing population.

The Citizen Soldiers

The call for public service cannot be met by professionals alone. We must revive the ancient ideal of citizen soldiers who answer their nation's call in time of peril. We need them on battlefronts where no guns are heard but where freedom is no less tested.

Here at the Woodrow Wilson School, you have done much to raise the sights of public service. I urge you to continue to promote excellence in all levels. We intend to do the same in Washington, sparing no effort to assist those who select this as their life work.

I have asked Chairman John Macy of the Civil Service Commission to head a task force which will survey Federal programs for career advancement. I have asked him to study an expanded program of graduate training which, with the help of the universities, can enlarge our efforts to develop the talents and broaden the horizons of our career officers.

I also intend next year to recommend to Congress a program of expanding opportunities for those who wish to train for the public service—we will assist:

—students planning careers in Federal, state, or local government;

—colleges and universities seeking to enrich their own programs in this field;

—state and local governments seeking to develop more effective career services for their employees.

Our concept of public service is changing to meet the demands of our time. A new public servant has emerged. He may be the scholar who leaves his study for the crucible of power in his state or national capital. Or he may be the young man or woman who chooses public service but does not abandon at its doorstep the techniques of scholarship and the search for knowledge.

These men and women will help us to answer the question Franklin Roosevelt asked thirty years ago: Will it be said, "Democracy was a great dream, but it could not do the job"?

He did not doubt the answer. Even as troubles mounted, he took the starting steps to strengthen a Federal structure capable of carrying this Nation safely through its crisis. He began to organize the modern office of the President and to bring American Government into the mid-twentieth century.

THE ESSENTIAL QUESTION

As we enter the final third of this century, we are engaged once again with the question of whether democracy can do the job.

Many fears of former years no longer seem so relevant. Neither Congress nor the Supreme Court shows signs of becoming rubber stamps to the Executive. Moreover the Executive shows no symptoms of callous indifference to the ills we must cure if we are to preserve our vitality. State and local governments are more alive and more involved than thirty years ago. And our Nation's private enterprise has grown many times over in size and vitality.

The issue for this generation is a different kind. It has to do with the obligations of power in the world for a society that strives, despite its worst flaws, to be just and humane. Like almost every issue we face, this is one in which scholars and public officials alike have an irrevocable stake.

Abroad we can best measure America's involvement, whatever our successes and failures, by a simple proposition: not one single country where we have helped mount a major effort to resist aggression—from France to Greece to Korea to Vietnam—today has a government servile to outside interests.

There is a reason for this which I believe goes to the very heart of our society: the exercise of power in this century has meant for the United States not arrogance but agony. We have used our power not willingly and recklessly but reluctantly and with restraint.

Unlike nations in the past with vast power at their disposal, the United States has not sought to crush the autonomy of her neighbors. We have not been driven by blind militarism down courses of devastating aggression. Nor have we followed the ancient and conceited philosophy of the "noble lie" that some men are by nature meant to be slaves to others.

THE RECENT LESSONS

As I look upon America this morning from the platform of one of her great universities, I see, instead, a Nation whose might is not her master but her servant.

I see a Nation conscious of lessons so recently learned:

—that security and aggression, as well as peace and war, must be the concerns of her foreign policy;

—that a great power influences the world just as surely when it withdraws its strength, as when it exercises it;

—that aggression must be deterred where possible and met early when undertaken;

—that the application of military force, when it becomes necessary, must be for limited purposes and tightly controlled.

Surely it is not a paranoid vision of America's place in the world to recognize that freedom is still indivisible—still has adversaries whose challenge must be answered.

THE STERNEST CHALLENGE

Today, of course, that challenge is sternest in Southeast Asia. Yet there, as elsewhere, our great power is tempered by great restraint. What nation has announced such limited objectives or such willingness to remove its military presence once those objectives are achieved? What nation has spent the lives of its sons and vast sums of its fortune to provide the people of a small, striving nation the chance to elect a course we might not ourselves choose?

The aims for which we struggle are aims which, in the ordinary course of affairs, men of the intellectual world applaud and serve: the principle of choice over coercion, the defense of the weak against the strong and aggressive, the right of a young and frail nation to develop free from the interference of her neighbors, the ability of a people—however inexperienced, however different, however diverse—to fashion a society consistent with their own traditions and values and aspirations.

THE SCHOLAR'S OBLIGATION

These are all at stake in that conflict. It is the consequences of the cost of their abandonment that men of learning must examine dispassionately. For to wear the scholar's gown is to assume an obligation to seek truth without prejudice and without cliché, even when the results of the search are at variance with one's own opinions.

That is all we expect of those who are troubled, even as we are, by the obligations of power the United States did not seek but from which she cannot escape.

Twenty-six years ago Archibald MacLeish asked of all scholars and writers and students of his generation what history would say of those who failed to oppose the forces of disorder at loose in Europe.

We must ask of this generation the same question concerning Asia.

MacLeish reminded that generation of the answer given by Leonardo when Michelangelo indicted him for indifference to the misfortunes of the Florentines. "Indeed," said Leonardo, "indeed, the study of beauty has occupied my whole heart."

Other studies, no matter how important, must not distract the man of learning from the misfortunes of freedom in Southeast Asia.

While men may talk of the "search for peace" and the "pursuit of peace," we know that peace is not something to be discovered suddenly—not a thing to be caught and contained. Peace must be built—step by painful, patient step. And the building will take the best work of the world's best men and women.

It will take men whose cause is not the cause of one nation but of all nations—men whose enemies are not other men but the historic foes of mankind. I hope that many of you will serve in this public service for the world.

Woodrow Wilson knew that learning is essential to the leadership our world so desperately needs. Before he came to Princeton, he attended a small college in North Carolina and went to classes every day beneath a portal which bore the Latin inscription: "Let learning be cherished where liberty has arisen."

Today, this motto which served a President must serve all mankind. Where liberty has arisen, learning must be cherished—or liberty itself becomes a fragile thing.

We dedicate this building—not only to the man; not only to the Nation's service—but to learning in the service of mankind.

There can be no higher mission.

*"Today . . . our Nation can declare
another essential human freedom . . .
freedom from ignorance."*
Message to Congress,
February 5, 1968.

In two centuries, America has achieved—through great effort and struggle—
one major educational advance after another: free public schooling; the land
grant colleges; the extension of the universities into the nation's farms and
homes; the unique venture that has placed a high-school education within
the reach of every young person.

I believe that our time—the mid-1960s—will be remembered as a time of
unprecedented achievement in American education.

The past four years have been a time of unparalleled action:

—The Congress has approved more than 40 laws to support education from
the preschool project to the postgraduate laboratory;

—The Federal Government has raised its investment in education to nearly
$12 billion annually, almost triple the level four years ago.

The real significance of what we have done is reflected not in statistics, but
in the experiences of individual Americans, young and old, whose lives are
being shaped by new educational programs.

Through Head Start, a four-year-old encounters a new world of learning.

Through Title I of the Elementary and Secondary Education Act, a disadvantaged youngster finds essential extra help—and school becomes a more
rewarding place.

Through the Teacher Corps, a bright and eager college graduate is at-
tracted to teaching and his talents are focused where the need is greatest.

These programs—all of them new—are enriching life for millions of
young Americans.

In our high schools, students find that once-empty library shelves are
filled; the most up-to-date laboratory equipment is available; new courses,
new methods of teaching and learning are being tested in the classroom.

A student who sets his sights on college is more likely than ever before to
find help through Federal loans, scholarships, and work-study grants.

Today's college student is more likely than ever to live and learn in new dormitories, new classrooms, new libraries and laboratories.

Today, thousands of parents who in their youth had no chance for higher education can say with certainty, "My child can go to college."

Above all, we can see a new spirit stirring in America, moving us to stress anew the central importance of education; to seek ways to make education more vital and more widely available.

That new spirit cannot be fully measured in dollars or enrollment figures. But it is there nonetheless. The achievements of the past four years have sustained and nourished it.

Yet for all our progress, we still face enormous problems in education: Stubborn, lingering, unyielding problems.

The phrase "equal educational opportunity," to the poor family in Appalachia and to the Negro family in the city, is a promise—not a reality.

Our schools are turning out too many young men and women whose years in the classroom have not equipped them for useful work.

Growing enrollments and rising expenses are straining the resources of our colleges—and the strain is being felt by families across America.

Each of these problems will be difficult to solve. Their solution may take years—and almost certainly will bring new problems. But the challenge of our generation is to lead the way.

And in leading the way, we must carefully set our priorities. To meet our urgent needs within a stringent overall budget, several programs must be reduced or deferred. We can reduce expenditures on construction of facilities and the purchase of equipment. But, many of our urgent educational programs which directly affect the young people of America cannot be deferred. But the cost—the human cost—of delay is intolerable.

These principles underlie my 1969 budgetary recommendations and the proposals in this message. My recommendations are tailored to enable us to meet our most urgent needs, while deferring less important programs and expenditures.

ELEMENTARY AND SECONDARY EDUCATION

It took almost a century of effort and controversy and debate to pass the Elementary and Secondary Education Act.

The great question was this: Can there be a system of large-scale aid to education which does not diminish the independence of our local schools and which safeguards the rich diversity of American education?

In 1965 such a law was passed. Today it is at work in nearly 20,000 school districts: strengthening state and local school boards, local school officials and classroom teachers, and improving the quality of education for millions of children.

It may take a decade or more to measure the full benefits of the Elementary and Secondary Education Act. But already evidence is mounting to support my belief that this is the most significant education measure in our history.

Last year, Congress extended this law, the bedrock of all our efforts to help America's schools.

This year we have an opportunity to make that law a more efficient instrument of aid to education; to make it more responsive to the needs of the states and communities throughout the country.

I urge the Congress to fund Title I of the Elementary and Secondary Education Act well in advance of the school year, so that state and local school officials can make their plans with a clear idea of the resources that will be available.

Our resources are not unlimited—and never will be. So it is all the more important that in assigning priorities, we focus our aid where the need is greatest.

That firm principle underlies a six-point program which I am proposing to Congress under the Elementary and Secondary Education Act and other authorities:

1. Two innovative programs to help America's youngest and poorest children have been proven in practice. I propose that funding for the Head Start and Head Start Follow Through programs be stepped up from $340 million to $380 million.

2. Last year, Congress authorized a special program to help Mexican-American, Puerto Rican, and other children who are separated by a language barrier from good education. I propose that we launch this bilingual education program with a $5 million appropriation.

3. We are still doing less than we should do to prepare mentally retarded and physically handicapped children for useful lives. I propose that our special programs for the handicapped be increased from $53 million to $85 million.

4. We must rescue troubled boys and girls before they drop out of school.

I propose full funding—$30 million—for a new stay-in school program, which will help schools tailor their own programs, from new and exciting methods of instruction to family counseling and special tutoring, to turn potential dropouts into high-school graduates.

5. Upward Bound, a program for poor but talented students, has directed thousands of young Americans into college who might otherwise never have had a chance. I propose that Congress increase funds for Upward Bound to serve 30,000 young Americans this year.

6. Adult basic education classes last year gave about 300,000 men and women an opportunity to gain new earning power, new self-respect, a new sense of achievement. I propose that Congress provide $50 million for this vital program.

If we can invest vast sums for education, we must also be able to plan and evaluate our education programs; to undertake basic research in teaching and learning, and to apply that research to the classroom. For these efforts, I propose appropriations of $177 million next year.

NEW STRENGTH FOR VOCATIONAL EDUCATION

Whatever else we expect of the local school, we demand that it prepare each student for a productive life. The high-school graduate who does not enter college needs not only knowledge enough to be a responsible citizen, but skills enough to get and keep a good job.

One and a half million young men and women will leave high school and enter the labor force this year—in a time of high employment, when skills are at a premium.

Too many of them will find that they have no job skills—or only marginal skills, or skills which are not really needed in their communities.

A high-school diploma should not be a ticket to frustration.

We must do more to improve vocational education programs. We must help high schools, vocational schools, technical institutes, and community colleges to modernize their programs, to experiment with new approaches to job training. Above all, we must build stronger links between the schools and their students, and local industries and employment services, so that education will have a direct relationship to the world the graduating student enters.

I recommend that Congress enact the Partnership for Learning and Earning Act of 1968.

This new program—streamlining and strengthening our vocational education laws—will

—give new flexibility to our system of matching grants so the states can concentrate their funds where the need is greatest;

—provide $15 million for special experimental programs to bridge the gap between education and work: for alliances between schools, employment services, and private employers; for new summer training programs combining work and education;

—totally revise and consolidate our existing vocations' education laws, reducing paperwork for the state, the schools, and other training centers;

—encourage the states to plan a long-range strategy in vocational education.

TRAINED PROFESSIONALS FOR OUR SCHOOLS

The value of all these measures—and indeed the effectiveness of our entire school system—depends on educators: teachers, teacher aides, administrators, and many others.

It would profit us little to enact the most enlightened laws, to authorize great sums of money—unless we guarantee a continuing supply of trained, dedicated, enthusiastic men and women for the education professions.

To advance this essential purpose, I propose:

—that Congress provide the funds needed to train nearly 45,000 teachers, administrators, and other professionals under the Education Professions Development Act of 1967;

—that Congress authorize and appropriate the necessary funds so that 4,000 of our best and most dedicated young men and women can serve our neediest children in the Teacher Corps.

HIGHER EDUCATION

The prosperity and well-being of the United States—and thus our national interest—are vitally affected by America's colleges and universities, junior colleges, and technical institutes.

Their problems are not theirs alone, but the Nation's.

This is true today more than ever. For now we call upon higher education to play a new and more ambitious role in our social progress, our economic development, our efforts to help other countries.

We depend upon the universities—their training, research, and extension services—for the knowledge which undergirds agricultural and industrial production.

Increasingly, we look to higher education to provide the key to better employment opportunities and a more rewarding life for our citizens.

As never before, we look to the colleges and universities—to their faculties, laboratories, research institutes, and study centers—for help with every problem in our society and with the efforts we are making toward peace in the world.

STUDENT AID

It is one of the triumphs of American democracy that college is no longer a privilege for the few. Last fall, more than 50 percent of our high-school graduates went on to college. It is our goal by 1976 to increase that number to two-thirds.

In the past four years, we have significantly eased the financial burden which college imposes on so many families. Last year, more than one student in five attended college with the help of Federal loans, scholarships, grants, and work-study programs.

But for millions of capable American students and their families, college is still out of reach. In a Nation that honors individual achievement, financial obstacles to full education opportunity must be overcome.

I propose the Educational Opportunity Act of 1968:

—to set a new and sweeping national goal: that in America there must be no economic or racial barrier to higher education; that every qualified young person must have all the education he wants and can absorb;

—to help a million and a half students attend college next year through the full range of our student aid programs, including guaranteed loans;

—to strengthen the guaranteed loan program by meeting the administrative costs of the banks who make these loans. With a service fee of up to $35 for each loan, this program can aid an additional 200,000 students next year, bringing the total to 750,000;

—to provide $15 million for new programs of tutoring, counseling, and special services so that the neediest students can succeed in college;

—to unify and simplify several student aid programs—college work-study, educational opportunity grants, and National Defense Education Act loans —so that each college can devise a flexible plan of aid tailored to the needs of each student.

AID TO INSTITUTIONS OF HIGHER LEARNING

Today, higher education needs help.

American colleges and universities face growing enrollments, rising costs, and increasing demands for services of all kind.

In ten years, the number of young people attending college will increase more than 50 percent; graduate enrollments will probably double.

Our first order of business must be to continue existing Federal support for higher education.

I urge the Congress to extend and strengthen three vital laws which have served this Nation well:

—The National Defense Education Act of 1958, which has helped nearly 2 million students go to college and graduate school.

—The Higher Education Act of 1958, which has helped nearly 1,400 colleges and universities meet growing enrollments with new classrooms, laboratories, and dormitories.

—The Higher Education Act of 1965, which, in addition to its student aid programs, has strengthened college libraries, involved our universities in community service, and given new vitality to 450 developing colleges.

I also urge the Congress to fulfill the commitment it made two years ago and appropriate funds needed for the International Education Act. This act will strengthen our universities in their international programs—and ultimately strengthen the quality of the men and women who serve this country abroad.

We must apply more effectively the educational resources we have. We must encourage better cooperation between the Nation's colleges and universities; and we should move to increase each institution's efficiency by exploiting the most advanced technology.

To serve these purposes, I recommend the Networks for Knowledge Act of 1968.

This pilot program will provide new financial incentives to encourage colleges and universities to pool their resources by sharing faculties, facilities, equipment, library, and educational television services. It will supplement the effort launched last year by the National Science Foundation to explore the potential of computers in education.

I also recommend three new measures to strengthen graduate education in America.

First, we should increase the Federal payment available to help graduate schools meet the cost of educating a student who has earned a Federal fellowship. At present, Federal fellowship programs are actually deepening the debt of the graduate schools because this payment is too low.

Second, we should launch a new program to strengthen those graduate schools with clear potential for higher quality. With enrollments growing, we must begin to enlarge the capacity of graduate schools. This program will underwrite efforts to strengthen faculties, improve courses, and foster excellent in a wide range of fields.

Third, I urge the Congress to increase Government-sponsored research in our universities. The knowledge gained through this research truly is power —power to heal the sick, educate the young, defend the nation, and improve the quality of life for our citizens.

A STRATEGY FOR HIGHER EDUCATION

The programs I am presenting to the Congress today are aimed at solving some of the problems faced by our colleges and universities and their students in the years ahead. But accomplishing all these things will by no means solve the problems of higher education in America.

To do that, we must shape a long-term strategy of Federal aid to higher education: a comprehensive set of goals and a precise plan of action.

I am directing the Secretary of Health, Education, and Welfare to begin preparing a long-range plan for the support of higher education in America.

Our strategy must:

—eliminate race and income as bars to higher learning;

—guard the independence of private and public institutions;

—ensure that state and private contributions will bear their fair share of support for higher education;

—encourage the efficient and effective use of educational resources by our colleges and universities;

—promote continuing improvement in the quality of American education;

—effectively blend support to students with support for institutions.

Such a strategy will not be easy to devise. But we must begin now. For at stake is a decision of vital importance to all Americans.

EDUCATION AND THE QUALITY OF LIFE

Every educational program contributes vitally to the enrichment of life in America. But some have that enrichment as their first goal. They are designed not to serve special groups or institutions, but to serve all the American people.

We have tested in the past three years a new idea in government: the National Foundation on the Arts and Humanities.

That experiment has been an impressive success. It has proved that Government can indeed enhance the Nation's cultural life and deepen the understanding of our people:

—With modest amounts of money, the humanities endowment has promoted scholarship in a wide range of fields and quickened public interest in the humanities.

—The arts endowment has brought new energy and life to music, drama, and the arts in communities all over America.

I believe the Foundation has earned a vote of confidence. I urge that the National Foundation on the Arts and Humanities authorization be extended.

We have acted also to launch an historic educational force in American life: public broadcasting—noncommercial radio and television service devoted first and foremost to excellence.

Last year the Congress authorized the Corporation for Public Broadcasting. This year we must give it life.

I recommend that the Congress appropriate the funds needed in fiscal 1968 and fiscal 1969 to support the initial activities of the Corporation for Public Broadcasting.

Last year I stressed the importance of a long-range financing plan which would ensure that public broadcasting would be vigorous, independent, and free from political interference or control. The problem involved is complex. It concerns the use of the most powerful communications medium in the world today. It should not be resolved without the most thorough study and consultation.

I am asking the Secretary of Health, Education, and Welfare, the Secretary of the Treasury, and the Director of the Bureau of the Budget—who have been studying this problem since the law was enacted—to work with the board of directors of the Corporation for public broadcasting and the appropriate committees of the Congress to formulate a long-range financing plan that will promote and protect this vital new force in American life.

THE FIFTH FREEDOM

On January 6, 1941, President Franklin D. Roosevelt set forth to Congress and the people "four essential human freedoms" for which America stands.

In the years since then, those four freedoms—Freedom of Speech, Freedom of Worship, Freedom from Want, and Freedom from Fear—have stood as a summary of our aspirations for the American Republic and for the world.

And Americans have always stood ready to pay the cost in energy and treasury which are needed to make those great goals a reality.

Today—wealthier, more powerful, and more able than ever before in our history—our Nation can declare another essential human freedom.

The fifth freedom is freedom from ignorance.

It means that every man, everywhere, should be free to develop his talents to their full potential—unhampered by arbitrary barriers of race or birth or income.

We have already begun the work of guaranteeing that fifth freedom.

The job, of course, will never be finished. For a nation, as for an individual, education is a perpetually unfinished journey, a continuing process of discovery.

But the work we started when this Nation began, which has flourished for nearly two centuries, and which gained new momentum in the past two Congresses—is ours to continue—yours and mine.

PART FOUR

The Reformation of Politics

Confessions of a Kennedy Man

By James MacGregor Burns

I am—and always will be—a Kennedy man. I watched John F. Kennedy take his first, faltering steps as a senatorial candidate in Massachusetts in 1952; campaigned with him through the Berkshire Hills and the Connecticut Valley in 1958; fought and bled and celebrated with him in his pre-Convention struggles; and as a delegate to the Democratic National Convention in 1960 I was one of a small band of "liaison men" that Bob Kennedy used to keep pressure on the delegations. Later, when I visited John Kennedy in the White House from time to time, he seemed to me as unaffected, arresting, and altogether attractive a person as when he had started his climb to power years before.

I remember only one time when I flatly disagreed with his political judgment and rebelled against it. That was when word came down to us on the Convention floor in 1960 that Kennedy had just chosen Lyndon Johnson as his running mate. I rushed about the arena seeking out liberal leaders seated in the delegations. Some of them were working up an abortive revolt. Most were acquiescing. One eminent liberal eyed me stonily. "That's what Jack wants and that's what Jack will have."

Two doubts assailed me about Lyndon Johnson. One was obvious. To me as an Eastern, academic liberal he was far too much the Democratic moderate who had opposed or watered down many of the proposals of liberal Democrats like Hubert Humphrey, Estes Kefauver, and even Adlai Stevenson. The other was that he was so much—and so proudly—the complete Senate man. To me the Senate was—and often still is—the seat of delay and deadlock. I had little use for the man who practiced and made a virtue of the brokerage and trading and erosion that had suffocated liberal bills or brought them through the upper chamber at a steep price.

When historians come to view the Johnson Administration in a fuller perspective, the question that will most perplex them, I think, will not be Lyndon Johnson's voyage from the moderate-conservative wing of the Democratic party to the liberal. Biographers will note the impact of his earlier years in a poor, populist land and perhaps will come to look on his Senate years as Majority Leader as an interlude between the New Deal-Fair Deal era and his years in the White House. Perhaps they will judge that the academic liberals, such as I, underestimated the early powerful progressive forces working on Johnson in his Texas environment, just as many other liberals overestimated the influence of conservative Catholic forces on John Kennedy's intellectual development.

What will baffle the historian far more, I think, will be how the complete Senate man moved so surely into the Presidency and began to employ from the start the levers of presidential influence. Within three days the Senate man seemed to have disappeared. In place of the legislative broker there was the executive man issuing instructions, using his staff, putting demands on Congress, taking over as party leader, filling the White House with his drive and purpose. How could this happen?

The range and quality of the President's speeches presented in this volume may in part reflect the transformation. Lyndon Johnson became President at a time when the White House staff had reached a peak of competence, authority, and versatility. It is hard to realize today that Presidents during much of the nineteenth century had to fight for their right to be chief executives. In this century even Franklin Roosevelt, with all his political dexterity and unparalleled support from the people, was badly beaten in an effort to maintain and extend control of the Executive branch. But Roosevelt's later partial success in strengthening the White House office and centralizing the Executive branch; the broadening of White House control during World War II; the enormous expansion of White House staff and machinery under Truman and Eisenhower; and the excitement and dedication and glamor that Kennedy imparted to the White House—all these were elements in an Executive Office that was ready to do the new President's bidding. Johnson had the wit and the will to use the executive machinery in terms of its own imperatives, just as he had mastered the legislative machinery earlier.

Machinery was not enough; it never is. But what the machinery did was to give Johnson resources to project his views and his policies on a national and world stage; more than that, it demanded as well as permitted action, because the machinery had its own momentum and direction. When people wonder who really writes President Johnson's speeches—as people have wondered about all Presidents at least since Jackson—the answer in part is his staff, because that too is part of the modern Presidency.

Johnson's inheritance of this kind of White House office raised still another question—was the new President simply a pawn of the presidential establishment? Had the Executive branch generally, and the White House office within it, become so vast, opaque, and autonomous an institution that it lay beyond the power of one man to control? This question was vital, since that one man happened to be the only elected official among 2 million or so Federal officials.

It is the mark of Johnson's impact on the Presidency that this question has hardly been raised in the last two or three years. Quite the contrary, Johnson went on not only to employ all the powers and machinery of the Presidency but to carry on centralizing and consolidating actions that have strengthened presidential authority over the far-flung executive establishment. One of these acts has been the internal reorganization of major departments to give their chiefs greater control over departmental policy and operations. The most conspicuous—but by no means the only—example was the Defense Department under Robert McNamara. A second marked trend under Johnson has been the further strengthening of the Budget Bureau as an agency of management as well as budgetary control. A third has been the conversion of the Civil Service Commission into a positive agency for recruiting executive talent, under the chairmanship of John Macy, who significantly has had as large a role in the White House on personnel matters as in his own agency.

Perhaps the most significant development under Johnson as Chief Executive has been the mysterious entity PPB. Planning–Programming–Budgeting has many uses, and perhaps some dangers, but its main significance for the President is that through the Budget Bureau the techniques of PPB can be used to integrate programs, strengthen presidential control and supervision, improve the whole planning process, and incidentally save money. PPB has tremendous potential for presidential leadership and impact. One of the vivid lessons of our long struggle against poverty and discrimination is that these fundamental ills cannot be cured by single-remedy approaches—by people who think that health or education or crime control or jobs or full employment or the right to vote or some other one channel is *the* royal road to a solution. Not only do these problems require action along a great many channels, but the action must be fully coordinated, because the forces for social advance are many times more speedy and effective when they mutually stimulate and reinforce one another. This cardinal fact has come to be recognized in the White House. "Because we are using a new method to analyze domestic problems for the first time—the 'systems' or 'total' method—we are beginning to recognize," presidential assistant Joseph A. Califano, Jr., has said, "that the only way to solve these problems is by attacking all of their many parts."

Still, mechanisms are not enough. What about the ends they are designed to serve? On this score the success of Lyndon Johnson as chief legislator or chief decision maker will turn on one's evaluation of his ideals and policies, and on these questions fair-minded men will disagree. It will be difficult, however, for anyone perusing the President's speeches—the fifty or so printed here or the thousand or so recorded in the pages of that invaluable journal, *The Weekly Compilation of Presidential Documents*—without being impressed by the sweep, depth, and above all the concreteness of the President's policy recommendations. Rhetoric there has been—perhaps too much of it— but the rhetoric has, it seems to me, been tightly bound to substance.

Many students of government—and of presidential personality—have been little surprised by Johnson's moves to strengthen government. They point out that he is the "strong" kind of President and naturally would secure and invigorate his means of control. Very true—but this makes all the more surprising the fact that the President has reached outside of the presidential establishment to call for reforms on the whole governmental system. He has urged that the federal-state-city "partnership" be reexamined and revamped to make this more than just a pretty phrase. He has urged extensive reforms of election procedures, campaign finance, lobby regulation, and of voting requirements, as his speech of May 25, 1967, reproduced here, attests. But certainly the most remarkable reform urged by this one-time Senate man is the four-year term for members of the House of Representatives, in his message to Congress of January 20, 1966 (included here). Shades of the separation of powers! For members of one department to interfere with the operations of another has long been anathema in theory and rhetoric (although actually done continually in practice) under the checks and balances. For the President to make such a definite recommendation on a matter so closely affecting the very political lives of Congressmen is a measure of the complete disappearance of Johnson the Senate hand. One can imagine the reaction of *Senate Majority Leader* Lyndon Johnson to any President who might have had the temerity to propose a four-year term for *Senators.*

So quickly are the pressures mounting on government, though, that even Johnson's sweeping proposals for reform may be inadequate for the years ahead. The man who takes the oath of office on January 20, 1969, will have to consider further extensive changes. I would suggest at least three:

1. The White House must be capable of conducting even more and better

long-term planning than it does today. The modern Presidency is far too much geared to the instant, the immediate, the present. My first change would be to remove every news ticker from the building. My second would be to introduce PPB even more intensively into the whole executive establishment with emphasis on its planning function.

2. The White House decision-making process has been too invisible under Lyndon Johnson. The President's passion for secrecy has been understandable in political and personal terms, but one result is that the whole White House decision-making operation has a bloodless and passionless quality. Under Johnson the White House has enlisted the advice and participation of some of the most brilliant minds in America, by systematically going out to the universities and searching out new ideas and information, but one would hardly know it from the impersonality and immediacy that characterize so much of the White House operation. The creativity, the policy innovations, the fresh thinking in the White House have been exciting in fact, but one would hardly know this by watching the White House from the outside.

3. Perhaps the most drastic change must come in fiscal machinery, especially tax policy. With our huge, powerful, volatile economy requiring close supervision and regulation, we must have adequate presidential control from day to day, not just year to year. Specifically, this means that Congress should grant the President power, for example, to set income and other tax rates on his own initiative within broad margins set by Congress, with Congress retaining the power, through a vote by both houses, to abrogate presidential action. This is the pattern of congressional control over administrative reorganization, which has worked well and should be extended to the all-important sector of fiscal leadership and coordination.

4. We will need to make decisive changes in our Federal system. As the Advisory Commission on Intergovernmental Relations reported early in 1968, the way in which we meet our sharp challenges at home "will determine if we can maintain a form of government marked by partnership and wholesome competition among national, state, and local levels, or if instead—in the face of threatened anarchy—we must sacrifice political diversity as the price

of the authoritative action required for the Nation's survival." We may need to experiment, for example, with devices enabling the national government to move strongly and directly on national problems and leaving only veto powers in the hands of state and local governments. We may find to our surprise that we can achieve "diversity in unity" and a pluralistic culture more effectively through making changes in our Federal system rather than letting it rigidify.

All this means a strong Presidency today—and an even stronger one tomorrow. An astute British observer, Henry Fairlie, has wondered whether we are breeding in the modern Presidency a new system of "Caesaropapism —that is, a consolidation of imperial (or federal) law and administration to create a commonwealth of citizens under one law, all of them persuaded of the ultimate justice of the regime to which they consent." As one thinks of the whirlwind of criticism that has enveloped Lyndon Johnson over Vietnam and other issues, one can hardly share such fears. My own worry is not so much about the Presidency, which must be strong in these turbulent and exacting times, but about the relative impotence, except perhaps during election time, of the Loyal Opposition. It is in the second party that we must hope for the great political innovations of the future—especially the strengthening and institutionalizing of a vivid and visible "leader of the loyal opposition." But that is one reform that surely lies beyond the long reach and leaping imagination of Lyndon Johnson.

A strong President is not automatically a great President. But these days a man cannot be a great President without being a strong President. And he cannot be a strong President unless he sees the uses and the limitations of the machinery of government. More than any other President, Lyndon Johnson has linked power and purpose, principles and policy. Both the principles and the purpose are laid out in this book: the citizen can assess them on his own. But to conceive that Lyndon Johnson is anything but deadly serious about carrying them out is to fail to take the measure of the man.

Lyndon B. Johnson

*"In our democracy, politics is the instrument
which sustains our institutions
and keeps them strong and free."*
The President proposes to Congress
measures for election reform, campaign financing,
regulation of lobbying, and residency voting requirements,
May 25, 1967.

Public participation in the processes of government is the essence of democracy. Public confidence in those processes strengthens democracy.

No government can long survive which does not fuse the public will to the institutions which serve it. The American system has endured for almost two centuries because the people have involved themselves in the work of their Government, with full faith in the meaning of that involvement.

But Government itself has the continuing obligation—second to no other—to keep the machinery of public participation functioning smoothly and to improve it where necessary so that democracy remains a vital and vibrant institution.

It is in the spirit of that obligation that I send this message to the Congress today. I propose a five-point program to:

—reform our campaign financing laws to assure full disclosure of contributions and expenses, to place realistic limits on contributions, and to remove the meaningless and ineffective ceilings on campaign expenditures;

—provide a system of public financing for Presidential election campaigns;

—broaden the base of public support for election campaigns, by exploring ways to encourage and stimulate small contributions;

—close the loopholes in the Federal laws regulating lobbying;

—assure the right to vote for millions of Americans who change their residences.

THE ELECTION REFORM ACT OF 1967

In our democracy, politics is the instrument which sustains our institutions and keeps them strong and free.

The laws which govern political activity should be constantly reviewed—and reshaped when necessary—to preserve the essential health and vitality of the political process which is so fundamental to our way of life.

In my 1966 State of the Union message I called attention to the need for a basic reform of the laws governing political campaigns in these words:

"I will submit legislation to revise the present unrealistic restrictions on contributions—to prohibit the endless proliferation of committees, bringing local and state committees under the act—and to attach strong teeth and severe penalties to the requirement of full disclosure of contributions. . . ."

A year ago this month, I submitted my proposals to the Congress in the Election Reform Act of 1966.

That measure reflected my concern, as one who has been involved in the process of elective Government for over three decades, that the laws dealing with election campaigns have not kept pace with the times.

The Federal Corrupt Practices Act was passed forty-two years ago. The Hatch Act was passed twenty-seven years ago. Inadequate in their scope when enacted, they are now obsolete. More loophole than law, they invite evasion and circumvention.

A sweeping overhaul of the laws governing election campaigns should no longer be delayed.

Basic reform—with an emphasis on clear and straightforward disclosure—is essential to ensure public confidence and involvement in the political process. On the cornerstone of disclosure we can build toward further reform —by charting new ways to broaden the base of financial support for candidates and parties in election campaigns.

I again ask the Congress to take positive action in this field as we work together to ensure continued and increased public confidence in the elective process.

I recommend the Election Reform Act of 1967 to correct omissions, loopholes, and shortcomings in the present campaign laws.

This Act embodies many of the same positive measures I proposed last May. Last October, after hearings, the subcommittee on Elections of the Committee on House Administration reported out substantially the bill I proposed "favorably and with bipartisan support." The Subcommittee Report called those measures "a vast improvement over existing law."

Full Public Disclosure

The heart of basic reform is full disclosure. This measure would, for the first time, make effective the past efforts of the Congress and the Executive to achieve full disclosure of political campaign funds.

Complete disclosure will open to public view where campaign money comes from and how it is spent. Such disclosure will help dispel the growth of public skepticism which surrounds the present methods of financing political campaigns.

Full disclosure efforts are frustrated today by gaps in the law through which have passed an endless stream of national, state and local political committees.

To ensure full disclosure, I recommend that:

—every candidate, including those for the Presidency and Vice-Presidency, and every committee, state, interstate, and national, that supports a candidate for Federal office be required to report on every contribution, loan and expense item over $100;

—Primaries and convention nomination contests be brought within the disclosure laws.

Effective Ceilings on the Size of Contributions

Closely related to full disclosure—the basic step in any election reform— is another equally demanding task. It requires that we make political financing more democratic by recognizing that great wealth—in reality or appearance—could be used to achieve undue political influence.

Current law limits to $5,000 contributions to a single candidate for Federal office or contributions to any national political committee supporting a candidate.

But the law does not prohibit an individual from making a $5,000 contribution to each of several national committees supporting a candidate or party—and there is no limit to the number of such committees. Moreover, state and local political committees are not even covered by existing law.

I recommend that a $5,000 limit be placed on the total amount that could come from any individual, his wife, or minor children to the campaign of any candidate.

Repeal of Artificial Limits on Campaign Expenses

With full disclosure and an effective ceiling on contributions we can move forward to cure another defect in our election campaign laws—the artificial limits on campaign expenditures.

—National political committees can raise and spend no more than $3 million. But the law does not limit the number of national committees.

—Senate candidates are limited to expenses of $25,000 and House candidates to $5,000. But the law does not limit the number of committees that can spend and raise money on the candidate's behalf.

These legal ceilings on expenditures were enacted many years ago, when the potential of radio in a campaign was virtually unknown and when television did not exist. They are totally unrealistic and inadequate. They have led to the endless proliferation of political committees.

I therefore recommend a repeal of the present arbitrary limits on the total expenditures of candidates for Federal office.

Barring Political Contributions by Government Contractors

Present law prohibits corporations and labor organizations from making contributions to campaigns for Federal office.

But there is an anomaly which must be corrected in the law relating to contractors with the Federal Government.

Noncorporate Government contractors are now prohibited from making political contributions at all levels of government—Federal, state, and local.

The bar on corporations with Government contracts, however, extends only to political contributions at the Federal level. These corporations are free to make political contributions at the state and local levels where finances are often intertwined with national political campaigns.

In the interests of consistency and good sense, I recommend that corpora-

tions holding contracts with the Federal Government also be prohibited from making political contributions at the state and local level.
Enforcement

To ensure that these reforms are strictly enforced, the Election Reform Act of 1967 would provide criminal penalties for violations of the law.

CAMPAIGN FINANCING

The proposed Election Reform Act of 1967 is corrective, remedying present inadequacies in the law. It goes hand in hand with the pursuit of another goal—to provide public support for election campaigns.
The Background

Democracy rests on the voice of the people. Whatever blunts the clear expression of that voice is a threat to democratic government.

In this century one phenomenon in particular poses such a threat—the soaring costs of political campaigns.

Historically, candidates for public office in this country have always relied upon private contributions to finance their campaigns.

But in the last few decades, technology—which has changed so much of our national life—has modified the nature of political campaigning as well. Radio, television, and the airplane have brought sweeping new dimensions and costs to the concept of political candidacy.

In many ways these changes have worked to the decided advantage of the American people. They have served to bring the candidates and the issues before virtually every voting citizen. They have contributed immeasurably to the political education of the Nation.

In another way, however, they have worked to the opposite effect by increasing the costs of campaigning to spectacular proportions. Costs of such magnitude can have serious consequences for our democracy:

—More and more, men and women of limited means may refrain from running for public office. Private wealth increasingly becomes an artificial and unrealistic arbiter of qualifications, and the source of public leadership is thus severely narrowed.

—Increases in the size of individual contributions create uneasiness in the minds of the public. Actually, the exercise of undue influence occurs infrequently. Nonetheless, the circumstance in which a candidate is obligated to rely on sizable contributions easily creates the impression that influence is at work. This impression—however unfounded it might be—is itself intolerable, for it erodes public confidence in the democratic order.

—The necessity of acquiring substantial funds to finance campaigns diverts a candidate's attention from his public obligations and detracts from his energetic exposition of the issues.

—The growing importance of large contributions serves to deter the search for small ones, and thus effectively narrows the base of financial support. This is exactly the opposite of what a democratic society should strive to achieve.

It is extremely difficult to devise a program which completely eliminates these undesirable consequences without inhibiting robust campaigning and the freedom of every American fully to participate in the elective process. I believe that our ultimate goal should be to finance the total expense for this vital function of our democracy with public funds, and to prohibit the use or acceptance of money from private sources. We have virtually no experience upon which to base such a program. Its risks and uncertainties are formidable. I believe, however, that we are ready to make a beginning. We should proceed with all prudent speed to enact those parts of such a program which appear to be feasible at this time.

PRESIDENTIAL CAMPAIGNS

The Problem

The election of a President is the highest expression of the free choice of the American people. It is the most visible level of politics—and also the most expensive.

For their free choice to be exercised wisely, the people must be fully informed about the opposing candidates and issues. To achieve this, candidates and parties must have the funds to bring their platforms and programs to the people.

Yet, as we have seen, the costs of campaigning are skyrocketing. This imposes extreme and heavy financial burdens on party and candidate alike, creating a potential for danger—the possibility that men of great wealth could achieve undue political influence through large contributions.

In recognition of this problem, the Congress last year enacted the Presidential Election Campaign Fund Act. By so doing, it adopted the central concept that some form of public financing of Presidential campaigns would serve the public interest.

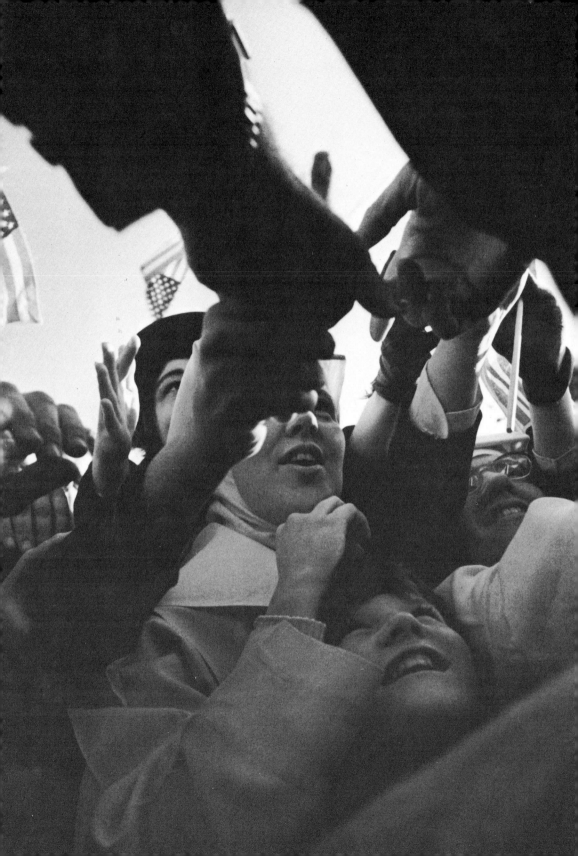

I did not submit or recommend this legislation. It was the creation and the product of the Congress in 1966. As you will recall, it was added as an amendment to other essential legislation. When I signed that Act into law last November, I observed that "it breaks new ground in the financing of presidential election campaigns" and that the "new law is only a beginning." It was my belief then, as it is now, that the complex issues involved in this new concept required extensive discussion and penetrating analysis.

Over the past six weeks, we have heard men of deep principle and firm conviction engage in a spirited and searching debate on the law. While there were honest and vigorous disagreements, they were voiced by those who share a common faith in the free ideals which are the bedrock of our democracy.

The Issues

The course of the debate has illuminated many of the issues which underlie the matter of Presidential campaign financing. For example:

—In what amount should Federal funds be provided for these campaigns?

—What limitations should be placed on the use of these funds?

—Should there be a complete bar on the use of private contributions for those aspects of campaign financing which would be regularly provided through appropriations?

—Can the availability of public funds result in an undue concentration of power in national political committees? If so, what steps can be taken to prevent it?

—Is the tax check-off method a sound approach or is a direct appropriation to be preferred?

—How can equitable treatment of minor parties be assured?

—What sanctions would be most effective to ensure compliance with the law?

—Whatever the ultimate formula, how can we preserve the independence, spirit, and spontaneity that has hallmarked American political enterprise through the years?

The Recommendations

Against this backdrop of concern for the political process, the protection of the public interest, and the issues that have been raised, I make these eleven recommendations to improve and strengthen the Presidential Election Campaign Fund Act:

1. *Funds to finance Presidential campaigns should be provided by direct congressional appropriation, rather than determined by individual tax check-offs.*

This approach would

—provide the opportunity for Congress to make a realistic assessment, and express its judgment, of what it would cost Presidential candidates or parties to carry their views to the voters. This assessment should consider the recommendations of the special Advisory Board to the Comptroller General, created under the Presidential Election Campaign Fund Act. The Board consists of representatives of both major political parties. Based on this review and recommendation, Congress could then appropriate the necessary funds.

—make the amount appropriated for the campaign fund more stable, by removing its uncertain reliance on tax check-offs, whose numbers might bear no reasonable relationship to the amount required to bring the issues before the public.

2. *The funds should be used only for expenses which are needed to bring the issues before the public.*

Under the procedure I recommend:

—the funds so appropriated would be used to reimburse specified expenditures incurred during the Presidential election campaign itself, after the parties have selected their candidate;

—the amount appropriated should be adequate to defray key items of expense to carry a campaign to the public and thus be limited to the following items: radio and television, newspaper and periodical advertising, the preparation and distribution of campaign literature, and travel;

—the amount of the fund for the major parties as finally determined by the Congress would be divided equally between them.

3. *Private contributions for major parties could not be used for those items of expense to which public funds could be applied.*

Private contributions, however, could be used to defray the costs of other campaign expenses. These would include the salaries of campaign workers, overhead, research and polls, telegraph and telephone, postage, and administrative expenses.

Citizens who want to make contributions to the party or candidate of their choice will be free to do so. Party workers at the grass roots will be able to pursue their neighborhood activities, a responsibility which is deeply woven into the fabric of American political tradition.

But under the measures I have proposed, the major burden of raising money for soaring campaign costs will be lifted from a presidential candidate's shoulders. No longer will we have to rely on the large contributions of wealthy and powerful interests.

4. *A "major party" should be defined as one which received 25 percent or more of the popular votes cast in the last election.*

A percentage-of-votes test is more realistic than the fixed number of votes (15 million) now in the present law. It recognizes our growing population with more Americans entering the voting ranks each year.

5. *A "minor party" should be defined as one which received between 5 percent and 25 percent of the popular votes cast in the current election.*

For the same reasons I described above, the eligibility test for Federal support should not be based on a fixed number of votes (5 million for "minor parties" in the current law), but rather on the percentage of votes received.

Third party movements can support the rich diversity of American political life. At the same time some reasonable limitations should be developed so that Federal financial incentives are not made available to parties lacking a modicum of public support—or created solely to receive Government funds.

Under this proposal, "minor parties" would receive payments based on the number of votes they receive in the current election. The payment for each vote received by a minor party would then be determined so as to be the equivalent of that made to the major parties.

For example, assume that two major parties received a total of 80 million votes in a prior election, and Congress had appropriated a $40 million campaign fund for those two parties. Although the major parties would share equally in that fund ($20 million each), the allocation would amount to 50 cents per vote cast for those parties. Using the 50 cents per vote as the guideline, a minor party receiving 5 million votes in the current election would be entitled to $2.5 million for its recognized campaign expenses.

6. *A "minor party" should be eligible for reimbursement promptly following an election.*

A "minor party" should be able to qualify promptly for Federal funds, based on its showing in the current election, rather than waiting four years until the next election. This added source of funds should enhance a minor party's opportunity to bring its programs and platforms into the public arena.

7. *The percentage of Federal funds received by a major or minor party which could be used in any one state should be limited to 140 percent of the percentage the population of that state bears to the population of the country.*

This would prevent the concentration of funds in any particular state and would minimize the ability of national party officials to reduce the role and effectiveness of local political organizations. At the same time, it would retain the flexibility necessary to carry a party's programs to the public. The Comptroller General should be empowered to issue rules for the equitable allocation, on a geographic basis, for national campaign expenses, such as network television.

8. *The Comptroller General should be required to make a full report to the Congress as soon as practicable after each Presidential election.*

This report should include:

—payments made to each party from the fund;

—expenses incurred by each party;

—any misuse of the funds.

9. *The Comptroller General should be given clear authority to audit the expenses of presidential campaigns.*

It is imperative that the strictest controls be exercised to safeguard the public interest. The General Accounting Office is the arm of the Government which I believe is best suited to monitor the expenditures of the fund.

Payments from the fund would be made only upon the submission of certified vouchers to the Comptroller General.

If the Comptroller General's audit reveals any improper use of funds, the following sanctions would be applied:

—the amounts involved would have to be repaid to the Treasury; and

—if the misuse is willful, a penalty of up to 50 percent of the amount involved would be imposed.

10. *To bring greater wisdom and experience to the administration of the Act, the Comptroller General's special Advisory Board on the Presidential Election Campaign Fund should be expanded from seven to eleven members.*

This Advisory Board is faced with a heavy and demanding task. It must "counsel and assist" the Comptroller General in the performance of his duties under the Act.

The membership of the Board now consists of two members from each major political party and three additional members. I recommend that the Board be enlarged to encompass the wisdom and experience of 4 distinguished Americans:

—The Majority Leader of the Senate,
—The Minority Leader of the Senate,
—The Speaker of the House of Representatives,
—The Minority Leader of the House.

11. *Criminal penalties should be applied for the willful misuse of payments received under the Act by any person with custody of the funds.*

The penalties should be a fine of not more than $10,000, or five years imprisonment, or both. Criminal penalties would also be applied against any person who makes a false claim or statement for the purpose of obtaining funds under the Act.

OTHER CAMPAIGN FINANCING

We should also seek ways to provide some form of public support for congressional, state, and local political primaries and campaigns.

Here, the need is no less acute than at the Presidential level. But the problems involved are as complex as the elections themselves, which vary from district to district and contest to contest.

Because the uncertainties in this area are so very great, and because the issues have not received the benefit of the extensive debate that has characterized Presidential campaign financing, I pose for your consideration and exploration a series of alternatives.

In 1961, President Kennedy appointed a distinguished, bipartisan Commission on Campaign Costs to take a fresh look at the problems of financing election campaigns. Although the Commission devoted its attention to the problems of campaign costs for Presidential and Vice-Presidential candidates, it pointed out that the measures proposed "would have a desirable effect on all political fund raising."

The Commission's 1962 report and recommendations were endorsed by Presidents Dwight D. Eisenhower and Harry S. Truman as well as leading Presidential candidates in recent elections.

Based on the Commission's recommendations and the later reviews and studies of campaign financing, there are several alternatives which should be considered. These alternatives all involve public financing of campaigns to a greater or lesser extent. Among them are

—a system of direct appropriations, patterned after the recommendations made herein for Presidential campaigns, or modeled after recommendations pending in the Congress;

—a tax credit against Federal income tax for 50 percent of contributions, up to a maximum credit of $10 per year;

—a matching incentive plan in which the government would contribute an amount up to $10 for an equal amount contributed by a citizen, whether or not a taxpayer, to a candidate or committee;

—a "voucher plan" in which Treasury certificates for small amounts could be mailed to citizens who, in turn, would send them to candidates or committees of their choice. These vouchers could then be redeemed from public funds, and the funds used to defray specified campaign expenditures.

I believe these deserve serious attention along with other proposals previously recommended and suggested to the Congress. Each alternative offers particular advantages. Thorough review may reveal that one is to be clearly preferred over the others, or that still other courses of action are appropriate. Whatever the outcome, any such review should reflect a realistic assessment of the amount of funds needed in these campaigns and the extent to which the funds should be provided by public means.

I recommend that Congress undertake such a review.

I have asked the Secretary of the Treasury and the Attorney General to cooperate fully with the Congress in its exploration of these alternatives in order to give all the help the Executive branch can to the Congress as it seeks the best congressional election campaign financing program.

These recommendations represent my thoughts on the issues at stake. I believe they highlight the problems in an area so new and complex that there is little experience in our national life to guide us.

I hope that these proposals will serve as guidelines for discussion and debate in the coming weeks. A penetrating and orderly review of these vital public issues, with all the wisdom that the Congress can summon, will in itself be an important educational process for the Nation in the art of government and politics.

I hope that Congress will proceed to consider promptly the problem of campaign financing and will enact appropriate legislation.

I make no recommendation as to the effective date with respect to such legislation. I leave that entirely to the judgment and wisdom of the Congress.

I have no desire to ask that the provisions be made applicable to any campaign in which I may be involved. On the other hand, I have no desire to request that any such campaign be exempted from modernizing legislation which Congress might enact.

Public financing of political campaigns presents the American people with an issue that is both significant and complex—departing as it does from the familiar practices of the past. It transcends partisan political considerations. I urge the American people and the Congress to consider this issue thoughtfully, on its merits, and on the highest and most objective plane, independent of any personalities now in office or seeking office.

Strengthening Federal Regulation of Lobbying

Full disclosure can serve the integrity of Government in another important area—the regulation of lobbying.

Lobbying dates back to the earliest days of our Republic. It is based on the constitutionally guaranteed right of the people to petition their elected representatives for a redress of grievances.

Yet to realize the American ideal of government, our elected representatives must be able to evaluate the varied pressures to which they are regularly subjected. In 1946, Congress responded to this need by enacting the Federal Regulation of Lobbying Act. Its purpose was not to curtail lobbying but to regulate it through disclosure. For the first time, individuals and groups who directly attempted to influence legislation were required to register.

More than twenty years of experience with the Act have highlighted its flaws. Through loopholes in the law, immune from its registration provisions, have passed some of the most powerful, best financed, and best organized lobbies. Although engaged in constant and intensive lobbying, they are not legally required to disclose their existence—because lobbying is not their "principal" purpose, the narrow test under current law.

The Congress has properly taken the initiative to meet this problem. Two months ago, the Senate passed S. 355 by a decisive vote. In that measure, Federal regulation of lobbying has been strengthened by:

—supplanting the "principal purpose" test with the broader test of "substantial purpose," thus extending the reach of the Act by a wider definition of those required to register;

—transferring the responsibility for administration of the law from the

Clerk of the House and the Secretary of the Senate to the Comptroller General.

I strongly endorse the Senate's action in strengthening Federal regulation of lobbying as an important step toward better government, and I urge the House to take similar action.

The Residency Voting Act of 1967

Voting is the first duty of democracy. H. G. Wells called it, "Democracy's ceremonial, its feast, its great function."

This Nation has already assured that no man can legally be denied the right to vote because of the color of his skin or his economic condition. But we find that millions of Americans are still disenfranchised—because they have moved their residence from one locality to another.

Mobility is one of the attributes of a free society, and increasingly a chief characteristic of our Nation in the twentieth century. More American citizens than ever before move in search of new jobs and better opportunities.

For a mobile society, election laws which impose unduly long residence requirements are obsolete. They serve only to create a new class of disenfranchised Americans.

An analysis of the 1960 election, the last election for which studies are available, shows that between 5 and 8 million otherwise eligible voters were deprived of the right to vote because of unnecessarily long residency requirements in many of the states. Almost half the states, for example, through laws a century old, require a citizen to be a resident a full twelve months before he can vote even in a Presidential election.

These requirements diminish democracy. The people's right to travel freely from state to state is constitutionally protected. The exercise of that right should not imperil the loss of another constitutionally protected right— the right to vote.

I propose the Residency Voting Act of 1967 which provides that a citizen, otherwise qualified to vote under the laws of a state, may not be denied his vote in a Presidential election if he becomes a resident of the state by the first day of September preceding the election.

Conclusion

Seventy years ago, the great American historian Frederick Jackson Turner wrote these words:

"Behind institutions, behind constitutional forms and modifications, lie the vital forces that call these organs into life and shape them to meet changing conditions. The peculiarity of American institutions is the fact that they have been compelled to adapt themselves to the changes of an expanding people. . . ."

This represents a valid exposition of the vitality of our democratic process as it has endured for almost two hundred years.

Over those two centuries Presidents and Congresses have strengthened that process as changing circumstances presented the clear need to do so. History has spared few generations that continuing obligation.

Today, that obligation poses for us the requirement—and the opportunity as well—to bring new strength to the processes which underlie our free institutions.

It is in keeping with the obligation that I submit the proposals in this message.

". . . Our country has developed the finest professional civil service in the history of the world."

Remarks on the creation of the new position
of the Executive Assistant to the President
of the United States and on the citation honoring
William J. Hopkins and appointing him to the new position,
July 15, 1966.

Every administration creates a phrase that describes its hopes for this great country of ours, this land we love.

It may be the New Deal—or the Fair Deal—or the New Frontier—or the Great Society. All the words themselves are a challenge. They are meant to inspire private citizens and public servants alike. They are meant to keep alive the vision of a just and a dynamic country.

The man who stands behind me this afternoon did not create those phrases. But for thirty-five long years now he has been a vital instrument— I would say a most indispensable instrument—in the struggle to make all of those phrases a reality.

For twenty-three years he has managed the business of this House: the bills that come from the Congress; the messages and orders of the President; the records of the entire Executive Office; the regulations that govern the duties of all of those who work in the Executive branch.

And for more than twenty-three years, through the Administrations of President Roosevelt, President Truman, President Eisenhower, President Kennedy, and President Johnson, the most commonly heard phrase in the halls of the White House has been:

"Check it with Bill Hopkins, before you turn it loose."

"Where is the farm bill? What has happened to the immigration bill? Can we send that safety message on Saturday? What is the per diem rate for a consultant? What did President Roosevelt say about that? What did President Eisenhower do when he was confronted with that situation? When is that report due for Congress?"

And the first answer to all of these questions has always been the same thing:

"Check it with Bill Hopkins, before you turn it loose."

If there has been a more valuable public servant on the rolls of the United States Government in that time—in the thirty-five years that I have been in that Government—I do not know his name.

Bill Hopkins' advice and counsel has been sought by the Presidents, by Cabinet officers, by military chieftains, by clerks and consultants, and by private citizens and it has always been given—freely, candidly, and discreetly—at all hours of the day and night, in all times of crisis and calm.

So this afternoon I am glad that all of you, my coworkers, could come here to join us, as we have met in this beautiful Rose Garden at the end of a long working day, to honor this man of stature, Bill Hopkins, and his twenty-three years of service as Executive Clerk of the White House.

This is a profoundly symbolic occasion. For in honoring Mr. Hopkins, we also honor the whole corps of dedicated civil servants of which he is so outstanding an example. I have said on many occasions that I believe our country has developed the finest professional civil service in the history of the world. And, as President, I have not merely expressed that opinion as idle words—I have acted upon it.

More than 40 percent of all the officials I have appointed to permanent positions in the United States Government in the almost three years I have been President have come from either the career civil service or the career foreign service.

I have looked to the career service, because I believe that the demands placed upon members of Government today are greater than at any time in the history of the Nation. And if we are to meet those demands wisely, with imagination and understanding, our top executives must be drawn from among the most able, the best prepared, and the most committed people that we can find in this country. In my experience, the career civil service is one place where such people are most likely to be found.

This conviction of mine is not hard to explain. For I am daily exposed to a man who combines in his own person the highest qualities of those who serve the public good.

When I explored the various awards available to me to present to Bill Hopkins on this anniversary, I learned that he had already received the highest awards that were available in the White House for that purpose. President Dwight D. Eisenhower selected Bill Hopkins for the President's Award for Distinguished Civilian Service—and it was richly earned. So, we had to innovate. We designed a very special award for him alone.

Bill, it is my great pleasure this afternoon to present this award to you as an expression of the high esteem, the deep appreciation, and the warm regard that all of your colleagues feel for you.

I should now like to read the citation:

CITATION

"The President of the United States of America awards this citation to William J. Hopkins with pride and appreciation on this your twenty-third anniversary as Executive Clerk of the White House. Your skill, dedication, and effectiveness have become hallmarks of excellence during a Federal career dating from 1929. Since 1931, your devoted service in the White House has been of immeasurable help to six Presidents. Throughout twenty-three years as the Executive Clerk you have performed a critical and sensitive assignment with a single-minded purpose: to render the highest possible service to the President and to the people of our country. We are limited in our ways to honor such ability and patriotism, yet I can offer one tangible evidence of our gratitude by promoting you today to the new position of the Executive Assistant to the President of the United States. You are a great credit to the career service and a credit to the United States Government.

"LYNDON B. JOHNSON

"The White House, Washington, D.C.
"July 15, 1966"

Now, ladies and gentlemen, that concludes the citation.

This promotion gives me very special pleasure, because, for once, instead of having to find a man to fill an office, we are creating an office that fits the man.

"Our democracy cannot remain static,
a prisoner to the past."
The President recommends to Congress
a four-year term for House members
and reform of the Electoral College,
January 20, 1966.

In 1816 Thomas Jefferson wrote: "Some men ascribe to the men of a preceding age a wisdom more than human, and suppose what they did to be beyond amendment. . . . I am certainly not an advocate for frequent and untried changes in laws and constitutions. . . . But I know also, that laws and institutions must go hand in hand with the progress of the human mind."

I believe that in the interest of progress and sound modern government—and to nourish and strengthen our creative Federal system—we must amend our Constitution, to provide a four-year term of office for members of the House of Representatives.

I believe that for the same reasons we must also eliminate those defects in the Electoral College system which make possible the frustration of the people's will in the election of their President and Vice President.

Four-Year Term for House Members

[I]

Debate over the length of the House term is not new. It began in the Constitutional Convention, where those who thought annual elections were essential to freedom clashed with others, such as Madison, who held that three years were required "in a government so extensive, for members to form any knowledge of the various interests of the states to which they did not belong," and that without such knowledge "their trust could not be usefully discharged." Madison's thoughts are ruefully familiar to members of the House today: he was certain that a one-year term would be "almost consumed in preparing for and traveling to and from the seat of national business," and that even with a two-year term none of the Representatives "who wished to be reelected would remain at the seat of government."

Between the advocates of a one-year term—those who, bearing in mind recent English experience, feared the despotism of a government unchecked by the popular will—and those who saw a tenure of three years as necessary for wise administration, a compromise of two years was reached.

Thus there was little magic in the number two, even in the year of its adoption. I am convinced there is even less magic today, and that the question of tenure should be reexamined in the light of our needs in the twentieth century.

[II]

The authors of the Federalist Papers said about the House of Representatives:

> As it is essential to liberty that the Government in general should have a common interest with the people; so it is particularly essential that the branch of it under consideration should have an immediate dependence on, and an intimate sympathy with the people. Frequent elections are unquestionably the only policy by which this dependency and sympathy can be effectually secured. *But what particular degree of frequency may*

be absolutely necessary for the purpose, does not appear to be susceptible
of any precise calculation; and must depend on a variety of circumstances
with which it may be connected.

The circumstances with which the two-year term is presently connected
are

—*the accelerating volume of legislation* on which members are required
to pass. In the first Congress, 142 bills were introduced, resulting in 108
public laws. In the Eighty-eighth Congress, 15,299 bills were introduced, of
which 666 were enacted into public law.

—*the increasingly complex problems that generate this flood of legislation,*
requiring members to be familiar with an immense range of fact and opinion. It is no longer sufficient to develop solutions for an agricultural nation
with few foreign responsibilities; now a man or woman chosen to represent
his people in the House of Representatives must understand the consequences of our spiraling population growth, of urbanization, of the new
scientific revolution, of our welfare and education requirements, and of our
responsibilities as the world's most powerful democracy.

—*longer sessions of Congress,* made necessary by the burden of legislation
and outstanding public issues. In less turbulent times, members of Congress
might conduct the public business with dispatch during elections years, and
spend the summer and autumn campaigning in their districts. Congress
adjourned in April of 1904, June of 1906, May of 1908, and June of 1910.
But increasing work loads have substantially extended the sessions. Thus it
was in August of 1958 that Congress concluded its work, in September of
1960, October of 1962, and again in October of 1964. The competitive
pressures imposed by the two-year term, when the incumbent must remain
in Washington into the fall to attend the public business, reduce his capacity
to do either task—campaigning or legislating—with the complete attention
his conscience and the public interest demand.

—*the increasing costs of campaigning* that biennially impose heavy burdens
on those who represent vigorously contested districts, and that magnify the
influence of large contributors, pressure groups, and special interest lobby-
ists.

It may be said that every elected official confronts similar circumstances
in the 1960s. Yet it can be said of none that his power for the public good
or ill is both so great as the Congressman's, and so sharply pressed in time.

For this public servant—part judge and author of laws, part leader of his people, part mediator between the Executive branch and those he represents —is scarcely permitted to take his seat in the historic Hall of the House, when he must begin once more to make his case to his constituency.

The Congressman's effectiveness as a legislator is reduced by this.

His district's right to be fully represented in Congress is diminished by this.

The Nation's need to be led by its best-qualified men, giving their full attention to issues on which our security and progress depend, is ignored by this.

In the states, in private business, and indeed in the Federal Government itself, the wisdom of longer terms for senior officials has come steadily to be recognized. State after state has adopted a four-year gubernatorial term.

This Administration has made every effort to extend ambassadorial tours of duty, to promote career civil servants to posts of higher responsibilities, and to retain Cabinet and sub-Cabinet officers on the job for longer periods than before. For we have learned that brief and uncertain periods in office contribute—not to the best interests of democracy—but to harassed inefficiency and the loss of invaluable experience.

[III]

Thus I recommend that the Congress adopt this Amendment to the Constitution in the belief that it will

—*provide for each member a sufficient period in which he can bring his best judgment to bear on the great questions of national survival, economic growth, and social welfare;*

—*free him from the inexorable pressures of biennial campaigning for reelection;*

—*reduce the cost—financial and political—of holding congressional office; and*

—*attract the best men in private and public life into competition for this high public office.*

I am mindful of the principal reason advanced for maintaining the two-year term—that it is necessary if the voice of the people is to be heard, and changes in public opinion are to be registered on the conduct of public policy. My own experience in almost three decades in public office—and, I believe, the experience of members of Congress today—is otherwise.

For we do not live in a day when news of congressional action requires weeks to reach our constituents, nor when public opinion is obscured by time and distance. Communications media rush the news to every home and shop within minutes of its occurrence. Public opinion polls, and mountains of mail, leave little doubt about what our people think of the issues most vital to them. I do not fear deafness on the part of those who will take their seats in Congress for a four-year term.

It is also vital to recognize the effect of a longer term on the authority of the House in making known the will of the people. Established in office for four years, the weight of the House in the councils of Government is certain to increase. For the sake of democracy, that is a development devoutly to be welcomed.

[IV]

I recommend that the amendment become effective no earlier than 1972.

It is imperative that each member of the House have the opportunity of campaigning during a Presidential election year. To divide the House into two classes, as some have proposed—one elected during the "off-year," one with the President—would create an unnecessary and wholly unfair division in that body. It would also create severe problems in every state: as reapportionment is ordered and redistricting takes place.

"Off-year" elections are notorious for attracting far fewer voters—perhaps as much as 15% fewer—than Presidential elections.

If our purpose is to serve the democratic ideal by making the people's House more effective in its performance of the people's business, then we must require that its Members be chosen by the largest electorate our democracy can produce. That, assuredly, is the electorate called into being during a Presidential year.

I do not believe the Congress will wish to make the House the least representative of our three elective elements by perpetually condemning half its membership to a shrunken electorate. Such a body could not long sustain its claim to be an equal partner in the work of representative government.

[V]

If this Amendment is to serve the public interest—if Members are to be free of campaigning for a period sufficiently long to enable them to master the work of the House—it is right that they should remain at that work during the entire term to which they are elected.

It would defeat the purpose of the Amendment, if a member were free to campaign for the Senate without resigning his seat in the House. Because we seek to strengthen the House, and through it, representative government —not to provide a sanctuary and platform for further electoral contests— I recommend that no member of either House be eligible for election as a member of the other House until his own term has expired, unless, at least thirty days prior to that election, he submits his resignation from the office he holds.

[VI]

Our democracy cannot remain static, a prisoner to the past, if it is to enrich the lives of coming generations. Laws and institutions—to paraphrase Jefferson—must go hand in hand with the progress of the human mind, and must respond to the changing conditions of life itself.

One law that should be changed limits the term of office for one of the great arms of our Government to a period too brief for the public good.

Let us no longer bind ourselves to it. Let us reform it. We shall better serve our people when we do.

Because I profoundly agree with former President Eisenhower, when he said, "Congressmen ought to be elected for four years, at the same time with the President," I urge the Congress promptly to consider a constitutional amendment extending the term of office for the House of Representatives to four years.

REFORM OF THE ELECTORAL COLLEGE SYSTEM

In my special message to the Congress last January, I urged an amendment to the Constitution to reform the electoral college system. I renew this recommendation and strongly reaffirm the need to reform the electoral college system.

There are several major defects in the existing system. They should be eliminated in order to assure that the people's will shall not be frustrated in the choice of their President and Vice-President.

First, there presently exists the possibility that the constitutional independence of unpledged electors will be exploited, and that their votes will be manipulated in a close presidential race to block the election of a major candidate in order to throw the election into the House of Representatives. This grave risk should be removed.

Second, if the election is thrown into the House of Representatives, the existing system suffers from other fundamental defects. In such an election, the House of Representatives would be empowered to elect a President from the three highest candidates. However, each state casts only one vote, with the result that the least populous states have the same vote in the election of the President as the most populous states.

As early as 1823, Madison reached the conclusion that "the present rule of voting for President by the House of Representatives is so great a departure from the republican principle of numerical equality, and even from the Federal rule, which qualifies the numerical by a state equality, and is so pregnant also, with a mischievous tendency in practice, that an amendment to the Constitution on this point is justly called for by all its considerate and best friends."

I firmly believe that we should put an end to this undemocratic procedure.

Third, if the electoral vote is indecisive under the existing system, the President is elected by the House of Representatives, but the Vice-President is elected by the Senate. This creates the possibility of the election of a President and a Vice-President from different parties. That possibility should not exist. To prevent its realization, the President and the Vice-President should both be elected by the same body.

Fourth, the Twenty-third Amendment makes no provision for participation by the District of Columbia in an election of the President by the House of Representatives, or of the Vice-President by the Senate.

I firmly believe that we should extend to the District of Columbia all the rights of participation in the election of a President and Vice-President which the fifty states may exercise.

Fifth, existing law fails to provide for the death of the President-elect or Vice-President-elect between Election Day and the counting of the electoral votes in December. There is also no provision in the Constitution to cover the contingency presented by the death of a candidate for President or Vice-President shortly before the popular election in November. These gaps should now be filled.

Elimination of these defects in our Constitution are long overdue. Our concepts of self-government and sound government require it.

Congress can now, in the words of Daniel Webster, "perform something worthy to be remembered," by uprooting the more objectionable features in the system of electing a President and Vice-President, and thereby helping to preserve representative government and the two-party system.

"Today in this crisis-ridden era
there is no margin for delay."

Remarks at a ceremony commemorating the ratification
of the Amendment concerning Presidential disability,
February 23, 1967.

It was one hundred and eighty years ago, in the closing days of the Constitutional Convention, that the Founding Fathers debated the question of Presidential disability. John Dickinson of Delaware asked this question: "What is the extent of the term 'disability' and who is to be the judge of it?" No one replied.

It is hard to believe that until last week our Constitution provided no clear answer. Now, at last, the Twenty-fifth Amendment clarifies the crucial clause that provides for succession to the Presidency and for filling a Vice-Presidential vacancy.

Two years ago I urged Congress to initiate this Amendment. I said that only our very amazing good fortune, and the remarkable stability of the American system, have prevented us from paying the price that "our continuing inaction so clearly invites and so recklessly risks."

Twice in our history we have had serious and prolonged disabilities in the Presidency. In 1881 President Garfield lingered near death for eighty days before succumbing to Guiteau's bullet. President Woodrow Wilson was virtually incommunicado for many months after a stroke, yet dismissed his Secretary of State for attempting to convene a Cabinet meeting. In each case there was controversy, but the Constitution provided no mechanism for installing the Vice-President in the Chief Executive's empty chair while the President himself was disabled.

Sixteen times in the history of the Republic the office of Vice-President—the office created to provide continuity in the Executive—itself has been vacant. Seven men have died while Vice-President, John C. Calhoun resigned, and eight others left the office vacant when succeeding to the Presidency. Again our American Constitution was silent on the selection of a new Vice-President.

Once, perhaps, we could pay the price of inaction. But today in this crisis-ridden era there is no margin for delay, no possible justification for ever permitting a vacuum in our national leadership. Now, at last, through the Twenty-fifth Amendment, we have the means of responding to these crises of responsibility.

We pay tribute here in the East Room today to some of those who have worked to provide those means—and thus to assure prompt and orderly continuity in the executive branch of the government. Herbert Brownell, J. Lee Rankin, and Nicholas Katzenbach were among those who helped to develop this vital reform in the Department of Justice. Senator Birch Bayh of Indiana and Representative Emanuel Celler of New York introduced the measure in the Congress, carried it through exhaustive hearings and many negotiations, and presided over its passage. Many of the members of Congress who contributed to its passage are here as our guests today. Many private citizens and organizations, and particularly the leaders of the American Bar Association, helped to gain broad public approval for it. And finally the legislatures of three-quarters of our states have made it the law of our land.

By this thoughtful Amendment, they have further perfected the oldest written Constitution in the world. They have earned the lasting thanks of the American people, for whom it has so long secured the blessings of liberty.

Envoy

"I shall not seek,
and I will not accept,
the nomination of my party
for another term as your President. . . ."
Television broadcast to the American people,
March 31, 1968.

Tonight I want to speak to you of peace in Vietnam and Southeast Asia.

No other question so preoccupies our people. No other dream so absorbs the 250 million human beings who live in that part of the world. No other goal motivates American policy in Southeast Asia.

For years, representatives of our Government and others have traveled the world—seeking to find a basis for peace talks.

Since last September, they have carried the offer that I made public at San Antonio.

That offer was this:

That the United States would stop its bombardment of North Vietnam when that would lead promptly to productive discussions—and that we would assume that North Vietnam would not take military advantage of our restraint.

Hanoi denounced this offer, both privately and publicly. Even while the search for peace was going on, North Vietnam rushed their preparations for a savage assault on the people, the government, and the allies of South Vietnam.

Their attack—during the Tet holidays—failed to achieve its principal objectives.

It did not collapse the elected government of South Vietnam or shatter its army—as the Communists had hoped.

It did not produce a "general uprising" among the people of the cities as they had predicted.

The Communists were unable to maintain control of any of the more than thirty cities that they attacked. And they took very heavy casualties.

But they did compel the South Vietnamese and their allies to move certain forces from the countryside, into the cities.

They caused widespread disruption and suffering. Their attacks, and the battles that followed, made refugees of half a million human beings.

The Communists may renew their attack any day.

They are, it appears, trying to make 1968 the year of decision in South Vietnam—the year that brings, if not final victory or defeat, at least a turning point in the struggle.

This much is clear:

If they do mount another round of heavy attacks, they will not succeed in destroying the fighting power of South Vietnam and its allies.

But tragically, this is also clear: many men—on both sides of the struggle —will be lost. A nation that has already suffered twenty years of warfare will suffer once again. Armies on both sides will take new casualties. And the war will go on.

There is no need for this to be so.

There is no need to delay the talks that could bring an end to this long and this bloody war.

Tonight, I renew the offer I made last August—to stop the bombardment of North Vietnam. We ask that talks begin promptly, that they be serious talks on the substance of peace. We assume that during those talks Hanoi will not take advantage of our restraint.

We are prepared to move immediately toward peace through negotiations.

So, tonight, in the hope that this action will lead to early talks, I am taking the first step to deescalate the conflict. We are reducing—substantially reducing—the present level of hostilities.

And we are doing so unilaterally, and at once.

Tonight, I have ordered our aircraft and our naval vessels to make no attacks on North Vietnam, except in the area north of the Demilitarized Zone where the continuing enemy buildup directly threatens allied forward positions and where the movements of their troops and supplies are clearly related to that threat.

The area in which we are stopping our attacks includes almost 90 percent of North Vietnam's population, and most of its territory. Thus there will be no attacks around the principal populated areas, or in the food-producing areas of North Vietnam.

Even this very limited bombing of the North could come to an early end —if our restraint is matched by restraint in Hanoi. But I cannot in good conscience stop all bombing so long as to do so would immediately and directly endanger the lives of our men and our allies. Whether a complete bombing halt becomes possible in the future will be determined by events.

Our purpose in this action is to bring about a reduction in the level of violence that now exists.

It is to save the lives of brave men—and to save the lives of innocent women and children. It is to permit the contending forces to move closer to a political settlement.

And tonight, I call upon the United Kingdom and I call upon the Soviet Union—as cochairmen of the Geneva Conferences, and as permanent members of the United Nations Security Council—to do all they can to move from the unilateral act of deescalation that I have just announced toward genuine peace in Southeast Asia.

Now, as in the past, the United States is ready to send its representatives to any forum, at any time, to discuss the means of bringing this ugly war to an end.

I am designating one of our most distinguished Americans, Ambassador Averell Harriman, as my personal representative for such talks. In addition, I have asked Ambassador Llewellyn Thompson, who returned from Moscow for consultation, to be available to join Ambassador Harriman at Geneva or any other suitable place—just as soon as Hanoi agrees to a conference.

I call upon President Ho Chi Minh to respond positively, and favorably, to this new step toward peace.

But if peace does not come now through negotiations, it will come when Hanoi understands that our common resolve is unshakable, and our common strength is invincible.

Tonight, we and the other allied nations are contributing 600,000 fighting men to assist 700,000 South Vietnamese troops in defending their little country.

Our presence there has always rested on this basic belief: the main burden of preserving their freedom must be carried out by them—by the South Vietnamese themselves.

We and our allies can only help to provide a shield—behind which the people of South Vietnam can survive and can grow and develop. On their efforts—on their determination and resourcefulness—the outcome will ultimately depend.

That small, beleaguered nation has suffered terrible punishment for more than twenty years.

I pay tribute once again tonight to the great courage and endurance of its people. South Vietnam supports armed forces tonight of almost 700,000 men—and I call your attention to the fact that that is the equivalent of more than 10 million in our own population. Its people maintain their firm determination to be free of domination by the North.

There has been substantial progress, I think, in building a durable government during these last three years. The South Vietnam of 1965 could not have survived the enemy's Tet offensive of 1968. The elected government of South Vietnam survived that attack—and is rapidly repairing the devastation that it wrought.

The South Vietnamese know that further efforts are going to be required:
—to expand their own armed forces,
—to move back into the countryside as quickly as possible,
—to increase their taxes,
—to select the very best men that they have for civil and military responsibility,
—to achieve a new unity within their constitutional government, and
—to include in the national effort all those groups who wish to preserve South Vietnam's control over its own destiny.

Last week President Thieu ordered the mobilization of 135,000 additional

South Vietnamese. He plans to reach—as soon as possible—a total military strength of more than 800,000 men.

To achieve this, the Government of South Vietnam started the drafting of nineteen-year-olds on March 1st. On May 1st, the Government will begin the drafting of eighteen-year-olds.

Last month, 10,000 men volunteered for military service—that was two and a half times the number of volunteers during the same month last year. Since the middle of January, more than 48,000 South Vietnamese have joined the armed forces—and nearly half of them volunteered to do so.

All men in the South Vietnamese armed forces have had their tours of duty extended for the duration of the war, and reserves are now being called up for immediate active duty.

President Thieu told his people last week:

"We must make greater efforts and accept more sacrifices because, as I have said many times, this is our country. The existence of our nation is at stake, and this is mainly a Vietnamese responsibility."

He warned his people that a major national effort is required to root out corruption and incompetence at all levels of government.

We applaud this evidence of determination on the part of South Vietnam. Our first priority will be to support their effort.

We shall accelerate the reequipment of South Vietnam's armed forces—in order to meet the enemy's increased firepower. This will enable them progressively to undertake a larger share of combat operations against the Communist invaders.

On many occasions I have told the American people that we would send to Vietnam those forces that are required to accomplish our mission there. So, with that as our guide, we have previously authorized a force level of approximately 525,000.

Some weeks ago—to help meet the enemy's new offensive—we sent to Vietnam about 11,000 additional Marine and airborne troops. They were deployed by air in forty-eight hours, on an emergency basis. But the artillery, tank, aircraft, medical, and other units that were needed to work with and to support these infantry troops in combat could not then accompany them by air on that short notice.

In order that these forces may reach maximum combat effectiveness, the Joint Chiefs of Staff have recommended to me that we should prepare to send—during the next five months—support troops totaling approximately 13,500 men.

A portion of these men will be made available from our active forces. The balance will come from reserve component units which will be called up for service.

The actions that we have taken since the beginning of the year . . .

—to reequip the South Vietnamese forces,

—to meet our responsibilities in Korea, as well as our responsibilities in Vietnam,

—to meet price increases and the cost of activating and deploying reserve forces,

—to replace helicopters and provide the other military supplies we need, all of these actions are going to require additional expenditures.

The tentative estimate of those additional expenditures is $2.5 billion in this fiscal year, and $2.6 billion in the next fiscal year.

These projected increases in expenditures for our national security will bring into sharper focus the Nation's need for immediate action: action to protect the prosperity of the American people and to protect the strength and stability of our American dollar. . . .

[Here the President discusses fiscal and monetary problems.]

Now let me give you my estimate of the chances for peace:

—the peace that will one day stop the bloodshed in South Vietnam,

—that will permit all the Vietnamese people to rebuild and develop their land,

—that will permit us to turn more fully to our own tasks here at home.

I cannot promise that the initiative that I have announced tonight will be completely successful in achieving peace any more than the thirty others that we have undertaken and agreed to in recent years.

But it is our fervent hope that North Vietnam, after years of fighting that has left the issue unresolved, will now cease its efforts to achieve a military victory and will join with us in moving toward the peace table.

And there may come a time when South Vietnamese—on both sides—are able to work out a way to settle their own differences by free political choice rather than by war.

As Hanoi considers its course, it should be in no doubt of our intentions. It must not miscalculate the pressures within our democracy in this election year.

We have no intention of widening this war.

But the United States will never accept a fake solution to this long and arduous struggle and call it peace.

No one can foretell the precise terms of an eventual settlement.

Our objective in South Vietnam has never been the annihilation of the enemy. It has been to bring about a recognition in Hanoi that its objective —taking over the South by force—could not be achieved.

We think that peace can be based on the Geneva Accords of 1954—under political conditions that permit the South Vietnamese—all the South Vietnamese—to chart their course free of any outside domination or interference, from us or from anyone else.

So tonight I reaffirm the pledge that we made at Manila—that we are prepared to withdraw our forces from South Vietnam as the other side withdraws its forces to the North, stops the infiltration, and the level of violence thus subsides.

Our goal of peace and self-determination in Vietnam is directly related to the future of all of Southeast Asia—where much has happened to inspire confidence during the past ten years. We have done all that we knew how to do to contribute and to help build that confidence.

A number of its nations have shown what can be accomplished under conditions of security. Since 1966, Indonesia, the fifth largest nation in all the world, with a population of more than 100 million people, has had a government that is dedicated to peace with its neighbors and improved conditions for its own people. Political and economic cooperation between nations has grown rapidly.

I think every American can take a great deal of pride in the role that we have played in bringing this about in Southeast Asia. We can rightly judge —as responsible Southeast Asians themselves do—that the progress of the past three years would have been far less likely—if not completely impossible—if America's sons and others had not made their stand in Vietnam.

At Johns Hopkins University, about three years ago, I announced that the United States would take part in the great work of developing Southeast Asia, including the Mekong Valley—for all the people of that region. Our determination to help build a better land—a better land for men on both sides of the present conflict—has not diminished in the least. Indeed, the ravages of war, I think, have made it more urgent than ever.

So, I repeat on behalf of the United States again tonight what I said at

Johns Hopkins—that North Vietnam could take its place in this common effort just as soon as peace comes.

Over time, a wider framework of peace and security in Southeast Asia may become possible. The new cooperation of the nations of the area could be a foundation-stone. Certainly friendship with the nations of such a Southeast Asia is what the United States seeks—and that is all that the United States seeks.

One day, my fellow citizens, there will be peace in Southeast Asia.

It will come because the people of Southeast Asia want it—those whose armies are at war tonight, and those who, though threatened, have thus far been spared.

Peace will come because Asians were willing to work for it—and to sacrifice for it—and to die by the thousands for it.

But let it never be forgotten: peace will come also because America sent her sons to help secure it.

It has not been easy—far from it. During the past four and a half years, it has been my fate and my responsibility to be Commander in Chief. I have lived—daily and nightly—with the cost of this war. I know the pain that it has inflicted. I know, perhaps better than anyone, the misgivings that it has aroused.

Throughout this entire, long period, I have been sustained by a single principle: that what we are doing now, in Vietnam, is vital not only to the security of Southeast Asia, but it is vital to the security of every American.

Surely we have treaties which we must respect. Surely we have commitments that we are going to keep. Resolutions of the Congress testify to the need to resist aggression in the world and in Southeast Asia.

But the heart of our involvement in South Vietnam—under three different Presidents, three separate administrations—has always been America's own security.

And the larger purpose of our involvement has always been to help the nations of Southeast Asia become independent and stand alone, self-sustaining as members of a great world community—at peace with themselves, and at peace with all others.

With such an Asia, our country—and the world—will be far more secure than it is tonight.

I believe that a peaceful Asia is far nearer to reality because of what

America has done in Vietnam. I believe that the men who endure the dangers of battle—fighting there for us tonight—are helping the entire world avoid far greater conflicts, far wider wars, far more destruction, than this one.

The peace that will bring them home someday will come. Tonight I have offered the first in what I hope will be a series of mutual moves toward peace.

I pray that it will not be rejected by the leaders of North Vietnam. I pray that they will accept it as a means by which the sacrifices of their own people may be ended. And I ask your help and your support, my fellow citizens, for this effort to reach across the battlefield toward an early peace.

Finally, my fellow Americans, let me say this:

Of those to whom much is given, much is asked. I cannot say and no man could say that no more will be asked of us.

Yet, I believe that now, no less than when the decade began, this generation of Americans is willing to "pay any price, bear any burden, meet any hardship, support any friend, oppose any foe to assure the survival and the success of liberty."

Since those words were spoken by John F. Kennedy, the people of America have kept that compact with mankind's noblest cause.

And we shall continue to keep it.

Yet, I believe that we must always be mindful of this one thing, whatever the trials and the tests ahead. The ultimate strength of our country and our cause will lie not in powerful weapons or infinite resources or boundless wealth, but will lie in the unity of our people.

This I believe very deeply.

Throughout my entire public career I have followed the personal philosophy that I am a free man, an American, a public servant, and a member of my party, in that order always and only.

For thirty-seven years in the service of our Nation, first as a Congressman, as a Senator, and as Vice-President, and now as your President, I have put the unity of the people first. I have put it ahead of any divisive partisanship.

And in these times as in times before, it is true that a house divided against itself by the spirit of faction, of party, of region, of religion, of race, is a house that cannot stand.

There is division in the American house now. There is divisiveness among us all tonight. And holding the trust that is mine, as President of all the people, I cannot disregard the peril to the progress of the American people and the hope and the prospect of peace for all peoples.

So, I would ask all Americans, whatever their personal interests or concern, to guard against divisiveness and all its ugly consequences.

Fifty-two months and ten days ago, in a moment of tragedy and trauma, the duties of this office fell upon me. I asked then for your help and God's, that we might continue America on its course, binding up our wounds, healing our history, moving forward in new unity, to clear the American agenda and to keep the American commitment for all of our people.

United we have kept that commitment. United we have enlarged that commitment.

Through all time to come, I think America will be a stronger nation, a more just society, and a land of greater opportunity and fulfillment because of what we have all done together in these years of unparalleled achievement.

Our reward will come in the life of freedom, peace, and hope that our children will enjoy through ages ahead.

What we won when all of our people united just must not now be lost in suspicion, distrust, selfishness, and politics among any of our people.

Believing this as I do, I have concluded that I should not permit the Presidency to become involved in the partisan divisions that are developing in this political year.

With America's sons in the fields far away, with America's future under challenge right here at home, with our hopes and the world's hopes for peace in the balance every day, I do not believe that I should devote an hour or a day of my time to any personal partisan causes or to any duties other than the awesome duties of this office—the Presidency of your country.

Accordingly, I shall not seek, and I will not accept, the nomination of my party for another term as your President.

But let men everywhere know, however, that a strong, a confident, and a vigilant America stands ready tonight to seek an honorable peace—and stands ready tonight to defend an honored cause—whatever the price, whatever the burden, whatever the sacrifice that duty may require.

Thank you for listening.

Good night and God bless all of you.

". . . To heal and to build . . .
is a noble task. . . .
Yet along the way I learned somewhere
that no leader can pursue public tranquility
as his first and only goal."
Speech to the National Association of Broadcasters,
Chicago, April 1, 1968.

Some of you might have thought from what I said last night that I'd been taking elocution lessons from Lowell Thomas. One of my aides said this morning—said things are really getting confused around Washington, Mr. President. And I said how's that? He said it looks to me like that you're going to the wrong convention in Chicago. And I said, well, what you overlooked was yesterday was April Fool's.

Once again we are entering the period of national festivity which Henry Adams called the dance of democracy. At its best, that can be a time of debate and enlightenment. At its worst, it can be a period of frenzy. But always it is a time when emotion threatens to substitute for reason. Yet the basic hope of a democracy is that somehow amid all the frenzy and all the emotion that in the end reason will prevail.

Reason just must prevail if democracy itself is to survive.

As I said last evening there are very deep and very emotional divisions in this land that we love today, domestic divisions, divisions over the war in Vietnam. With all of my heart I just wish this weren't so. My entire career in public life—some 37 years of it—has been devoted to the art of finding an area of agreement because generally speaking I have observed that there are so many more things to unite us Americans than there are to divide us.

But somehow or other we have a faculty sometimes of emphasizing the divisions and the things that divide us instead of discussing the things that unite us.

Sometimes I have been called a seeker of "consensus"—more often in criticism than in praise. And I have never denied it. Because to heal and to build in support of something worthy is, I believe, a noble task. In the region of the country where I have spent my life, where brother was once divided against brother, this lesson has been burned deep into my memory. Yet along the way I learned somewhere that no leader can pursue public tranquility as his first and only goal.

Because, for a President to buy public popularity at the sacrifice of his better judgment is too dear a price to pay.

This nation cannot afford such a price and this nation cannot long afford such a leader. So the things that divide our country this morning will be discussed throughout the land and I'm certain that the very great majority of informed Americans will act as they have always acted to do what is best for their country and what serves the national interest.

But the real problem of informing the people is still with us and I think I can speak with some authority about the problem of communication. I understand far better than some of my severe and perhaps intolerant critics would admit my own shortcomings as a communicator.

How does a public leader find just the right word or the right way to say no more or no less than he means to say, bearing in mind that anything he says may topple governments and may involve the lives of innocent men?

How does that leader speak the right phrase in the right way under the right conditions to suit the accuracies and contingencies of the moment when he's discussing questions of policy so that he does not stir a thousand misinterpretations and leave the wrong connotation or impression?

How does he reach the immediate audience and how does he communicate with the millions of others who are out there listening from afar?

The President, who must call his people and summon them to meet their responsibilities as citizens in a hard and enduring war often ponders these questions and searches for the right course.

You men and women who are masters of the broadcast media I think surely must know what I am talking about. It was a long time ago a President once said "the printing press is the most powerful weapon with which man has ever armed himself." And in our age the electronic media have added immeasurably to man's power.

You have within your hands the means to make our nation as intimate and as informed as a New England town meeting. Yet the use of broadcasting has not cleared away all the problems that we still have of communication.

In some ways, I think, sometimes it has complicated them. Because it tends to put the leader in a time capsule. It requires him often to abbreviate what he has to say. Too often it may catch a random phrase from his rather lengthy discourse and project it as the whole story.

How many men, I wonder, Mayor Daley, in public life have watched themselves on a TV newscast and then been tempted to exclaim: "Can that really be me?"

Well, there is no denying it. You, the broadcast industry, have the enormous power in your hands. You have the power to clarify. And you have the power to confuse.

Men in public life cannot remotely rival your opportunities, because day after day, night after night, hour after hour, on the hour, you shape—and the half-hour sometimes—you shape the Nation's dialogue. The words that you choose, hopefully always accurate, hopefully always just, are the words that are carried out for all the people to hear.

The commentary that you provide can give the real meaning to the issues of the day or it can distort them beyond all meaning.

By your standards of what is news you can cultivate with them or you could nurture misguided passions. Your commentary carries an element of uncertainty.

Unlike the print media, television writes on the wind. There is no accumulated record which the historian can examine later with the 20-20 vision of hindsight, asking this question: How fair was he tonight? How impartial was he today? How honest was he all along?

Well, I hope the National Association of Broadcasters, with whom I have had a pleasant association for many years, will point the way to all of us in developing this kind of a record, because history is going to be asking very hard questions about our times and the period through which we are passing. And I think that we all owe it to history to complete the record.

But I did not come here this morning to sermonize in matters of fairness and judgment. No law and no set of regulations and no words of mine can improve you or dictate your daily responsibility. All I mean to do—what I'm trying to do—is to remind you where there's great power there must also be great responsibility.

This is true for broadcasters just as it's true for Presidents, and seekers for the Presidency.

What we say and what we do now will shape the kind of a world that we pass along to our children and our grandchildren. And I keep this thought constantly in my mind during the long days and the somewhat longer nights when crisis comes at home and abroad.

I took a little of your prime time last night. I wouldn't have done that except for a very prime purpose. I reported on the prospects for peace in Vietnam. I announced that the United States is taking a very important unilateral act of deescalation which could—and I fervently pray, will—lead to mutual moves to reduce the level of violence and to deescalate the war.

As I sat in my office last evening waiting to speak I thought of the many times each week when television brings the war into the American home. No one can say exactly what effect those vivid scenes have on American opinion.

Historians must only guess at the effect that television would have had during earlier conflicts on the future of this nation. During the Korean War, for example, at that time when our forces were pushed back there to Pusan. Or World War II, the Battle of the Bulge, or when our men were slugging it out in Europe, or when most of our Air Force was shot down that day in June, 1942, off Australia.

But last night television was being used to carry a different message. It was a message of peace and it occurred to me that the medium may be somewhat better suited to conveying the actions of conflict than to dramatizing the words that the leaders use in trying and hoping to end the conflict.

Certainly it is more dramatic to show policemen and rioters locked in combat than to show men trying to cooperate with one another.

The face of hatred and of bigotry comes through much more clearly, no matter what its color, and the face of tolerance I seem to find is rarely newsworthy.

Progress, whether it's a man being trained for a job or millions being trained, or whether it's a child in Head Start learning to read or an older person, 72, in adult education, or being cared for in Medicare, rarely makes the news, although more than 20 million of them are affected by it.

Perhaps this is because tolerance and progress are not dynamic events such as riots and conflict are events.

So peace in the new sense is a condition. War is an end. Part of your responsibility is simply to understand the consequences of that fact, the consequences of your own acts. And part of that responsibility, I think, is to try as very best we all can to draw the attention of our people to the real business of society in our system, finding and securing peace in the world, at home and abroad. And for all that you have done and that you are doing and that you will do to this end, I thank you and I commend you.

I pray that the message of peace that I tried so hard to convey last night will be accepted in good faith by the leaders of North Vietnam. I pray that one time soon the evening news show will have not another battle in the scarred hills of Vietnam, but will show men entering a room to talk about peace. That is the event that I think the American people are yearning and longing to see.

President Thieu of Vietnam and his Government are now engaged in very urgent political and economic tasks which I referred to last night and which we regard as very constructive and hopeful. And we hope the Government of South Vietnam makes great progress in the days ahead.

But sometime in the weeks ahead immediately, I hope President Thieu will be in a position to accept my invitation to visit the United States so he can come here and see our people, too, and together we can strengthen and improve our plans to advance the day of peace.

I pray that you and that every American will take to heart my plea that they guard against divisiveness.

We have won too much and we have come too far and we have opened too many doors of opportunity for these things now to be lost in a divided country where brother is separated from brother.

And for the time that is allotted me, I shall do everything in one man's power to hasten the day when the world is at peace and Americans of all races and all creeds and of all convictions can live together without fear or without suspicion, without distrust, in unity and in common purpose, because united we're strong, divided we're in great danger.

Speaking as I did to the nation last night, I was moved by the very deep convictions that I entertain about the nature of the office that it's my present privilege to hold.

The office of the Presidency is the only office in this land of all the people.

Whatever may be the personal wishes or the preferences of any man who holds it, a President of all the people can afford no thought of self. At no time and in no way and for no reason can a President allow the integrity or the responsibility or the freedom of the office ever to be compromised or diluted or destroyed because when you destroy it, you destroy yourselves. And I hope and I pray by not allowing the Presidency to be involved in division and deep partisanship I shall be able to pass on to my successor a stronger office, strong enough to guard and defend all the people against all the storms that the future may bring us.

You men and women who have come here to this great progressive city of Chicago led by this dynamic great public servant, Dick Daley, are yourselves charged with a peculiar responsibility.

You are yourselves the trustees—legally accepted trustees, legally selected trustees—of a great institution on which the freedom of our land utterly depends.

The security, the success of our country, what happens to us tomorrow rests squarely upon the media which disseminate the truth on which the decisions of democracy are made. We get a great deal of our information from you, and an informed mind is the guardian genius of democracy.

So you are the keepers of a trust and you must be just. You must guard and you must defend your media against a spirit of reaction, against the works of divisiveness, against bigotry, against the corrupting evils of partisanship in any guise.

For America's press as for the American Presidency, the integrity and the responsibility and the freedom—the freedom to know the truth and let the truth make us free—must never be compromised or diluted or destroyed.

The defense of our media is your responsibility. Government cannot and must not and never will, as long as I have anything to do about it, intervene in that role.

But I do want to leave this thought with you as I leave you this morning. I hope that you will give this trust your closest care, acting as I know you can to guard not only against the obvious but to watch for the hidden, the sometimes unintentional, the often petty intrusion upon the integrity of the information by which Americans decide.

Men and women of the airwaves fully as much as men and women of public service have a public trust, and if liberty is to survive and to succeed that solemn trust must be faithfully kept.

I do not want and I don't think you want to wake up some morning and find America changed because we slept when we should have been awake, because we remained silent when we should have spoken up, because we went along with what was popular and fashionable and "in," rather than what was necessary and what was right.

Being faithful to our trust ought to be the prime test of any public trustee in office or on the airwaves and in any society all you students of history know that a time of division is a time of danger, and in these times now we must never forget that eternal vigilance is the price of liberty.

Thank you for wanting me to come. I've enjoyed it.

Epilogue:
The Pride and the Greatness

By Eric Hoffer

When I read in the newspapers about America or talk with professors about America—I feel like I'm talking about mysterious people living on a mysterious continent. I don't know what they mean when they talk about the masses. What do they know about us?

We elected Roosevelt four times in the teeth of all the newspapers, in the teeth of Wall Street. And we elected Truman when all the newspapers said that Dewey was elected.

I remember the picture when Truman was sworn in—all the great brains standing around and wondering, "Look who is being sworn in as President." Now the Trumans are a dime a dozen in this country. You can almost close your eyes, reach over to the sidewalk, and make a man President—and he'll turn out to be Truman. Show me any society on earth or in heaven that can supply potential leaders like that. It's breathtaking.

Who among the great intellectuals could have predicted that a machine politician, patronized by the Knowlands here in Oakland, would become Chief Justice Earl Warren? We are the most mysterious people in the world. Who could have predicted that a hack politician endorsed by the Ku Klux Klan would become Justice Black?

I have lived with Trumans and Johnsons all my life. To me they embody the pride and the greatness of this country. It's they who built this country, and they know how to defend it. When a Johnson gets a job you do not presume to tell him how to do it. You have faith in his competence and his capacity to learn. You know he will do whatever he does the best way he knows how. This is as much as anyone in heaven or on earth can demand. You also know that the Johnsons don't scare, and will not swerve from their path.

It is the unique greatness of this country that it has many Trumans and Johnsons. To us, a Johnson in the White House is not a hero but one of us, saddled with the toughest job in the world and trying to do his best.

If he fails, we fail; if he succeeds, we succeed.

A CHRONOLOGY

The Presidency
of Lyndon B. Johnson

[1963]

November 22:
Arrival at Andrews Air Force Base from Dallas: "We have suffered a loss that cannot be weighed. . . . I will do my best. That is all I can do. I ask for your help—and God's."

November 23:
Proclamation of National Day of Mourning for President Kennedy: Executive Order Closing Government Departments and Agencies on November 25, 1963.

November 25:
Message to the Members of the Armed Forces: "You may know that the policies and purpose of your country are unchanged . . . in seeking honorable peace."

November 27:
Address Before a Joint Session of the Congress: "No memorial oration or eulogy could more eloquently honor President Kennedy's memory than the earliest possible passage of the civil rights bill for which he fought so long. We have talked long enough in this country about equal rights. We have talked for one hundred years or more. It is time now to write the next chapter, and to write it in the books of law."

November 29:
Executive Order Designating Facilities in Florida as the John F. Kennedy Space Center.

November 29:
Appointment of the Warren Commission.

December 7:
First Press Conference.

December 11:
Letter to Senate and House Committee Chairmen on renaming the National Cultural Center in honor of President Kennedy.

December 17:
Address Before the General Assembly of the United Nations: "The United States of America wants to see the Cold War end, we want to see it end once and for all. . . . The United States wants sanity and security, and peace for all, and above all."

December 28:
Chancellor Erhard visits LBJ Ranch.

[1964]

January 3:
Appoints a Special Assistant for Consumer Affairs and establishes the President's Committee on Consumer Interests, giving the American consumer direct representation in the White House.

January 8:
First Annual Message to the Congress on the State of the Union.

January 10:
Assistant Secretary of State Thomas Mann ordered to the Canal Zone to report on anti-American rioting and snipers.

January 14:
First State visit: President Segni of Italy.

January 21:
On the reopening of the Geneva Disarmament Conference, the President outlines five major types of potential agreement between the U.S. and the USSR.

January 23:
The President announces the adoption of the Twenty-fourth Amendment to the Constitution, abolishing the poll tax.

January 27:
Special Message to the Congress recommends the establishment of a new Cabinet Department of Housing and Community Development.

February 5:
Special Message to the Congress on consumer interests: ". . . for far too long the consumer has had too little voice and too little weight in Government."

February 7:
The President declares United States determination to guarantee the security of the Naval Base at Guantánamo. This statement followed the Cuban Government's cutting off of water supply to Guantánamo.

February 10:
Special Message to the Congress on the Nation's health: "I recommend a hospital insurance program for the aged."

February 11:
Names Sargent Shriver to direct the program to eliminate poverty.

February 26:
Signs the Tax Bill, an $11.5 billion reduction, largest in U.S. history.

March 16:
Special Message to the Congress proposing a nationwide war on the sources of poverty: "Today we are asked to declare war on a domestic enemy which threatens the strength of our nation and the welfare of our people."

April 3:
Signs a joint declaration with Panama.

April 28:
Transmittal of the Bill for the Appalachian Region: "I have seen the despair and hopelessness in the faces of these citizens. What exists in this area is a challenge to the ingenuity as well as the compassion of the Congress."

May 18:
Special Message to the Congress transmitting request for additional funds for Vietnam.

May 22:
"Great Society" proposed in speech at the University of Michigan, Ann Arbor.

July 2:
Signing the Civil Rights Bill: "Those who are equal before God shall now also be equal in the polling booths, in the classrooms, in the factories, and in hotels, restaurants, movie theaters, and other places that provide service to the public."

July 9:
Signs the Urban Mass Transportation Act.

August 3:
Instructs the Navy to take retaliatory action in the Gulf of Tonkin.

August 4:
Reports to the American people on renewed aggression in the Gulf of Tonkin.

August 5:
Special Message to the Congress on U.S. policy in Southeast Asia.

August 7:
Passage by Congress of the Joint Resolution on Southeast Asia.

August 10:
Signs Joint Resolution for the Maintenance of Peace and Security in Southeast Asia.

August 20:
Signs the Economic Opportunity Act: "Today for the first time in all the history of the human race, a great nation is able to make and is willing to make a commitment to eradicate poverty among its people."

August 26:
Recommends that the Democratic National Convention nominate Hubert Humphrey as Vice-President.

August 27:
Accepts the presidential nomination of Democratic party.

August 31:
Signs the Food Stamp Act.

September 2:
Signs the Housing Act.

September 3:
Signs the Wilderness Bill and the Land and Water Conservation Fund Bill.

September 7:
Opens 1964 Presidential election campaign at Cadillac Square, Detroit.

September 24:
Receives the Warren Commission Report.

October 18:
Radio and television report to the American people on successful Chinese nuclear device.

November 2:
Addresses the American people on Election Eve.

December 18:
Announces decision to build a sea-level canal and to negotiate a new treaty with Panama.

[1965]

January 4:
Annual Message to the Congress on the State of the Union: "We seek to establish a harmony between man and society which will allow each of us to enlarge the meaning of his life and all of us to elevate the quality of our civilization."

January 7:
Special Message to the Congress—"Advancing the Nation's Health": "I . . . strongly urge the Congress to enact a hospital insurance program for the aged."

January 12:
Special Message to the Congress—"Toward Full Educational Opportunity": President asks for one billion dollars to aid schools serving children of low-income families.

January 13:
Special Message to the Congress on Immigration: calls for elimination of national origins quota system—"that system is incompatible with our basic American tradition."

January 18:
John T. Connor sworn in as Secretary of Commerce.

January 20:
Inaugural Address: "We can never again stand aside, prideful in isolation."

February 8:
Special Message to the Congress on Conservation and Restoration of Natural Beauty.

February 13:
Nicholas deB. Katzenbach sworn in as Attorney General; Ramsey Clark sworn in as Deputy Attorney General.

March 2:
Special Message to the Congress on the Nation's Cities: asks Congress to establish Department of Housing and Urban Development, proposes "rent supplements" program.

March 8:
Special Message to the Congress on Law Enforcement and the Administration of Justice: "We must arrest and reverse the trend toward lawlessness."

March 15:
Special Message to the Congress—"The American Promise": "At times history and fate meet at a single time in a single place to shape a turning point in man's

unending search for freedom. . . . So it was last week in Selma, Alabama. . . .
It is not just Negroes, but really it is all of us, who must overcome the crippling
legacy of bigotry and injustice. And we shall overcome."

March 15:
Special Message to the Congress on the Right To Vote.

March 18:
Statement by the President in response to a telegram from the Governor of Alabama: "If he [Governor Wallace] is unable or unwilling to call up the Guard and
to maintain law and order in Alabama, I will call the Guard up and give them
all the support that may be required."

March 31:
Special Message to the Congress on the Food for Peace Program.

April 1:
Henry H. Fowler sworn in as Secretary of the Treasury.

April 7:
Address at Johns Hopkins University: "There may be many ways to . . . peace:
in discussion or negotiations with the governments concerned; in large groups or
in small ones; in the reaffirmation of old agreements or their strengthening with
new ones. We have stated this position over and over again, fifty times and more,
to friend and foe alike."

April 11:
Signs the Elementary and Secondary Education Bill.

April 28:
President orders troops into the Dominican Republic.

May 2:
Radio and Television report to the American people on the situation in the
Dominican Republic.

June 1:
Partial withdrawal of Marines from the Dominican Republic.

June 4:
Commencement Address at Howard University: "It is not enough just to open the gates of opportunity. All our citizens must have the ability to walk through those gates."

July 3:
Further withdrawal of U.S. forces from the Dominican Republic.

July 20:
Arthur J. Goldberg nominated as U.S. Representative to the United Nations.

July 26:
Establishment of the President's Commission on Law Enforcement and Administration of Justice.

July 30:
Signing the Medicare Bill, with President Truman in Independence, Missouri: "Through this new law every citizen will be able . . . to ensure himself against the ravages of illness in his old age."

August 6:
Signing of the Voting Rights Act: "This is a victory for the freedom of the American Negro. But it is also a victory for the freedom of the American Nation."

August 17:
Presentation of Draft Treaty to prevent the spread of nuclear weapons (in Geneva): ". . . bind[s] its signers in a pledge to refrain from actions which would lead to any further increase in the number of nations having the power to unleash nuclear devastation on the world."

August 18:
Dr. John W. Gardner sworn in as Secretary of Health, Education, and Welfare.

September 30:
Signing of the High-Speed Ground Transportation Act.

October 2:
Signing of the Water Quality Act of 1965: "Today we proclaim our refusal to be strangled by the wastes of civilization."

October 20:
Signing of the Clean Air Act Amendments and Solid Waste Disposal Bill.

October 22:
Signing of the Highway Beautification Act of 1965: "Beauty belongs to all the people and so long as I am President, what has been divinely given to nature will not be taken recklessly away by man."

November 3:
Lawrence F. O'Brien sworn in as Postmaster General.

November 8:
Signing the Higher Education Act of 1965 at Southwest Texas State College: ". . . to provide and permit and assist every child born in these borders to receive all the education that he can take."

[1966]

January 12:
Annual Message to Congress on State of the Union: "This Nation is mighty enough, its society is healthy enough, its people are strong enough, to pursue our goals in the rest of the world while still building a Great Society here at home."

January 18:
Robert C. Weaver sworn in as Secretary of Housing and Urban Development.

January 26:
Message to Congress recommending a program for cities and metropolitan areas: "I propose a Demonstration Cities Program that will offer qualifying cities of all sizes the promise of a new life for their people."

January 31:
Resumption of air strikes on North Vietnam.

February 8:
Discussions in Honolulu with Chief of State Thieu and Prime Minister Ky of Vietnam.

March 2:

Message to Congress on Transportation: "I urge the Congress to establish a cabinet-level Department of Transportation."

March 9:

Special Message to Congress on Crime and Law Enforcement: "The safety and security of its citizens is the first duty of government."

April 14–15:

President Johnson in Mexico.

August 19:

First of 1966 campaign trips.

October 17–November 2:

Trip to Asia: Hawaii, American Samoa, New Zealand, Australia, the Philippines, Vietnam, Thailand, Malaysia, South Korea.

November 3:

Signing of the Truth-in-Packaging Act: "The housewife should not need a scale or a yardstick or a slide rule or computer when she shops."

[1967]

January 10:

State of the Union Message: "I have come here tonight to report to you that this is a time of testing for our Nation."

January 16:

Alan S. Boyd sworn in as Secretary of Transportation.

January 23:

Message proposing increases in Social Security.

January 27:

Signing the treaty governing exploration of outer space: "The moon and . . . orbiting manmade satellites will remain free of nuclear weapons."

February 8:
Message to Congress concerning America's children and youth: "No ventures hold more promise than these: curing a sick child, helping a poor child through Head Start, giving a slum child a summer of sunlight and pleasure, encouraging a teen-ager to seek higher learning."

February 28:
Message to Congress concerning Education and Health in America. Requests for fiscal year 1968 a 10 percent increase in spending for education, a 22 percent increase in spending for health.

March 10:
Ramsey Clark sworn in as Attorney General.

March 14:
Urban and rural poverty message: "Let it be said that in our time we pursued a strategy against poverty so that each man had a chance to be himself. Let it be said that in our time, we offered him the means to become a free man—for his sake, and for our own."

March 16:
Consular convention with the USSR.

March 20:
Conference on Vietnam held on Guam.

April 11–14:
American Chiefs of State meet at Punta del Este, Uruguay.

April 23–26:
To Germany to attend funeral services for Chancellor Adenauer.

May 16:
Completion of Kennedy Round negotiations: "The way is now clear for the conclusion of a final agreement covering billions of dollars' worth of trade among more than fifty countries."

May 25:
In Montreal for EXPO '67.

June 4–10:
Middle East crisis. Use of "hot line" with Chairman Kosygin regarding Middle East.

June 14:
Alexander B. Trowbridge sworn in as Secretary of Commerce.

June 23; June 25:
Glassboro, New Jersey, meeting with Chairman Kosygin.

July 24:
The President authorizes Federal troops in Detroit.

July 27:
Establishment of Advisory Commission on Civil Disorders.

August 9:
Recommends expansion of guaranteed loan program for college students.

August 14:
Recommends a broadened communications program: "No technological advance offers a greater opportunity for meeting the challenge [to communicate] than the alliance of space exploration and communications."

August 16:
Visit of Chancellor Kiesinger of Germany.

September 19:
Visit of President Saragat of Italy .

September 26:
Recommends a United States contribution of up to $200 million to the new special funds of the Asian Development Bank.

October 2:
Launches a pilot program to enable industry to provide jobs and training in areas of hard-core unemployment.

October 16:
Remarks at ceremony marking the entry into force of the Outer Space Treaty: "By adding this treaty to the law of nations, we are forging a permanent disarmament agreement for outer space."

October 18:
Visit of Prime Minister Lee Kuan Yew of the Republic of Singapore.

October 23:
Edwin N. Griswold sworn in as Solicitor General of the United States.

October 28:
Chamizal Declaration of the Presidents of the United States and of the United Mexican States: "We thus lay to rest a century-old dispute."

November 7:
Signs the Public Broadcasting Act of 1967.

November 14:
Visit of Prime Minister Eisaku Sato of Japan.

November 20:
Signs bill to establish National Commission on Product Safety.

November 21:
Signs Air Quality Act of 1967. "It is not the first clean air bill—but it is, I think, the best."

November 27:
Transmits to Congress copy of the Multilateral Trade Agreements: "The agreement brings to a successful conclusion what we all know as the Kennedy Round of trade negotiations."

December 4:
Signs bill amending Mental Retardation Facilities Construction Act.

December 12:
Addresses national convention of AFL-CIO: "You took up the fight for the kind of programs that would make this country better for your children than it had been for you."

December 15:
Signs bill amending the Meat Inspection Act, with Upton Sinclair among his guests.

December 16:
Signs bill barring improper age discrimination in employment.

December 19–24:
President's Round-the-World Trip: Prime Minister Holt's funeral in Canberra; Honolulu; Pago Pago; Canberra; Khorat; Thailand; Cam Ranh Bay, South Vietnam; Karachi, Pakistan; Rome. "The enemy cannot win, now, in Vietnam. He can harass, he can terrorize, he can inflict casualties . . . but he just cannot win."

[1968]

January 2:
Signs Social Security Amendments: "Measured in dollars of insurance, the bill enacted into law today is the greatest stride forward since social security was launched in 1935."

January 7:
Meets with Prime Minister Levi Eshkol of Israel.

January 17:
State of the Union Message.

February 8:
Meets with British Prime Minister Harold Wilson.

February 28:
Awards outgoing Secretary of Defense Robert McNamara Medal of Freedom.

March 1:
Clark Clifford is sworn in as the new Secretary of Defense.

March 6:
C. R. Smith is sworn in as Secretary of Commerce.

March 22:

President announces nomination of Wilbur Cohen to be Secretary of HEW.

President announces nomination of General William Westmoreland to replace General Harold Johnson as Chief of Staff of the Army.

President announces nomination of Sargent Shriver to be Ambassador to France.

March 31:

Address to the Nation: President announces bombing halt and unilateral deescalation of conflict in Vietnam and asks that peace negotiations start right away.

President announces decision not to seek reelection.

April 5:

Proclaims April 7 a national day of mourning for the Reverend Dr. Martin Luther King, Jr.

April 5–7:

President sends Federal troops to restore law and order in Washington, D.C., Baltimore, and Chicago.

April 10:

President names General Creighton Abrams to succeed General William Westmoreland in Vietnam.

April 11:

Signs Open Housing Legislation: "I do not exaggerate when I say that the proudest moments of my Presidency have been times such as this when I have signed into law the promises of a century."

April 15–17:

President goes to Honolulu to confer with President Chung Hee Park of Korea and to discuss Vietnam peace prospects.

May 3:

President announces Paris as site for negotiations with Hanoi.

Events Scheduled 1968–69

August 1–5: Republican National Convention
August 26–30: Democratic National Convention
November 5: Election Day
January 20: Inauguration Day

Index

491

PHOTO CREDITS: pages 186–187: Fred Ward, Black Star; page 228: Adlemann; page 327: Arthur Shatz; pages 394–395: Jack Mitchell.